SAN BRUNO PUBLIC LIBRARY
701 Angus Avenue West
San Bruno, CA 94066

New Amsterdam

New Amsterdam

Elizabeth Bear

Subterranean Press 2007

First Edition

Trade Hardcover Edition
ISBN: 978-1-59606-106-4

Subterranean Press
PO Box 190106
Burton, MI 48519

www.subterraneanpress.com

Portions of *New Amsterdam* appeared in somewhat different
form in *Interzone* and *Subterranean.*

LUCIFUGOUS

(March, 1899)

THE ZEPPELIN *HANS GLÜCKER* left Calais at 9:15 in the evening on a cold night in March, 1899, bound for New Amsterdam, the jewel of British North America. Don Sebastien de Ulloa, known to the Continent as the great detective, passed his departure on the promenade, watching the city lights recede through blurring isinglass. He amused himself by taking inventory of his fellow passengers while enjoying the aroma of a fairly good cognac.

The *Hans Glücker* was nearly empty, aside from cargo. So empty, in fact, that Sebastien wondered if she would not have delayed her Atlantic voyage for want of passengers if she were not also a mail dispatch and carrying diplomatic papers. Her capacity was over sixty, but this trip she bore only fourteen.

The longest-term travelers were a couple who had been with the airship since Shanghai, Mr. Cui Jioahua and his wife, Zhang Xiaoming. They had passage as far as the Spanish settlement of San Diego, on the west coast of North America, where they intended to join family—if the intersection of their limited Arabic and German and Sebastien's equally flawed Cantonese could be trusted.

It seemed a tremendous journey, but the trans-Siberian and then trans-Atlantic route by airship was actually faster and more secure than the month one might expect to spend on a steamer east across the Pacific. Mr. Cui was willing to risk his household furnishings to the pirates infesting the Windward Isles, but, being of a practical bent, he was not willing to risk his own life or that of his lovely wife.

Another six comprised a touring group of five Colonials and one European that had been with the *Hans Glücker* since Ukraine. The touring group, which had boarded in Kyiv after traveling by rail from Moscow, were all plainly well-acquainted already, and what with one casually overheard conversation and another, Sebastien had pieced together a good deal about them. The eldest passenger, though by a few years only, was Madame Pontchartrain, a stout, gray-eyed matron enroute to her family's estate in French Mississippi by way of New Amsterdam. She accompanied a young

Colonial relative of apparently impeccable breeding and small estate, a Mademoiselle LeClere, who said she was travelling home to Nouvelle Orleans. The resemblance between them was strong enough that Sebastien thought Madame Pontchartrain must have been a very great beauty in her youth. He also thought them lucky that the *Hans Glücker*'s route—new the previous September—spared them a trip by rail across the interior of the North American continent. Various treaties with the Native nations would have made it possible, but far more rigorous and perilous than a modern journey by air.

Next was Oczkar Korvin, an aristocratic Hungarian with hair as dark as Sebastien's and an equally patrician bearing. A platinum chain leashed his pocket watch, and though he had the sallow Habsburg coloring, he was undisfigured by the famous deformed jaw. A collateral branch, no doubt.

The loveliest of the group was also the most famous. She traveled with an entourage and claimed three cabins. Dressed outrageously in a man's suit and cravat, Lillian Meadows, the American moving picture star, crossed her ankle over her knee and smoked Virginia cigarettes in a long tortoiseshell-and-jet holder, gesturing extravagantly with fingers studded with sapphires and diamonds. She was returning to Atlanta—where the studios were—from a European junket. Her white-blonde hair had been arranged in delicate waves around jeweled pins, and the English couple—who like Sebastien had boarded at Calais—avoided her.

One of her traveling companions was a man nearly as beautiful as she was, and also blond. He wore his darker gold hair slicked back against his skull, a handlebar moustache accentuating planed cheekbones and a defined jaw. His name was Virgil Allen, and he was a wealthy farmer's son from South Carolina, and a playboy by reputation.

The other was a woman, the Boston authoress Phoebe Smith. She a fair-haired, bespectacled, sensible small woman with a stubborn tilt to her head, straight-spined in widow's black that did not suit her, her hands usually folded before her. She carried a little bag with a black paper-bound notepad and fountain-pen, and every so often she would take them up and scribble a line.

A further six passengers had boarded at Calais. Two were Sebastien and his companion, Jack Priest, who presented every appearance of being a young man of excellent family. In truth, his breeding was no better than Sebastien's. But—also like Sebastien's—his education was unparalleled, and a work in constant progress. He was seventeen years old and looked fifteen, with delicate bones and tousled fair hair like a girl's.

Three and four were Michiel and Steven van Dijk, Dutch businessmen travelling only as far as New Amsterdam, where even under English colonial rule there was still a thriving Dutch community. Michiel was the elder, forty-ish, round-cheeked under graying, wavy fair hair, and plump without seeming heavy—as light on his feet as if he was filled with the same hydrogen that bore up the dirigible. Steven—pronounced *stay-van*—was taller and younger and also plump, his dark hair cropped short, his cheeks usually flushed and his eyes glittering with good cheer. He kept a green miniature parrot in his cabin, or occasionally on his shoulder, and Jack was instantly enamored of them both.

And the final two—the ones who seemed determined to avoid all of the Colonials, both the British colonials and the Frenchwomen—were a couple in their twenties. Hollis and Beatrice Leatherby were Londoners moving house to take advantage of a political appointment in the Pennsylvania colony, where an ambitious young man could advance faster than in Albion. She was darkly lovely while he was a freckled redhead: a striking pair.

Sebastien learned those things easily enough. Observation was a long-honed habit, though he intended merely a minor distraction for the hours until he could decently be seen to retire. The journey overland had not been easy and Jack had been delayed, only joining him in Calais that afternoon. Sebastien could not afford to be seen in good light until they had had a few minutes alone.

And so, from his solitary post at the dark end of the promenade, away from the too-revealing electric lights, Sebastien observed the other passengers and watched Jack.

Jack held court forward along the promenade, his admirers a potential source of amusement or inconvenience. He was drinking champagne rather than liquor, but his laughter told Sebastien enough about his conversation with Steven van Dijk and the Leatherbys to swamp that raft of faint reassurance in a sea of potential tribulations. He *would* flirt. And right now he was flirting with Mrs. Leatherby, immediately under her husband's oblivious eye—and sparing a little charm for van Dijk, as well.

Sebastien cupped his glass before his face, and pretended to taste the cognac. The sharp, drowning scent was good. It blunted his hunger, which threatened to grow overwhelming, and the snifter gave him something to occupy hands that wanted to tremble with desire.

The social dance was not distracting him tonight. He could feel it in the cut-glass edge on his senses, the heaviness of limbs that would transform into mercurial quickness when he required it. Too much more and his restraint would fail. He'd waited too long.

Discipline was always a matter of degree to such as Sebastien, and it had required a certain subterfuge and sleight of hand to free himself of old friends and allies. That alone had consumed days. His court would be displeased when they came to understand that he had abandoned them. He would be missed, and their protests would have carried the day if he had paused to listen; Sebastien de Ulloa was notoriously too soft-hearted. But he could not remain in Europe. It held no savor for him now, and boredom and sorrow were ever more dangerous adversaries than any merely human agency.

There was some risk in travelling in secret, in shedding his court. He should have left Jack, too…but Jack would almost certainly leave *him*, soon enough (as his proteges always did) and he couldn't travel without an entourage. The rail journey from Helsinki to Calais alone had taxed his strength and ingenuity. But he had needed to be free of Europe, so full of secrets and history, and all of Evie's friends.

He closed his eyes. His restraint would hold through this endless, tiresome evening, and then he would have what he needed. Jack would take care of him. And once he came to the Colonies—well. If he could not make a new beginning in America, then he would find an end.

He opened his eyes again, watching Jack tease and flirt and please himself. Meanwhile, someone was slipping up on him, and Sebastien was meant not to notice. The warm scent of her skin carried over the cognac, though, even if he hadn't observed her movements or heard the scuff of her shoes on the deck. Still, he pretended oblivion, because it amused him to.

It was Mrs. Smith, the blonde American novelist, and he feigned startlement when she touched his arm.

"So intent," she said. "What is it that you see, I wonder?"

Sebastien tipped his untasted glass at Hollis Leatherby. "More than he does, in any case."

She bore a red wine cupped in her hand, the stem falling between her fingers, as if she meant to warm the contents with her palm the same way Sebastien could not manage to warm his cognac. She smiled, her glasses lifting as the bridge of her nose crinkled. "Are you certain?"

"My dear lady," Sebastien said, "I am certain of nothing. But I will speculate. And my first speculation concerns a charming American, yes? And her agenda in approaching a sullen stranger at a remarkably boring cocktail party."

"You're a striking man. A mysterious Continental stranger. With a certain notoriety. That's supposed to be enough, isn't it?"

Sebastien shook his head, amused. It had been some time, admittedly, but when last he'd consulted a looking glass, he had been of slightly better than average height (for a modern man) and somewhat swarthy complexion—convenient, as it concealed his frequent pallor—with dark hair, thin lips, and a hooked nose. He had no reason to believe much had changed since then. Passable, certainly; his court had never complained of his ugliness. But *striking* was quite plainly in the eye of the beholder.

"At least you didn't call me *handsome*," he replied. "Jack would never let me hear the end of it. But come, now—don't we both prefer honesty, Mrs. Smith?"

She sipped, then swirled the fluid in her glass to release the aromas, and considered him. "Will you treat a lady novelist to a demonstration of your storied powers?"

Ah. Well, that neatly explained why she had sought his darkened, solitary corner. He was *material.*

And Jack had noticed that Sebastien had company. He caught Sebastien's eye over Beatrice Leatherby's head, offering a little smile that whispered *you'll pay later,* then turned back to Steven van Dijk and the five-inch-long grass-green bird who perched on Steven's forefinger, eyeing Jack as if his nose might be some sort of undiscovered delicacy.

Well, Sebastien would cheerfully abet anyone's quest for a continuing education, especially a smart young woman's. He reminded himself to breathe and said, "On whom shall I inform? And are you in the mood for gossip, dear lady, or for parlor games?"

"At all costs, gossip."

He turned from her quirk of smile and cast his eye over the other passengers. During Sebastien's brief distraction, the Captain—Konrad Hoak—had extricated himself from conversation with Oczkar Korvin and Michiel van Dijk and joined Jack's group, pretending a fascination with the parrot to cover a fascination with Beatrice Leatherby. Curiously, Hollis Leatherby seemed far more cognizant of the Captain's flirtation than of Jack's—or perhaps there was simply more of concern in a grown man's attentions to one's wife than those of a fresh-faced lad, no matter how pretty.

In any case, a frown tugged the corners of Leatherby's mouth as he excused himself, added his wife's empty glass to his own, and made his way down the promenade stairs toward the rolling bar in the dining room. He brushed past Mme. Pontchartrain stiffly, flinching from her effusive greeting while handing over both glasses.

Perhaps Mrs. Leatherby was the jealous one. She certainly glowered sharply enough when she took note of the conversation, though Sebastien did not think Mme. Pontchartrain was the sort of woman who would drive most wives to jealous rages.

Meanwhile, Mr. Leatherby waited as the bartender, a strapping fair-haired Hun of the sort epidemic among the *Hans Glücker's* crew, mixed martinis and added olives and onions. But Leatherby too couldn't resist a glance over his shoulder while he waited, or a wince when his wife dimpled prettily at the captain.

So Leatherby was also jealous. But not the type to cause a scene.

And any fool could see it, so it would hardly serve to impress an intelligent woman. And Sebastien did feel the urge to impress her, though he mocked himself for it. *Haven't you left all this behind, Sebastien? Haven't you sworn it off, the flirtations and seductions? A clean start, wasn't it?*

Ridiculous, of course. He was what he was, and had been far longer than this enjoyable young woman had been alive.

And there was Jack. So not a clean start, exactly. But Sebastien could no more leave Jack behind than his grief and his memories. And like those memories, Jack was perfectly capable of chasing him all the way to New Amsterdam.

It was the hazard in taking apprentices.

"Well?" Mrs. Smith said, shifting close enough that he could feel her warmth on his arm. "I'm still waiting to be amazed."

He wanted to impress her, but he had hidden in his dark corner for a reason; he was in no mood to perform for anyone. Perhaps he could distract her. "Your impoverished Frenchwoman," he said, with a smile. "Do you suppose she plans to marry American money?"

He didn't need to point. On their left was the outward-slanting wall of isinglass that showed the sea below and the fading lights of the French coast. On their right was the dining room and the bar, from which Leatherby was emerging with his offering to his wife. Meanwhile, Mme. Pontchartrain, perhaps one or two sherries over her limit, was engaged in a conversation with Zhang Xiaoming that involved a good deal of handwaving and laughter on both sides. She was, however, keeping one drooping eye on the same thing that had drawn Sebastien's attention: Mlle. LeClere, who perched on the bench of the airship's ultra-light aluminum piano alongside Virgil Allen, playing the low notes while he played the high, and together producing a somewhat abused version of "The Lights o' London."

"She'll be disappointed," Mrs. Smith said. "Virgil's a second son."

"I'm surprised the girl's guardian permits it either way," Sebastien said. "Has she spent the entire trip at the bar?"

"She does tipple a little," Mrs. Smith admitted. "Though one doesn't like to judge. After my Benjamin died—" Her voice trailed off, and she sipped her wine. "Well, one copes as one can. And short of turning to necromancy or mediums, alcohol has its mercies."

Her lingering sorrow was contagious, awakening his own. Sebastien wished, for a moment, that he could risk the cognac in his glass. "And Mlle. LeClere?"

"Ah," Mrs. Smith said. "A beautiful, guileless, impoverished heiress. And all the men of good estate flock 'round...."

"My dear," Sebastien answered gallantly, "I prefer a woman who knows her own mind."

"Well, there's enough of those on this tub." The wine made her sparkle. Or perhaps the wine was an excuse to shed a little reserve; one could never be too sure. "You won't go lonely."

"Madame," he said, sincerely, "if only it were so."

Some time later, Mrs. Smith excused herself to visit the ladies' washroom, leaving Sebastien to his own devices. Eventually, someone was bound to notice that he'd been standing in the same corner, swirling the same cognac in his glass for hours. Hunger wouldn't make him wobbly or vague, but it would make him sharp-set, unnerving. And he did not care to leave his fellow passengers...unnerved. Attention now could lead to suspicion later.

Sebastien picked his way down the steps toward the bar, to relieve himself of his undesired burden. He would collect Jack (who had descended to the dining room) make his excuses to the captain, and retire.

The steward took Sebastien's full glass with a smile and slipped it under the bar. Sebastien winked at him; he found he could generally rely on the international conspiracy of bartenders for discretion. Especially as Sebastien was always well-behaved.

He turned away.

It was Jack leaning against the piano now, while Oczkar Korvin tried his hand at a little Bach. The result was generally superior to the English parlor tunes, not in the least because no-one attempted to sing. Korvin's hands were long and gaunt, knobby-fingered, and his hair fell over his eyes as he leaned forward, arms akimbo over the keyboard. He glanced up as Sebastien came over and settled in beside Jack. "Don Sebastien."

The effort to speak did not appear to affect his concentration. "Korvin úr," Sebastien answered, giving the other man's name the Hungarian honorific before continuing in the same language, "A pleasure to make your acquaintance. How *did* you come to be travelling with so many lovely women?"

Korvin laughed and let his hands fall silent on the keys as he answered in English, perhaps noticing Jack's furrowed brow—a patent fraud, as Jack spoke Hungarian like a native. "I noticed the notorious Mrs. Smith had cornered you. Beware of that one. She'll have your secrets out of you like a pocket handkerchief."

"Indeed?" Sebastien folded his arms and settled his weight on his heels. "You met her in Kyiv?"

"Moscow. With the other ladies, and Mr. Allen, ten days ago. The airship's route took us across most of the Baltic states. The *Hans Glücker* is not what you would call a—" He snapped his fingers as the English word eluded him.

"Express," Jack supplied.

"Thank you." The shared smile made Sebastien's neck hairs prickle. "Moscow," Sebastien prompted, more from curiosity than towards a purpose. Pretending he did not see Jack's smile, he said, "I am preternaturally nosy."

"That is why they call you the detective, I presume," Korvin said, with reasonably good humor. "Have you noticed the Leatherbys? I would not have expected them to be any more acquainted with either of the Colonial parties—American or *americain*—than I was, but I would say that they have a quite developed aversion to Madame Pontchartrain. Although"—his fingers lifted from the keys to adjust his cravat—"they get on well enough to our Dutch friends."

"So not just English standoffishness, then?"

Jack stirred and cleared his throat before Korvin could answer. "Madame Pontchartrain," Jack said. "How good of you to join us."

She was carrying water now, not sherry, and walking quite steadily, though with a certain degree of care. She paused a few feet away and smiled. "I beg your pardon, gentlemen," she said, in French. "I had come to see if I could prevail upon you for a little more music."

Korvin lifted his fingers from his lap and stretched them. "For the right tithe," he said, "I might even sing. Master Jack, would you see if the bartender has a bottle of cognac back there?"

"Indeed he does," Sebastien said, nodding permission to Jack. "Good evening, Madame—"

She rolled her shoulders over a corset that gave her the general appearance of the prow of a battleship, and curled one loose strand of her uptwisted hair around her finger in a gesture that would have been coquettish, were she young. "And good evening to you, Don Sebastien. I've spent a good deal of time in Spain, and you are the first of your family I've met. Might I inquire where you are from?"

He laughed and turned it aside, hiding his discomfort. "New Amsterdam, as of today. I am emigrating."

"Along with your…pupil?"

"My ward," he said. He lifted his chin to watch Jack's negotiations with the steward, the jerk of his thumb over his shoulder as he said, no doubt, *the drink is for Mr. Korvin.*

"A likely lad." Her voice purred a little, just this side of insinuating, and Sebastien drew himself up.

"Very likely," he answered, and made himself scarce. It was late enough to permit a dignified escape. If Jack wanted to stay up and flirt with the ladies—and not just the ladies, apparently—he could perfectly well follow when he was ready. Sebastien would survive until he got there.

As it happened, he didn't have to survive long. Jack arrived no more than ten minutes later, brushing aside with one hand the curtain that covered the doorway. He peered through and slipped inside, pausing just within. "You should have said something."

Sebastien was sitting on the lower bunk, a gothic novel open upon his knees. He paused with one page delicately uplifted between his fingers, and looked up. "I hadn't the wit left to divert Mme. Pontchartrain's determined questioning. Fortunately, I had the wit to realize it, so I pled a cognac headache and fled. You seemed to enjoy yourself this evening."

His voice went sharper than he'd intended, but Jack just smiled and turned to be certain the curtain was closed. "Put out the light, Sebastien."

Sebastien stood and pulled the shade down. There were no windows in the cabin, but an electric porthole light—of all the futuristic contrivances—provided illumination. It was operated by excess power from the *Hans Glücker's* six motors and easily darkened by a shade should the occupants desire. Electrical switches could cause a spark, considered undesirable in a hydrogen-filled vehicle. The dim rooms suited Sebastien very well. Much better than any sailing vessel might have.

The cabin seemed even closer with the lights out. Sebastien could see exceptionally well in the dark, but he closed his eyes to feel Jack moving. Sebastien heard him unbuttoning his collar, untucking his shirt, hanging his jacket in the dark, and sliding his braces down. He kicked his shoes off, and Sebastien heard his shirt and trousers fall, as well. "Jack?"

"Come here."

Sebastien went to him, catfooted. He folded his arms around Jack and pressed his mouth to warm, uptilted lips. He breathed Jack's scent; released from his clothes, it hung about him like the drapery on a Grecian statue. Jack's fingers pressed Sebastien's cheeks and he clucked, not liking what he found. "Don't wait that long again."

"I was alone."

Jack's hands slid across Sebastien's face and knotted in his hair, pushing him to his knees, pressing Sebastien's cold face against his skin. Jack leaned against the bedframe. "Well," he said, "for Christ's sake, don't wait now."

Early the next morning, when the *Hans Glücker* was well away over the Atlantic, Madame Pontchartrain was discovered missing from her cabin and, in fact, the entirety of the dirigible. Mademoiselle LeClere, sleeping in the top bunk, claimed to have heard nothing in the night.

Sebastien could no more travel unescorted than could a respectable woman, although in his case the difficulty was of well-being rather than social standing. They retired separately; Jack slept in the bottom bunk, closer to the curtained doorway. Sebastien did not sleep, but lay listening to the *Hans Glücker*'s deep silences, the creak and strain of her superstructure, the muted breathing of the nearest passengers. Both men would have preferred a room with a door—even a door of spruce splints and doped cloth—but there was no such luxury to be had aboard the dirigible.

So when someone pounded with a nervous fist against the aluminum doorframe beside the curtain, the wall rattled against the bunk, waking Jack with a start. Sebastien was already sitting upright in the filtered gloom when his companion rolled out of bed. "Coming," Jack called.

Sebastien slipped from the top bunk and withdrew into the room's most shadowed corner, shrugging his dressing-gown over his nightshirt. Jack checked that he was halfway presentable before flicking the curtain aside.

"Detective! You are needed! Madame Pontchartrain is gone!" A crewman's voice, by the coarse German accent. Jack glanced over his own shoulder at Sebastien. "A mystery," Sebastien said, with an impatient turn of his hand. "How quaint."

Jack turned back to the crewman and let the curtain fall wide while Sebastien stepped forward to stand at his shoulder. Jack's German was better than the crewman's English, so he spoke in that language. "You wish to speak to the detective?"

"The captain does," the crewman said, his cap clutched to his breast. His eyes flicked around the dark cabin, taking in the blacked-out light, the two rumpled beds. He swallowed.

"Excellent." Sebastien drew his dressing gown closed across his chest, as if he felt a chill. "I'll meet him in the salon in half an hour."

He reached over Jack's shoulder and flipped the curtain shut in the surprised crewman's face. Jack waited until he heard footsteps and stepped back, pressing his shoulder to Sebastien's arm. "No holiday for you," he said.

Sebastien, turning away, paused to tousle Jack's hair. "Pull your trousers on, there's a good lad, and go and check the salon for me, would you?"

"Already done," Jack said, crouching by his trunk. "Use the center stair. I looked last night. It's away from any windows."

Sebastien flipped his valet case open and searched compartments for his cufflinks. "And get yourself some breakfast," he said without raising his chin. "You're pale."

The cabins, lounge, and dining room were on the main deck, in the belly of the seven-hundred-foot-long airship. The promenades lined that same deck, their isinglass windows angled down, following the curve of the dirigible's body, and showed the passing earth and sea below; direct sunlight would not be a problem except at sunset and dawn.

There was a second promenade one flight up, and the lower deck, while mostly crew quarters, also contained the galley, the washrooms, the smoking room—with its asbestos ceiling and tin floor—and the salon.

Which was empty but for Mrs. Smith when they entered. Barely twenty minutes had elapsed; Sebastien could be ready very quickly when he chose.

The salon was a pleasant room, windowless and in the center of the lower deck as a courtesy to passengers of delicate disposition who might find the *Hans Glücker's* altitude or motion unsettling, and thus it was very well suited to Sebastien's needs. The steady drone of the zeppelin's motors was a constant accompaniment as he collected a china cup of tea from the small banquet laid along one wall, then chose a leather wing-backed chair beside the door. Meanwhile, Jack piled jam on scones to suit an adolescent's appetite.

Mrs. Smith was already seated on the divan, applying a silver fork to the pastry on her canary-yellow Meissen cake plate. She had acknowledged Sebastien earlier. Now, he touched the teacup to his lips before he set it, and its saucer, on the side table. "Mrs. Smith," he said. "You seem very calm."

Her eyebrows rose over the frame of her spectacles. "I'm screaming inside," she said, and laid the fork down beside her plate. "But that's no reason not to eat."

"Did you hear anything last night?"

"I thought you'd ask how I learned of the mystery."

"Actually," he said, "I'm curious how you knew to be in this room. As my message was for the captain alone, I believe."

She sipped her own tea. "I eavesdropped." She smiled. "My German is excellent."

The door at the base of the stair swung open. It was a fragile thing, fabric stretched over a wooden frame, closed by a wooden latch for lightness of structure. Sebastien and Jack stood as Captain Hoak entered the salon alone, his hat pinned against his side by his left elbow. Mrs. Smith remained seated, as was proper, but set her teacup down.

"Mrs. Smith," the Captain said, in English. "Good morning. And *guten Morgen*, Don Sebastien, Master Jack. Is Mrs. Smith—" He wavered, uncertain as to whom he should be addressing.

"Mrs. Smith is just leaving," the authoress said. She abandoned her cup and plate and made sure of her reticule before standing. "I shall be in the observation lounge if I am required. Thank you for the excellence of your company, Don Sebastien." She offered her gloved hand. He took it and bowed over it lightly. "Master Jack," she concluded, with a teasing smile that sent high color across the young man's face, and swept past the Captain with a little gracious nod.

The Captain turned to watch her go. He was a tall man, blond hair graying, and he carried the beginnings of a small, hard paunch. He sighed lightly as the door latch clicked and went to fetch his own coffee. "How much have you been informed, Don Sebastien?"

Sebastien reclaimed his chair as the Captain sat. He lifted his cooling tea and blew across the saucer. Jack, who had already finished two scones and was toying with the crumbs on his plate, sat as well. Sebastien expected a steward would be along to tidy when their conference was done. "Only that Madame Pontchartrain is…gone, I believe the word was. Not dead, I take it then?"

"Vanished," the Captain said. "Dead, perhaps. If she fell, certainly, but there's no evidence she did. No breach in the hull, and the passenger doors are sealed—and she did not enter the control cabin."

"Have you searched the lifting body?" Sebastien's hand rose, an extended finger indicating the ceiling and the giant framework of aluminum beyond it. Within the streamlined lifting body were thirteen donut-shaped gas containers filled with hydrogen and harnessed by netting within the dirigible's frame.

"We are searching it now," Captain Hoak said. "But there has been no sign of her there. And of course, even if a woman of her…dignity could be expected to be clambering up ladders, the hatchways are kept locked."

Sebastien picked up his cup and saucer and stood smoothly, without reliance upon the arms of the chair. "By all means," he said. "Let us examine the lady's cabin."

Madame Pontchartrain's cabin was no different from Sebastien's, except in that women's clothing—a dozen or so dresses, half of them rich with velvet and silk, and cut for a more generous figure than the plainer muslins and wools—and two nightgowns—hung from the bar at the foot of the bunks, and the upper bunk had been tidied. Sebastien and Jack searched the cabin thoroughly, to the Captain's stiff-lipped dismay, and found little of note. The lower bed lay as it had been left, the covers smoothed roughly over a bottom sheet that was rumpled but not creased; hardly typical of what Sebastien had observed of the chambermaids' military efficiency. There was no blood, and no sign of a struggle, although Madame Pontchartrain's papers seemed to be in some disarray inside her portfolio, and her cabin bag was less neatly packed than one might expect.

"Dear boy," Sebastien said, while the Captain posed rigidly beyond the door, erect as a hungry hawk upon a glove, "do you suppose a woman of

Madame Pontchartrain's age and breeding is inclined to creep from her bed at night—to any purpose—without smoothing the sheets respectably?"

"Perhaps if she were very ill," Jack said uncertainly. He stood a little closer to Sebastien than decorum warranted, but the Captain seemed disinclined to comment. "And very much in a hurry."

"Captain," Sebastien said. "I believe we must examine the ladies' washroom."

The ladies' was innocent of any sign of violence, and like Mademoiselle LeClere, the attendant had heard nothing. After their inspection, Sebastien accompanied Jack to the dining room for an early luncheon, switching plates discreetly when Jack finished his own steak and salad and began eyeing Sebastien's poached salmon. He was halfway across the serving and eating methodically when his fork hesitated in midair and his chin came up, blue eyes catching the filtered light.

Sebastien, who was sitting with his back to the windows so he would not be dazzled by even indirect sunlight, saw their bright shapes reflected in Jack's irises.

"Ah," he said, observing the deepening furrow between Jack's eyebrows. "The nightgowns."

"Two nightgowns," Jack agreed. "Hanging, and one unrumpled. Madame Pontchartrain never went to bed last night."

"Indeed she didn't," Sebastien said, holding his wine under his nose before tilting the glass, and flicking his tongue out to collect just a drop on the tip, for tasting's sake. "So the question remains, who rumpled her bunk?"

"And why did Mademoiselle LeClere lie?" Chewing a last bite of salmon, Jack laid his fork across his plate—more yellow Meissen, with cabbage roses and gilt edges. The tablecloths were eyelet linen, white and fine. "Speaking of which, there's the young lady herself. With Miss Lillian Meadows, no less."

Sebastien lifted his knife and turned it so the silver blade reflected the dining room behind him. He saw two blonde heads bent close together as the ladies were seated, Miss Meadows tight-trousered and drawing sidelong glances—admiring or censorious—and Mlle. LeClere scandalous with her shawl wound about her neck like a scarf rather than covering the white expanse of her bosom. "While the duenna's away—" Sebastien began, but then his eyes were drawn to the white cloth twisted around Mlle. LeClere's long pale throat.

Jack cleared his throat. "I *know* where *you* were last night."

"Indeed." Sebastien laid the knife crisply across Jack's plate, abruptly grateful that he could not blush. "So do I. And also I think it's time for a stroll. Do you not agree?"

Silently, Jack rose, folding his napkin. And together they left the table.

———⁂———

"Do you think it's Miss Meadows?" Jack asked, when they were safely away from the dining room, strolling the promenade. It was only a little past noon, so the sun was safely blocked from the long windows by the shadow of the airframe, and if anyone did harbor suspicions about Sebastien, it would do no harm for Sebastien to be seen by midday.

"One doesn't find many of the blood in theatre." Sebastien licked pale lips. "Matinees."

"But she's a motion picture actress—"

"And how might she explain an inability to shoot outdoor scenes in daylight?"

"Ah," Jack said. He raked at his hair, pale curls stretching between his fingers and then springing back. "Besides, why would she turn to Mlle. LeClere when she has two travelling companions of her own?"

"Mrs. Smith was wearing an open-necked shirtwaist," Sebastien pointed out.

In answer, Jack touched his own loosely-knotted cravat. He did not affect the London and Milan fashion of high collars, as Sebastien did. "Mrs. Smith may not be prone to bruising—"

"She is a *very* pale blonde."

"—or she may be a more intimate friend of Miss Meadows' than Mlle. LeClere, leaving the evidence…inobvious." Jack finished, smugly.

"I am scandalized," the great detective answered, a small smile warming his lips. They warmed further when Jack checked over his shoulder, and then brushed them with a quick peck.

"If not Miss Meadows…." Jack said, stepping back.

"You make assumptions," Sebastien said. A cardinal sin, and Jack winced to be caught out. "*If* there is another of the blood aboard this ship…and *if* Mlle. LeClere is of her court"—the polite term, in preference to any of the myriad crass ones—"it would be the rankest sort of stupidity to murder an old woman."

They turned at the wall, and began walking back.

"Because suspicion would naturally fall on any passenger discovered to be of the blood."

"Prejudices die hard," Sebastien said.

"I've known a few Jews," Jack said. The dryness that informed his voice was no happenstance. He *was* one, blond curls and blue eyes and good plain English alias aside. "It's the same everywhere. And it needn't be your folk, Sebastien. A disappearance in the absence of any evidence suggests black magic to me. Teleportation, transmutation…what if someone turned her into a frog?"

"Or a green parrot? And us without a forensic sorcerer anywhere to be found."

Jack cleared his throat. "We've seen the parrot and Madame Pontchartrain in the same place. So if it is one of yours, and not Miss Meadows, who?"

"Korvin úr," Sebastien said, automatically. And then he checked himself. "At a guess."

"Good guess," Jack said. He lowered his voice; they were still alone on their side of the promenade, but below, in the dining room blurrily visible through the interior isinglass, Virgil Allen and Hollis Leatherby had entered and paused beside the drinks caddy. "I'm trying to remember if I've heard his name—"

"Have you?" The tone was sharper than Sebastien had intended. He did not care to be reminded of Jack's past.

There were clubs in most cities, places where those who courted the blood congregated, and where those of the blood who were far from their courts and their courtesans could go, for sustenance and for companionship. Names were whispered in those places, and secrets traded.

It was in one such, in a basement in Budapest, that Sebastien had discovered Jack, a gamin child of eight or nine years, and where he—against his custom and better judgement, and in much the spirit with which one might haggle for a starved dog chained to a railing—had purchased the boy.

It was three hundred and fifty German marks Sebastien considered very well spent indeed.

Jack chewed his lip, and then shrugged. "It was a long time ago. I don't recall."

—⁓—

Jack was still tired from a difficult night, while Sebastien buzzed with energy. It had been unsafe attending to his needs aboard the *Hans Glücker*, but it would be more unsafe to spend three days and part of a fourth in human company with his skin cold and waxen and his hunger growing.

Sebastien wondered if Korvin úr had found himself in similar straits. It was unusual for one of the blood to travel without a companion. Or three.

Or perhaps the handsome stranger to eye with suspicion wasn't Lillian Meadows or Oczkar Korvin, but the pale and delicate Mrs. Phoebe Smith. Virgil Allen had a southerner's bronzed glow, but that could be counterfeited with cosmetics…

Sebastien paused in the passageway and shook his head, leaning one hand on a cornerpost of the corridor wall. Those, at least, were solid enough to hold his weight, unlike the cloth stretched between them. He was committing the same sin he'd accused Jack of, speculating on small and circumstantial evidence, looking for a monster to explain away what was most likely mere human veniality. Speculation, rather than deduction, and that was no way to solve a crime.

Assuming any crime had been committed. Which, admittedly, seemed like a fairly safe assumption—but one assumption tended to lead to another.

He straightened up and squared his shoulders under his coat. The next step must be to interview the witnesses. Particularly, he thought, Mlle. LeClere.

He was halfway down the spiral stair to the day parlor, following her scent, when something else occurred to him. Her scent. In particular. It had been present in the cabin she shared with Mme. Pontchartrain. As, indeed, had the scents of Mme. Pontchartrain—both her own bodily aroma, and the funereal bouf of roses and chrysanthemums she habitually wore. But there had been no third person's aroma, and, as Jack had noted, Mme. Pontchartrain did not appear to have even slipped on her nightdress.

So why *had* her bunk been rumpled? And not, he thought, rumpled as if someone had slept therein, but rather as if someone had stripped the covers back in hasty investigation, and then smoothed them carelessly.

That mystery distracted Sebastien to the bottom of the stairs, where he paused and cast left and right, sniffing delicately, for the aroma of lilies, powder, and warm girl that identified Mlle. LeClere.

Instead, he smelled lilacs and civet and a different warm girl entirely, the scent vanguarding a swish of sensible English wool. "My dear Mrs. Leatherby," he said, and turned.

She startled, which had been his intention, and drew herself up short, her skirts swinging heavily about the ankles of her button boots. Gray kid-gloved fingers tensed on the handle of her reticule; there was a tiny snag on her left thumb, a little hole she hadn't yet sewn up. "Don Sebastien," she stammered. "I beg your pardon—"

"I have excellent hearing," he said, stooping a little to offer her an arm. She accepted it, her fingers curling as convulsively on his sleeve as they had on her handbag.

"As it happens," Mrs. Leatherby said in a small voice, "so do I. Which is what I wished to speak with you about, if you do not find me too forward, Don Sebastien."

Her steps tarried so he must cut his own stride for fear of dragging her off her feet. He ducked his head to introduce the appearance of intimacy. "Do continue."

"I'm sorry," she said, shivering delicately. "I'm all aflutter. If there's a killer aboard...."

"Quite." He patted her arm, grateful of the long sleeves that would prevent her from noticing how his skin was chill.

"Last night—" She glanced over her shoulder, and he soothed her with a hand on her hand again. "Last night I heard voices. You must understand that Hollis is a very sound sleeper, Don Sebastien, and he snores quite dreadfully."

"Indeed," he answered, letting her annoying overuse of his name pass unremarked, though it led him to unworthy speculation on whether Mr. Leatherby had perhaps been less oblivious than he seemed to Jack's shameless flirtation with his wife that first night in the salon, or if the sighs he had breathed had been of relief rather than jealousy. "And this is significant because?..."

"We sleep away from the other passengers," Mrs. Leatherby said. "Out of consideration."

A benefit of the nearly-empty passenger quarters. "You heard something?" Sebastien asked, understanding dawning. His hair slid down his forehead, and he tossed it back, taking a moment as well to consider the particular hell of a nervous woman with acute hearing paired with a heavy snorer.

"A man and a woman," she said, her chin jerking in small, sharp nods. "Speaking French. I recognized the man's voice as Mister Korvin's, and is he really a viscount?"

"Vikomt, in Hungarian," Sebastien said. "And I have not heard Korvin úr make such a claim. If only this were a sailing vessel, one could examine the peerage in the ship's library."

"Silly me," Mrs. Leatherby said. "I'm sure you think me a right fool, but it's so exciting, being abroad and meeting exotic personages with their European manners." Her hand flew to her mouth, releasing his somewhat crumpled sleeve. "Oh, Sebastien, I'm terribly sorry."

"It's quite all right," he answered. "No offense taken." Released of her grip, he took a half-step toward the salon. She tripped after.

"But I haven't told you the worst," she said. Her voice rose, but she had the art of the breathless shriek, like so many Englishwomen, and it wouldn't carry. He wondered when the pocket handkerchief would emerge, or if she'd skip directly on to the fainting spell.

"Indeed, Señora," he said. Perhaps he should resort to his own handkerchief; the lilac was about to make him sneeze. "What *did* you hear?"

"I didn't understand the words, of course, but it had the sound of an argument," she said. "And afterward...there were other things." Her lips made a moue of distaste.

"Ah," Sebastien said. "Say no more. Did you recognize the lady's voice?"

"They were speaking *French*," she repeated, insistently.

"Of course," Sebastien answered. With a great and distancing show of gallantry, he stepped forward and opened the door to the salon for her, sweeping an outrageous bow. "That does narrow the field somewhat, now doesn't it?"

Unfortunately, his intention of speaking to Mlle. LeClere was foiled by the continuing presence of Miss Meadows. The ladies had been joined by Mr. Allen and Korvin úr, and judging by the way Mlle. LeClere was leaning on Oczkar Korvin's arm, Miss Meadows' presence was all that was preventing a scandal—an irony which Sebastien savored, briefly.

He understood the urge. A young woman rarely—perhaps never—found herself released on her own recognizance. It must seem a heady interlude in such a constrained life, and he couldn't grudge her taking advantage of it, when it would be back to her ordained task of trapping a man when she made landfall. The *Hans Glücker* was, in any case, a relatively safe place to sow wild oats.

Or should have been, to all rights, if there had not been a potential murderer aboard.

As soon as Sebastien could decently extract himself from Mrs. Leatherby, he went in search of the infinitely preferable American lady, Mrs. Smith. At the very least, she could no doubt tell him a little something about Miss Lillian Meadows and Mr. Virgil Allen.

He found her on the promenade. Lingering would become a tricky proposition as the sun slid down before the nose of the dirigible, but for now the long shadows kept him safe. Phoebe Smith stood at the forward-most reach of the promenade, under the nose of the airframe. She held her hard-backed black notebook left-handed and scribbled busily with the right, her ink-stained fingers embracing the grip of a tortoiseshell fountain pen.

She sniffed as he came up beside her, and said, with great satisfaction, "Did you know, Don Sebastien, that were we to ascend very much further, the drop in air pressure would cause the ink in my pen to expand, resulting in an oozing mess?" She turned to him, and held it up beside her face for in-spection. The nib gleamed dully in the indirect light, a hairline of black demonstrating the split, but Sebastien focused past it. At her face, her pal-lor, the whiteness of her lips where they tightened over her teeth, the faintly visible capillaries warming her pale cheeks.

"You're staring, Don Sebastien."

He glanced quickly down so she would not see him fail to blush. "So it would appear. Is the material any good?"

"I beg your pardon?"

He gestured to the crawling sea below the isinglass. "You must be work-ing on a novel."

"Only scribbling observations. It's what I do."

"Scribble?"

"Observe."

"And eavesdrop."

"That, too." And yes, she *could* blush, a delicate seashell glow across her cheeks. "Fortunately, I am discreet."

"And unshockable."

"Quite," she said, after a short pause. She capped the pen and clipped it to a cord around her neck, so that it slid out of sight between her breasts. She marked her place in the notebook with a ribbon and stowed that, as well, in her reticule. "Your young ward thinks highly of you."

Sebastien could no more blanch than he could blush, and this once he thanked Providence for it. They had been quiet—ferociously quiet, *fiercely* quiet—but Jack had not been able to stifle a gasp against his fist, or the sharp single flex of his hips that had shaken the aluminum frame of the bunk when Sebastien's fangs slipped in.

At that, he was quieter than Sebastien had been in his own time.

"He is very dear to me as well," Sebastien answered. "And your travel-ling companions? Do you think highly of them?"

Her true smile dazzled. Gone was the contrived, ladylike lift of her mouth at the corners. This was honest mirth, and it included Sebastien rather than mocking him. "I find them a font of human detail," she said. "A veritable education."

"On what do they educate you?"

"On the unpleasant nature of seduction," she said, in a softer tone. She leaned forward, hands braced on the promenade railing, to stare down at the sea below and the *Hans Glücker*'s attendant flock of gulls. The white birds did not seem to care that the ship they followed flew rather than floated. "I would not ever care to find myself on the sort of string upon which Miss Meadows keeps Mr. Allen."

It struck home. Sebastien leaned against the railing beside her, and spoke in French. "Or upon which I keep Jack?"

She tilted her head, watching him from the corner of pale eyes. She didn't shift away, and when she answered it was in the same language. "I didn't say it."

"Did you need to?"

"Don Sebastien," she said. "Is it you who has the young Mr. Priest on a string? Or perhaps the other way around?"

"Ach." He pushed himself straight against the railing. "Mutual dependency. How unflattering."

"How very like a marriage." She fiddled one pearl earring, refusing to meet his eyes. "No, perhaps you should look to Korvin úr and Mlle. LeClere, if you wish to see a troublesome partnership breeding."

"Are they partners?"

"He makes her cry," Mrs. Smith said, dropping into English again. "And while she seeks refuge and distraction with Lillian—with Miss Meadows—she does not return Korvin úr's notes unread, either."

"She encourages him."

"She *breathes* for him, Don Sebastien," Mrs. Smith said. "And Lillian thinks it's funny."

— ❧ —

When Sebastien returned to the salon, he watched for it. Conveniently, Allen, Korvin, Mlle. LeClere, and Miss Meadows were still present, playing whist under an electric light. Ladies were partnered against gentlemen, and Mlle. LeClere and Miss Meadows were winning—on brass moreso than chivalry.

Sebastien swirled a cognac in a balloon glass and lounged in the armchair he'd appropriated, back in the corner beside the door, pretending to read a four-day-old Times of London. He had a knack for vanishing into the shadows when he cared to, and as long as he didn't snap the paper or rattle his cufflinks the card players in their armchairs seemed to have more or less forgotten him. Except for Oczkar Korvin, who never glanced over at all, as if he were consciously ignoring Sebastien's presence.

The Hungarian was of a yellowish complexion, which could have been natural, but also made it more difficult to tell if he blanched where his hand pressed the cards. But then Mlle. LeClere stood between tricks, laying her hand tidily face-down and fetched drinks for the table—sherry for herself, whisky for Miss Meadows and Mr. Allen, and a plum brandy for Korvin úr. Mademoiselle slipped the glass into his hand rather than set beside him so she had the excuse to brush her fingers across his palm. And then, Sebastien saw him lift the glass to his lips, his throat working as he swallowed.

Korvin murmured something in Mlle. LeClere's ear that made her blush. When he turned and saluted Sebastien, the level of the gold-tinged transparent fluid had fallen. Sebastien toasted him back and raised the cognac to his lips, heady fumes searing his nostrils. He tilted the glass, so the cognac touched his lips, and feigned drinking, watching Korvin's smile, and wondering what, exactly, he was up against.

Observing the dynamics at the table made an interesting pastime. The four played intently, without excess table talk. They were all subdued and prone to starting at small noises, but Sebastien judged that more likely the nervousness of the herd when it cannot place the predator than any effect of guilt.

Allen kept his eyes on Miss Meadows rather than on his partner, as Mrs. Smith had predicted. As a result, he gave away easy tricks, plainly displeasing Korvin. As for Mlle. LeClere, she made an interesting subject. She sat across from Miss Meadows, and kept her gaze almost exclusively on the actress' face in a manner that might have mimicked infatuation if it was not for the narrow line between her brows. The expression made her seem less like love's supplicant, and more like a dog eagerly seeking any clue to its master's mind.

Amidst this, however, she turned the rare fawning glance on Korvin, and seemed only to speak to Allen to apologize to him—peculiar, after her friendliness of the previous evening. Whatever had transpired, however, it wasn't sufficient to keep her away from the table, and there didn't seem to be any enmity between them. Just a sort of chariness like two cats ignoring one another's presence on the bed.

The impasse persisted unaltered until the door slipped open and Hollis Leatherby entered. Sebastien was the only one present who did not startle spectacularly. He had the advantage of having heard and identified Leatherby's step in the corridor, but he feigned a little rustle anyway.

The sound of the paper caught Leatherby's attention. He turned from the ladies and the gentlemen at the card table as if they did not exist—not quite a cut direct, but sharp enough—and took a place opposite Sebastien, in the second of three matching chairs. Across the salon, play continued uninterrupted after the first brief flurry of glances. "Don Sebastien," he said.

"Mr. Leatherby," Sebastien answered. He folded the paper in half and set his drink on the side table, centering it carefully on a cork and wicker coaster. "You seem refreshingly unaffected by the general air of nervousness."

"Do I?" Leatherby leaned forward, elbows on the arms of the chair, and hunched between his shoulders. "I wonder, have you seen my wife?"

"Half an hour or so ago. I left her here, but when I returned—" Sebastien shrugged. "I have not seen her since."

"Damn it," Leatherby said, a flash of real temper roughening his voice. "She wasn't on the promenade."

"Perhaps she went to lie down. She seemed rather peaked."

"And what's that supposed to mean?" Leatherby's voice escalated enough that Korvin's head turned, though the other three kept their shoulders set and stared firmly at their cards, a reversal of earlier roles that Sebastien would once have found amusing.

Sebastien held up his hand, mildly, the palm open and facing Leatherby. "It was merely an observation. Really, sir, you are so quick to take offense. One might almost suppose a guilty conscience."

It was provoking, and meant to be. He didn't like Leatherby: didn't like the way he'd dismissed Jack, for one thing, and furthermore didn't like his sharp temper, now that he'd experienced it himself. *Careful, Sebastien.*

Leatherby drew himself out of the chair, his chest puffed up. "Are you accusing me of something, Don Sebastien?"

"Oh, not at all," Sebastien said. "But I'm also not casting aspersions on the delightful Mrs. Leatherby. So please, there's no need for hackles raised." As he said it, he couldn't remember if it was a common English expression. The languages would run together.

Judging by Leatherby's eyebrow, it wasn't. Ah, well. Quirks of speech were the least of Sebastien's problems. Steadfastly, he refused to stand. "Really," he said. "I imagine she went to lie down. You might look for her there."

Leatherby gave him one more brow-crumpled look and headed for the door. Sebastien heaved a sigh of relief when it closed behind him, and looked up to meet the eyes of Virgil Allen, who was paused beside the caddy, pouring whisky into a still-damp glass. "My money's on the Chinese. For what it's worth."

"I see." Sebastien reached for his cognac, wishing he dared to drink it. "Any reason in particular?"

"Just a feeling," Allen answered. "Could be nothing. Probably is," he amended, when Sebastien's arched eyebrow did not waver. "Still, you know those Chinese have got magicians we don't know anything about in the West."

"I've heard that," Sebastien said. "I've also heard a lot about your American hexes and…gris gris, is it?"

"Voudou," Allen supplied. "Mademoiselle LeClere could tell you more about it, I imagine. The Carolinas are civilized; that's her country."

Jack appeared fifteen minutes later. His color was recovering, though he looked entirely too bright-eyed to have slept the afternoon away. He arrowed straight to Sebastien and plunked down beside him, lifting the cognac glass from his hand without so much as a greeting. His fingers stroked Sebastien's and Sebastien flinched, but managed not to glance guiltily at Korvin úr.

"It makes you dizzy," Sebastien said.

"Medicinal purposes," Jack said, and sipped the amber liquor. "The sun's under the bow."

"Thank you. I've strolled enough for one day."

"I think you'll stroll more, when I tell you what I learned."

"When you were supposed to be resting."

Jack shrugged. "Ask me who the officer of the watch was last night," he purred, waiting for Sebastien's eyebrows to rise before nodding. "Captain Hoak."

"You're entirely too smug for that to be all."

"The logbook," Jack said, and paused for a sip of cognac, his cheeks hollowing as he rolled it over his tongue. He flirted at Sebastien through lowered lashes, and Sebastien folded his newspaper with a snap that turned Virgil Allen's head. The American cleared his throat and glanced quickly back at his cards. "Shows some inconsistencies. It would appear that the

Captain's pen ran dry of ink, and he refilled it, but the blacks do not match. One is a German black, and one is French, and greener. He must have bought ink in Calais."

"What was amended?"

"The time of the three a.m. tour was entered, I would guess, simultaneously with the data for the five a.m. tour. But rest of the entry was written earlier. And the pen was not skipping, which indicates that somewhere between entering the notes and entering the time, the captain did some other writing. Or perhaps changed pens."

The words were low, more shape than breath, for Sebastien's ears alone.

"Jack, you're a marvel," Sebastien said. And then he paused, amused pride replaced by an irrational spike of jealousy, as if he'd bought more of Jack than his freedom, that night in Budapest. And after years of work in making Jack understand that Sebastien didn't *own* him, and never meant to. "And how did you gain access?"

"Sebastien," Jack said, suddenly serious, his voice still soft, as Sebastien swallowed and sat back, his teeth cutting his gums and the inside of his lips in violent—and unwarranted—reaction. "All I did was flirt."

"One might almost say that all you *do* is flirt," Sebastien said, sourly, but then forced himself to sit back in his chair. "I'm sorry, Jack. That was unkind."

Jack only smiled, his delicate hands cupped around the bell of the glass. "One scandal draws attention from another," he said, and let one shoulder rise and fall, graceful as a girl. When he gestured with Sebastien's glass, he led with his wrist, as languidly as Miss Meadows could have managed.

"Terrible boy," Sebastien said, hiding his relief more successfully than he'd hidden his jealousy. *And what will you do, Sebastien, you old fool, when he's a grown man and wants more of a life than you can offer him?*

Not too much longer now. And Sebastien had no answer.

Sebastien's opportunistic stalking of Mlle. LeClere came to naught, as she left with Korvin úr—ostensibly to change for dinner, but in actuality trotting alongside him with quite pathetic focus—after the card game broke up. *Will the girl never be alone?* he thought, and settled behind his paper so Miss Meadows and Mr. Allen would not see him seem to rush out after, while Jack made a ceremony of dispensing with the dirtied glass and adjourning up the stairs. He'd keep an eye on Mlle. LeClere, and if Sebastien could not catch her alone, perhaps she'd be more amenable to Jack's pale beauty.

Mr. Allen packed up his cards and offered Miss Meadows his elbow and they too adjourned a moment later, nodding to Sebastien as they passed. As for Sebastien, he set the paper down and leaned his head back against the chair, closing his eyes, to wait out the day. So Korvin was not of the blood. Even that much liquor would have made him terribly sick, if he were. And—as Jack had noted—the sun was under the bow. Sebastien himself would not risk wandering the airship—he checked his pocket watch, stroking the pad of his thumb over the cool, engraved surface—for at least another fifteen minutes.

He rose from his chair and began to pace. If Korvin were not of the blood, he could be so many other things—a ghul, a necromancer…a garden-variety rapist and murderer, for that matter. Sebastien did not fool himself that such men limited their predations to beautiful maidens, or even that a rapist's particular intent was lust, whatever the erotic fantasies expressed in tawdry paperbacks.

Sebastien, as it happened, knew a thing or two about predators.

And would Mlle. LeClere lie for such a man? As smitten as she was, Sebastien had no doubt at all. In addition, Korvin úr was at least trying to give the impression that he knew something about Sebastien.

Sebastien mused on that for a few moments, straightening pictures that did not need it, and shook his head. There were still pieces missing.

He checked his watch again, though he knew the time, and turned toward the door. He would dress in his evening clothes, and if he could not cut Mlle. LeClere out of the crowd for a word in private, it was time to beg the captain's assistance in the matter. There were only two days and a few hours more until the *Hans Glücker* made landfall in New Amsterdam. And if Mme. Pontchartrain had not yet been discovered—in the passenger quarters or in the airframe—Sebastien did not believe she would be.

If that made him a cynic, well then, so be it.

As he was reaching for the doorlatch, however, he paused. Someone was on the other side. Someone male, and by his breathing, he was nerving himself to some action.

Sebastien paused and stepped back, waiting with his hands at his sides. The American, Allen, by his scent. And nervous rather than angry, praise God for small mercies.

If only it were that easy to identify another of the blood—but contrary to common myth, Sebastien's brothers and sisters in immortality smelled no different dead than they had alive. And his ears weren't *quite* acute enough to listen for the sound of a human heart. Alas. It would be nice to be more than mundanely supernatural.

Sebastien stood and waited, and at length the door slid open. Virgil Allen started to see him waiting there, hands at his sides, but recovered quickly. "Don Sebastien," he said. "May I enter?"

"This is a public space," Sebastien said, but made no move to surrender the center of the chamber.

Virgil Allen stepped inside, and shut the door behind himself. He coughed and cleared his throat. "Miss Meadows wishes to make an offer." He extended his right hand, staring resolutely at the floor between Sebastien's boots while blushing furiously. A folded sheet of cream-colored paper rested between his thumb and forefinger. Sebastien extracted it, broke the still-warm seal, and flipped it open while Allen twisted his boot against the rug.

The letter was brief.

> *My dear Señor de Ulloa*
>
> *I hope my note does not seem too forward, but it seems to me that I have heard your name—and that of the delightful Mr. Priest—before. It wasn't until this afternoon that it came to me; of course, we are mutual acquaintances of Mr. Iain MacDonald of Edinburgh, and I believe you and he are members of the same club.*
>
> *While I myself do not have that honor, I would be very gratified if you would agree to join me for drinks and conversation after dinner tonight. My dear Virgil will be happy to bear your reply.*
>
> *Yours truly,*
>
> *Miss Lillian Meadows*

Iain MacDonald was a bookseller. And a bit more than that; he was also, as Miss Meadows suggested, an old friend of Sebastien's and the proprietor of one of the less shady of the underground meeting places. Casually, Sebastien folded the note and slipped it into his breast pocket. "Thank the lady, Mr. Allen, but I will be unable to join her tonight."

"She—" Allen hesitated, obviously both relieved by Sebastien's answer and concerned that the news would be unwelcome. "She said, if you were other otherwise occupied, to inquire as to whether you understood her offer."

"I do," Sebastien said. "And I thank her, but no. I cannot oblige."

Mr. Allen nodded and stepped back, clearing Sebastien's path to the door.

"Gracias." Sebastien stepped forward. He paused with his hand on the latch, and said over his shoulder, "Mr. Allen?"

"Sir?"

"You shouldn't permit her to take such advantage of you, Mr. Allen. It's undignified." The American was still gaping after Sebastien as the detective took his leave with a nod, before stepping into the corridor.

Jack was fretting in their stateroom, or rather, the cubbyhole that passed for it, but he was dressed for dinner and had Sebastien's evening clothes laid out and brushed. Sebastien paused with the curtain in his hand, and said, "Are you my valet, now?"

"No," Jack replied, turning to the mirror to settle his bow tie, "he's following by steamer with our luggage. Unless you sacked him, too...Oh. You did, didn't you?"

"Sacking, in your colorful idiom, would indicate I found some flaw in his service."

Jack sighed, giving Sebastien his shoulder. "I just thought you'd appreciate it if your clothes were ready. Tomorrow, I'll crumple them in the corner."

"I'm sorry." Sebastien let the curtain fall closed behind him. "I didn't mean it that way." He hesitated, and went to pick up the suit on its hanger. "Did you discover anything about Korvin úr and Mademoiselle LeClere?"

"She's going to have some fast explaining to do on her wedding night," Jack said, in Greek. "It would tell us why she didn't hear anything last night, if she slipped out of the cabin. And what if it was her nightgown that wasn't rumpled? I suppose keeping Madame Pontchartrain silent about something like that would be as good a reason as any to kill her. You don't suppose Mademoiselle LeClere stands to inherit?"

Sebastien harrumphed. "We shall ask the captain for access to Madame's papers, again."

Jack raised a perceptive eyebrow. "What's upsetting you, Sebastien?"

"Is it so obvious?"

"To me," Jack said. He took the evening coat out of Sebastien's hands, set it aside, and began untying Sebastien's necktie and unbuttoning his collar. "You'll want a fresh shirt."

"Yes, dear," Sebastien said, and suffered himself to be dressed like a girl's paper doll. "Miss Meadows knows, Jack."

Jack paused in his work and looked up. He would never be a tall man, but he *was* a man, and Sebastien was never more disinclined to forget it than when Jack primped into his fey, adolescent persona. "Isn't that the point of all this?" A fluid, dismissive wave. "I'm of age, if anyone asks. And don't I remember you making me wait until I was. How many times did I offer before I turned sixteen?"

"One hundred and thirty-one," Sebastien said. "And no. I mean she's in the club."

"What about the matinees?" Jack stepped back, Sebastien's collar draped limp as a dead snake over his hand.

"Not of the blood." He let it hang until Jack's frown deepened from a pin scratch to a furrow. "An admirer."

"Oh, no you don't," Jack muttered. He tossed the collar aside and reached out, knotting his hands in Sebastien's hair. "Just because I've got to give you back to whatever court you assemble in New Amsterdam, Sebastien, doesn't mean this trip isn't mine. You *promised.*"

And what would his blood brothers think, Sebastien wondered, if they could see him now, pinned down and soundly kissed by a courtesan two-thirds his size?

They would think he was eccentric, of course, and too lenient with his pets.

But Sebastien was old enough to be excused a certain measure of eccentricity. And he'd long ago realized he preferred the mayfly society of humans to that of the blood. The blood took everything so *seriously*, as if they passed into that stage of human aging when mortals realized that the world turned like a wheel, and then through it, to a place where the natural cycles of success and catastrophe must be arrested. Before they could inconvenience—or worse, *annoy*—anyone.

Jack stopped kissing him before he'd rumpled his evening clothes, but after Sebastien's teeth—sharpening in reaction—had furthered their earlier damage to his own lips and gums. Fortunately, he healed fast.

Jack wouldn't have. And it was mad of him to tempt Sebastien so soon after a feeding; Sebastien could control himself, and—barring disaster—he wouldn't need more until they were well grounded in New Amsterdam. But Sebastien also needed far more than Jack had to give. Which was why those of the blood who did not care to hunt for their suppers had courts and courtesans, and not simply a favorite or two. A pint a month, any healthy adult could spare. The same twice a week was slow death—even though the blood, in Sebastien's considered opinion, was merely a metaphor for something more...exalted.

It warmed Sebastien as thoroughly as that mouthful of blood would have, though, to see Jack's jealousy.

Dinner passed uneventfully. Jack demonstrated a certain hesitancy in circumventing the pork roast, but—given two lunches—he extemporized around the fish and salad courses and, with the addition of Sebastien's dessert to his own, made a satisfactory supper. Sebastien disarrayed his food artfully to produce the illusion of dining, a sleight of hand that had served him well over the years.

After dining, the ladies excused themselves before the men adjourned to the smoking room. Sebastien took advantage of the exodus to plead a headache and an aversion to cigars and make his own escape. If Sebastien ventured into the smoking room, he'd be smelling stale tobacco for days. Jack, who numbered cigars among his bad habits as well as brandy—quite the young rakehell, he was growing into, and Sebastien had no-one to blame but himself—would report if anything interesting transpired.

Sebastien had fairer prey.

The passenger room at the head of the stairs was the least desirable, and on an airship as unpeopled as the *Hans Glücker*, it was understandably deserted. Sebastien slipped inside, leaving the light fixture shrouded, and settled on the lower bunk to wait.

A human—or even a younger blood—might have brought reading material, something with which to while away the hours. Sebastien simply closed his eyes in the dark, leaned his shoulder on the bedpost, and listened to the *Hans Glücker* drift.

An airship was no more silent in her passage than a sailing vessel. Through the deck, Sebastien could feel the thrum of engines, the almost-subliminal vibration of the cables containing the gas bags within the lifting body, the way the giant aircraft moved in response to the wind plucking at its control cabin and fabric skin. He listened to the ship in the night, and let his mind wander. It was a kind of meditation, and sometimes it helped him uncover surprising truths.

Now, it led him back to Mme. Pontchartrain's cabin, and the disarrayed papers, and the amended logbook. But those items refused to resolve into a pattern, no matter how many angles he turned them to or stared at them from. He found himself instead musing on Mrs. Leatherby, and her blatant attempt to feed him information. Probably accurate information, as it happened. But he was not blind to the manipulation.

A step on the stair and the swish of a woman's skirt brought him from his reverie. A small woman, by the weight of her footfall, and so either Mrs. Smith or Mlle. LeClere. And while he would have been happier to see Mrs. Smith—he was beginning to give some serious thought to wooing her; he would need friends and courtesans in America—he hoped it was, at last, Mlle. LeClere.

Alone.

He smoothed his hair with both hands, the mirror no use to him, and stepped into the corridor. And almost into the young Frenchwoman's arms.

She gave a startled squeak and might have toppled down the stairs if he hadn't caught her wrist and landed her. Instead she tottered and collapsed forward into his arms; he took two quick steps back to set her at arm's length. "Mademoiselle," he said. "Forgive me. Are you all right?"

"Fine," she said, and shrugged his hands off. "I'll just—"

"Not at all." He stepped aside, and then fell in beside her when she advanced. "I've been meaning to speak to you alone."

"That's hardly seemly, monsieur." She stepped faster, but he kept up with ease.

"I did not think you the sort of young lady who concerned herself with appearances," he countered. The reached the cabin she had until recently shared with Mme. Pontchartrain, and Mlle. LeClere moved as if to push Sebastien aside. He caught her elbow and turned her.

"Monsieur," she said. "I will shout."

"And I will tell the Captain that you lied about where you were last night."

She held herself stiff for a moment, her chin lifted, her lips pressed suddenly thin. And then, abruptly, she deflated, sagging inside the confines of her corset. "Damn you," she whispered. "What do you want?"

"Mademoiselle," Sebastien answered, "we all have secrets. I wish only to discover what became of your chaperone. Will you tell me where you were last night?"

"With Oczkar," she said, hopelessly. "I knew Mme. Pontchartrain had a taste for laudanum, you see, and sometimes she did not even remove her clothes of an evening, when she had indulged—"

"And your absence would not wake her from her dreams."

"Indeed," she said, hopelessly. "But I did not kill her. I did not even provide the drug—"

"Hush," Sebastien said. He brushed her cheek with cool fingers. "You do not need to justify yourself to me."

—⁂—

"Was she lying?" Jack asked, in the darkness.

"I don't believe so." Sebastien did not sleep. But he occupied his pajamas nonetheless, and lay on Jack's bunk beside him, listening to Jack breathe, inches away in the quiet darkness. "So what do we know, then?"

"That we can cross Korvin and LeClere off our list of suspects." Jack spoke very softly, just for Sebastien's ears, both of them aware of Mrs. Smith sleeping peacefully on the other side of the doped fabric wall. Faintly, distantly, Sebastien could hear Hollis Leatherby snoring.

"Unless they did it together."

"Then no-one has an alibi."

"Not even you."

"Alas," Jack said. He shifted under the covers, leaning his head on Sebastien's shoulder. "We know Mrs. Smith is an inveterate eavesdropper. We know Captain Hoak—or somebody feigning his handwriting—made an inconsistent entry in the logbook. We know Mme. Pontchartrain disappeared between drinks and breakfast. We can speculate that Korvin and Meadows had some sort of prior arrangement to travel together, or that Corvin and LeClere did—aside from the tour group, I mean. Five colonials and one European, that's a bit odd, isn't it? Is that something you can inquire after with Mrs. Smith?"

"I thought you didn't approve of Mrs. Smith."

"She's just your type," Jack said, feigning placidity. "And I know very well that we can't get along in America, just the two of us, without friends."

"You are a practical soul, dear boy," Sebastien said, and turned to kiss Jack's forehead. "We also know that Beatrice Leatherby has some agenda that involves incriminating Korvin."

"Or Mademoiselle LeClere."

"Just so. Extending that last point, we know that there is some mysterious tension between the Leatherbys and the other passengers. We know Korvin úr may very well be something other than he seems, but that he is not of the blood."

"We know Miss Meadows knows that you *are*." Sebastien could hear Jack's frown in his voice.

"And we know that this dirigible is currently host to any number of unsavory relationships."

"Is that so?" Jack asked, propping himself on his elbows, his silhouette barely visible in the dim light that slipped around the edges of the lampshade.

"Unfortunately," Sebastien answered, sitting up, "it appears to be a motif. You should sleep, Jack."

Jack caught his wrist. "Madame's papers appeared to have been riffled. Hurriedly. But you said no one but she and Mlle. LeClere had been in the cabin."

Sebastien nodded. "I did, didn't I? I wonder if I could have been mistaken."

"Anise oil confuses bloodhounds," Jack said, slyly.

Sebastien snorted.

"We also now know that Madame Pontchartrain was an opium addict."

"Such harsh terms for a little genteel laudanum use." And then Sebastien stopped, freed his right hand, and used it to stroke Jack's curls, thoughtfully. "Jack, when we searched Madame Pontchartrain's room—"

Jack stiffened. "No laudanum bottle."

"Indeed," Sebastien answered. "And isn't that a curious thing?"

Long before first light, when Jack was sleeping soundly, Sebastien dressed and slipped from the cabin. This time, the lack of doors that locked and fastened abetted him. He paused in the corridor, listening for activity, and heard only even breathing and faint snores. Slowly, he descended the stairs, which neither creaked nor settled under his weight, and paused at the bottom landing.

Pretend you are a murderer, Sebastien thought, and permitted himself a smile he would never have worn around a mortal, friend or foe. It even *felt* unpleasant on his face.

If I wanted to murder someone, though—

No. He turned back, and regarded the stairs, lit green by emergency lights. Sebastien was considerably stronger and more agile than a human man, and he could not have maneuvered even a small unconscious woman down those stairs without waking the ship. The forward stairs were no better—and closer to the occupied sleeping chambers. If she had come this way, she had not been dragged.

Which meant that if Mme. Pontchartrain had not gone *up*, into the airframe—and the search there had revealed no sign—then, barring sorcery, she had come down under her own power.

And, also barring sorcery, Mlle. LeClere had lied again, because if she had left Mme. Pontchartrain drugged insensate, then there was no way Mme. Pontchartrain could have gotten down these stairs.

In the absence of a Crown Investigator or a Zaubererdetektiv, Sebastien found he must reluctantly shelve the idea of sorcery—at least until they made landfall in New Amsterdam. Where, it happened, there was a Detective Crown Investigator, the most notorious of the scant three the British-American colonies boasted.

Under German law, while he was no more welcome in most men's houses than…than Mrs. Zhang and Mr. Cui, he was not *proscribed*. In British America, however, the blood were outlawed. Those Crown rules had not been generally enforced since the seventeenth century, but were kept on the books for convenience's sake in *troublesome* cases.

And so, it would be entirely best for Sebastien to have this mystery resolved by the time DCI Garrett arrived on the scene—or the scene, as the case might be, arrived in her jurisdiction.

So it had better not be sorcery, hadn't it?

He paused. Of course, there was one very easy way to tell if it potentially *could* be sorcery. And that could be addressed in the morning. In the meantime, however—

Sebastien heard crisply military footsteps, and started forward. A few steps took him around the corner, and into the path of the watch officer. Tonight, it was the first mate, who tipped his hat and kept on walking, obviously accustomed to sleepless passengers.

"Guten Morgen," he said, the first mate echoing his words. As he passed, Sebastien checked his watch. Three oh eight. "Herr Pfrommer?"

The first mate checked his stride and turned back. "Ja, mein Herr?"

Briefly, Sebastien outlined what he proposed, and when it seemed as if the officer would protest, held up his hand. "Please check with the captain," he said. "I will abide by his decision."

Herr Pfrommer clicked his heels, a tradition Sebastien had considered happily buried until that moment, and carried on with his rounds. And Sebastien sighed and took himself down to the control cabin before the officer returned, or the sun came up.

The *Hans Glücker* didn't have a hanging gondola, as a smaller dirigible might. Most of its passenger and crew facilities were inside the airframe, with only a small control cabin protruding underneath the nose of the ship. Sebastien walked forward past the salon and smoking room, down the white-walled corridor which provided access to the washrooms, crew quarters, and the galley by means of German-labeled doors. The hum of the engines was louder, here. They extended from either side of the ship on sets of pontoons, and one of the main struts ran through behind the forward door that would have brought him into the control cabin.

It was locked, of course.

Fortunately, among all his other skills, Jack could pick a lock. And it was Sebastien who taught him.

Sebastien unpinned his cravat—the jewel was set in gold, but the stick pin itself was steel—and with its offices and those of a bit of wire, he managed the lock by touch in seconds. He opened the door and let himself through, and proceeded down a short flight of stairs.

The pilot didn't turn. He spoke, though—in German, of course. "You're back very soon, Herr Pfrommer."

"I am not Herr Pfrommer," Sebastien said, and when the pilot started and turned, producing a weapon, Sebastien stood with both hands raised and open, having dropped wire and pin into his pocket. "I am sorry. The door was open, and I—"

"You are *investigating*?"

"Yes." Sebastien smiled. "How many pilots are on this ship, sir?"

"Two," he answered. He checked his controls and locked them in position, and then turned back to Sebastien.

"Heel and toe watches?" Twelve hours on and twelve off, that meant. A grueling schedule.

"Yes, mein Herr."

"So it was not you to whom my ward spoke this afternoon."

"I went to my bunk at six—" the pilot began, and then pressed his lips together. "What did your young man tell you about Franz?"

"Just that he was charming," Sebastien lied, taking the opportunity to survey the control cabin. It was small, and while there was an exit door, it was clearly visible from the pilot's position. "And that he gave Jack a tour of the control cabin. Tell me, mein Herr, did you leave your post at all last night?"

"Only to visit the washroom," the pilot said. "And for my coffee and dinner breaks. The officer of the watch takes control during that time." He checked his watch—a wristwatch, favored by aviators, rather than a pocket watch. "I'll take my second break as soon as the first mate returns from his rounds, in fact. My relief arrives at six hundred hours."

"Your dinner break is at three hundred."

"Three twenty," the pilot corrected.

"Thank you," Sebastien said. It was perhaps three twelve. "I can show myself out. Oh—" He paused with his hand on the latch. "Can you tell me where rubbish is disposed of, please?"

"There are receptacles in the washrooms—"

"No, I mean once it is collected. Is it hauled on to New Amsterdam?"

"That would be a waste of the weight allowance," the pilot said. "It's cast overboard. It helps to counterbalance any hydrogen leakage that occurs via diffusion through the gas bags."

"And it's dumped from where?"

"The side corridor outside the galley," the pilot said. "There are rolling bins to collect the trash, and a chute."

"*Thank you*," Sebastien said, and took himself outside again.

When Jack awoke, Sebastien was waiting. He leaned against the wall beside the porthole light. The cabin's sole piece of furniture besides the bed was a luggage stool for the cabin bags. That stool stood on Sebastien's left hand, under the light, and a white tented shape occupied its flat top. "Sebastien?"

"Cover your eyes," Sebastien said. Jack obeyed, and Sebastien flipped up the shade on the light. Jack lowered his hands, blinking, and pushed himself upright on the bed, tousled and puffy-cheeked as a child.

"What did you find?"

"Laudanum," Sebastien answered, and uncovered the glinting, pale blue rectangular bottle, still full almost to the bottom of its long neck. "And barely a mouthful gone."

There were new technologies that might be used to recover latent fingerprints from smooth, imporous objects, such as the surface of a glass bottle. The materials—lamp black, fine brushes, adhesive cellophane tape—which Sebastien would need to carry out such research would be available in New Amsterdam. As would the infamous—and, by reputation, formidable—DCI Abigail Irene Garrett. The Crown Investigator would wield an arsenal of forensic sorcery, and numbered among its functions would be spells capable of linking the murder weapon to the murderer. Assuming the laudanum was the murder weapon, and not a middle-aged widow's comfort, as Mlle. LeClere had suggested.

"Boss!" Jack exclaimed, bounding out of bed.

In the morning, they strip-searched the passengers.

The process required some orchestration, as of course neither Sebastien nor Jack could examine the female passengers. This inconvenience was surmounted by sending Mlle. LeClere, Mrs. Smith, Mrs. Zhang, Miss Meadows, and Mrs. Leatherby aside as a group to examine each other, with the airship's two chambermaids and one female washroom attendant acting as matrons in the smoking room, while the men occupied the larger lounge. From the giggling that ensued, either all eight of them were in collusion, or all eight of them were agreed that men, in general, were a ridiculous species though perhaps best humored.

Meanwhile, Sebastien and Captain Hoak examined the unclothed chest of each of the men.

It was not an absolute test, of course, but if any of them were a university-trained sorcerer (as opposed to a hedge-wizard or conjurer) he would have borne on his chest the ineradicable mark of his training, a sigil tattooed over the sternum. The mark would be red for the great universities at Oxford, Wittenberg, Paris, Rome, and Kyiv, black for lesser colleges.

There were no schools for sorcerers in Spain.

The sigil would be an outline for a wizard who had matriculated, fully inked for a graduate. But it would be there.

It came as little surprise to Sebastien that Oczkar Korvin, who had maneuvered to be last in line, said softly "I believe this is what you are looking for," and unbuttoned the breast of his shirt to reveal a black-inked design the size of a cigarette case. "Prague," he said. "Eighteen seventy-nine. Are you going to arrest me?"

"Not only on the strength of that," Sebastien said. "Mademoiselle LeClere, however, has twice lied—and claimed you as her alibi. Tell me—did she hope to inherit, when Madame Pontchartrain was gone?"

"Neither Mademoiselle LeClere nor I had anything to do with Madame's disappearance," Korvin said. "Nor do I expect you have anything but circumstantial evidence to suggest it."

Sebastien smiled, his shoulders and chest tightening as he considered the probable course of events. "Circumstantial evidence is enough to hold you and your young lady for questioning, however. And Mademoiselle LeClere hardly exhibits the marks of a clean conscience."

"It's no crime to study sorcery." Korvin úr calmly rebuttoned his shirt. "If we're condemning on history and circumstances, Don Sebastien, what about yourself?"

It had been inevitable. If Miss Meadows knew, then likely so did her entire coterie. Sebastien opened his mouth to respond—

Oczkar Korvin raised his right hand, fingers and palms bent around a hollow concavity, and Sebastien's world went white.

He folded reflexively against the light, shielding his face, his face scorched and the flesh on his hands and wrists searing. He groaned, or perhaps screamed; his ears were full of the roaring of that terrible light, and he couldn't hear anything except, suddenly, Jack's voice shouting.

The pain fell away. The white brilliance darkened, a shadow protecting him: Jack had lunged between Sebastien and the light and then the light was gone, whisked away, as Korvin slipped the enchanted lens into which he had summoned sunlight back inside his waistcoat pocket.

Jack turned, still covering Sebastien with his body, and reached out tentatively to touch his hair. "Are you—"

"I'll live," Sebastien answered, and Jack managed a cramped little laugh as Mr. Cui said something quite unintelligible.

Whatever it was, the captain answered with a quick shake of his head.

The skin on Sebastien's hands was peeled, scorched, pulling back from the flesh in thick curls like a two-day-old sunburn. It ached and itched abominably, already healing now that the affront was ended. Sebastien drew his arms against his chest like a dog protecting an injured paw.

"So," Korvin said. "Shall we hold the wampyr for questioning, too?"

Sebastien forced his fists to loosen, and disciplined himself into standing straight, to face the silent room without rubbing at his peeling face. The connecting door to the smoking lounge swung open and the blurred face of Mrs. Smith appeared around it. Sebastien, still dazzled, recognized her chiefly by the flash of light off her spectacles and the startling paleness of her hair. She shoved the door wide and stepped through, the other women following behind her.

Mrs. Leatherby came last, still hastily rebuttoning her collar. Sebastien heard her gasping. Her bosom must be heaving over the top of her corset as if the brief run had winded her. She tugged some blurred object—a comb?—from her disordered hair, releasing a wave of perfume as locks fell over her shoulders. The scent sharpened his teeth—a room, full of warm humans, and with his scalded flesh sapping his strength—

The injury would heal, but it would cost Sebastien, cost him resources…and Jack, understanding, would inevitably offer. Sebastien was anticipating that conversation with even less pleasure than the one he was about to have.

Captain Hoak reached out left-handed and grabbed Jack's wrist, almost hauling him off his feet as he yanked him away from Sebastien. Jack squawked and struggled free, tearing his shirt-cuff in the process, and shied away from Captain Hoak, towards the women. Beatrice Leatherby detached herself from that little group and stepped toward her husband. Sebastien thought she clutched Leatherby's elbow; in any case, she slid her hand through the crook.

"Don Sebastien," Mrs. Smith said. She started forward, her quick steps arrested when Korvin caught her arm. She must have glared over her glasses, or shaken him off, because he stepped back abruptly, his raised hands white against the dark suit coat.

"Don't interfere," Korvin said.

"Merci à Dieu," Mlle. LeClere said, pressing her fists to her bosom. "He earlier accosted me on the stairs, Captain. If I had known my danger—"

The captain spared her a glance before turning to keep an eye on Jack. "Lad, no one's going to make you stay with him. You may think you've nowhere to go, but we can make arrangements—"

Sebastien, still blinking tears from his eyes, couldn't see it. But he could imagine quite plainly that Jack paused, turned—slowly—and balled his hands into fists before pursing his lips into the most condescending consideration imaginable. He would stare the captain in the eye until Hoak flushed and dropped his gaze, and then he would drawl—

"Oh, I think not."

It was as well that Sebastien's face hurt too much for smiling, as he heard the hesitancy in the captain's voice as he said, "Lad?"

"I'm of age," Jack said. "Eighteen in December, before you ask, and also before you ask, I know everything I need to know about Sebastien de Ulloa. He saved my life, and you'll have to kill me to take me away from him." He lifted his chin, arms crossed, the smallest man in the room—shorter than two of the women, in fact—and though Sebastien couldn't see it, he knew Jack glowered.

Sebastien swallowed a ridiculous, hurtful pride, feeling like a man watching his terrier stare down a room full of mastiffs. "Jack—"

"Shut up, Sebastien," Jack said. "Let me handle this. Captain, Germany's laws against vampirism were repealed in the eighteenth century, along with the witchcraft laws. Sebastien has done nothing wrong."

"Nothing besides child slavery and—" the captain glanced over his shoulder, at the ladies clustered like hens by the door to the corridor, and did not say the words *rape* or *prostitution*.

Into his embarrassed silence, Miss Meadows stepped, slim and elegant in her men's clothing as she sidled between the corseted ladies. She posted herself a little to Captain Hoak's left, making quite a contrast to the stout, graying captain. She seemed cut more from the same fragile white-gold cloth as Jack. "Jack, darling. How old were you when he bought you?"

Several flinched at the word, and now Sebastien's vision was clearing enough to tell who. Mrs. Smith was one of them, though Sebastien was wishing he was still dazzled enough to pretend he didn't see her face. Instead, he focused on Miss Meadows—and was surprised to see that her furrowed brow was an expression of concern, not reproach.

"Seven," Jack said, folding his arms. "My parents couldn't afford to feed me; they indentured me at five. There would have been three years left to run on my bill of service by now."

And that, finally, brought a look of dawning uncertainty to the captain's face. "Would have been?"

"Yes," Jack said. "Sebastien emancipated me when I turned fourteen. And settled a considerable trust on me, as well. I'm *quite* independent, and no more in need of rescuing than Miss Meadows, here." And then he smiled at the captain and tilted his head, more like the dove he played at than the falcon as which he stood revealed. "And I also know precisely where Sebastien was the night before last, and I assure you, it *wasn't* with Madame Pontchartrain. Now, may I see to my patron's injuries, Captain, or are you going to make me force your hand?"

The last time Sebastien had been so eager to absent himself from the public eye, it had involved an angry Parisian mob with pitchforks and torches, and that was leaving aside all hyperbole. This, at least, was less physically hazardous. But just as humiliating, as Jack guided him up the stairs—while Sebastien's eyes had recovered enough that he had been able to see fairly well in the bright salon, the dimness here defeated him, and his fingers were numb under the throbbing pain of the burns—and brought him to their chamber. Once Sebastien was settled, Jack went for water and bandages himself rather than trusting an attendant.

Sebastien sat in the dark with his eyes closed, healing. The flash had been brief, intended to injure and mortify rather than maim or kill. And it had been effective, indeed. He was quite thoroughly humiliated—and quite thoroughly defanged, at the risk of a terrible pun. In one dramatic gesture,

Korvin had rendered it impossible for Sebastien to continue investigating any crime aboard the *Hans Glücker*. And, Sebastien thought, listening to the footsteps of the crewman who was now wearing a path in the decking outside the cabin, he'd also neatly distracted attention from himself and Mlle. LeClere as suspects.

Sebastien sat forward and opened his eyes. The dazzle was fading, and even in the dim room, he saw plainly now. In particular, he saw the upholstery cabin-bag that he had left beside the door when he and Jack went downstairs to conduct the search. The cabin-bag which had held the bottle of laudanum he'd fished from *behind* the carts beside the trash chute.

The bottle would not have fallen there, he thought, unless someone was stretching *over* the carts to dispose of something in the chute. Straining, struggling with something heavy. Sebastien was now reasonably certain that chute had been Mme. Pontchartrain's route to a final resting place at sea.

The bag was not where Sebastien had left it.

He crossed the cabin in one and a half quick steps, crouched beside the bag, and pulled it open. The contents were in no disarray. But the bottle, which should have been slipped between his shirt-collars and underthings, was nowhere to be found.

And there was no scent of anyone on the air, other than Jack and himself, the crewman in the hall, and the chambermaid.

Sebastien was abruptly reminded of his burned face as his eyebrows crept up his forehead. Standing dizzied him. He needed to feed, to recoup the strength he was expending regenerating his face and hands. And Jack—

Jack's voice in the hallway, cheerily greeting their watcher in German. The watcher's embarrassed mumble. Jack's footsteps, and the scent of clear water. "Sebastien?" Jack said, from beyond the curtain. "My hands are full."

Sebastien kicked his bag back against the wall and pulled the curtain aside, frowning at Jack's wince when Jack saw his face. "That bad?"

"Get the light, would you? And you mean you don't know?"

Having raised the lampshade with his aching hands, Sebastien silently tilted his head at the tiny mirror.

Jack choked out a laugh. "Stupid question. Yes. It looks bad." Jack set the basin on the stool and crouched beside it, unfolding a clean muslin towel over his knee. He glanced at the half-open curtain and switched from Spanish to Greek. "I thought these would do for bandages. The ship's medic was significantly absent from the surgery. If you still need bandages, after—how much do you need?"

"No, Jack."

"It's not open for discussion. I'll be fine—"

"Jack," Sebastien said, softly, "you were beautiful down there. You were fierce and wonderful and I in no wise deserve you"—Jack snorted, in that inelegant manner he reserved for Sebastien alone—"and I *will not* risk you that way. Two days is too soon."

"You haven't another option," Jack said. He tore a strip of toweling and folded it in a pad. Leptodactylous fingers broke the surface of the water in the basin as he wet it. "Come here into the light, so I can see what I'm doing."

Sebastien came forward and dropped a knee beside the stool. Jack tilted his face up left-handed and dabbed with the cloth held in the right. The cool water was soothing, though Sebastien winced as ruined flesh rubbed free of raw new skin. "I do have."

"Have what?"

"An option," Sebastien said. He paused, too long. Jack was already tensing in protest when he finished, "Will you take a message to Miss Meadows for me, Jack my love?"

Silence.

"Jack?"

"Damn you," Jack said, and wet the cloth again.

Perhaps Sebastien had been foolish in expecting Miss Meadows to meet him alone. Instead, she came to his rooms attended not just by Jack-as-guide, but also in the company of Virgil Allen.

Sebastien was warned of their arrival by brief, firm words exchanged with the ludicrous corridor guard. He didn't catch what was said, but the tone in Miss Meadows' voice was enough to coerce her way through, Jack and Mr. Allen beside her.

Allen entered the cabin without knocking and took a post in the corner by the foot of the bunks, stern and glowering under his moustaches. Sebastien was cognizant of the bulky weight in the South Carolinian's coat pocket. A revolver, no doubt, suitable for a well-armed American gentleman.

The advisability of carrying firearms on a hydrogen-filled airship aside, Sebastien could muster no more than an inward shrug for the weapon. If Allen felt the need to shoot him, it would sting less than Korvin's suncharged lens.

"Señor de Ulloa," Miss Meadows said. She paused with the curtain in one hand, Jack behind her in the hall, and framed herself in the doorway with an actress's trained unconscious grace. "I am sorry for your injury." She eyed his face. "Although it seems much improved."

"Not without cost," he said. He swayed when he stood, and steadied himself against the bedframe. He was lightheaded, his stomach cramping. Behind Miss Meadows, Jack shifted from foot to foot, barely restraining himself. "Miss Meadows," Sebastien continued, "I am uncomfortable in bringing this up again, especially in the wake of my earlier refusal...."

She stepped into the cabin, holding the curtain until Jack relieved her of it, while appearing not to notice him at all. Sebastien swallowed on a growl, but made a point of meeting Jack's eyes over her shoulder. Jack bit his lip and turned away.

As for Miss Meadows, she stripped her gloves off with a negligent gesture and shrugged under her jacket. Gracious in victory, she smiled. "I understand," she said. "Our needs may change unexpectedly."

She turned to the left and Allen was there, waiting to take her gloves from her hand. She laid them across his palm, and began unbuttoning her collar as Jack stepped into the cabin and let the curtain fall.

It was crowded and close, four people in the tiny room, and Sebastien considered himself fortunate that he did not *require* breath except for speech, or to detect scents.

"Would you prefer privacy?" Sebastien asked.

Again, Miss Meadows deployed that studied shrug. "Señor, as long as the cameras are not rolling, this *is* privacy."

She slid her jacket off and gave that to Allen as well. His face might have been a plaster mask; his expression was frozen in lines stretching from the corners of his nose to the corners of his mouth. Even Jack's irritated frown was more mobile.

"And you are not new to this?"

Jack made a small noise of protest and folded his arms, turning to face the door like a eunuch guarding a harem. The set of his shoulders said everything he bit his tongue on.

"Quite accomplished." Miss Meadows pushed her hair aside, disarraying carefully coiled lovelocks, and turned her head.

The scars were small, delicate dimples in her skim-milk skin, only visible where the light hit them at an angle. "Yes," Sebastien said, "I see."

He reached out as she closed her eyes, Allen's glower searing his neck, and took her by the shoulders. With one hand, he steadied her head as she drew her hair further aside. He was enough taller that he had to stoop to kiss her throat, despite the advantage of her heeled boots.

She shivered in anticipation, her right hand flexing rhythmically where it curved around his wrist. He wondered whose courtesan she had been, and how she had come to leave that relationship.

Her scars were old.

He kissed soft flesh, breathed her scent and her perfume, felt his teeth sharp in response. His stomach knotted. "Yes?" he asked, requiring consent, and she moaned her answer.

"Yes."

Sebastien could barely remember the name he had been born to. He had forgotten the name of the village he had been born *in*—it had changed since—or the year in which that birth had occurred. He no longer recalled his own age, except in the vaguest of terms.

But he remembered how it had been, when he became a wampyr's courtesan, and he remembered *her* name very well.

Eudeline—Evie—had been young, new to the blood, lonesome as only the newly turned can be. Sebastien had loved her with a passion he had sworn was eternal, and she had been inexperienced enough to believe him.

He had been wrong, so it happened. Mortal love was never meant to last forever. Fifty years. Perhaps even a century was possible, though Sebastien could not attest it. But not forever.

Their romance had not outlasted the Christian millennium. But he still recalled her kiss.

First there had been the cool touch of a wet mouth on warm skin, the press of tongue seeking the pulse. The expert courtesan knew how vital it was to remain motionless for the kiss, as Miss Meadows now remained motionless for him, though her outward appearance of calm was belied by trembling hands and a racing heart.

Sebastien found the pulse and unsheathed his fangs, letting the tips indent her skin. She whimpered through closed lips, and Sebastien heard the rustle of cloth as Allen halted himself half a step into intervening.

Sebastien's memory was perfect, in this. First the prickle of the fangs, and then the pain, tremendous, *scathing*, all out of proportion to the injury, the two swift stabs that merely nudged the skin aside. The vein must only be punctured, never severed or torn. And the punctures must be tidy and straight, to heal properly.

Sebastien's fangs were triangular in cross-section, designed to pierce flesh and leave no lasting injury. It was of no more benefit to the blood to kill their prey than it was to a milkmaid to slaughter her dairy cows.

And after the pain—so impatiently endured—the pleasure. Transporting, incomparable. He knew when she felt it, because the measured breaths she had used to ride the pain faltered, replaced by a great, rattling intake of air. Her body melted against his, her hips rocking against his thigh, the grasp of her clutching hands both desperate and fragile, her head lolling against his supporting hand. The blood was rich and warm, a salty-metallic froth that pulsed over his tongue, surged down his tightened gullet, and flushed his skin with heat. Her heartbeat rang in his ears, world-filling, and he forced himself to sip delicately, gently…and then to pull against her clutching, surrendered hands, unsheathe his fangs from her flesh long before either of them was sated, and seal the wound with his closed lips while she trembled against him, silently pleading for more.

He almost liked her, a little, for that moment.

Virgil Allen had leaned away from the bedpost, his hand in his pocket, his impassivity cracked into a scowl. The set of Jack's shoulders hadn't changed.

Sebastien lifted his lips from Miss Meadows' neck, kissed her slack mouth quickly, a formal thank you, and set her back at arm's length. Jack, his motions impersonal and brisk, stepped between them and pressed to her throat a clean pad folded from the same torn muslin that he'd used to doctor Sebastien.

"Thank you, Miss Meadows," Sebastien said, and bowed over the hand she hadn't pressed against Jack's.

"Thank *you*," she answered, and let Jack catch her as she wobbled against his shoulder.

"Mr. Allen," Sebastien said, "the stool, if you will."

"Eugenie LeClere is a quite reprehensible person," Miss Meadows said, when she returned to herself. She was paler and more lovely than ever, a testament to the reasoning behind certain wampyrs' legendary preference for blondes. Sebastien, seated on the bottom bunk beside a stiff-shouldered Jack while Allen hovered over her like an anxious mother, reserved his sarcasm.

What had a wampyr to say about morality?

He didn't blame Jack his anger. But either Jack would allow Sebastien to make it up to him, or Jack would leave him—as Jack eventually must, because *Sebastien* was old enough to understand that there was no such creature as eternal loyalty, nor was it fair to ask—and in either case, Sebastien had done no more than he needed to.

"If you're going to attempt to direct my investigation to Mademoiselle LeClere, Miss Meadows, rest assured, it needs no further guidance."

"Call me Lillian, if I may call you Sebastien," she said, adjusting a pincurl in its diamond barrette without benefit of the mirror. "And I don't think Eugenie killed her. I think she was trying to get *away* from her. There's very little I would put past Eugenie. But not murder."

"Miss—Lillian, forgive me." Sebastien stood, moving fluidly again, his strength restored as hers was lessened. "But I think the information you're hinting around would be better plainly expressed."

"Ah." Lillian glanced at Allen, who shrugged. He handed her a silver flask—taken from the pocket which did not hold the revolver—and she sipped, winced, and recapped it before shaking her head—very slightly, so as not to disturb her bandages. "Eugenie loves Oczkar."

"So Mrs. Smith said. I am drawn to the inescapable conclusion that you all were acquainted before this flight commenced. Am I incorrect in that?"

She could, of course, be drawing him out, playing the game of misleading and misdirection that tended to permeate any murder investigation. But he had something to bargain. Something she wanted.

If only the captain were here to make his ever-so-delicately phrased charge of whoredom now. "We met in Moscow," she said. "I had lost someone, and was grateful for the company. You know how strangers can make you bear yourself up as you could not manage, in the company only of friends?"

He didn't answer. She pressed her fingertips to her bandage.

"Sebastien?"

"Yes, I know it well. And the Leatherbys?"

"I had not met them before. Although they appeared to know Madame, and did not seem to care for her. Or perhaps it was simply a matter of her reputation preceding her. If you take my meaning?"

He did not, and beckoned her to continue.

"Eugenie and Madame Pontchartrain—Leonelle—well," Lillian said. "They were not what they pretended. Either of them. Their grand tour of England and Europe was a…fishing expedition. You see, Madame Pontchartrain never married. And Eugenie was not merely her travelling companion; she was her bastard daughter. They had no family, and no estates. And their means of making their way in the world…." she permitted her voice to trail off suggestively, and gave the flask a regretful glance before handing it to Allen.

"Entrapment," Sebastien said, understanding, on the same breath that Jack said, "Blackmail."

"Eugenie wanted free of her."

"And yet you insist she did not kill her?"

"How Shakespearean," Lillian said. "And how unnatural, don't you think? For a child to murder her mother, no matter how opportunistic or unloving?"

"And she refused to turn Korvin úr over to her mother?"

"She was not supposed to approach Oczkar at all. He is unmarried, a sorcerer—what more could an affair do to his reputation? No, she was meant to accuse my darling Virgil of rape." She turned her head and smiled at Allen, experiencing no such difficulty with the word as the captain had. Allen's lip quirked under his moustache, and he tipped an imaginary hat. "Virgil is not well-off, of course, but Madame Pontchartrain believed I would pay to silence them."

"But Mademoiselle LeClere came to you with her story instead."

"Is it so hard to believe I pitied her?"

Jack, from the recesses of the bottom bunk, said, "I wouldn't have thought you had pity in your makeup." He stood, shouldering past Sebastien in the strained silence that followed, and edged around Virgil Allen. He paused by the curtained door and turned back, as if wavering on the edge of another unpleasantness. Gratitude—or manners—won over jealousy, and he swallowed hard and continued, "Miss Meadows, Mr. Allen, would you join us for lunch? It's nearly the hour, and Miss Meadows should certainly eat."

She stared him down for a moment, but gave the ground, obviously aware that this was a competition she could not win. "But surely," she said, as Allen helped her wavering to her feet, "Sebastien—"

"Oh," he said, straightening his collar, "I wouldn't keep my public waiting. Besides, I think I need a word or two with Mademoiselle LeClere and Korvin úr. Don't you?"

The crewman pacing in the hallway didn't try to stop them from descending, but he did follow at a discreet distance. Sebastien made a little ceremony of seating Lillian, and he was sure every eye in the place was trained on the four of them, side by side at a round table meant for six. Already seated elsewhere were the Chinese couple—most skilled at looking without seeming to be looking—and the Dutch brothers, who dined with their heads bent together conspiratorially and stared with perfect frankness when Sebastien's party entered. Steven actually essayed a small smile, however, and Michiel spared Jack a nod, which was more than Sebastien would have predicted. Meanwhile, Lillian smiled with bright falseness across the dining room, her bandages a small bulge under her high-collared blouse that everyone avoided staring at, their gazes veering away as precipitously as if she had strolled in naked.

Sebastien, at least, was spared the annoyance of pretending to dine. The maitre d' himself came and cleared Sebastien's place setting, providing a goblet of clear ice water, then brought the bread and butter for the other diners with his own hands. Sebastien thanked him, and offered that—if the burly crewman now lingering inside the door, at attention like a footman, should require a meal and a rest—Sebastien had no plans to leave the dining room for at least an hour.

The maitre d', Sebastien noticed, blushed most appetizingly.

Sebastien hated this, the mingled obsequiousness and fear. And Jack's sly sideways smile told him that Jack was enjoying a small, Schadenfreude-soaked revenge in Sebastien's discomfiture.

Sebastien sighed, and fiddled with his water glass. The service of the soup was notably slow. Lillian chattered gaily with Virgil and Jack, who was putting forth even more of an effort than usual to be his best, most charming self. Sebastien found Jack's knee under the table and gave it a grateful pat, and Jack's answering smile was a touch less sly. Had Sebastien had a heart to beat, it would have accelerated in relief.

He would be forgiven after all.

Virgil was pouring a second round of wine—the waiter having exhibited a curious hesitancy to approach their table except when forced to deliver dishes—when Mrs. Smith entered unaccompanied. She cast her eye over the room, tucked an errant strand of hair behind the earpiece of her spectacles, and beelined for their table, barely acknowledging the other diners. "May I join you?"

Without glancing at her tablemates for approval, Lillian gestured Mrs. Smith to a chair. "My dear Phoebe, if you can stand the stench of scandal."

"Is that scandal?" Mrs. Smith set her notebook beside her plate. "I was afraid it was the soup." She snapped her napkin open and spread it across her lap. "Don't worry, Don Sebastien. My good opinion of you is unchanged. Although you may find yourself the victim of a barrage of correspondence should I come to write a novel featuring one of—is the polite term *the blood?*"

"The polite term is whatever you say with a smile," he answered, gratified. "I am pleased not to be pre-judged. I had thought you might avoid my company after this morning's unpleasantness."

Mrs. Smith accepted a wine glass from Virgil, who remained thoughtfully silent. "Am I supposed to sprain myself avoiding being seen dining with the wampyr, or with the adventuress?"

"What about the sorcerer?" Jack said, gesturing to the door as Oczkar Korvin entered. "That should liven up the place."

"Jack," Sebastien said. Korvin úr, he noticed, left a stout-thewed crewman by the entry, too. Sebastien wasn't the only one under close observation. "We needn't be unpleasant."

One could *see* Jack assembling the persona, if one caught him at it, like a knight girding on his armor. Sebastien had never asked Jack about his childhood—he rather, in fact, hoped Jack didn't recollect overmuch of it—but it had taken three or four years of taming before the fey speechless child Jack had been was willing to relax that armor at all.

Without looking at her, Sebastien heard Lillian's taken breath. An actress recognized the signs of a character falling into place. "Oh, very well," Jack said, then, casually. "If you insist." He raised his voice. "Korvin úr, aren't you going to join us?"

The parade of expressions across Oczkar Korvin's face would have been humorous under other circumstances. But to his credit, he mastered them, and came to take the chair remaining between Virgil and Mrs. Smith. He seated himself, collected and precise, with his posture folded in onto itself. "Señor de Ulloa," he said, "I owe you a rather abject apology."

"You made your point," Sebastien said. Now he rather wished he had a plate; utensils to manage would make a welcome distraction. "Won't Mademoiselle LeClere be dining with you?"

"She is unlikely to be down to lunch," Korvin said. "Judging by the hysterics that consummated our recent conversation."

"Your remorse does not extend to her?"

Korvin turned his water goblet with his fingertips. "A man doesn't like to be manipulated into doing a woman's dirty work for her," he said. "I made an unfortunate choice in listening to Eugenie—to Mademoiselle LeClere."

"She suggested your trick with the burning glass?" Sebastien asked, leaning forward.

"She said that you were going to accuse her—and me—of murder. That Madame Pontchartrain had disappeared while she and I were together, and—" an eloquent shrug. "Even sorcerers who are under a crown's control are viewed with a certain amount of suspicion."

"I'm acquainted with prejudice," Sebastien said. "What's changed to bring you to me now?"

"I had a word with Mr. Leatherby," Korvin said. "Mademoiselle LeClere and he had some unhappy history, it appears, and he was kind enough to warn me—"

"She was blackmailing him." Lillian set down her spoon and picked up her wine glass, slouching against the chair-back in a manner which she never could have managed in a corset. Mrs. Smith gave her an envious glance.

"Or her guardian was, with her assistance." Korvin said. He lowered his voice as the waiter came to take the soup away.

"Miss Meadows seemed to think Mademoiselle LeClere might attempt reform for your sake," Sebastien said.

"Who could ever trust her? Fortunately, I was not overfond of the girl."

Just willing to use her affection for you. Sebastien bit his tongue. Korvin wasn't the first or last of his kind. Not that Sebastien was any better, he thought, with a sidelong glance at Jack, who fiddled his cuffs, seemingly oblivious.

But, that piece in place, Sebastien abruptly remembered Mrs. Leatherby hurrying into the salon behind the others, her blouse still unbuttoned at the collar. He remembered her pulling the comb from her hair, and the scent of her perfume filling the room as her hair tumbled over her neck.

He put his water goblet down sharply enough to slop fluid on his hand. "Mrs. Smith," he said. "Or Lillian...I don't suppose either of you recalls *when* Beatrice Leatherby arrived in the lady's washroom to be inspected for a tattoo?"

"Late," Lillian said. "Out of breath."

And Sebastien nodded, the completed understanding filling him with lazy satisfaction. Jack was looking at him, smiling, and Sebastien wondered if the triumph were so transparent on his face. "Summon the Captain," he said. "She and her husband are the murderers."

—⁂—

The Leatherbys walked into quite a different luncheon than they must have been anticipating. Captain Hoak was waiting for them, flanked by the burly crewmen—alike as a brace of hounds—who had been guarding Korvin and Sebastien. "Your bags will be searched for a bottle of laudanum and for a magical hair-comb, which Korvin úr will inspect for enchantments related to concealing the presence of the wearer." he said. "You are accused of the murder of Leonelle Pontchartrain, and as master of this ship, I am placing you both under arrest."

"*Konrad*," Beatrice Leatherby said, and laid a hand on his arm. "Surely—in front of all these people—"

The captain flushed red to the roots of his hair. In the corner by the piano, Mr. Cui bent down to whisper something in his wife's ear, and she covered her mouth with both hands. Michiel van Dijk laid down his silver fork, but did not stand. "We'll not speak of it now."

Hollis Leatherby retained his composure, and bulled forward, pulling his wife away from Captain Hoak. "On what evidence?" His gaze swept scornfully over the assemblage, hot enough that Sebastien almost felt it curl the fine hairs on his skin. "I suppose the vampire and the sorcerer have joined forces to save their necks?"

"That's the tone I object to," Sebastien murmured in Mrs. Smith's ear, drawing a short sharp laugh before stepping forward, around her and away from Korvin and Jack. "Mr. Leatherby," he said, "would you like a *list*?"

"By all means, Mr. de Ulloa," Leatherby said. He stepped away from his wife and the captain, but there was nowhere for him to run on a dirigible, and Sebastien wasn't worried. "List away." He stuffed his hands in his pockets, frowning intently.

"You snore," Sebastien said, lifting his finger to tick off the first point. "Abominably. And yet I do not recall hearing your snores, even muffled by distance, the first night of the voyage. I have abnormally acute hearing, Mr. Leatherby. Interestingly, I would have thought nothing of it if your wife hadn't commented that your snoring had kept her awake, so that she happened to notice an argument between Korvin úr and Mlle. LeClere. Which was Mrs. Leatherby's first attempt to cast suspicion on them." He drew a breath. "Additionally, someone was able to come and go, both in my cabin and in Madame Pontchartrain's, without leaving any evidence—and your wife has a hair comb that masks her scent and prevents trace evidence—fibers and fingerprints and such—from being left behind. A pretty toy, and one I hadn't seen before, though Korvin úr assures me that they are not uncommon in Prague and Moscow, where certain of the security forces are staffed by wampyr and lycanthropes. And last, but not least, Mrs. Leatherby was the only passenger unaccounted for when my bags were riffled and evidence stolen."

Mr. Leatherby glanced at his wife and swallowed. "That implicates Beatrice, sir. Not me."

"*Hollis*," she said, in exactly the tone in which she'd said *Konrad.* "Hollis, you can't—"

"Oh, but I can," he said.

"Never fear, Mrs. Leatherby. We know your husband disposed of the body."

"You can't know that either," said Leatherby.

"But.I can," Sebastien said. *Nothing* gave the sense of satisfaction this did: watching a murderer scramble to avoid justice—and failing—was a most fulfilling side effect of his avocation. "Because I know that your wife met Captain Hoak on his three a.m. rounds, promised to come to the control cabin to meet with him while the pilot was on his dinner break, and there distracted him so thoroughly that he forgot to enter the time of his three a.m. rounds until much later, when he also entered the data of the five a.m. rounds. Between those times, he filled out other paperwork, or perhaps he wrote a letter to his wife, and in the course of those tasks he emptied and re-filled his fountain pen. I know that you, Mr. Leatherby, had arranged to meet with Madame Pontchartrain by the washrooms a little after three, ostensibly to deliver the next installment of her blackmail demands. After having arranged to take this particular flight solely to encounter her. In any case, it would be the least conspicuous place to meet, as you'd both have ample excuse to visit them on midnight errands. Your wife had already poisoned Mme. Pontchartrain's supply of laudanum, and when, after a stressful conversation, Madame slipped into the ladies' washroom to refresh her nerves, you remained waiting outside. Disposing of the body was easy, but unfortunately, when the bottle of laudanum fell from Madame Pontchartrain's clothes and was lost behind the rubbish bins you did not notice.

"Afterwards, when your wife left the Captain, she crept up to Mme. Pontchartrain's cabin and liberated her blackmail papers, and also the remaining poisoned opium. Because what opium eater would travel with only one bottle of her drug? I imagine those joined Madame Pontchartrain in her journey down the garbage chute?"

Hollis Leatherby stared at Sebastien with white-rimmed eyes.

Sebastien shrugged. "It must have been very difficult for you to meet her payments—and such a tragic result to a brief dalliance, wasn't it, and perhaps an ill-considered note or two to Mademoiselle LeClere. Your wife's gloves need mending, and your collars are worn. And no doubt, your new position in the Puritan atmosphere of the Colonies would place you in an even more fragile position. Were the blackmailers increasing their demands?"

When Beatrice Leatherby fainted dramatically, sliding out of Captain Hoak's arms, Sebastien was ready. Hollis Leatherby backpedaled under cover of the flurry of activity surrounding his wife, and Sebastien was half a step behind him—but when his hand emerged from his pocket clutching the requisite gun, Sebastien hesitated.

He would let the criminal withdraw into the hallway, he decided, and then intervene. Gunfire on a dirigible in mid-ocean was an unacceptable risk.

Unfortunately, Virgil Allen responded like a frontiersman. His revolver was in his hand far faster and more smoothly than Hollis Leatherby's had been, and he cleared his field of fire with a quick crabwise sidestep. "Put it down, Hollis."

Leatherby's hand tightened convulsively on the pistol, his other hand groping behind him for the door latch. "You won't fire."

Sebastien was just calculating his angle of attack when Jack slipped past him. Jack *did* know how fast he could be, and dodged his grab as slickly as the guttersnipe he had been. Sebastien's fingers brushed Jack's wool suitcoat, and before he could grab again Jack had walked between the men with the guns, his arms spread wide.

"*Neither* of you is going to fire," he said. He faced Leatherby, his back to Allen, and Sebastien saw Allen's hand tremble. And he also heard the soft, near-silent scrape of chair legs on the carpet's pile, and knew that Michiel van Dijk was standing, cautiously.

Please don't, Sebastien thought, wondering if he was fast enough to intercept a bullet, if that was what it took.

"Dammit," Allen said. "Get to one *side*, boy."

And how ridiculous was it for a vampire to pray? He did, anyway; if he'd been a breathing man, he would have held his breath. And beside him, all but forgotten, Lillian gave a little squeak.

"Mr. Allen," Jack said, "put up your weapon. There's nowhere for Mr. Leatherby to run."

"He could sabotage the airship," Allen argued, and Jack shrugged.

"So he could. And you could set us all on fire over the North Atlantic. Let him go for now. He's got nowhere to run to, until we reach New Amsterdam."

Allen shuddered, shook his head, and leveled the revolver again. He closed one eye, the revolver at arm's length, and squinted at the iron sight.

He was going to try to shoot past Jack, Sebastien saw, and he almost turned aside. Almost. Instead, he drove his nails into his palms and forced himself to watch.

"Your logic is impeccable," Virgil Allen said, and with a single crisp motion, elevated the muzzle of his gun.

No one intervened as Leatherby coughed out a labored breath and fumbled with the door. He slipped through it, back first and gun following.

Sebastien heard him moving on the far side of the doped fabric the way a cat hears rustling mice. Sebastien was much stronger than a cat, and much faster than a man, though Allen and van Dijk were both lunging for the door by now, along with one of the brawny crewmen. He simply *moved* through lathe and fabric, shredding it like crepe.

And on the other side, he broke Hollis Leatherby's right arm in two places in the process of relieving him of his gun. A spiral fracture, a nasty one.

It would likely never heal quite right.

Jack came to find him after dark. Sebastien stood on the promenade, his hands laced behind his back, and stared out at the air. The vast curve of the airship blocked any chance of stars, but the night was soothing, and there was moonlight in the east. They stood silently for a little, shoulder to shoulder, and Sebastien sneaked a sideways glance.

Jack stared straight ahead, his spine stiff. "I've been thinking," he said.

Sebastien winced. "What you said to Captain Hoak is true, you know."

"That I'm a free man? I know it." Jack sighed, and let his hands fall to his sides. "They'll take the Leatherbys and Mademoiselle LeClere back to Germany for trial on their charges of murder and blackmail, respectively. And I don't think any of the passengers for America will spread tales about you. I had a word with Miss Meadows and with Korvin úr."

"Thank you, Jack. Actually, we've been invited to visit Boston."

"We?"

"Oh, yes," Sebastien answered, letting his teeth show when he smiled. "You know, I think our Mrs. Smith quite fancies you."

They fell silent again. For a little while, Sebastien listened to Jack breathing, and considered what to say, to let Jack know it was all right, that Sebastien wouldn't hold a grudge. Jack frowned sideways at him, and Sebastien shrugged, and smiled slightly. But Jack spoke first. "Forgive me?"

"What's there to forgive?" Honestly startled, Sebastien turned and looked at Jack. And—at last—Jack was looking back.

"I was unreasonable about Lillian."

"You are never unreasonable," Sebastien answered.

"Will you visit her again?"

"Atlanta is far from New Amsterdam."

"Actresses and wampyr both tend to travel."

Sebastien shrugged. "I won't, if you forbid it."

They stood for a little while, becalmed in silence, until Jack spoke. "I talked to her a little. Her patron…she burned."

Sebastien winced. Vampires only passed one way: by violence, either at their own hand or that of another. Suicide was far more common than angry mobs, these days. And Sebastien knew very well that there were mornings when it would be far too easy to walk into the sun.

She burned.

"Whose was she?" he asked, because he had been avoiding asking.

"Jayne Fortescue," Jack answered, quickly. He'd been prepared with the name.

Sebastien sighed—a human habit he had never quite lost. He'd never heard of her. "An American?"

"I don't know." Jack licked his lips. "There aren't supposed to be any of the blood in America. It wasn't Evie, Sebastien."

"Of course not." Evie Péletier was the name she had burned under, but he had met her as Eudeline la Noire.

Names changed; the woman never.

Sebastien continued, "Evie burned years ago."

Almost five years, and Sebastien had only just learned of it, hadn't he? Five years of silence, not so much as a letter, and he'd thought nothing of it. They'd encounter one other by chance sooner or later, he reasoned, in Paris or in Bonn. Europe was small, and unlife was long.

And there would always be time.

Burned, this Jayne Fortescue. As his Evie had burned, all alone in tiny, crowded Europe with its clubs and lineages and complicated alliances and agreements and rules. All alone, and empty with it.

"Lillian's scars are old," Jack said. "The casually visible ones, anyway. You might have thought—"

He *had* thought, though he silently thanked Jack for permitting his dignity the lie. It would have explained too easily how she knew his name, and on some level, he had *wanted* to believe.

He shrugged and said, "That must be very hard for Lillian."

It didn't fool Jack. He caught Sebastien's sleeve and forced him to turn, to look Jack in the eye. "Promise me you won't."

"Jack—"

"Promise, Sebastien."

"You didn't know Evie." *What shall I tell you, Jack Priest? That it's very odd realizing that you are the oldest person that you are ever likely to know? That it is also very lonely?*

At least in America, I shall be able to pretend I have a reason to feel so alone.

"No," Jack said. "But I know how I feel about you. Don't think I don't know what this sudden emigration is about. You've left everything. Sold your house, lied to your court. You're never going back to Spain."

"And what of it?"

"Nothing." Jack turned and pressed a warm hand to Sebastien's cheek. "But you're not going to shake me that easily. That emancipation means you don't get to tell me to go away any more than you get to tell me to stay."

Mulishly, Sebastien plowed ahead. "I can't give you a *life*. Life is for the *living*, not the undead."

Jack dropped his hand and stared at Sebastien, chin tilted up. "Don't be an idiot."

"Jack?"

Shaking his head, Jack lifted himself up on tiptoe and kissed Sebastien quickly on the mouth. Sebastien closed his eyes for a moment, to savor the passing warmth, and so happened not to see when Jack turned on the balls of his feet and strode away. He'd gone three steps by the time Sebastien stirred himself to movement and caught up. Without looking at him, Jack coughed and ran one frail-seeming hand through his hair. "I don't need you to *give* me a life, you old fool. Or haven't you noticed that I've got my own?"

Sebastien blinked. Slowed his steps, so that Jack slowed to stay alongside him. "There's no such thing as forever."

"That's all right. *I* haven't got forever. So if you leave me like Lillian got left, I shall be quite cross. *Promise.*"

It was harder than it should have been, so he knew he wasn't lying.

Sebastien touched Jack's arm, and said, "I promise."

ꙄAX
(April, 1901)

No one slept well that night.

A little after three a.m., as a cold whispering rain fell over steep-gabled slate, husbands silently pulled wives close in the clammy darkness. Nurse-maids rose from narrow beds to check bundled babes; massive-headed mastiffs whined by banked hearthfires as household cats insinuated between dream-running paws; and in their warm, summer-smelling loose boxes, arch-necked carriage horses stamped and rolled white-rimmed eyes, leaning against the barred partitions to press flank to flank. The City of New Amsterdam tossed restlessly.

Detective Crown Investigator Abigail Irene Garrett had no one to turn to for comfort on a dismal night in April. When the chill slipped like an unwelcome guest between sheet and featherbed and her faded blue eyes came open, Garrett's hand crept automatically to the pistol under her pillow. Her half-awakened intellect checked her wards and guards. Intact. Despite the muffled impact of her heart against her ribcage, she was as alone as she should have been.

The pearl grip cool and heavy in her hand, Garrett sat up, swinging her legs over the edge of her black wood bedstead. Her left hand resting on the ornate spiral of a bedpost, she ran through her wards again. At her feet, her ragged patchwork terrier whined into the darkness.

"Hush, Mike. I know."

Nothing. She slipped her revolver back under the pillow and stood, belting a cream lace negligee over her nightgown. Her wand—ebony capped in silver, as long as the span from elbow to fingertip—lay on the nightstand, and this she lifted and touched to the wick of a gnarled beeswax stump. The candle sparked into light and Garrett drew a long, tight breath, trying to ease the clenching in her belly. Thirty years in the service of the Crown, and she had never felt such apprehension.

Setting her wand aside, she crossed rug-scattered tile to the credenza, where she poured herself whisky without water and sipped it slowly. Mike scampered close at her heels. She opened the casement one-handed, rain-beaded glass icy on her fingertips, and leaned out into a gaslamp-jeweled night. Falling water trickled down her neck, washed her face like tears. The woeful exhalation of a late-arriving steamship, packet boat from England or places more distant, hung on the night. The black stone windowledge gouged a cold furrow across her belly. Mike shoved dustmop paws against the wall, too small to reach the windowledge. She reached down and ruffled his ears.

When the first inch of liquor warmed the chill from her shoulders, Abigail Irene Garrett straightened from the window, unwound white fingers from her tumbler, and began to dress.

— ⟡ —

"Grisly," Garrett commented—an uncharacteristic sentiment.

And an understatement. The rain had slowed to a mist, but the flag-stoned walk lay puddled under her feet. Her eyes narrowed as she gathered the navy-blue skirts of her walking dress in her hands. She lifted them clear of the bloodstained stoop of a wide-fronted three-story brownstone as she minced up the steps. Stringy, clotted runnels dripped down them like paint.

She glanced at uniformed representatives of the Colonial Police and two of the Duke's city Guard, looking apprehensive and outnumbered. "Who can tell me what happened here?"

A patrolman stepped forward, avoiding the DCI's gaze—and avoided following the direction of it when she turned her back on him, bending toward the body crumpled against the scored wooden door. She couldn't keep her boots out of the clotted blood, but uniformed officers had already walked through it. *And a detective or two who should have known better, I warrant,* she thought. *Well, we're not all cut out to be sorcerers.*

She glanced over her shoulder, pinning the hapless patrolman on a nee-dle-pointed gaze, wondering which of her notorieties occupied his attention. *Perhaps it's just the scent of blood paling his face.* "Well?" *Perhaps.*

"DCI, I was first on the scene."

"And?" Garrett drew herself upright, ash-laced blonde hair falling in a wing across her forehead. *Don't smile at him, Abby Irene, or you'll never get another word of sense out of him, and he might very well piss himself. And you know Division would have something to say about that—disgrace to the uniform and so on.* The thought quivered her lips. She fought the smile to a standstill and converted it into an expectant frown.

"He was dead when I arrived, DCI. I heard the screaming…"

"I see." She let him see her lean forward to note the number on his shield. "Did you identify the bystanders? At what time?"

He took a half-step back. "Sunrise, ma'am. Perhaps an hour ago. There were no witnesses present when I arrived."

"No-one came to his assistance? You heard screaming—"

The officer trained his gaze on the blood-spattered leaves of a just-budding rose alongside the wrought-iron fence. "It was over quickly. Ma'am. As I arrived, the neighbors began coming out of their houses. I was only around the corner."

"No-one has touched the body since?" *Poor lad. He couldn't have been more than fifteen. What was he doing out so early in the rain?*

"Officers entered. But they climbed through the window."

She could see that from the footprints. Thankfully they had sense enough not to move the body to open the door. Garrett planned to go inside once she had finished her work with the victim. She was too old to climb through windows in the rain.

I wonder what's become of his spine? She leaned forward to examine the damage. *The skull is cracked, and I would wager the poor lad's brains have been scooped out. If a human being could do that, I'd say so violent an attack was personal.* She crouched to investigate a scatter of pale flecks on the steps, like a splash of milk frozen in place.

The patrolman swallowed loudly. Red hair and freckles, couldn't have been four years older than the victim. Despite herself, Garrett took pity on him. "What's your name, officer?"

"Forester," he replied. His face gleamed white around a fevered flush spotting the center of each cheek.

She sighed, seeing her own imperious face reflected in his eyes. Twenty years ago, she had been thought a great beauty. Boys like Forester had been so far beneath her notice that she had not even realized it was possible for them to *have* feelings. *Times change, Abby Irene.* "I am a sorcerer, lad, not a cannibal. You did as well as could be expected." She turned away.

"Ma'am?"

"Dismissed," she confirmed. "Go back to your dispatch for debriefing, Forester. You were right to call me in. This is a matter for the Crown." She knew perfectly well that the summons had come from the city Guard, and not from the Mayor's Colonial Police, but it was polite to lie.

Sometimes—but only some times—Garrett could almost admit a

sympathy for the Mayor and his push for home rule. Her true loyalties, however, lay with the Crown. And the Duke.

Except, she mused, bootheels clicking as she made her way back to her waiting carriage, the Crown was an ocean away on the other side of her self-imposed exile, and in these days of threatened hostilities with the French and Iroquois it seemed to prefer to forget the Colonies existed. And the Duke, loyal Patriot that he was, had problems of his own.

Still, it rankled: in London, she could have counted on a specialist sorcerer and at least one additional DCI for so gruesome a murder. In the entire reach of the Colonies, from the Atlantic to the Iroquois territories West of the Appalachians, Garrett's only colleagues were in Boston and Philadelphia. One doddered through the closing years of a white-bearded wizard's career; the other was a puling idiot who never would have achieved his Th.D without judiciously applied nepotism.

Yes, unequivocally—and especially since the Iron Queen's death and her eldest son's succession—Garrett was on her own.

Her driver, huddled miserable on the box, touched his cap. The renewed patter of rain on the cobbles told her to hurry. Uniformed officers held the gathering crowd back while Garrett rooted in her blue velvet carpetbag, kept dry in the enclosed coach. Quickly, she found what she needed and returned.

It was nasty work, sketching a circle around the corpse, and the hem of her dress was black with sucking mud and daubed red as well by the time she closed it. Renewed murmurs ran through the onlookers. Garrett shook her head, not troubling herself to look up. *They can't have only now figured out who I am.*

But deliberate steps clipped along the bloodsoaked walk, and a silken voice close behind her said, "Crown Investigator."

Garrett pinched the bridge of her nose, thinking very hard about the silver flask of brandy in her carpetbag. She knotted the circle off so that it would hold during her distraction and turned to face the intruder.

"I see the officers recognized you, Viscount," she said, briefly distracted by hazel eyes under a fall of brown-black hair. Princely cheekbones, a caballero's noble nose, and the sensual lip of a Rumanian aristocrat.

Garrett bit down on a sigh.

"Please," said the notorious amateur detective, extending his grey-gloved hand, voice melodious with the interwoven tones of his native language. "So lovely a lady must by all means call me Sebastien. Besides, your English titles are so confusing."

Garrett transferred her wand to her left hand and allowed him to bend over her right. Much as she despised the man, she had to admit to a certain agreeable shiver when his lips brushed her glove. Don Sebastien de Ulloa straightened and smiled, gesturing to the mangled remains of the boy with the tip of his walking stick. "And so, my dear investigator—what have we here?"

Garrett pursed her lips in frustration, but kept her voice level. "I'm not certain yet," she said. "I've just finished containing the scene. There are a few interesting anomalies...."

"That is candlewax." Don Sebastien leaned forward, laying a hand on Garrett's arm to steady himself away from the circle.

"It appears to be," she answered, shifting from the touch. "Interesting, is it not? Other than the mud and blood, it is obvious that the doorstep and facade were immaculately kept; probably scrubbed daily, if their housekeeper is anything like my Mary. So the wax can be no older than a day."

Don Sebastien was no sorcerer, and she largely ignored him while she dipped mingled salt and lampblack out of a little pouch and spread those around the circle, pretending she did not notice the cold water dripping down her collar. Don Sebastien seemed untroubled. "What intrigues me, Crown Investigator, is the swiftness of the attack. Have you eliminated a human agency?"

She tucked the little pouch into her pocket. "I've ruled out nothing," she answered, feeling as if he tested her. "But I must admit, I can see no way around suspicions of sorcery. Unless it was a beast." She let her voice drop. "In which case, we can expect further attacks."

Don Sebastien pursed sensual lips. Rain spattered from the brim of his hat. "May I call you Lady Abigail? It is so much less unwieldy than 'Crown Investigator.'"

"My name is 'Abigail Irene.' And I would prefer to be addressed by the title appropriate to the situation. 'Garrett' will do if you are pressed for time, Don Sebastien."

"I meant no disrespect. DCI, have you considered some of the more unpleasant possibilities?"

"Such as?"

"Were-thing. Wampyr. Summoned demon, improperly bound."

"What would you consider the more *pleasant* possibilities, Don Sebastien? A deranged lunatic with the strength to peel a man's spine out of his back?"

"Ah. I take your point, Investigator. Although I admit, I am still exceedingly curious about the candlewax."

Garrett chuckled. "So am I, Don Sebastien. So am I. And curious as well, where the other residents have gotten off to. Shall we proceed?"

Once the coroner had moved the body, Don Sebastien wrapped the brass door-pull—which had already been examined—carefully in his handkerchief and tugged it open, stepping aside so that Garrett could precede him. "Crown Investigator, may I join you?"

"Thank you, Don Sebastien. If you must, you may." She shook her gore-daubed skirts and knocked the worst of the mire from her boots before she crossed the threshold; it didn't help. Wet cloth still clung to her knees when she crouched. "Well."

Don Sebastien reached up and pulled a taper from the sconce upon the wall, keeping the drip shield at its base. He set it alight with a silver lighter, drawn from his coat pocket, and dropped to one knee facing Garrett, tilting the candle to give her light. Shadows scrolled about them. "More candle-spatters," she said. "Beeswax, and a good quantity of it, too."

"Do you maintain your good opinion of the housekeeper?"

She lifted her chin and glanced around, hair moving against the nape of her neck. Don Sebastien's eyes were on the scrollworked secretary beside the door. Garrett reached out and ran a kid-gloved fingertip along its edges. She examined the results in the glow of the taper, which was of good enough quality not to drip even when he angled it. "Even the back is clean," she said. "And a family of some means, if they were spending so on candles. And *that* candle does not drip like this." She drew out a penknife and flaked a few dribs of wax into a glassine envelope.

"Your reputation does not do you justice," Don Sebastien said, and stood, offering Garrett his assistance. "The intruder's light, do you think?"

"If there was an intruder." His flesh was cool even through her glove. "Don Sebastien, you were too long in the rain."

"I am always cold," he answered, and released her lightly once her balance was sure. "The trail appears to lead this way. Shall we have a look upstairs, Crown Investigator?"

"By all means. Lead on, Lucifer." *Light-bearer.*

He laughed and held the candle high. "I have been called worse. You have noticed the angle of the drippings?"

"Of course," she answered. "They fell from the candle of someone *leaving* the house."

"Indeed." They entered the front room. He stood aside again, to allow her to precede him up the sweeping stair.

Very pretty. For a hobbyist. Does he think because a Crown Investigator is also a woman, she needs an expatriate Spaniard as her shadow to solve a murder? And then, since he was only looking at the back of her rain-wet head, she allowed herself a little, mocking smile. *Perhaps he's just hoping to catch a glimpse of your ankles.* "There is more wax up the stair runner."

"And on the banister."

"And across the landing—interesting. The droplets crisscross the hall." She bent again, gesturing for the light. Don Sebastien was beside her as silently as a cat in his patent-leather boots, dabs of mud marring their mirror shine. "The intruder spent a fair amount of time here."

"Do you suppose he came in through an upstairs window? Two were open; strange on a stormy night."

"Do you suppose he was a *he*?" Garrett answered mildly, moving to the closest of the bedrooms, from which a cold draft flowed. The door stood open; mud on the threshold told her the officers had been through it, and she wished she knew if the door had been closed or open when they arrived.

She paused in the frame of the doorway, letting her eyes take in the room. A young man's, by the schoolbooks and fencing gear, and the bed had been slept in—disconsolately, judging by the crumpled and thrown-back covers and the disarray of the pillows. Unlike the downstairs entryway, there was light enough in this room to see the spatters of wax on the floor, although there was no candle in the holder by the bed.

A chill lifted the hair on Garrett's neck. She moved to the window, aware of Don Sebastien behind her, although the wide wooden boards scarcely seemed to flex under his weight. "Are you a swordsman, Don Sebastien?"

"A notorious one, in my youth," he answered, giving it the slight inflection of a double entendre. Her lips twitched. She did not look, instead leaning down beside the windowframe and tilting her head to examine it against the slanted light. The floor beneath was damaged, the wood already swollen from rain falling inside. That rain had washed away any traces that might have been on the windowsill; Garrett stared until her eyes crossed and found nothing. Still her skin crawled.

"He is restless," Garrett said, straightening and stepping away from the casement. She whirled, noticing Don Sebastien's sudden stillness, as if he set himself for an attack. Garrett pulled her eyes from the Spaniard and paced quickly to the bed. "He rises. He—"

"—kindles a light," Sebastien interrupted. "There is a burnt match in the candle holder, and the box in the nightstand cubbyhole."

"Very good. Except he's neglected a candle—"

"—or perhaps he pulls the candle from the holder."

"To what purpose?"

"I do not know." Their eyes met, and Garrett released the deep-drawn breath she had been holding. *The thrill of the chase.*

"Were you restless last night, Don Sebastien?"

"I am always restless at night, DCI."

"Then perhaps—" she advanced with a firm step like a duelist's "—you would be better served at home, resting in your bed." She didn't smile to soften it, and again their gazes crossed. Garrett fancied she could hear the ring of steel. "This is still a Crown investigation, Viscount."

Don Sebastien reached up to tip his hat, which he had not removed when they stepped inside. "I am very restless," he answered. "And, too often, very bored. And I do not imagine that this is *anything* but your case, Crown Investigator."

"As long as you understand me."

She turned away and went to the window again. She was leaning out to grasp the edge of the casement with the intention of swinging it closed when he spoke again from close beside her. "Oh, never that, Abigail I—"

His body struck hers a moment before she properly registered that he had stopped speaking mid-sentence, slamming her forward, belly against the windowsill and her arms flung out like a diver's. Her corset took the brunt of the impact, whalebone bruising her at belly and breast, and she shouted outrage and scrabbled at rain-slick wood. She teetered, Don Sebastien's weight pinning her, and kicked wildly, expecting any moment to feel his hands on her ankles tilting her forward into a sickening, tumbling fall.

She didn't think the rose-bushes would break her fall enough to save her. Especially if she hit the fence. *Why would the Great Detective murder a wealthy East Side boy?* Amazed by the calm precision of her own thoughts even as she twisted, bringing her gloved hands up to fend him off.

His strength was irresistible. He simply wrapped hands as hard as barrel-hoops around her wrists and—

—hauled her spluttering back into the room and down onto the floor. "Are you hit?" he asked, patting her cheek anxiously. His hat had tumbled off and fetched up in the far corner, and his glossy, hard-looking hair stood up in disheveled spikes.

"Hit?"

"The carriage—" He shook his head. "You didn't see." And rolled on his back, away from her, and raised his right hand to point across his face to the ceiling directly overhead. "There was a rifleman down on the street."

Detective Crown Investigator Garrett certainly knew the look of a fresh bullet-hole in plaster, when she saw one. "Ah," she said quietly. "Someone must be taking an interest in the case."

— ❧ —

A little before noon, Garrett marked time in the antechamber outside the Mayor's office, grateful at least for the chance to shed her soaked oilcloth. Although the rain had stopped falling and the clouds had thinned shortly before Don Sebastien took his leave, the afternoon promised a continuing overcast.

Blood and mud still smirched the hem of her walking dress, and it might have been politic to return to her rooms and change. However, his Lordship, Peter Eliot, Mayor of New Amsterdam, had made it known that he expected to see her with all deliberate speed, and far be it from her to think of preserving the man's prized Persian carpets under such circumstances. Garrett swallowed a pleased smile.

By the watch pinned to her bodice, she'd been waiting at least twenty minutes before the door opened and the Mayor's confidential secretary—a well-made young man with dark blue eyes, whom she noted appreciatively— gestured her in. Garrett smiled; she'd taken the opportunity to rifle his desk while he was away, and had one of his visiting cards slipped inside the cuff of her glove. *Simon LeMarque, M.Th.S.* Another sorcerer. *And French. How interesting. The Mayor must be more worried about the Duke and me than he admits. Although, given the number of times he's tried to*—embarrass—*us both, I shouldn't be surprised.*

She swept past Simon LeMarque, holding her soiled dress well aside, and glided to a halt before Peter Eliot's enormous mahogany desk. The Mayor didn't trouble himself to look up from the papers that occupied his attention, and Garrett gave her sodden skirts an extra shake to settle them. "Your Lordship."

Eliot glanced up. "I understand there was some trouble in the city this morning, Detective."

"Crown Investigator, sir," she answered. "And yes."

He nodded judiciously, setting his papers aside. "Have you identified a suspect yet? I'm under pressure from the press, you understand. The gruesome aspect of the murder…."

You blithering idiot, I've been at the crime scene for six hours. I've barely begun my investigation, and you know it. But he isn't a blithering idiot, and I'd better remember that. "Respectfully, sir, because of the possibly—*probably*—arcane nature of the crime, it's a Crown matter now. You shall have to address the press's inquiries to the Duke's office."

"I'd hate to have them jump to the conclusion that the Duke's officers are impeding a murder investigation."

Ah. The threat made manifest. "The Duke is quite capable of handling his own public affairs, your Lordship."

Eliot smiled, uncoiling from his desk. He was a long, narrow man, grey hair thinning at the top, waistcoat tight across the small bulge of his paunch. Probably not much older or taller than the intensely annoying Don Sebastien. Despite her professional dislike for the so-called Great Detective, Garrett found herself comparing the Mayor unfavorably to the Spanish aristocrat. "Ah, yes, the Duke. Has he taken an interest, then?" Garrett didn't miss the jeweled-serpent glitter in the man's eyes.

She knew she was one of Richard's—the Duke's—biggest political weaknesses. And she suspected the Mayor knew as well, or at least suspected. *But he cannot prove a thing, and that is the important part. And my service record is impeccable, for all I am a woman.*

"I have yet to speak to him regarding the case, sir. Usually he prefers not to be involved until the evidence is more complete, and in any eventuality, I have not yet even had time to write up my notes. But you appreciate that I can discuss nothing relating to a Crown investigation with anyone who is not in my chain of command." *And here in the god-forsaken West, my chain of command begins and ends with the Duke. You have no power over me.*

Well, other than the power to endlessly complicate my life. With the exception of Garrett and the city Guard, New Amsterdam's law enforcement reported to the office of the Mayor. And Garrett desperately needed to keep her access to the resources of the Colonial Police.

"And I know you like to keep a very personal hand on your investigations, Detective…Crown Investigator."

Familiar ice stiffened Garrett's spine, and she let it freeze her professional smile on her face. "Surely, sir, I have no idea what you might be insinuating."

"Ah, of course not. You will keep me apprised?"

And that's what this is about. An offer to betray Richard for a place at Peter Eliot's right hand? Oh, how will I ever resist the temptation. Years of practice kept the ironic tinge from her voice. "Of course, your Lordship."

Eliot came around his desk and laid a hand on her upper arm, turning her gently toward the door. "I would be indebted to you, Lady Abigail. I hope you know how impressed we all are with your work. So many women consider themselves fit to fill any man's shoes—it is always refreshing to meet one who can actually do a job. There are always opportunities for people like you."

Ah, yes, the carrot and the stick. The touch, warm through damp cotton, made her skin crawl, and she was again moved to contrast the Mayor with Don Sebastien. She frowned, pushing disloyal images aside. *You despise the man, Abigail Irene.* The self-reminder amused her; she let that amusement color her tone. "You will be the third to know, your Lordship. Possibly the fourth."

That brought him up short, or perhaps he merely stumbled, spit-shined shoes catching on the nap of the richly knotted carpets. "The fourth?"

"Ah, yes," Garrett said, taking advantage of his momentary distraction to disengage her arm and break for the door with all the dignified haste she could muster. *Two years of finishing school not entirely wasted. At least I can manage an imperious exit.* "Don Sebastien de Ulloa appears to have interested himself in the case." *And he has no loyalty to the Duke, but neither bears he any love for you.*

It was too much to hope that the Mayor would not have her followed, so Garrett did exactly as he would expect. Resuming her carriage, the Crown Investigator gave instructions to her driver to wake her when they arrived at the Duke's residence, in Queens.

But she could not sleep. Somewhere along the way, the clouds broke and a slanted line of sunlight glanced off rain-frosted stones, gilding the city. Garrett took a breath of cold air, rich with the promise of spring, and let it out again on a sigh. *That's what you do it for, Abby Irene,* she thought. *Seven million souls, thirty percent of the population of the Colonies, and the capitol of the British Protectorate of North America. So what if it's not London?*

She chuckled at the comparison. *Well, it's just not London. That's all. But you live with your decisions, Abigail Irene. And if living in the would-be-Plutocratic chaos of the Colonies is what it takes to fulfill your duty, so mote it be.*

After crossing the Elizabeth Bridge, her driver turned the rattling coach down Brewster Street, and Garrett smoothed her dress. The mud had somewhat dried; she slipped her gloves off, cracking the powder off her hem.

Then she dug in her reticule for lotion to smooth her face and disguise her exhaustion. Not that she had anything to hide from Richard, Duke of New Amsterdam, but old habits died hard.

She was tugging the fingers of her gloves back into place when the carriage jolted to a halt on the gracious circular drive of the Duke's massive white Colonial. Garrett nodded coolly to the groom who rushed to hand her down, and made her way up the broad, shallow steps to the portico.

The Duke's servants opened the door before she reached the landing. They ushered her into Richard's study, where she shooed a two-hundred pound Mastiff out of the loveseat and settled herself before the fire with a brandy from the sideboard. Candles blazed on the marble mantle; the gaslights were not lit. The fair-haired, fiftyish Duke himself joined her before she had halfway finished the glass.

She set it on an end table and would have stood, but he raised one hand and shook his head. "Keep your seat, Abby Irene. And finish your brandy. I can see that you need it." He poured a glass for himself before coming to sit beside her, curling his long legs to the side. His hair was wavy, silver at the temples and the nape, the rich ashen color of tree bark. She wanted to run her fingers through it, and instead she sipped her brandy.

"You can't be ready to make me a report on that murder yet," he said, leaning toward her.

She gave him a troubled smile and put her other hand on his knee, first glancing past him to make sure the door was latched.

"I locked it," he said.

"People will talk."

"People do," he said. "Someday you'll tell me what brought you to America, Abby Irene. My curiosity keeps me up nights."

She sipped her brandy. "I don't think it was curiosity, Richard. Not last night, anyway."

He offered her an expression of frank surprise. "Really? You didn't sleep well either?"

"No one did, it seems. And one boy's night-time wandering may have led to his death."

"Ah, yes. Tell me about the murder."

"There's little enough to tell." She let her hand slide across the tailored dark fabric of his trousers before leaning back, curling against the arm of the loveseat in a manner that would have horrified her tutors. "Don Sebastien has involved himself, but he is—as is his wont—playing his cards close to his chest. And whoever it was that arranged the vanishments and the murder isn't above a little rough play with a hunting rifle." Sebastien had dug the flattened bullet out of molded plaster. Now Garrett slipped it from the cuff of her glove and dropped it with a clink into Richard's brandy glass.

His lips thinned. "You were not harmed." Flatly, as if he would accept it no other way.

"Thanks to de Ulloa. I was not harmed." She swirled brandy on her tongue, watching Richard fish the bullet out between thick fingers and hold it up to the light. Her voice was more petulant than she had intended when she spoke again. "If I could find the rifle that came from, I might be able to prove who fired it. And I *wish* you would let me have that Peter Eliot assassinated."

"Abby Irene...."

"I know, my love. I'm not—*quite*—serious. Yet. But you know he'd rather have your nephew in your place."

"David is too young." The Duke raked a hand through his hair and bit his lip. "Which is why Peter would want him in my place. Of course, I'd have to be dead."

"Dead or abdicated." She did not permit longing to enter her voice.

"There is that. And there are days when the temptation to divorce is overwhelming. But then I think of Mayor Peter Eliot. And the French and Iroquois on our Western border. And," he continued bitterly, "King Phillip, and his Eastward-looking eye."

"I wouldn't have you anyway, Richard." Trying for levity.

He toasted her, one eyebrow raised, his voice rich with irony. "What sensible woman would marry a man she knows to be unfaithful?" Into her silence, he continued, "The murder."

She finished her brandy. "Grisly," she said, standing to pour herself another. "Inhuman, I think. Nasty."

"Ah." He frowned as she turned back.

She saw him taking in the disarray of her dress, and drew herself up a little prouder. *You were a famous beauty once, Abigail Irene. If you're stupid enough to sleep with your superior, you'd best be smart enough to use whatever you have left.* "Also, the murdered boy was slain on his own doorstep. Mud to your ankle, and not a footstep. No marks and no signs anywhere, except two windows open and his whole family missing."

The Duke leaned forward, all but ready to jump to his feet. "*Missing?* How many?"

"Mother, father, adolescent sister, housekeeper. Strange."

"Indeed. Continue."

Garrett shrugged. "Most odd was the wax."

"Wax? Candlewax?"

"Droplets of it. Scattered throughout the house. Splashed. Near the boy's body as well."

"I see. And yet no leads?"

Garrett shook her head. "If I locate the candle—presuming it is a candle—I'll be able to use the principles of contagion, similarity and sympathy to prove that the wax originated with that particular one, and we'd have a case. But...."

"But?"

"Well.... Richard, I have nothing. I haven't even a trail to follow, and four people are missing who may very well be alive and in danger somewhere."

Across the room, he nodded. "I see."

"Do you?"

No smile creased Richard's face now. "You say that Don Sebastien has taken an interest?"

Garrett nodded curtly.

"Use him," Richard said, coldly. "Use whatever it takes. I'm relying on you, Abby Irene."

"Richard," she answered softly. And: "My Lord."

Garrett seldom entertained at home, and when she did, they were usually the sort of guests one received in the den, or the library. Her laboratory was on the first floor of her townhouse, immediately behind the parlor, where one might have anticipated a dining room. The room itself was half study and half chemistry, with books and chairs lining the walls and long stone-topped benches running parallel.

Cleanly clothed, now, and gowned in a white canvas smock to protect her dress, Garrett moved crisply between her granite-topped workbench and the thaumaturgic circle inlaid in red and white stone tiles amid the slate-blue field of the floor. She laid out the samples she'd isolated from the body of the murdered boy: earth, fingernail clippings, scraps of his clothing and scrapings from the steps on which he had died. She piled each sample in a shallow watch glass placed in one of the isolation circles. Those smaller peripheral circles also held beakers of clotted blood and an Erlen flask of rainwater, along with samples of hair that she had retrieved from the toiletries of the missing individuals—a bit of everything she meant to eliminate from the parameters of her spell. At the very center of the circle, over the gas flame, a crucible warmed. A low table set beside it held a small heap of candles brought from the victims' house and several more watch glasses.

Three of these shallow dishes each contained a bit of the waxlike substance. The last one cradled splinters from the gouges in the blue wooden door.

By seven o'clock, Garrett was on her second pot of tea. Mike had come in to find her after his supper and was dozing in his basket. Straightening from her bench, she had just thought of pausing for her own meal before the evening's real work when a familiar tap on the door brought her head around. Mike pricked up his ears and hopped to his feet as she opened the door.

"Supper already, Mary?" Garrett asked the dark, narrow-shouldered housekeeper standing in the hallway.

Mary's eyes twinkled. "If it please you, m'Lady, there's a right handsome gentleman caller to see you. I've invited him in." Mary extended an ornate silver tray so that Garrett could pick up the visiting card lying on it.

"Ah. Indeed?" She didn't think she needed to glance at the name—the slightly oily feel of parchment between her fingertips told her everything. "Engraved. Very nice. Send Don Sebastien in, please. I will receive him in the laboratory." Mike wagged his coiled plume happily after Mary; she ducked her head and left.

Mary must have taken the gentleman detective's overcoat and hat, but Garrett noticed that the shoulders of his coat were damp through. "Is it raining again, Don Sebastien?" Absently, her hand came up to press the place between her breasts where a sigil tattooed in crimson marked her training. She felt as if his gaze burrowed through cloth to notice it.

"Indeed," he said, bowing over her hand, making no comment on her stained smock. Again, his lips brushed the back of her fingers—ungloved, this time—and sent a shiver down her spine.

Her terrier withdrew to his basket and watched the tall stranger warily. She snapped her fingers for Mike's attention, and his tail flipped twice, but he merely lay there, watching with disturbing, alert eyes.

"Have you had any success, my dear Crown Investigator?"

She sighed and turned away, gesturing toward the circle. "As you can see, I am just about to commence. What have you discovered, Don Sebastien? As I recall, when we parted company, you were on your way to research the boy's family."

"And so I was. May I sit?"

"As it pleases you," she answered. He selected a wingbacked chair against the wall, pushed away from Garrett's equipment and opposite Mike's basket, not far from the hearth.

When he was settled on the olive brocade and had refused tea, he began to speak. "The lad's name was Bruce Carlson, home on Easter break from a school in Westchester. His family, as you no doubt noticed from the house, were not without resources, which proved fortunate for them, because the lad seems to have been something of a troublemaker."

"Really?" Garrett turned up the flame under her crucible and began breaking the candles into it. "What sort of trouble?"

"Well." The handsome Spaniard rubbed his hands together, leaning toward the fire. "There were whisperings—nothing proven, you understand, or even openly charged—that he was less than honorable to a maidservant who left their employment last year."

"English girl?" *Even a servant should have been able to go to the Colonial Police if her master's son laid hands on her.*

"Irish," Don Sebastien answered, his frown raising him an inch or two in Garrett's estimation. Her own history gave her a certain sympathy to pariahs of any stripe—Irish, Negro, even the Romany and Indian halfbloods who were welcome nowhere—but few aristocrats harbored fellow-feeling for their 'inferiors.' "No family I've been able to locate. Not even a last name."

"What became of her?" *What is your agenda, Don Sebastien? What is it you want of me? Of New Amsterdam?*

He shrugged expressively, smoothing his damp hair behind his ear. "I do not know. I understand she may have been—*embarazada,* although such things are not openly spoken of."

"So we have a motive for the killing. A potential motive, at least. Sorcerous blood runs strong in those old Irish families."

Don Sebastien nodded. "There may be other motives as well. The father is a member of Colonial Parliament. House of Commons."

Garrett stirred wax with a glass rod, the hot scent filling her head. "They must be better off even than the house shows."

"Not necessarily. The father—Robert Carlson—has familial links to Mayor Eliot. And the Mayor's patronage."

"Ah." The wax was clearing. Garrett fished the wicks out of the bottom of the crucible and trapped them against the rim, scorching her fingers slightly as she pinched them out. She blew on the scalds. "Would he not have been the target, then?"

"Perhaps. We cannot be certain he was not—he is, after all, gone. And we also cannot rule out other, unknown, enemies."

Garrett lifted the first of the watch glasses and held it over the seething pot. "What troubles me is the consents," she said. "The boy was killed outside the door of his house. Outside its protection. But the family—although that upstairs window was open, there is no trace of forced entry."

"Continue, Crown Investigator." She thought she saw respect in his eyes. *Perhaps his open-mindedness about the worth of things extends to Irish and women both. Will wonders never cease?*

"Human agencies can come and go as they please. Magical ones—the forms must be observed. One of the forms is consent, expressed or implied."

"Ah, yes," he said. "I am familiar with the theory. And of the difference between implied and informed consent, and that one will serve as well as the other." He smiled as if something amused him. "So, in adherence to the principal tenets of magic, if no human agency entered the house—excepting the officers of the Colonial Police—"

She stirred the contents of the watch glass into the wax. "—then a consent must have been issued to whatever did. Did you note the damage to the door?"

"*Sí.*" He watched her intently now, eyebrows rising as she frowned at the contents of her crucible.

"That's odd."

"Crown Investigator?" He stood from the wing chair and would have come to her, but she raised one hand to forestall him before he crossed into the circle.

"A moment," Garrett said, selecting another glass. "As I was saying, whatever killed the boy—and I too become more convinced it was a whatever and not a whomever—made an attempt at the door and was barred from entrance. However, it—or something else—apparently managed to enter the house almost immediately and remove the residents tracelessly."

"Except…." His long fingers indicated the shallow dish in her right hand.

"Candlewax. Yes." She nodded and upended it.

Don Sebastien leaned forward, curiously, his boots firmly on the outside of the tiled circle. "What are you looking for?"

"Antipathy," she answered, and looked up long enough to shoot him a brief, real smile.

"What every woman wants."

Garret laughed and set the dish aside, rather more casually also capsizing the third one into the vessel. She did not lift the one containing the splintered bits of door. "I've learned something interesting, Don Sebastien. You may enter the circle now, I'm finished. Come and see."

—◈—

Mary served them dinner on a card table in the book-paneled library, where Garrett normally took her solitary meals. Silver candelabra decorated the table, and when Garrett commented on the extravagance, Mary remarked that she'd gotten a bargain on candles. Don Sebastien lifted his Windsor-backed chair and placed it adjoining Garrett's, rather than across. Amused or contemplative, she permitted the familiarity. He tasted his wine and picked up the heavy, long-tined silver fork gingerly, investigating the salmon on his plate.

As he teased the flaking fish apart, he glanced up and met her eyes, smiling. "You did not find what you expected," he said.

Garrett ate carefully but with good appetite. "One tries not have expectations, precisely," she answered. "But yes, I would have to say that I did not expect the splashed wax to exhibit similarity with the candles remaining in the house. You saw how the wax in the crucible accepted what I introduced to it?"

Don Sebastien nodded. "I could see no difference."

"The principle of antipathy states that two substances which do not share an identity will not normally commingle. This tells me that the splashes of wax which we retrieved from the Carlsons' house are magically identified with the candles they were using."

"Those candles were from several sources, however. Beeswax and paraffin, you had." Don Sebastien laid his fork down by his plate. Rain drummed on the windows.

"But what is important in this case is that they were bought by the same person, with the same sense of purpose—that of lighting her home. The will of the individual who uses a thing is very important. A bullet and a gun, for example, are manufactured separately—but a bullet may be traced back to the gun from which it was fired, using the principle of sympathy—which is the converse of that of antipathy. Do you understand?" She peeled buttered bread apart with her fingers and offered a tidbit to the terrier, her expression challenging Don Sebastien to say anything as the little dog nipped her fingers with sharp white teeth.

He smiled, amused, swirling wine in his glass. "Very well, I think. So the splashed wax came from candles inside the home."

"Precisely. Which means...."

Sebastien effortlessly picked up her thread. Annoying or not, it was a pleasure to talk to a man with a wit. "...our lad must have gone out to the stoop to investigate something—some noise, some cry—and been carrying a candle in his hand."

"Then we are left with another question, Don Sebastien."

"*Sí*, DCI. What became of the candle?"

"At dinner, Don Sebastien, you may call me Abigail Irene if you so desire." She lifted her glass and drank deeply. "From the evidence of the wax, there was nothing special about it. I wonder if it was picked up by a bystander, perhaps?"

"Perhaps."

"Don Sebastien, you've barely touched your dinner."

He shook his head slightly, smiling. "This is not what I am hungry for." And then he sighed and glanced toward the windows. Mike, curled watchful near the door, whined. "I wonder what this night will bring."

"Rain," Garrett said, and—weary to the bone—kissed him on the mouth.

Later, in the darkness of her bedroom, he paused with his cool face pillowed on her belly. "This is what I hunger for, Abigail Irene."

"A request for consent, Sebastien?"

He nodded against her skin.

"What harm will come to me of it?"

"A day's weakness. Or two. No more, I promise; I would not take from you the sun."

With some slight idea of what she offered, she smiled into the darkness and whispered, "Yes."

And screamed against her muffling fists as he turned his head and sank fangs like spikes of ice and flame into the inside of her thigh.

Sometime in the night, the rain stopped, and Sebastien slipped from beneath the covers to dress. Garrett stirred sleepily, the stiffness in a blackening bruise tightening her leg. "Stay until morning?"

"I cannot, my lady. The clouds are breaking.... and I cannot risk the sunrise." Shirtsleeved, a pale ghost in the darkness, he bent over the bed to kiss her. She tasted the harsh metal of her own blood on his tongue. "I will return, if you will have me." He ducked his head and kissed the tattoo of a sorcerer, nestled just between her breasts.

"Ah," she said, one hand still on his arm. "I...cannot promise fidelity, Sebastien. Or any acknowledgment of this."

"Secrets," he answered, "are a stock in trade." He straightened away from her. Outside the door, Mike—silent for hours—scratched and yipped.

Garrett's hand rose to her throat. "I feel it." She fumbled for her wand and kindled a light. The stub of candle flared.

Don Sebastien moved toward the door, listening with an ear pressed to the wood. "Nothing," he said, and cracked the door open so that Mike could scramble in. The dog lunged across the floor, scattering throw rugs, and hurled himself into his mistress' arms to bathe her face with his little clean tongue.

Gathering him close, Garrett rose to her feet, her pistol ready in her other hand. Her dressing gown lay forgotten on the foot of the bed. "This is just like last night," she whispered.

Sebastien came to stand beside her. "Our quarry," he said. "I'd warrant it."

For a long moment, they stood side by side, listening to the nightfall. Nothing disturbed the spring chill of the bedroom. Garrett shivered and set her dog down. He whined, cuddling close.

"Don Sebastien," she said, suddenly formal in her nakedness. "Have you a way to track the source of that unnatural chill? A poltergeist, would you say?"

He shook his head. "Yes, and I do not."

She frowned. "Learn what you can of Robert Carlson. I will call on you before lunchtime. Unless you will be sleeping."

He smiled, and bent to kiss her on the cheek. "A woman both brave and fair," he said. "I never sleep." He raised an eyebrow at her, bowed, and was gone through the door and down the stairs.

Morning did indeed dawn bright and clear: Sebastien's instincts proved correct. Garrett, exhausted by a second sleepless night, did not trouble herself with the Mayor's office hours. Instead she presented herself at his home on Manhattan, fronting the park, before breakfast. Her groom offered her a conspiratorial wink as she disembarked. He knew very well how long Don Sebastien's carriage had waited.

And what would you say if you knew the Spaniard was an immortal drinker of human blood? It explained many things.

There were always a contingent of Colonial Police by the Mayor's door, and Garrett nodded to one of them as she passed, recognizing the redhaired youth. He blanched when she met his eye, and she fought a grin. *Wait until the rumors of your wampyr lover get around. Ah, to be a stranger to scandal…but what fun would there be in that?*

The mayor greeted her in the echoing marble-pillared entryway, flanked by servants and the dark-haired young Master of Thaumaturgical Sciences. Now she saw him clad in a dressing gown, and clearly made out the sigil inked black under the notch of his collarbone. *Private sorcerer, not personal secretary. And the Mayor keeps him at his side at all times. Interesting. Can he truly be so frightened of Richard?*

"Sir, you did not tell me," Garrett said, ignoring the pleasantries, "that one of the missing was your political ally."

"It did not seem significant," Peter Eliot answered. "And I would never use my office to the advantage of my friends, of course. Detective, will you join us for coffee?"

Garrett bit her tongue, contenting herself with a shake of the head. A moment later, when she'd brought herself back under control, she continued: "Are you taking precautions, sir, to prevent an attack upon your person?"

"I am," he answered, and she noticed the significant glance that passed between sorcerer and Mayor. "I will send messengers to the Duke, as well. Perhaps it is some plot of the French or Iroquois. I would not put raising demons past them."

"Raising demons?" Garrett snorted, smoothing her hair back. "Would that were all, your Lordship. Would that were all."

Halfway along the long route from the Mayor's house to the Duke's, the clamor of hooves racing too fast for a city street drew alongside her carriage. "DCI!" A city Guard, one of the Duke's men, resplendent in red on a lathered dark bay. "There's been another murder, Ma'am. The Duke is there."

"Tell my coachman to bring the horse around then," she said, leaning through the curtains. "Lead on, good man. Lead on!"

Thirty minutes later, the carriage clattered into an exclusive neighborhood not far from the Mayor's house. Her heart sank as she recognized the address—the townhome of William, Earl of New Haven, another Member of the Colonial Parliament. House of Lords, and one of Richard's closest allies.

Richard handed her down from the carriage, to all appearances formal and distant—but she felt the squeeze of his hand and caught the comforting smile in his eyes, even if his lips showed nothing. She felt obscurely guilty, and forced herself to return the smile. *You owe him nothing:* remembering the hard, slick texture of Sebastien's hair.

"The same as last time?"

Richard shook his head. Garrett wanted to smooth the tight creases from the corners of his eyes. Frustration curled her fingers. She forced herself to listen. "They're just—gone. The entire family. Seven staff. The groom and stableboy are present and unharmed, but everyone who slept in the house has vanished."

"More wax?"

"Spattered on the floor. Otherwise clean as a whip."

Garrett, dizzy with exhaustion, followed the Duke inside, thoughtful as he led her from room to room. "The groom called the Guard, which is why we are here and not the Colonial Police."

"Politics," Garrett said, too much a lady to spit. "But whoever is behind this doesn't seem to be choosing sides."

"What do you mean?"

"One of yours, one of the Mayor's. Were the windows open when you arrived?"

"Two in the bedrooms only. And what you just said—not precisely true." Alone in the servant's stair, he laid a hand upon her shoulder. She turned to him, and they kissed furtively, a moment's embrace.

"Oh?" she asked, breathless. Her heart pressed, enormous, in her throat.

The Duke's eyes crinkled at the corners, but it wasn't exactly a smile. "Robert Carlson, the house of Commons fellow—he passed information to us, Abby Irene."

"Us?"

He nodded. "The Patriots. He was opposed to home rule. Not that Peter Eliot ever knew it."

"Ah." Garrett leaned against the wall for a moment, considering. "Or maybe he did."

Richard laid the palm of his hand against her cheek, breaking her train of thought. "Abby Irene...."

His tone rang alarms. She stiffened, did not answer. He continued. "A man was seen leaving your house late last night."

Garrett stepped back. "Don Sebastien de Ulloa," she replied. "What of it? I am not a married woman, and I am old enough to make my own decisions, Richard."

His lips twitched, his eyes dark with concealed pain. "You are beholden to no man," he said, very quietly.

Garrett laughed low in her throat, tired and giddy. "That's right, Richard. Not you. And not him either. Do you understand?"

He took a breath, let his hand fall to his side, and leaned forward slowly, touching his lips to the center of her forehead. "Perfectly," he said, and turned away.

"I have the maidservant's name," Sebastien said from the darkness of the parlor doorway. "Where were you this afternoon?"

Garrett dropped her velvet carpetbag inside the front door and leaned against the frame. Mary would not thank her for the clutter, but she was too exhausted to care. "I was with the Duke, and then at University. There have been more disappearances. Why are you here?" She was too exhausted for politeness, either. She stripped off gloves and cast them on a side table.

"You did not keep our date. I was concerned."

Mary bustled down the hallway to take Garrett's coat, clucking over the mess.

The bruise on Garrett's thigh ached, and more than anything she wanted to be left alone. She wove unsteadily on her feet. "So you came to check on me when darkness fell. Thoughtful."

Sebastien ignored the dig. "We need to talk in private."

Garrett bit her lip and nodded acquiescence, leading him up the stairs. "I'd bet a guinea the Mayor's somehow behind this," she said. "He's got a sorcerer dancing attendance—black mark, not red, so he could have graduated from any little backwater college of magics and I have no way of knowing what his ethics are. Furthermore, I've learned that the man who vanished yesterday was working for the Duke on the sly."

"Interesting. Was there another dismemberment, or merely the disappearance?"

Mike ran at their heels, determined not to be left behind. Abruptly, Garrett stopped and crouched, offering her hand to the patchwork dog. "I'm sorry, boy. I should have said hello when I came in." He wriggled adoringly, and she tousled his head before she straightened. Don Sebastien caught her arm to keep her afoot. "Disappearances. A whole household again, which sent me to the library for the balance of the day. I can think of only one reason for attacking entire households."

"And what is that?" They attained the landing; Sebastien opened her chamber door. Mike gamboled past him, having decided that wampyr made acceptable houseguests after all.

"Fear," she said. "To engender fear."

"I keep asking myself," Sebastien commented, "what was different about the boy? Why did he need to die so terribly, when the others just...softly and silently, vanished away?"

Garrett staggered again. "I need to lie down."

"Of course you do. A sleepless night, and the blood you gave to me...on top of the work of the past two days. Forgive me." He scooped her into his arms like a child—like a doll—and carried her to bed. Mary had made it, tidied the counterpane, placed a new candle on the bedside table to replace the one burned out the night before.

Blackness like an undertow, Garrett tried to remember the last thing. She yawned jawcrackingly. "Sebastien. You said...."

"Ah, yes," he answered. "The missing maidservant. I haven't found her yet, but I have her name. Forester. Maeve Forester."

Sleep sucking her under, Garrett knew to a certainty that there was something enormously important about that name, but she was damned if she could remember what it was.

A chill awakened her in the small hours of the morning. Sebastien lay curled beside her, but his body offered no warmth, and her heart hammered in her chest as if she awakened from nightmare. Mike whined by her feet, huddling into the covers.

"Sebastien?"

"I feel it," he said. "Like last night."

But it wasn't. Similar. But colder and stronger, and it froze her to the bone. The curtains on the casement windows fluttered—*odd*, she thought, *those should be tight shut.* And she could see that they were, see the glass reflecting the gaslights from the city below. *Where is the draft coming from?* Teeth chattering, Garrett reached for her wand and struck a light.

The temperature dropped sharply. Garrett clutched her wand to her chest. Mike growled his terrier's growl, voice of a much larger dog in a little dog's throat. Meanwhile, Sebastien swung his long legs out of the four poster and stood. When he spoke, even his cool breath frosted in the icy air. "Ghost?" he asked.

"Sebastien!"

Garrett threw herself across the bed, away from the nightstand, jumping up with her back against the far wall, the coverlet dimpling under her feet. Mike scrabbled toward her, crowded her ankles growling, all sharp teeth and powderpuff defiance. Slowly, Sebastien turned....

The candle on the nightstand ascended into the air and was joined and circled by others that materialized out of the darkness. A vast, lumpy darkness, clawing with enormous hands like annealed black clots of wax, a ring of candles blazing on the gnarled stump that might have been its head.

Garrett screamed as the thing reached for her. She leveled her wand at it and spoke a word. A spark flashed between them, did nothing. Mike snarled and would have lunged after the threat, and Garrett swept her leg aside, knocking her indomitable companion from the bed. He yelped, and she flinched, but for a second he was safe from the squelching abomination that examined her face with familiar pale eyes.

It grabbed for her and she twisted away, falling half into the crevice between bed and wall. In a moment, those slick, sucking hands would touch her flesh. "Sebastien! The candles!"

Sebastien hesitated, hands half outreached as if to grab the monstrosity and haul it away. Candlewax dripped from its crown, spattering the tile floor; droplets that touched its black hide vanished without a trace.

"What do you mean?"

"Don't touch it! The candles! Put them out!"

Mike growled low in his throat as he found his feet again, eyes gleaming in the flickering brilliance. Something moved through the blackness, flaring light. Candlewax dripped, spattered, ran.

The thing lurched closer, stepping onto the bed. Sebastien glanced about wildly, caught up a rug from the floor, and swung just as Garrett, half-pinned, shouted a word of magic and hurled her wand like a throwing knife.

The rug came down on the dark thing's crown, dashing candles out. Garrett's wand vanished into its breast, silver tip first. The thing wailed, spinning wildly, reaching for Sebastien with groping, malformed paws. He skittered aside like a toreador, swinging the rug again, smashing the thing in the face. A final candle fluttered out as it fell forward, keening, clutching Sebastien's shirtfront, and Garrett saw the horror in his eyes as it started to enfold him in devouring blackness.

And then it sagged to its knees, slid downward, cloth tearing in the grasp of its suddenly human hands. It fell, curled inwards, and buried its face in its knees, dappled moonlight shaking in short red curls.

Duke Richard waited for her in her parlor, flanked by city Guards. The early afternoon light crept in through white eyelet lace, gilding his hair. He had his hat in his hand, as if he did not intend to linger, but Mike sat on his shoes, tongue lolling.

When she entered, he dismissed the Guards.

"Richard," she said, when the door was closed.

"Investigator Garrett."

She came a few steps closer, and did not let her hurt show in her face. "I'm glad to see you, your Highness."

His jaw worked, and the hat tumbled from his hands as he came to her, pulling her close, all but crushing her in his arms. "Abby Irene." His voice broke.

She leaned into the embrace for a long, quiet moment, listening to the pounding of his heart. When he finally let her step back, she did. "I'm safe."

"But barely. And I wasn't there to protect you."

"Sebastien was," she said, and regretted it immediately. "What's to become of Officer Forester?" He'd been taken away in chains before sunup.

"He's cooperated. Named his accomplice. Or his handler, more like— the Lord Mayor's pet sorcerer."

"Neither one implicated the Mayor?"

"Stayed silent as the grave. To hear Forester tell it, LaMarque—the sorcerer—offered him revenge against the lad who ruined Forester's sister. Forester took him up on it, not knowing the price. And then LaMarque— and Peter Eliot, of course, but neither one of them has or will admit that— used that consent, once granted, to enslave him. From what he said, he killed the Carlson family first, consumed them...and then chased the lad out into the street to deal with him more messily."

Garrett shuddered. "What about the splintered door?"

"Misdirection. A smart lad. He'll hang, of course."

"Of course." The door was shut; the curtains were drawn. She laid a hand on his shoulder, leaned her face against his sleeve. "They must have thought I was close."

"You were." He put his arm around her shoulder. "I would have been next, no doubt."

She nodded. *This is wrong. And yet... what else can we do?* "It is a pity that we cannot arrange a search of the Lord Mayor's domicile. I feel certain that we would find a rifle which I could match to the bullet fired at me."

He let the silence hang for a moment before he continued. "What I don't understand is how Forester got admittance to the houses. I know there are rules of consent and so forth, for these dark things to do their will." He looked away. *And he's not mentioning Sebastien, although it's costing him something not to.*

"Each of the houses invaded had apparently received a surprising bargain on candles recently. And an action can provide consent as easily as a word."

"I am afraid I'm not following you, Abby Irene."

Garrett counted breaths before she answered, pressing her face to his arm. "Consent must be offered," she said. "Express or implied. But think. You awaken, cold and alone. In darkness with a banked fire. You feel a presence looming over you. What is the first thing you do?"

"Reach for my pistol."

"After that."

"Strike a light. Oh!"

"Strike a light, yes. And reach for the candle by your bed."

WANE
(March, 1902)

GARRETT LOWERED HER GAZE from the beaten-copper diameter of a rising moon to regard the soft-eyed wampyr beside her. The dark fabric of his sleeve lay smooth under her fingertips. A breeze still tasting of winter ruffled the forensic sorcerer's carefully arranged hair and shifted the jewels in her earlobes. "Thank you for coming, Sebastien."

"On the contrary, Abby Irene," the Great Detective murmured through lips that barely moved. "What man could refuse your company of an evening?" A lifted eyebrow made the double entendre express. The moonlight lay like a rush of blood across his cheeks, making Sebastien look almost alive. "Was this the face that launched a thousand ships/ And burnt the topless towers of Ilium?"

"Perhaps in my youth."

"To a connoisseur, value increases with time."

She permitted herself an unladylike snort. Sebastien waited until it was plain she wouldn't answer. "In any case, I'm flattered by the invitation. Although I fear we must be home by dawn. From what I hear of her Grace's parties, we'll miss the best part. Shall we go inside?"

"I suppose we must. The Mayor will be here."

"Simply *everyone* will be here, my dear. On all sides of the issue—come to fawn on the Prince, or spit on his back." Sebastien handed her up the sweeping front steps of the Duke of New Amsterdam's palatial residence, and she presented her invitation to the butler.

"Detective Crown Investigator Abigail Irene Garrett," the Duke's gentleman said. "And Don Sebastien de Ulloa. Be welcome in my master's house."

"Lady Abigail Irene will do tonight, Seamus," Garrett replied with a formal smile. "Unless you plan to host a murder."

"Oh, no—" But Garrett was already tugging Sebastien over the threshold. She might stumble or bolt if she delayed, so instead she forged ahead to the ballroom. She knew the way.

Sebastien chuckled and hurried to keep up. "What a time for a ball," he said into her ear. She felt the coolness of what passed for his breath.

"The eve of war seems to you a strange time to celebrate?"

The wampyr smiled sideways at the dryness of her tone, leaning close enough that she could smell his skin, like dead leaves in autumn. "Exiles must celebrate where they may."

Shaking her head slightly, closing her eyes in rue, Abigail Irene Garrett entered her rival's den. Jacqueline, the Duchess of New Amsterdam, was renowned for her velvet soirees, for fantasies and folderols, for balls and banquets. Renowned for making the most of whatever society the New World had to offer, and making it her own.

She was the wife of the man Garrett loved.

"You're flushing," Sebastien whispered into her hair. "You need champagne, I think." He led her across to the ballroom and fetched a glass, collecting another that he retained untouched.

"The guest of honor isn't here yet." She let her hand drop from his arm and turned to observe the room, raising the flute to lips incarnadined with paint.

"Ah, yes." Sebastien cocked his head to one side, listening. "His Highness Prince Henry of Britain, brother and heir to King Phillip and favored emissary, on his tour of the Americas. At least once a decade whether they need or not. The dirigible arrived from Tenochtitlán yesterday."

"I'm surprised you didn't come to view the landing. It was spectacular." The colonies didn't see as much airship travel as the cities of Europe, even in the dawning years of the 20th century. Peter Eliot, the Lord Mayor of New Amsterdam, had been there with his wife in her French gown and her diamonds, every artifact of dress a political statement in these days of near-open warfare between the Empire and the French. Mohawk sorcerers might have been blamed for the massacre at St. Johnsbury in the Green Mountains, but Garrett knew that the Native warriors must be supplied with modern weapons out of Quebec. The Mayor, she suspected, would cheerfully turn to the French if it meant home rule for the colonies.

"In the balmy afternoon sun? Abby Irene, I believed you thought more highly of me." He took the empty glass from her hand and replaced it with his own. Lightly, so quickly she didn't think anyone in the room would have noticed, he brushed a fingertip across the scarlet sorcerer's tattoo over her breastbone, just visible in the décolletage of her gown. Daring for an older woman, but Garrett believed in getting away with whatever she could. "There. A much more becoming flush, I think. You're upset for your Duke, señora?"

The light laughter sounded forced even to her. "It's not the Duke, Sebastien. And you know I never married."

"Señorita." He awarded her the point with a smile. "Or the Duchess either?"

She sighed. "It's the Prince."

"Abigail Irene. You do impress."

"Long over," she replied. "I came to America."

"I wondered why. Does Richard know?"

She finished Sebastien's champagne. "Duke Richard?" The lightest possible emphasis. "I rather imagine he wouldn't have let his wife invite me, if he did. He has an eye for propriety, our Duke. Shall we dance?"

"Unless you care for another glass of champagne." A kiss of irony as he lifted the glass from her fingers and set it aside.

She felt eyes upon her as she straightened a hothouse rose in his buttonhole. The damasked petals felt like silk. She imagined they matched the flush marking her cheeks. "I'm giddy enough," she said, and glanced up, expecting Richard's gaze pale under bark-brown curls or a fish-eyed glare from Peter Eliot.

Instead, dark eyes glittered in a sailor's deep lined squint as Henry, Prince of England, looked back at her and offered up a slow, deep, self-possessed smile. He wore a goatee now, she observed—even as her breath jammed in her throat and tore—though his curls were still black as Japanese lacquer. He stared at her over the shoulder of her lover, Duke Richard, who bent close to whisper in his ear. The Prince laid tapered fingers on the Duke's shoulder, shook his head once gently to end the conversation, and came down the steps. A cool breeze from some open window brushed Garrett's cheek.

"Excuse me," Garrett turned to whisper to Sebastien, but the wampyr had already slipped away. She smelled citrus and ambergris and bit the inside of her cheek until her eyes stopped stinging. It was only a moment, but by the time she looked forward again, Henry of England was bowing over her hand. She would have thought herself numb enough to feel nothing, but his fingers tickled her skin through kid; she almost closed her eyes. "Your—Highness."

"Abby Irene," he answered, and *now* she felt the Mayor's eyes searing the nape of her neck, felt Richard's and Jacqueline's gazes on her face like hands raised to her cheek in question. "The New World has been kind to you."

"Intermittently. Champagne, your Highness?"

"I think I had better not." The smile carved deeper furrows beside his eyes. A green jewel dripped rakishly from his left earlobe. "I recognize your escort, by the way. Do you know—"

"It's a well-kept secret, but yes."

"Ah."

He stared at her throat. She was glad she'd worn the low-cut gown and suffered her hair to be piled up tall. The small white scars weren't on her neck: Sebastien was considerate. She smiled through the numbness. "He's a friend. How's your wife?"

"Pregnant again. May I call on you in private tomorrow, Crown Investigator?"

The title drew her back. Henry never said anything he didn't mean to carry several meanings. *This is official.* "Highness? Could I deny you?" *Would I, if this were a personal visit?* She didn't know the answer, even now. The Atlantic, it seemed, hadn't been as wide as she had thought.

"Anon, then." A quick bow, and he was gone, leaving Garrett to hide her urge to stand and stare after the Prince's retreating back like a terrified doe. She turned in time to catch the Lord Mayor's eye still on her, his lanky red-haired wife posed beside him in marten and gold and emeralds. The fabric falling back from her fashionably pale hand was a royal blue so dark it was almost violet, and Garret wished she had a wine glass to raise in a silent, mocking toast. Instead, she twined fingers in the jade moiré silk of her skirts and let her steps carry her toward the Eliots, Peter and Cecelia. A blonde head moved through the crowd: Duchess Jacqueline trying to intercept her, but Richard's wife would not be quick enough.

Cecelia had evaporated by the time Garrett reached her goal, but she succeeded in catching up with the Lord Mayor. She reached past him to liberate a canapé from the refreshment table. "This must be quite uncomfortable for you."

"Crown Investigator?" His expression gave her to understand he had no idea what she might be insinuating.

She licked a crumb free of her lip varnish. "A party in His Highness's honor. I'm surprised you found it appropriate to attend, given your politics."

"Because a man is loyal to the needs of his own home over the demands of a distant emperor, does not mean that that man doesn't wish the opportunity to discuss matters discreetly and in a mannerly fashion. Or perhaps I'm just here to flirt with the lovely Duchess." Eliot smiled his fishy smile, and Garrett winced as she swallowed the second bite of canapé.

Creamy goat cheese tasted like crumbled lard and ash, but she managed with dignity.

"She's lovely enough to warrant it."

Eliot leaned forward. "I had no idea you were so intimate with the Crown."

She let herself laugh; she had practice. "It's my job. To uphold the Crown and the law."

"Even when the Crown is above the law?"

"Parliament would disagree with that contention, Lord Mayor." The Duchess came up beside them at that moment, and Garrett saw Eliot smile thankfully. *Interesting that his hatred for Richard doesn't extend to Richard's wife.* Garrett excused herself, refusing to squirm under Jacqueline's raised eyebrow, and went looking for the Duke through the gentle swirl of music drifting across the floor.

A compact, strong-shouldered man in evening clothes intervened. She studied him without seeming to—as was her habit—as he bowed and handed her a bit of parchment sealed in violet. "Compliments of his Highness." He had an aquiline, pockmarked face and grass-green eyes, strange in mahogany skin but matching the beryl in his cravat-pin. She took the note, imagining the crisp oiliness it would have on her flesh. Gloved fingers brushed hers. "You are as lovely as your reputation, Lady Abigail."

"Please," she said, feeling something—a chain?—shift inside the packet as she touched the corner to her lip. "Abigail Irene. May I know your name, sir?"

The smile rearranged his face under the terrible scars. "Nezahualcoyotl. Michel Nezahualcoyotl. Charmed."

"Aztec! Are you an ambassador from the Emperor?"

"I am." His accent was slight and cultured. "Five years in the court of King Phillip. This has been my first chance to visit my home, however. And my first time in your fair city: very lovely by moonlight."

"I saw it rise," she said. "Gorgeous indeed. Nearly full."

"On the waning side." His smile gentled the correction. "My father's people say the shapes on its face make the outline of a rabbit, but my mother taught me it was an old man. What do your New Amsterdam people see?"

"I'm from London." She changed the subject. "You have very charming eyes. I've never met an Aztec before: I had thought you would have eyes as dark as a Mohawk."

"My mother was white." A trace of coolness in that? "It's why I survived the smallpox, and why I was sent to England when a diplomat was needed."

"It is no doubt to his Highness' eternal benefit that you did." She shook the packet again, lightly, to hear it rustle. "Were there instructions with this?"

"He only asked me to deliver it. My Lady." And he bowed slightly and turned away.

Garrett took a half-step after him, squinting as her skirts belled forward and then settled, swaying, about her hips. She tilted the parchment once more, again felt some weight slide within it. *A note? Something I need to open now? Or is it best kept for home?* She raised her chin to search for Richard and saw him in wary conversation with the Lord Mayor.

And where has Sebastien gotten off to?

That breeze touched her face again, and she turned to seek its source. Bellied draperies revealed some passageway beyond them, and Garrett chose to investigate.

Rather than a window, the draperies concealed a doorway to a tiny balcony, just large enough for two. It was unoccupied, and Garrett pushed weighty silk velvet aside and stepped onto pale marble gleaming blue in the moonlight. She drew her right glove off and draped it over her arm before lifting the seal on the packet with her fingernail. Night wind scarfed her skirts and petticoats around her thighs. She tilted the packet and the contents slid and dropped.

A gold chain fine as a breath of wind fell across her hand. She closed her fingers quickly, before the swinging weight of the pendant could drag it loose, and raised it to the light. A dark stone shaped like a tear swayed in a shaft of moonlight. "Henry."

There was writing inside the parchment. She slipped the jewel into the cuff of her glove, forgetting to replace the other one, and folded the letter open.

For fondest remembrance, it said, and was unsigned. A peace offering, then, and not a deeper gesture. A breath she had not known she was holding hissed between her teeth; the perfume of forsythia and daffodils filled her throat, dizzying. She clutched the rail, not knowing if what she felt was grief or gratitude, and didn't notice until she opened her eyes again that her glove had slid down her wrist and dropped over the railing.

"Bother." Garrett tucked the note into her remaining glove, collected her wits, picked up her skirts, and—when another quick glance around the ballroom showed no trace of Sebastien—began her descent into the gardens to retrieve it. She was halfway down the sweeping stairway when she heard the scream.

DCI Garrett was something of an expert on screams. She placed this one as female, aristocratic, and as the discoverer rather than a victim of an atrocity. She turned on the stair, somehow managing her gown, and sprinted back up as fast as she could run.

Cecelia Eliot lay across the striped silk divan in the ladies' lounge with her head pillowed on the scrolled mahogany arm, pale and empty in a way that made Garrett think of a discarded stocking. A torn discarded stocking, ripped from heel to hem…for Eliot's chest was torn open, her throat slashed from ear to ear, and her royal blue gown as spotless and dry as the silk of the couch. Jacqueline stood beside her, trembling, pale hands clutched white-knuckled in front of her mouth.

The little room smelled of cloved oranges, lavender and face powder. Garrett almost gagged. She kicked a vanity bench in front of the door to hold it open and laid her ungloved hand on the Duchess's arm. "Your Grace, come away." Jacqueline looked at her, but Garrett didn't think the woman saw her. "Come away." She heard running footsteps—servants, the Aztec ambassador, the Lord Mayor, and—God bless—the Duke. *Richard!* Garrett stopped her cry just in time, as Sebastien came up the front stairs four at once. Garret bent her attention to Jacqueline. "Duke Richard. Your Lady needs help." Gently but firmly, she placed Jacqueline into his care and focused on Nezahualcoyotl. "The Mayor," she said, and Nezahualcoyotl turned to intercept the man before he could see his wife in such disarray.

Garrett turned back to the body, crouching beside it. She raised her hands before her as if drawing in a net, but she did not touch. "Don Sebastien." She didn't need to look up to know when he knelt at her side.

"Crown Investigator." Her title now, and his voice rose cool and professional over the sound of a woman's sobbing.

"Detective, what do you notice about the scene?"

She saw the slight smile quirk the corner of his mouth, heard the low resonance of Nezahualcoyotl's voice as he led Peter Eliot away. Jacqueline had recovered herself and was speaking to Richard in a voice that carried soft, urgent command.

The wampyr's gaze swept the bloodless body, the terrible wounds. A thoughtful pause, and then: "Her jewels are gone."

Garrett nodded and waited, knowing there would be more.

"And there are no marks on her arms or hands. Also, the blood is missing—"

Richard's voice interrupted them, as he leaned between their close-bent heads. His words stopped Garrett's heartbeat in her throat. "So is the Prince."

The burgeoning moon had long drifted into slumber, the sun was well-risen and Sebastien had fled the morning hours before Abigail Irene, exhausted, managed to return to her townhouse. Her servant Mary snored in the chair by the door, and did not awaken at Garrett's key in the lock. Mary wore yesterday's apron and her wiry coils of hair had frizzed free of her bun. Garrett was reaching out a hand to shake Mary awake when she realized that her dustmop terrier, Mike, was nowhere in evidence. A reflexive check of her wards told her no-one had entered the house uninvited, but revealed a presence upstairs.

Garrett's carpetbag lay in the front hall closet beside her umbrella, but her wand was in her boot, and from there quickly in her hand. Without wakening Mary, she first checked the lower level and then crept up the stairs to her bedroom door. She was about to turn the smooth, hard doorknob stealthily when the scent of oranges and musk tickled her memory.

She opened the door. Her bedroom drapes were drawn to muffle any sunlight, and Mike came bounding to her from the corner by the fire where she kept two leather-covered chairs. She scooped the patchwork dog up and held him tight to her breast, unmindful of the green silk of her gown. "Your Highness," Garrett said into the darkened room. "We've been tearing the city apart." *Henry. What ever possessed you....*

"I imagined you would think your wampyr awaited you." The tall black-haired Prince came out of the shadows towards her, and she saw that he had slept—if at all—in snatches. The darkness under his eyes lay as hollow and black as that rimming her own.

"I recognized your cologne." She shut the door behind her and threw the bolt. "Henry—"

"I know." He closed the space between them. She turned away and laid her wand on the French-waxed half-round table by the wall, still holding Mike close. The wallpaper in her bedroom had a narrow silver stripe and subtle traceries of wisteria; she studied it as he spoke. "I vanished. New Amsterdam is in an uproar. I had a reason—"

"Let me see your hands."

"Pardon?"

She set Mike down by her feet. He gamboled around her ankles for a moment, and then went to sniff the gleaming shoes of his long-absent friend the Prince. "Let me see your hands, Henry."

Wordlessly, he held them out to her, and she took them in her own—her left one clad in kidskin, the right one bare. She'd forgotten her glove after all. Henry had bourbon on his breath—not much, a trace, from the decanter on her washstand—and as she examined his manicured nails he leaned close as if to breathe the perfume from her hair. "How have you been, Abby Irene? Really?"

His hands were clean, undamaged. She let them fall. Mike whined by her ankle and Henry crouched to tousle his fur, like brown-and-cream milk-weed fluff across those capable fingers. A breeze stirred the draperies and a shaft of morning sunlight glittered on the pirate gemstone in the Prince's ear. "I've been well," she said. She took two steps back and sat down on the edge of her bed, patchwork counterpane dimpling where her hands clenched. "Well enough. I—I like the earring."

"A royal gift from our Aztec friends. Phillip had a fit." Same eyes, same smile. The creases a little deeper.

"Phillip will put up with it unless he gets a son."

A low chuckle trickled out of his mouth. "He will at that. He's had no luck yet. Fortunately, I have three. The sorcerer-midwife tells Elaine it will be a daughter at last, this time."

"Your wife must be pleased." She made herself stop twisting the counterpane before it tore. "Why did you leave the ball?"

"I was told my life was in danger, and—" He stood, boots silent on her thick, layered carpets as he measured and re-measured a path from bed to wall.

"And."

"—not mine alone, if I stayed. This was the safest place I could think of. I've not been in New Amsterdam before."

It twisted her strings to think he would come to her for protection. After everything. After she had come to America when his mother, the Iron Queen, died and he became heir, when their relationship became a potential embarrassment. She was a Crown Investigator, beholden—only—to the Crown. She had gone to King Phillip without telling Henry.

She had gone without saying goodbye. "Not your danger alone if you left, either."

He stopped mid-stride, turned from his pacing, fixed her on a look. "What do you mean?"

"The Lord Mayor's wife is dead."

— ⚜ —

Garrett woke Mary and sent her for Richard's carriage, knowing the Duke's men would recognize the Crown Investigator's housekeeper and do as she bid. She put Henry to bed in a guest room—it amused him—to get what rest he could, and cast a minor working over herself to ensure wakefulness. She didn't remember the necklace until she drew hot water and began to undress. When she dropped her one remaining glove on her vanity, a golden chain slipped from the pale kid like a serpent from its den. The stone clinked on marble, and when she picked it up and held it to the light it glittered green, the twin of the one in Henry's ear.

She lifted the long chain over her head and let the stone hang against the crimson sigil between her breasts while she bathed. She was dressed again, decent in a high-necked blue-grey linen gown, by the time Mary returned perched beside the coachman on the bench of Richard's carriage, and with Richard inside.

Garrett waited for the Duke inside her door. "The Prince?" he asked. Before he even had his hat off.

"Asleep," she answered. Richard bent to kiss her and she turned her face away so that his lips brushed her cheek. She gazed up the stairs. "He felt unwell."

"I imagine. And you?"

She shrugged and hung his hat. "Concerned. How is Eliot bearing up?"

"Badly. He insists on the arrest of the Prince."

Garrett swallowed and staggered. Richard caught her arm before she could fall over the hem of her dress. "The—*Henry?*"

"Yes."

"But—"

Richard lead her to a chair. "There was a similar crime in London six months gone, before the airship departed for Tenochtitlán. The woman killed was—a favorite of his Highness'. It's rumored, anyway."

Garrett was pleased that she did not flinch. "What would the Prince want with Cecelia's emeralds, Richard?"

The Duke seated her and released his grip on her arm. Gently, he smoothed a disarrayed blonde strand back from her eyes. "Misdirection? It's easily explained away. Given the Prince's disappearance just before the murder, when the guests were accounted for and questioned…Telegrams have been sent: Parliament approves the action."

"I am not in the pay of Parliament," Garrett said quietly. "And neither are you, your Grace. What does his Majesty say?"

"His Majesty is silent," Richard replied, bending his head low over hers. "But in the absence of a better suspect…."

"I can offer one, Richard."

Garrett's head turned, as did the Duke's. Henry stood at the foot of the stair, his hair combed and the shadows under his eyes somewhat lightened. "Your Highness!" She hastened to her feet, Richard's hand still resting on her shoulder.

"Sit, Abby Irene," the Prince said kindly, and Garrett heard Richard's breath stop short, felt his fingers clench on her arm. "I can see you are unwell."

She glanced at the Duke but he would not look at her. His forehead was white: she imagined his flesh must feel as cold as if all the blood in his body had run down into his *boots. And now you know, as you've often asked me, why I left London, my love.* She obeyed her prince, and sat. "Another suspect, your Highness?"

Henry nodded and crossed the intricately tiled entryway to stand before them. Richard drew his hand off Garrett's arm. "Forgive me for eavesdropping. I overheard what you said, Richard, about the similarities to the murder in London. I was not even in London at the time: I had the details from a friend."

Richard nodded; his throat worked, but he didn't speak.

Garrett felt a strange tautness in the skin of her face, as if it stretched toward a shout. *No. Henry. No.*

"One of the guests at your ball, New Amsterdam, had both motive and opportunity for the crime. The Spaniard, de Ulloa. It was my contention that the crime in London was the work of an unclean beast…and here we find another such crime and another such creature in close proximity. The coincidence is unnerving."

"Beast? The 'Great Detective'?" Richard glanced down at Garrett, a knife line drawn between his eyes. "DCI?"

She closed her hands on the carved wood of the chair and stood, forcing herself to steadiness. She raised her eyes to the Duke's and made her voice strong. "Sebastien's a wampyr, Richard. That's what his Highness is so gently insinuating. Did you expect—what? Stoker's *Dracula* or Dumas' *Gosselin?*" She smiled bloodlessly at the Prince, the jewel burning between her breasts like a star. "I suppose we can place Prince Henry and Sebastien both in protective custody. Just until we get things sorted out. We'll have to wait until nightfall to collect Sebastien." She pinned Henry with a look. "Your Highness, consider it a gesture to reassure your people that you do not consider yourself above the law."

The Prince opened his mouth, met Garrett's steel-blue gaze, and subsided with a curt, ungracious nod. Henry had always been the smarter of the two royal brothers. Garrett glanced at the Duke: the look Richard gave her was startled admiration, and she kept her gaze on him because she couldn't stand to meet Henry's.

After they had seen to the Prince's comfort—which mostly involved feeding his Highness and seeing him drawn a hot bath—Garrett found herself in the salon with Richard, relaxing on a velvet-covered couch and sipping brandy while his Mastiff laid a head that weighed more than a stone upon her foot and sighed. "Did anyone happen to collect my glove from the garden?"

"I'll ask Seamus." He swirled cinnamon-scented liquor in his glass and leaned against the arm of the curved couch they shared. "Will Don Sebastien come if we send a messenger?"

"I don't see why not. He'll need a darkened room for day."

"I can't just lock him in the wine cellar?" But Richard half-smiled and Garrett's startled retort faded.

She let the brandy roll over her tongue, savoring an almost creamy texture. "Where's Jacqueline?"

"The Duchess—" Richard frowned. "Spent the night at her siser's. I expect she'll be home after dinner. The Lord Mayor, I am told, has taken to his bed." Richard's opinion was plain in his voice. "You never told me you had an affair with the Prince."

"I never told the Prince I had an affair with you. When you have Sebastien in your clutches, my Lord, will you see to it that the house burns down and be rid of them both?"

"If only I could get away with it." But he smiled. "Can you link the criminal to the crime? If we have them both in the house, can you eliminate them as suspects through sorcery?"

"I can try," she said. "It depends whether the assassin kept the device used to commit the murder far away from himself until it was needed, and then discarded it, or if he kept it close. Perhaps if we can discover what became of the poor woman's blood…." She shook her head. "It wasn't Sebastien, Richard. For one thing, he came up the stairs behind me, and if he had gone down so close in advance I would have seen him."

"He could have leapt from a balcony. If he's what you say?"

"He could. But—"

"A wampyr wouldn't kill, if the mood took him?"

"That's prejudice, Richard, and utterly unfair. Or is it just jealousy?"

"I…." He reached down and smoothed the dog's velvet ears. Sipped his drink. Fiddled with a stick-pin she hadn't seen before. "Yes," he said sharply. "Would you rather I didn't care?"

Something wild flared in her breast. "Sebastien," she said with utter clarity, "doesn't need to *take*."

Her words seemed to hang between them for an hour. Richard stared into the depths of his glass, and spoke very slowly, as if he had no heard her at all. "We have to—Abby Irene. We have to prove the Prince's innocence. If there is any doubt. Any *shade* of doubt—" He left the thought unfinished. *The Lord Mayor will turn it into another article in his endless list of reasons the Colonies must secede from the Empire, and throw ourselves on the mercy of the silk-fisted French. Not just neglect, taxation, King Phillip's desire to build his Empire eastward.*

Not just neglect, but malevolence.

She stood and finished her drink, gently extricating her foot from under the dog. "Send the message to Sebastien now: his servants will see that he gets it. Send another servant for a scrap of Cecelia Eliot's dress. I'll need it tonight. When I check on the Prince. Or the prisoner, if you prefer."

"As you wish," Richard said, his foot flipping restlessly. He set his own glass aside, fingers lingering on the mouth-blown glass. She shivered in an almost-physical recollection. "You should rest beforehand, Abby Irene."

"Where is Mr. Nezahualcoyotl sleeping?"

"The ambassador? He's got rooms on the fourth floor. In the East Wing, near the Prince's suite."

"I need to speak to his Highness before I rest: I need some items from him. I'll take the south guest bedroom, after. The green one." Down the hall from Richard's room, connected by a side door to the third-floor library. A pair of three-hundred-year-old elms screened the windows. Richard cocked his head at an angle and arched his eyebrow at her—a silent question.

Garrett forced one narrow smile before she left.

Richard left her before teatime, brushing her emerald necklace aside to plant a final, lingering kiss on her sorcerer's tattoo. Garrett stretched against the velvet coverlet on the canopied bed and closed her eyes just for a moment as the door to the library closed behind him. When she opened them again, the sky blazed crimson through sheer cream lace curtains, and she swore; she had wanted to speak to Henry before Sebastien arrived. She rose and dressed quickly, wincing as she yanked a comb through unfashionably short hair, and turned back just as she was leaving to snatch up her dark velvet sorcerer's carpetbag and the envelope with the scrap of dress in it. She took the servant's stair because it was faster and scandalized a chambermaid in the process, but arrived at Henry's suite before the red sun dipped under the horizon. She knocked, and the Prince in his dressing gown opened the carved door so quickly he must have been waiting.

She had thought that Richard's touch fresh on her skin would make it easier. She looked into Henry's smile and cursed herself for a fool. *You're too old for lovesick, Abby Irene.* Same refrain. It never helped. "Ready for the spell, your Highness?"

"Of course."

He shut the door behind her and locked it, came to her and laced his fingers through her hair tight enough to hurt when she stepped away. Almost as much as stepping away from the warm smell of musk and lemon peel that surrounded him hurt. She did it anyway. "Henry."

"I adored you," he said.

"It's not beyond Phillip to have you killed if you become an embarrassment, you know."

"Is that treason, Lady Abigail Irene?"

"It's fact," she said coldly. She turned up a gaslamp and lit a candle from her bag: an old one, translucent wax lumpy with bits of shattered quartz and pungent with rosemary needles. She set it on the cherrywood dresser and looked up at him. "Did you get what I asked for, your Highness?"

Wordlessly, he handed her a snippet of thick white linen. She recognized it: a bit of the hem of the shirt he had worn to the ball. She drew a silver spoon and an ordinary nail-scissors from her carpetbag and clipped a corner of the blue dress fabric, rested both in the spoon, and held it over the candleflame.

"Don't you need to cast a circle?"

"The smoke must move freely," she answered. She looked up at him; the rising moon cast a copper light through the eastern window, a little less full than the night before. It touched Henry's cheek with color as it had Sebastien's. "Let's watch."

Garrett knew the smoke would rise in two distinct streams, parted by still, unbreakable air, and drift about the room aimlessly as a bored kitten. The inverse principle of similarity would make the two smokes irreconcilable, unless the natures of the two fabrics—manufactured half a world apart—had been fused into a single whole by some act of violence.

The streams rose pure and red-lit by the rising moon, conjoined as if they were one thing.

As they were. Garrett dropped the spoon into the candle, snuffing the flame. She snapped a glance over her shoulder at Henry, but the Prince simply watched her, a frown drawing the corners of his mouth down. "What have you done?" she whispered.

"Nothing," he said, waving a hand to disperse the stream of smoke that coiled around his throat like a noose. "This is some trick. Nothing. Tell me you believe me: have I ever lied to you?"

She shook her head and blew the smoke away. "You never have," she said, and when the pooled wax had hardened, she swept her tools into her bag. "You should dress for dinner, your Highness. We'll have guests."

The tension at the long table all but soured the meat and wine, glittered off the silver and crystal like the gaslight from the chandeliers. Sebastien had arrived with a wry smile on his face and a fresh rose in his buttonhole fifteen minutes before service. He sat on Garrett's left and flaked his fish aimlessly across his plate with a heavy silver fork. She drew a great and secret amusement from watching the cleverness with which he pretended to dine: he'd very nearly fooled her, when they met.

The wampyr caught her looking and presented her with the thin edge of a smile. He swirled his wine in the glass, and touched it to his lips, inhaling the aroma. Garrett found she didn't have much appetite either, sitting among guarded men with Michel Nezahualcoyotl making polite forays into conversation.

Sebastien had scarcely set the glass down when the Aztec ambassador leaned forward. "What brings you to the Americas, Don Sebastien? You are Spanish, of course—" Nezahualcoyotl left the thought unfinished. The

British alliance with the Aztec Empire dated from a time when both great powers found themselves with a common enemy: the then even greater power of Spain. "—I would have thought you'd go to the great trade city of San Diego, if you wished to explore the new world."

"San Diego is lovely," Sebastien said, laying his fork aside and letting his left eye drift closed in a smiling wink. "But I prefer a cooler climate for my exile."

"No-one comes to America for the climate." Garrett watched Richard's face as she said it. He smiled faintly: he'd been born in New Amsterdam, made his fortune by twenty-one in the service of the Iron Queen, and married the old Duke's daughter and heir so he could protect the city and the colony he cherished.

"Some come to New Amsterdam to escape the consequences of previous actions," Henry commented without looking up from his food. "But I think most come out of—well, I won't call it cowardice. Perhaps it would be better to say, a desire to start anew. I suspect most of those merely wind up making the same mistakes over again. A *man* faces up to his errors, after all, and fixes what he can."

Garrett felt the pressure of Henry's eyes on her, his anger and his desire, and smelled again the smoke of scorching cloth. The anger she thought she should feel paled under white scorn at his cruelty, and her unease at the messages in the smoke. *You broke his heart, Abby Irene. And he is angry. But what reason would he have to kill Cecelia? It only hurts the crown. Now, if it were the Lord Mayor...Perhaps this was an attempt to frame Sebastien?* She saw Sebastien formulating a rejoinder, more incensed on her behalf than his own, and interceded casually. "It's a better exile than some."

"There are many sorts of exile," Nezahualcoyotl said. The Aztec seemed to eat with good appetite. "It's hard, being kept from your home." A self-deprecating smile touched the corners of his strange light eyes, and then he glanced at Henry. "But not too onerous; one finds good friends wherever one travels—"

The sound of footsteps in the hall silenced him. Richard half-stood from his chair, moving to place his body between the Prince and the door. Garrett pushed her chair back, a half-step behind Sebastien—who moved like oil on water when he wanted to—and slipped her silver-tipped ebony wand from her pocket as she came up beside the Duke.

She relaxed only incrementally when she realized that the figures framed in the archway were the blonde, reserved Duchess and the widowed Lord

Mayor. *Are they having an affair?* she wondered—but they stood an unmeasured distance apart, and no awareness flowed between their bodies. *No.*

Could Eliot be behind the murder? He wouldn't be the first husband to sorcerously do away with his wife. And she knew he'd hired a black mage not twelve months earlier to weaken Richard's political position and to try to kill Garrett herself, although Garrett had been unable to prove it.

"My lord husband," Jacqueline began. She stepped into the dining room, gaslight glittering on her earrings and playing over the fine silk of her dress. "I happened upon the Lord Mayor in the drive as he was arriving. Shall we invite him to dine?" Her eyes measured Garrett for a coffin as she spoke.

"The offer is kind," Eliot interjected before Richard could answer. "But I won't sit at table with a killer. I suppose you've made no progress in your investigations, Detective Crown Investigator?"

His expression shook Garrett's cool assessment of the man as a bastard: there was pleading in it. Richard stepped halfway in front of her, and she bit back a snarl, but Sebastien laid a steadying hand on her elbow and moved aside, drawing her from behind the Duke's fair-haired bulk. "The *Crown* Investigator," Richard said, "is making every effort to bring the case to a speedy resolution."

"Richard," Jacqueline began. He tried to silence her with a glare: she raised her chin and stepped forward. "It is his *wife.*"

"I'll bet," Eliot said simultaneously, stepping past Jacqueline and striding forward to confront Richard nose to nose. "In *loyal* service to the Crown."

Garrett heard the scrape of a chair as Henry stood. She didn't look. "That's sedition," Richard said softly.

"It's fact." Eliot turned his head and spat. "Arrest the Prince, Richard. Prove once and for all you care for something other than your Ducal seat. That you care for the colonies, and for New Amsterdam." He turned his head and stared Garrett in the face. "DCI. Do you know who killed my wife?"

Richard moved to put himself between them again. He walked into Sebastien, who had coolly set himself for the block. Garrett pushed forward and laid her hand on the Lord Mayor's arm. She looked over his shoulder, caught a complex expression on the Duchess' face. "When I have conclusive evidence—" *You have conclusive evidence, Abigail Irene.* "—Lord Peter, you will know what I know."

He stared her in the eye for a long, sharp-edged second before he turned and strode away.

—⟨≫⟩—

Garrett wasn't quite certain how Sebastien spirited her away from the dining room. She remembered his hand on her arm, quick footsteps and the eventual pause, breathless, under a rising moon that painted the gravel garden path under their feet in knifelike shadows. "Don Sebastien, I am in your debt again," Garrett said, leaning into the shadows of a towering forsythia, fighting crawling shivers.

"I think we're past the point of friendship where we need to keep accounts," he replied. "Was Richard always such a pig?"

She laughed, winding her arms around her body. "He's jealous. And a patriot: he sets no loyalty before the Crown. I think he sees that you are not jealous, and to him it seems another bit of evidence that you are heartless and cold."

"I learned that it was foolish to try to possess things." Sebastien shrugged and put his arm around her, for all he had no warmth to share. "Or women. What sort of a life could I offer?" A thoughtful pause. "Is it Prince Henry, Abby Irene? I cannot deduce another answer, and I cannot understand why he would do such a thing."

She leaned back against his shoulder and watched the rising moon dye the facade of the Duke's manor the color of skimmed milk. She shook her head, her hair moving against his jacket, the rose in his lapel brushing her ear. "Was this the face that launched a thousand ships/And burnt the topless towers of Ilium?"

"You realize, if they had listened to the women, Troy would still be standing? Helen tried to warn them, and Cassandra too."

"After she was cursed for spurning Apollo. And yet she and Helen take the blame." The scent of the forsythia hung over them, raw and sweet, less flower than vegetable. The moon rose another finger's width, waning from full, shaped like a sail bellying in the rising wind. "Don't the years grow long alone, Sebastien?"

"Look." He pointed. "You can see the rabbit in the moon."

"Did you bring me a bit of the shirt you wore last night?"

"I did," he answered, and held her strong hand in his cold one as they walked with measured paces back inside. "I'll ask Duchess Jacqueline if I may have the room beside yours, if that suits you. I somehow don't think she'll mind."

—◈—

Smoke rose by smoke, two streams plainly divided in the dappled moonlight that made its way through the branches of those ancient elms.

Garrett closed her eyes and leaned back against the wall beside the locked door to the library, breathing a sigh. *Exactly as it should be.*

The wampyr was innocent. She laid the silver spoon in an ashtray and snuffed the candle out with licked fingertips just a moment before a light tap rattled her door. The hall door: she had been prepared to ignore a furtive tap on the other, having little patience for Richard tonight. If he was fool enough to come to her under the same roof as his wife.

Garrett padded to the door barefoot and slid the bolt back, letting the door drift open on well-oiled hinges. She was unsurprised that Henry stood revealed beyond. "I apologize," he said as he brushed by her, pulling the knob from her hand and swinging it silently closed. She noticed with annoyance that he turned the key in the lock. "I was boorish at dinner. I don't know what possessed me, and I hope—" he paused. "I hope you can forgive me."

Garrett stepped to the side, and began putting the tools of her sorcery away. "No apology is needed. Thank you for the necklace, Henry. It's lovely."

"Necklace?" His voice was tight and heavy as if he wept. The floor creaked behind her.

Garrett whirled, carpet burning the naked ball of her foot, and grabbed for the wand in her open bag. Not fast enough. His hands—those strong, tapered fingers—reached for her throat, lengthening as she watched, strange hollow-pointed claws curving from the nailbeds in a welter of puckered flesh.

Garrett shouted at the top of her lungs. Henry's eyes shone blankly glossy, glazed by the moonlight. Talons pricked her skin and she heard—as if through cotton wool—the sound of someone pounding on the heavy, ancient door. She drew a breath to scream but—alien, dagger-tipped, not the hands she remembered so well—his hands closed on her throat and he pressed her back against the bureau still littered with her instruments of sorcery.

Garrett reached out right-handed and tore the emerald out of his ear.

Henry jerked away with a cry, blood racing over suddenly human hands as he clapped them to ripped flesh.

One more resonant thump: the lockplate shattered with a splintering crash. Sebastien and Richard burst through the door. They halted at the spectre of blood and moonlight, at Garrett tearing her gown open and wrenching the emerald necklace from her throat as Henry swayed and went to his knees.

"Richard, your stickpin!" She pointed at his collar, and he flung the jewelry away like a serpent discovered in a pocket.

"Abby Irene—" Sebastien started.

"It's the ambassador," she said. Henry looked up at her, the sanguinary flow still staining his hands and his shoulder. Sebastien turned, Richard half a step behind him.

"No."

A voice accustomed to obedience, and both men froze in the doorway as Henry forced himself to his feet. A slow red drip trickled down his jacket. He didn't seem to notice. "I'll handle this."

Garrett supported herself against the dresser. Sebastien and the Duke stepped aside, but turned to follow as the Prince pushed through the shattered door and stomped out of sight.

Silence ensued for some minutes, and Garrett found the strength to go and seat herself on the bed. She wondered when a servant would be along or worse, Duchess Jacqueline. But some time later, Sebastien stepped in from the hallway and reported: "He kicked the door in."

"Oh."

Henry followed no more than ninety seconds later, Richard at his side. He held something clenched in his fist like a shed snakeskin, and he held it out to Garrett like a man offering his best hound the fox's tail. "Your glove, my lady?"

Garrett took the limp, bloodstained thing and dropped it on the floor between them. "He needed a binding. The emeralds to limit it, to bind you and identify the target. Some personal item to trigger. He must have done the same in London."

"I left before the killing—"

"Did you?"

"I...." Henry pushed bloodstained fingers through his hair. "Yes. I don't remember. But how could I not remember?" His arm dropped to his side as if his own touch disgusted him.

Garrett moved away from the dresser, into the center of the room. "He said his mother was white."

"French," Prince Henry answered. "A concubine to the Aztec Emperor. She died of the same pox that scarred him as a boy. When the Aztec court came to England, when we were both boys." The Prince had too much courage to turn away. "I taught him English. We were—friends."

"The Emperor found uses for him, I take it. But they didn't suit his ambitions?"

"Or maybe his taste for revenge." Richard shrugged.

"Bastards and second sons—" irony dripped from Henry's tongue "—make good ambassadors."

"We can't let anyone know he used you for his scheme, Highness. You've no guilt in this thing." The Duke coughed into his hand. Garrett studied Richard's face, and Henry's. And the wampyr's, though Sebastien stood silent by the door.

Henry swallowed and looked down at his hands. "I can't…lie about this, Richard."

"You're asking him to conceal evidence of a murder." Garrett was surprised at her own voice, level and disbelieving.

"It could mean the revolt of the colonies if you don't. The end of our alliance with the Aztecs: this is the Emperor's bastard son. Everything the French could have wanted."

Henry looked at Garrett, his deep-set eyes glistening, stricken in the bluing moonlight. Garrett looked away. She knew what he wanted her to say. She touched her throat, felt the torn edges of her dress. "I serve the Crown," she whispered.

She pushed away from the dresser, stepped past Henry, past Richard, toward the door. She stopped. Glanced over her shoulder.

"I have to confess this," Henry said, drawing himself up.

A harsh scent of burned cloth and blood tainted the air, overwhelming the scent of oranges.

"It will mean lives if you do, your Highness." She didn't need to look at Henry to know how his lips pursed in struggle, didn't need to look at Richard to see him drop his eyes to the floor. "Mine, perhaps. The Duke's. Maybe even your own. It will mean war. And it will mean only your honor if you don't."

"I know." His hands flexed helplessly, stretched and clenched. "What would you have me do, Abby Irene? What will *you* say of all this?"

"I will do as my King bids me do," she said. And then she stood and watched the moonlight move upon the wall, and waited for them to argue. Don Sebastien never moved from his place beside the door.

"Sebastien," she said, some time later. "Sebastien, take me home."

LIMERENT
(October, 1902)

THE DEAD MAN SAT in a wing-backed chair before a cold fireplace. The butler had shut the gas lamps off from the hall. His rooms were dark and still.

Detective Crown Investigator Abigail Irene Garrett paused in the open doorway, and did not yet enter. First, she set her lantern and her blue velvet carpetbag outside the door and drew white kid gloves onto her hands. Then she slipped the pouches drawstringed with ribbons—her housekeeper Mary had cleverly sewn them from linen handkerchiefs—over her shoes, and bound them tight. She shook out her skirts in the hall, and retrieved her silver-tipped ebony wand.

Taking up the lantern, the white beeswax candle flickering only slightly, she went to the corpse's side.

The smell of death was familiar.

As she approached, she became aware of a soft, organic rumble. She cast around for the source, alert to sorcery. But the sound emanated from a large orange cat curled, kneading, on the dead man's lap. It looked well-kept, sleek and worried, and as Garret watched, it bumped the dead man's hand with its smooth skull, rubbing ears and cheek against his fingers, purring loudly enough to shake its whiskers. Coaxing, hoping.

"He's not for eating," Garrett said to the cat. She preferred terriers. Nevertheless, something about the hand that the cat rubbed so determinedly caught her attention.

She reached out gingerly and stroked the cat between the ears with her gloved hand. It turned mad golden eyes on her, affronted, and she chuckled, tucked her wand under her arm, and set the lantern down on the table beside the chair. She slipped her fingers into the dead man's softly cupped hand.

She drew forth something small and dark, neither a cylinder nor a sphere, and rolled it between her fingers. "Las rosas," said a familiar voice, pitched to carry from the hall.

Garrett did not startle, but the cat did, leaping from the dead man's lap to the floor and vanishing behind a plant stand in one sharp, fluid motion.

"Sebastien." She permitted herself a smile as she turned to face the detective. "Roses? It's a rosary bead, yes. How did you know?"

He came forward, even more silent than the cat, and picked the bead from her fingers. "It's one of the old ones," he said, and ran it delicately under his nose. "made of rolled flower petals. It's aromatic. Is there any sign of violence?"

She gave him her shoulder and lifted the cover of the inverted book that the dead man had lain over the arm of the chair with the tip of her wand, meticulously, just enough to read the title page. "Do you smell any *blood*?"

"He could have been poisoned."

"He could," she said. "Do you smell any of that?"

"Not yet. But he was expecting trouble."

"How do you know?"

Sebastien smiled. "Lift the book a little more."

She lifted an eyebrow as well, but obliged him. And sighed. Under the open pages lay a derringer, unfired, balanced on the broad arm of the chair. "I suppose you smelled that as well?"

"Powder and gun oil. Very distinctive, you know," he said, with an apologetic shrug. "But perhaps he died in a locked room, alone, with a pistol to hand and a cat on his lap—at peace, with just time to lay down his novel."

"It's a history." Garrett pointed to the title page. *Discours sur les révolutions de la surface du monde, et sur les changements qu'elles ont produits.* "And stranger things have happened."

"So first," Sebastien said, "we find out how he died. Do you suppose his son will want the cat?"

—⤜⤛—

The dead man was Emmett Goodwood, and Garrett was slightly surprised to discover that he was the mogul behind the Goodwood patent shoe fortune. He had employed over seven hundred young woman in one cramped and steaming stitchery in the Bronx alone, with other factories in Worchester, Hartford, and Philadelphia.

The Lord Mayor of New Amsterdam, Peter Eliot, would just as soon have kept her out of the case entirely. But the corpse of a millionaire, contained in a locked room, was just the sort of reason that Crown Investigators existed. The Colonial Police—who reported to the Lord Mayor—had a murder squad, but it was not equipped to deal with black sorcery.

Still, Eliot had his own ideas as to the proper authority of the Crown in its Western colonies, and interfering in the quotidian administration of his city lay outside that scope. And so Garrett did not herself question the household staff. The role of Crown Investigators, ideally, was to work in tandem with less arcane branches of law enforcement, and she did not expect this to be a terribly difficult case.

She sealed the scene, remanded the body for autopsy, and left the unsorcerous detective inspectors of the Colonial Police's Murder Investigations Office to remonstrate with Goodwood's next of kin. Finally, at about the fourth hour after midnight, she turned to find Sebastien standing at her shoulder, the marmalade tom ensconced in his arms.

"Would you do me the honor?" he asked.

"Of accepting an armload of tabby?"

The cat, purring, narrowed its eyes. "I had thought you might agree to share my carriage," Sebastien said. "It will be light soon, and—"

Garrett checked over her shoulder. "Sebastien, are you inviting me to come home with you?" She had never been to his house, though they had been friends and occasional lovers since April of 1901.

About time, perhaps.

A tip of his head, self-deprecating. She studied him; he did look drawn, with the waxen countenance she had come to associate with his need. "I'd love to," she said, and cracked her jaw with a yawn. "But I can't promise to be any good to you tonight. Have you a footman we could send to my Mary for a bag?"

"Jack will see to it," he said.

It was not until much later that it occurred to her that she would have been wise to have asked, *who is this Jack?*

Sebastien lived in an end-row townhouse fronting Jardinstraat, which was named not for the park it formed the eastern border of, but—along with the park—for the seacaptain Karel Jardinstraat, Dutch hero of the wars of a hundred years before. Jardinstraat, along with New Amsterdam and the rest of the Dutch colonies, had been ceded to the British for the duration of the French occupation of Holland, which stretched until 1815. At the end of the war, the Iron Queen's grandmother Eleanor had been regent for a George who did not live to take the throne; she returned Captain Jardinstraat to the Dutch, but not so the park named for him or the colony it belonged to.

Her grand-daughter, born in 1822, had been named for the end of the last great war with the French: *Alexandria Victoria*. The Iron Queen.

It was her death that had brought Abigail Irene to the city Queen Alexandria's grandmother claimed as a spoil of war, because it was one thing to be the lover of a dashing, martial younger prince. It was quite another to be the lover of the heir to the throne. Especially when one was scraping by in society on a courtesy title as the elder sister of a wastrel lordling.

Sebastien, however, seemed as if he could not care less for any of that. He'd never asked, and when he'd learned, he'd greeted the news without so much as a shrug. Duke Richard, by contrast, had been tempests of sighs and unconcealed jealousy.

And now, Sebastien let her doze against his shoulder in the rocking carriage, as the orange cat dozed on his lap, only rousing her when they came up to the house. If Garrett fell in love anymore, she'd be tempted. Whatever peculiar dietary habits he professed.

He gave the cat to the footman and handed Garrett down from the carriage. He was a lean man of slightly more than medium height, with strength in his arm that did not admit of her weight. She felt sticky and disarrayed, stumbling on cobbles, but he caught her and she straightened automatically, posture drilled and corseted into reflex. She fumbled her carpet bag from the carriage before the footman shut the door.

Sebastien said, "When was the last time you ate?"

"This afternoon." She had to pause to remember. The sky was paling behind the roofs, though the sun had an hour or so 'til rising. Sebastien had left himself plenty of time.

"Yesterday afternoon," he corrected, and led her to the side-entry.

The mudroom was dim and still, the only light filtering through a narrow window beside the door. The small room smelled pleasantly of lemon wax and hothouse flowers. The footman set the orange cat down and stepped back outside the door, no doubt to assist the coachman in getting the horses unharnessed. It shut behind him with a click, and Sebastien, one-handed, shot the bolt. He cracked the inside door so the cat could enter the house—it did with all speed—and then he shut it again, sealing himself and Garrett in the narrow entry.

And then he was against her, his hands in her hair, tipping her head back to kiss her hard, his tongue at first cool and dry, drawing warmth and moisture from her mouth. She gasped and pressed against him, supporting herself on his shoulders until she got herself against the wall between the coats and scratching coathooks and leaned back. Then she fisted her kid-gloved hands in her skirts and hoisted them to her waist. Sebastien leaned against her, slipped between her thighs, made a small, inarticulate sound to find her as bare under her petticoats as any dance-hall can-can girl. "You should eat first," he said, and for answer she put her forearms over his shoulders and pushed down, trailing ruffles and flounces.

He was cold in her arms, his face cold as he pressed it to the heat of her thighs, his hands cold as he stroked her sweating skin. She drew a deep breath, bracing for the expected agony that would lead to pleasure beyond speech, and instead felt his shivery kiss, the insinuation of his tongue. "Sebastien—"

He caught her wrists, dropped her skirts over his head and shoulders and held her until she tugged free and pressed a double fistful of gabardine to her mouth, muffling the sounds she couldn't help. And only then, while she was panting, slack, his steadying hands on her hips keeping her upright against the pounding surf of her pulse, did he kiss her mons softly and slide sideways, tongue the hollow of her thigh, part the flesh over the artery with an adroit nudge.

Garrett made another noise against the crumpled wool, this one of sharp duress, but Sebastien's hands gentled her, an abject apology, and then a moment later she lost herself in the narcotic rush of his kiss, a sweet asphyxiating pleasure that bore as much resemblance to their foreplay as champagne did to soda water. She arched like a figurehead, face turned, temple pressed to the wallpaper, and sobbed against her skirts.

When she recollected herself, Sebastien still knelt under her lifted dress like a pilgrim at a shrine, his handkerchief pressed to the scratch on her thigh. "Thank you," he said, peeling the cloth aside to see if the wound had sealed. He dabbed his lips with the same linen as he stood; she saw it by the faint movement of white cloth in the near-dark. She dropped her skirts and gave them a shake, but leaned on his arm harder than she liked until she found her balance.

He continued, "I am much restored. And now for you—"

He opened the door into the side parlor, where there was light. Someone stood by the far wall, holding a candle. Garrett shaded her eyes, caught the glint of flame on fair curls. "Sebastien?" A young man's voice, light and flexible, with an upper-class snap. "Is all well?"

"Very well," Sebastien said. "Jack, I should like you to meet Detective Crown Investigator Abigail Irene Garrett. Abby Irene, Jack Priest, my very dear friend."

More than that, Garrett thought, if Sebastien was giving him precedence in the introductions. Mr. Priest came forward, the candle in his left hand, and took Garrett's glove in his right. "Charmed," he said, and did not sound it. He was shockingly young—seventeen? Perhaps? No, he looked like a lad, but he carried himself with a man's confidence.

He glanced at Sebastien, as if to record the wampyr's dewy complexion and restored glow. "Lady Abigail Irene, do you require refreshment?"

She was about to demur, the undercurrent of tension in the room too much in her current state of exhaustion, afterglow, and blood loss, but Sebastien intervened. "Don't wake Consuela," he said. "But if we could find her cider and an egg on toast, perhaps a bit of black sausage?"

Mr. Priest nodded, turning silently with his candle, and led them down a long hallway to the kitchen, where he shaded the windows for Sebastien's safety before he lit the gas lights and the burners. "By the way, Jack," Sebastien said, as the young man was cooking, "have you just seen an orange cat?"

Mr. Priest, his sleeves rolled up to his elbows, hooked a thumb in the pocket of a borrowed apron, and did not look away from the egg and sausage sizzling on the stove. "Bringing home strays again, are we?"

Garrett woke in a darkened room, and did not know the time. The shades were closed and the drapes were drawn, the door cracked open. There was no warm weight across Garrett's feet, where her terrier Mike should be, and she heard voices, thready and thin. An argument, if she could only pick out the words, but one carried out in low and level tones.

Her wand was on the nightstand, where Sebastien, who knew her, had left it. She reached gingerly; Sebastien's hearing was as good as his sense of smell. Warm ebony slipped into her fingers. A generic focus, not as powerful as a dedicated one might be, but it would halfway serve.

She sketched a quick sigil in the air, and mouthed the words. And faint, but distinct, the voices came to her.

—It's my house too, Sebastien.

—Do you think I brought her here idly?

—That woman? I don't know what to think. I know you've been dancing attendance on her since last year, and now I see she'd never even heard my name—

—Jack.

A pleading note, nothing Garrett had ever heard in Don Sebastien's voice. She stilled an icy spike of jealousy, and almost pulled the warm silver tip of her wand from her ear. But no, it was better to know.

Sebastien had never pretended to be faithful, as she had never pretended with him.

A long silence, and then:

—I'm being unreasonable.

—It is an unreasonable situation, mi cariño. But you will understand I hold the lady in some affection, yes?

—Yes, Mr. Priest said, unwillingly. —I suppose you would like it if I tried to make friends.

—I do not expect miracles outside church, Sebastien answered dryly, and Mr. Priest, still reluctant, laughed.

—Were you unwell last night? Or injured? he asked, in a different tone all together. —You had your due of me not so long ago, to find yourself in such straits.

—It is no matter.

—It *does* matter.

Despite herself, Garrett smiled to hear Sebastien bullied. Someone needed to undertake it.

—I grew tired at the murder house, Sebastien admitted. —But Abby Irene was well enough, and we were together the whole time. I think I am only overwrought.

And Garrett had not the faintest inkling why that might be. She frowned, and resolved to ferret it out—between murders. It wasn't, she assured herself, that it was intolerable that young Jack Priest knew something about Sebastien that she did not. Surely there were many such somethings. Sebastien was…

…she didn't know how old he was. Decades? Centuries? More?

—Here, he said to Mr. Priest. —Look at this. Can you find out from your Irish friends what it might be doing in a dead man's hand?

—What makes you think my Irish friends will know anything about it?

—It's a rosary bead, said Sebastien. —A paddereen.

—That's also their word for *bullet.*

—I know, Sebastien said. —I know.

—⋘—

Garrett padded downstairs uncorseted, wrapped in Sebastien's dressing-gown, which he or Mr. Priest had left on the bedpost. The interior of the house was bright enough for comfort unless one meant to read, shades and drapes in the front room and parlor thrown wide, the den behind them lit by reflection through the open door. Sebastien was in that den, working the ciphers in the Sunday paper. She envied him his freedom from sleep, a need that often affronted her. Her envy wasn't quite strong enough to tempt her with the cure, however.

"So," she said, when he glanced up and smiled, "Have I slept the day away?"

"Just the morning. Are you well?"

She settled in the chair beside his. "Nothing a little beefsteak and brandy won't cure. What do we know about the murder?"

A game they played; sometimes listing the facts made a pattern come plain, like the transposed digits in the broadsheet puzzlers. He rang for a servant, and began. "I am the fabulously wealthy Emmett Goodwood. Who wants me dead?"

"My heirs and assigns," Garrett said promptly. "My mistress. Do I have a mistress?"

Sebastien licked his pencil and made a note in the margin of the newspaper while Garrett restrained the urge to warn him against antimony poisoning. You couldn't get French graphite in the colonies any more. But wampyr, as far as she knew, were no more subject to long-term harm from toxins than from bullets.

And—witness Sebastien's cavalier handling of the rosary bead—tales of allergies to holy relics were myth as well.

"If I don't have a mistress, why not?"

"I love my wife?" Garrett suggested, and Sebastien noted *wife* below *mistress* on the yellow newsprint. He also wrote down *brother, sister, son.*

"Goodwood seems like it should be an English name, doesn't it?"

"Nothing Englisher," Sebastien answered. The orange tom appeared beside his chair and made an imperative noise, and Sebastien reached down to scratch it behind the ears. "So why did he die with a Fenian death-wish clutched in his hand?"

"Does he have any family in the old country?"

"Mary is no doubt in receipt of a small mountain of documents wired from London by now," Garrett said. "Do you think Finn's Boys might have done away with him as a message to a relative in the heart of the Empire?"

"English colonial politics are not my forte. But it supports investigation, I should think." He held the pencil in his left hand now, and the right still dangled toward the floor, scratching the cat under its chin. Garrett could hear it purring again, and the sound brought with it smell of the dead man's room. She waited to see if Sebastien would give her anything more—a hint of Mr. Priest's investigations, of his illicit contacts. But he petted the cat one last time and sat upright, saying, "If he thought the Fenians sought his death, he'd have no little reason for the locked door and the derringer."

The cat blatted at him, and Garrett laughed as he blocked his lap and newspaper with the hand holding the pencil. "I had no idea you were so fond of cats."

"They aren't often so fond of me as el Capitán here, are they, gato?" Sebastien said the last as if in direct address to the cat, which smoothed its whiskers at him. Even Garrett's fearless terrier had not been so fearless, at first, of the well-dressed predator.

Cat eyed wampyr, and after a brief battle of wills the wampyr stood, surrendering the chair. "Mary sent over fresh clothing. You'll want to get back on the case, of course."

There were a thousand things she could have said. She laid a hand on his forearm, stroking the fabric of his coat. "I've never been in your house before," she reminded. "May I have the tour?"

"Of course. That is the parlor. You'll pardon me if I introduce the front rooms from the doorway."

He made her laugh. It was the deadpan as much as the conspiratorial tone. She moved forward, into the well-lit parlor, letting her toes seek out the direct rays of the sun where they warmed the carpet. She turned to see him, framed through the door. "Why *are* all your windows open? That seems incautious—"

"It presents a grim façade from the street if everything is sealed, don't you think?" He wasn't quite looking at her, but rather into the shadows by the cold fireplace. "The light doesn't dazzle me if I don't stare at it directly, and I'm no more likely to stray into a sunbeam than you are to lay your arm across a hot stove-lid. Also, the servants prefer a little light." Then, delicately, like a testing cat himself. "And Jack."

"Ah yes. Jack." He let her have the silence while she selected her words. "Sebastien, who *is* Mr. Priest?"

"An emancipated and quite capable young man," he said. "Anything else, he should tell you himself."

"Your pet?"

He still wasn't looking at her; now he stared down at the cat, quite cozy in his abandoned armchair. "One would think they were seeking the warmth, no?"

"One would think," she said. "Do you love him?"

His dark eyes shone when he glanced up at her, though she did not think wampyr could weep. "Don't be foolish." He made a gesture as if blowing the fluff from a dandelion clock. "One cannot love dust. One might as well put the hook in one's heart oneself. You'd better go along, Abby Irene. I shall join you tonight, and tell you what Jack has uncovered in his travels. He's out among the lower element, seeking the provenance of the 'paddereen.'"

He must have observed her shock as she came back to him; he arched his brows and tilted his head in silent query. "I thought you were keeping secrets," she said. Anything more would be a confession of eavesdropping— as if he didn't already know. But he'd just more or less told her that Mr. Priest associated with the Fenians, without telling her anything in a way she could not deny.

But then, she was already a wampyr's lover—and that was illegal, too.

He smiled, and kissed her mouth without touching her elsewhere. "I am."

He cares for me, she thought, with a kind of amazement. And the next instant, brutally pitied him.

—⁂—

The raisin-sized nugget rested in the middle of a white linen handkerchief, surrounded by candles, a goblet of water, a goblet of wine, a dish of salt, and the magnetized blade of Garrett's arthany. With her silver-tipped ebony wand—just the length from elbow to fingertip—she made passes in the air above it, and pronounced the requisite words.

The table was of a size for eight, without the leaves in place, though she'd pulled the chairs away for unfettered access and gotten Sebastien and his manservant Humbert to roll up the rugs so she could cast a circle in salt.

The paddereen looked ridiculously tiny on Garrett's improvised altar in Sebastien's dining room. Inaptly named, perhaps, except obviously someone ate there. Mr. Priest?

In any case, the little lump of preserved flower petals showed no signs of having been magicked, not even with a trigger or a focus spell. No sorcery had been cast on it or through it, in other words, though there were lingering traces of an ancient Catholic blessing, layered and relayered so many times that it clung to the bead like lacquer.

It also revealed no traces of poison. Not that she'd expect it to—she'd only handled it with gloves, but Mr. Priest had touched it bare-handed and come to no harm.

If she had suspects, she could write their names on slips of parchment, array them around the edges of the altar-cloth (or Sebastien's handkerchief, as the case might be) and see which one was drawn into the center. No proof positive of ill-will, not with the bead apparently innocent, but it could have directed an investigation.

As it was, the thing was utterly inert, and might as well be useless. She made a cutting gesture with her wand, severing the circle of protection, and dropped the ebony stick beside the altar. Her hair was lank with sweat. She wiped it from her forehead.

"The carriage is ready, Abby Irene," Sebastien said from the doorway. She had not an inkling how long he'd been standing there, waiting for her concentration to break. He was that silent. "Have you any luck, mi corazón?"

She swallowed uncomfortable dryness at the unprecedented endearment, trying not to remember that he'd been as affectionate to Mr. Priest when she was not meant to overhear. How could he feel anything for her that was any greater than the casual affection for a pet, the fondness he already betrayed for the orange tomcat? She'd be gone as if in instants, she realized, dead to him between one breath and the next.

Not that he breathed.

"Thank you, Sebastien," she said, and began bundling her tools into the bag. He crossed the circle, stepping over the rolled-up carpet and scuffing the salt with his foot, and stayed her with a hand when she would have lifted handkerchief and rosary bead. "Leave it, por favor," he said. "Unless you must maintain it for evidence? I think that Jack may find a use, before the week is out."

"Of course," Garrett answered, and kissed him on the cheek before she drew off her white gloves.

It had been kind of Sebastien to loan her his carriage again—"I won't need it until sunset"—and though it rattled her teeth, Garrett was grateful not to brave the crowded subway. She had long since stopped finding it ironic or eerie that the city at large paid no attention to a murder, whether the victim was a prominent citizen or a guttersnipe.

And in all reality, it shouldn't. Life went on; there were apples in the markets now, and squash, and cabbages and potatoes to set by for winter. It was Garrett's job to be concerned with justice and the dead. And this particular case seemed to be falling together more or less neatly—but, so often, they did. Murder was usually quite simple and solving it routine.

Unlike politics, which were typically messy, she mused, her attention drawn by the unusual number of redcoats and even a few of what the Frogs would call grasshoppers—green-coated riflemen—in the streets. Garrett wondered whose homes they'd been garrisoned in, and whether they were New England men, or troops sent from the old country in anticipation of continued trouble along the border with Quebec.

She was home by teatime, and Mary, bless her heart, had it waiting. Doubly fortuitous, because Mary also refused to let Garrett see any of the paperwork until she'd eaten. Mike at first spurned her, sulking in his basket, but eventually Garrett's groveling and bribes of tea-cake moved him to resume his post on the chair beside hers.

He was about the color, shape, and size of an ostrich-feather duster, and suited Garrett much better than either of them suited the décor in her townhouse. She'd bought it furnished; it ran to Oriental carpets and perfectly nice carved cherry. Garrett was far more attached to the dog than to the needlepoint chair cushions.

Mary laughed, though, when she came in with fresh cream and found Mike sitting upright on the chair, determinedly ignoring the proffered lemon cake.

"Just like a man," Mary said. She was a thin middle-aged mulatto, her fingers so spare of flesh as to seem rectangular in cross-section. "Never let them know they have the advantage, or you'll be running after them all the rest of your life."

Garrett laughed too and ate the lemon cake herself, licking her fingers for the icing. She stretched inconspicuously. Her leg ached, but no more than normal. The food set aside the last of her lightheadedness, which she almost mourned. She pushed her plate away and swept the crumbs into her palm. "May I have those papers now?"

Mary huffed, but brought them. Telegrams from London, on the undersea cables. She laid them on the table while Garrett dusted her hands over the empty plate, pretending not to notice when Mary set another cup of tea with cream and sugar to hand. The surprising thing was, Mary approved of Sebastien.

Garrett wondered if that would continue if she knew about Mr. Jack Priest.

The telegrams were written in a thaumaturgic code, keyed to the oath and useless to anyone but a Crown Investigator. They contained more information than their size would indicate, and while it took some time to extract it, Garrett had her answer in no more than a quarter hour.

The useful telegram came from the archivist of the Enchancery at Christchurch Greyfriars on Newgate Street, the main London headquarters of the Crown Investigators. The Shambles, the Crown's Own called it, for the slaughterhouses that had given the parish its previous name: St. Nicholas Shambles—as discrete from the Bridge, which was their shorthand for the laboratories, safely isolated over and insulated by running water in the mansions of Old London Bridge, now closed to traffic as a safety precaution.

The Shambles was the administrative and archival anchor of Crown Investigators scattered to the corners of the Empire. And Goodwood's fingerprint and aura pattern were on file.

He wasn't Emmett Goodwood—if any such person had ever existed. Colm Sheridan, on the other hand, was the son of Owen Sheridan. And Owen Sheridan's was a name Garrett knew well from her time in London. The old Fenian bastard, an Irish hedge-sorcerer, had been the special project and the bane of the Crown's Own for close to fifty years, until he was felled by nothing more mysterious than a heart attack.

It didn't tell Garrett who had killed Sheridan, of course. But the available evidence was falling into a satisfying pattern. This might even be an easy case.

And if the case proved as straightforward as it seemed, there would be a certain pleasure in bringing down a Fenian sorcerer who used his power to kill.

She was setting aside the last yellow flimsy when the doorknocker thumped. Reflexively, she glanced at the window. The sun was still above the horizon; it would not be Sebastien.

Garrett's dining room had long ago been converted into a laboratory. She took tea in the library, and so she clearly heard the voice that greeted Mary when she opened the door. Richard, the Duke of New Amsterdam.

She closed her eyes and hurriedly finished the sweet, rich tea, wishing there was brandy in it. There was, however, brandy on the sideboard, and she poured two—her own quite stiff—before Mary could bring Richard in.

The Duke was a big, broad-shouldered man with bark-colored hair that might once have been blond, or brown. He swirled the brandy in the glass and tasted it, then watched as Garrett took two large sips of her own. Mary, clearing the tea things, vanished in her thin brown manner, as if she were just another stick of furniture, but Garrett never forgot she was there.

"Don't worry," she said dryly, after Mary had left the room, "he's not turned me into a vampire, Richard."

Richard set his glass down and frowned. "How can you trust him?"

"Because he's trustworthy." She finished her drink and poured another. "Have you come to denigrate my friends, or would you like to stay to supper?"

It made him laugh, which was what she wanted. "Actually, I came with news. Before Eliot heard it. And to ask what you've learned regarding the Goodwood murder."

"Sheridan," she said. "Goodwood was an alias. He was Colm Sheridan. What's your news?"

Richard paused, considering what she'd said in all its implications, and then silently handed her a telegram. The flimsy paper crackled as she unfolded it. Unlike the ones she'd been perusing before tea, it was brief.

MY SISTER EXPECTING HEIR STOP PLEASE INFORM OUR FRIEND STOP HENRY END

Garrett's control was legendary. The paper didn't crumple in her fist. It barely trembled. Prince Henry's 'sister' was his sister-in-law, Anne of England. If he was confident enough to send Richard a telegram, even an oblique one, then a sorcerer-midwife had confirmed that the child was healthy and male. If it was born alive, Henry would no longer be his brother's heir.

It changed so many things.

"Oh," she said. "May I keep the telegram?"

Richard nodded. "I thought you might wish to."

She pleated it carefully and tucked it into her neckline, where the paper rustled against her skin. "Is that all?"

He shook his head. "Mayor Eliot is a major shareholder in the Goodwood Patent Shoe Company."

Garrett poured more brandy. His had vanished as unaccountably as her own. "I'll have his finances checked."

She would have preferred he left by the time Sebastien arrived, but it was not to be. The sun set a little after six. Sebastien's carriage crunched to a halt in the street while twilight still lingered.

At least the Duke's coach was still in evidence at the side of the house. His rival's presence would not take Sebastien by surprise.

He returned the courtesy. Garrett had long granted him liberty of her house, but this time Mary preceded him, bearing a salver upon which rested two visiting cards. One was Sebastien's, the familiar slightly-greasy parchment. The second was crisp white linen-finished cardstock, and read *Mr Jonathan Priest, 184 Jardinstraat, New Amsterdam.*

Garrett wondered if that was his real name. "Show them in," she said. Mary winked on the side away from Richard, but her frown never broke.

As Garrett had anticipated, she did not approve.

She ushered the new arrivals in, however, and set about fussing with the fireplace, as if the four of them were children or testy dogs who could not be trusted to maintain standards of behavior. But Richard gave her the lie, greeting Sebastien with excruciating politeness, and Sebastien responded with a bow that was well-nigh medieval in its elaborations. He then turned to introduce Mr. Priest—"my assistant."

That minefield navigated, Garrett poured the young man a drink and replenished her own glass. Richard was not yet in need, and Sebastien could stomach no alcohol. Nor anything else but living blood, if it came right down to it.

When the unpleasantries were dispensed with, Garrett cleared her throat and said, "His grace has told me something interesting."

Richard cast her an apprehensive glance, but didn't interrupt. "It seems the Lord Mayor has a financial interest in Goodwood Patent Shoes. And I've learned that the Goodwood Patent Shoe company has blood links to the Fenians." Quickly, she explained about the Sheridan connection.

Sebastien smiled faintly through it, looking directly at Garrett rather than Richard or Mr. Priest. Garrett let the silence linger, shocked at herself. She should not be keeping Mr. Priest's secrets for him.

There were, she temporized, sound reasons why Mr. Priest, as Sebastien's associate, might infiltrate New Amsterdam's Irish underground. And they were not reasons that Richard—as Sebastien's rival or as the Duke of the City in his own character—would be inclined to appreciate.

These things were true. But the fact of the matter was that if Garrett loved Richard—and she had certainly lived the past years of her life in the presumption of that love—she had discovered in those same years that she did not like him much.

How I have fallen, Garrett thought, and held her tongue.

Sebastien, meanwhile, waited until Mr. Priest had gotten himself around the better part of the brandy and Mary had kindled the fire against the spring night's rawness. Garrett's house was without gaslights, and as twilight faded, Garrett took herself about the library, striking lucifers and kindling paraffin lamps. It reminded her of an early night spent in Sebastien's company, and her hand trembled under the flame.

When the room was bright enough for those without a wampyr's advantage and Mary had withdrawn again, Sebastien said, "Jack has learned a little today as well."

The young man in question cupped his glass against his chest, elbows tucked to his ribs. He held his poise, though all eyes were on him. Garrett admired him despite herself.

"Well," he said, "I think the paddereen came in the post. I spoke with Paul Goodwood this morning. He recalled his father receiving a lint-filled envelope, very light, that seemed to disturb him greatly."

"Paddereen?"

"He died holding a rosary bead, your Grace," Garrett explained.

"It seemed to suggest Irish involvement," Mr. Priest said. "Following a hunch, I visited some of the right sort of public houses today."

A dramatic pause, which Garrett did not interrupt. Richard made a soft noise, amplified by his raised glass.

"There is a fair body of rumor," Mr. Priest continued, the picture of insouciance now where before he had been tight-wound, tense, "that suggests Goodwood was laundering money. The people who are talking—which is, I should remind you, not very often the people who know the secret truths—think that if he was murdered, it was by the King's men, begging your pardon, your Grace. At least the lower echelon believes him to have been a loyal son of Ireland. Also, the son, Paul, was born in the Colonies to a Dutch mother. I shouldn't be too certain he knows anything."

Richard seemed to choose his words with care, "Do we assume that the funds for the shoe factory came from the Fenians?"

"I'll put the constabulary on it at once, my lord," Garrett said.

"The City Guard," Richard corrected. "Considering the Lord Mayor's possible role."

"Your grace—"

Richard looked past her, catching Sebastien's eye. "Excuse us," he said. "I need to speak to the Crown Investigator in confidence."

"Of course," Sebastien said, and took Mr. Priest by the elbow to lead him to the hall. When the door was firmly latched, Richard stared at Garrett, and stared away.

"I want Eliot this time, Abby Irene."

The brandy came back up her throat. "Richard—"

But he stopped her with a lifted palm. "He's tried to kill us both," he said. "Last spring, through the French sorcerer. And again six months before that, when his confederates lured us to the Earl of Westchester's country house. Do you honestly believe he's not involved in this, whether we can prove it or not?"

"You're asking me to bear false witness."

"I'm asking you to prove what we already know to be true."

She had no facile answer. *An easy case,* she thought, bitterly, and swallowed to rid the burning in her throat. She forced one calm breath, another. Like magic: if one could fool the body into *acting* calm, it could *become* calm. "I took an oath. If it is not inviolable, then I am useless. If I am not inviolate, my magic is not inviolate."

He was about to say something else. She took the glass from his hand. Two brandy glasses made opening the door awkward. She set them on an end table and gave the cold brass handle one hard jerk. "I'm sure the Duchess is expecting you. Good night."

Sebastien and Mr. Priest were just a little way down the hall. He could have caused a scene, but scenes weren't Richard's métier. Instead, he gave her a look that promised further discussion, nodded to the wampyr and his apprentice, and without another word went to collect his hat.

— ⊛ —

"What was that?"

"A private matter." She put a hand on Sebastien's arm and didn't care if Jack Priest saw. "Stay me with flagons, comfort me with apples," she quoted, "for I am sick of love."

He kissed her on the head. "Will you settle for apple brandy?"

"I've had my share." But she took the glass Mr. Priest handed her, though she did not know if it was her own, or Richard's. Mr. Priest retired to the corner, and she saw him set his back against the paneling and square his shoulders in a silent dare. *Go ahead and ask me to leave.*

She had her own bravado. She finished the brandy—not apple, but good New Holland grape—and rummaged in her bosom for the telegram. Silently, she gave it to Sebastien, and silently, he read it.

Twice.

"Your prince is in danger?" he asked, when he was done.

"He's hardly *my* prince."

Sebastien gave her the yellow rectangle, slightly damp from her skin. "You never told me how the murder case ended."

The murder in question had been that of the Lord Mayor's wife. And Garrett, in other circumstances, might have expected the outcome of that case to endear her to the Lord Mayor.

Eliot had gotten something he'd wanted: King Philip's heir, Prince Henry, returned to England in well-concealed disgrace. Duke Richard might have sworn Garrett to secrecy, but the truth was that Henry had killed Eliot's wife. Sebastien hadn't asked. But then—he wouldn't. However old he was, if patience hadn't been among his native gifts, the years had taught it to him. And it was a test, too, to see how much she'd give him in front of Mr. Priest.

With sharp certainly, it struck her: she was being invited into the family. If Sebastien and Mr. Priest could be called a family, precisely. Sebastien was offering something. Something she had to rise to.

She wished she hadn't finished the brandy. Or that she'd drunk more. "Henry wanted to confess." She wasn't wearing gloves. She fidgeted her sapphire ring. "And I told him I would abide by his brother's command."

"I recall," Sebastien said gently. He didn't touch her again, but she stood at his side and that was strength enough. He'd been present for the first argument. Not for the second, though. "And then?"

"King Phillip commanded, and I abided," she said, without audible irony. "I swore an oath to serve and obey the Crown."

"You also swore an oath to seek the truth."

"So I did." She turned and ran a stare through him. He stared right back. "Of course, you eavesdropped, just now."

"I overheard." He had the grace not to excuse himself with a shrug. "As one does."

She snorted, familiar with the excellence of his hearing. "As it happens, before I was forced to decide which oath to break, Henry shouldered the burden. He agreed to remain silent, and I was spared." And then she must ask, "And of what you overheard?"

Sebastien neither looked down nor stepped away. "At my age, one loses the conceit that one's actions have a positive effect on the larger world," Sebastien said. "Or that the exigencies of politics are of any lasting import. One is left with the options of withdrawing from the world, or with the conviction that whatever small kindnesses and justices one can accomplish are more useful in the long run than revolution. People will be unhappy no matter what you do, Abby Irene. One helps where one can."

"Unhappy under law, then, or unhappy under anarchy?"

"I have devoted the last several hundred years to catching clever criminals," he said. "Whatever my feelings on the equal inutility of political systems, surely you can have no doubt as to where my allegiance lies."

It wasn't the answer she wanted. She glanced at Mr. Priest, who still stood with folded arms, like an allegorical stature representing obduracy.

"I know a lot of people," he said. "But it doesn't mean I agree with them. I'm not an Irish nationalist, D.C.I., if that's what that glare is asking so eloquently."

"No," she said. She rather suspected he was another kind of revolutionary, entirely. Not unlike Peter Eliot.

Sebastien and Mr. Priest stayed through supper. Afterwards, during more brandy, Sebastien arranged a convenient absence to take the air. Garrett knew it was a convenient absence, because Sebastien didn't breathe, and the sort of euphemistic accommodations required by wampyr were rather different than those of ordinary humans. "He did that on purpose," Mr. Priest said, when he'd vanished down the corridor toward the back garden.

Garrett toasted him with her glass. "He's leaving us alone to get to know each other, do you think? Matchmaking?"

She was, she admitted, trying to shock him. If she wasn't two and a half times his age, she hadn't a day.

But, "You're of Sebastien's court," Mr. Priest said, with a fine display of unconcern. "It would be easier on him if we didn't throw fits and jealous squabbles." And then he smiled up at her through his lashes, a beautiful golden child.

"I'm difficult," he finished, as if he shared a great secret.

The coquettish flirtation left her uneasy, even as she laughed. But she didn't think of herself as a vampire's courtier. Surely the power in their relationship was shared, not taken. "I'm Sebastien's friend," Garrett corrected.

"Yes. Sebastien is considered something of an eccentric."

"How old *is* he?"

Mr. Priest stopped, and stared. "He doesn't know."

And that was kind. He could have toyed with her, gloated over knowledge she did not share. *Oh? He never told you?*

"Roughly?"

"He remembers the Black Death," Mr. Priest said. "He remembers the millennium. He saw Vladimir the Great baptized a Christian in Kyiv. And Evie had already left him, by then, and he says they were together forty years or so—"

"Evie."

The blond boy tipped his head. "The one who gave him his first… taste."

"He's *a thousand years old*, Mr. Priest?"

"My best guess? I make it about eleven hundred. He sometimes mutters to himself in a particularly incomprehensible dialect of medieval vulgar Latin when he's not pretending to that ridiculous Spanish accent. It might be Galicean. *He's* Galicean. Or Asturian, rather, if I have the dates right."

"But you're not sure?"

Mr. Priest shrugged. "He says he doesn't remember. He says he starved, during the plague, and forgot a great deal."

"And you believe that?"

He tilted his head. His smile slid from cherublike to conspiratorial. For a moment, they were allies. "I think *he* wishes to believe it."

The Lord Mayor's summons arrived in the first morning post, shortly before sunrise. Garrett read it in her nightgown, lingering over tea spiked with lemon, honey, and a trace of brandy. The summons was phrased as an invitation to luncheon; Garrett penned a reply before she moved on to the rest of the mail.

There were the usual assortment of personal notes, invitations, correspondence, and bills; she set the latter aside for Mary's attention and retained the rest. It being Wednesday, she also had both morning papers, the *New Amsterdam Courant* and *The New World Times*, the second of which actually concerned itself with little more than New England, New Holland, and Virginia.

The news was ill. The redcoats and green-jackets she'd noticed the previous afternoon were fresh on ships from Africa, and garrisoned on Manhattan, where they could take what rest they might and also serve to reinforce the city.

Some three hundred were quartered with local householders, and, as might be expected, some of those—but not all—protested. The Lord Mayor demanded the troops be withdrawn or that their hosts be compensated. The Duke welcomed the aid from abroad.

Garrett flipped to the second page and looked for reports of continued skirmishing in the Green Mountains. She found nothing, but that didn't mean there was nothing to find, only that the newspapers were not printing it.

Richard considered his mandate to extend to the suppression of uncomfortable truths.

Garrett had no stomach for the rest of her tea. She pushed the tray away, left the letters on the table, and padded up the stairs to dress with more than her usual care.

The Lord Mayor's offices opened at nine. Garrett presented herself in the antechamber at precisely half one, squaring her boots on the Persian carpets before the secretary's desk between bongs from the grandfather clock. There was no assistant in evidence, and the desk was clear and dusted. The ink on the blotter was fresh.

Garrett was about to announce herself with a sharp rap on the double doors to the Lord Mayor's private office when the right one swung open. Peter Eliot himself peered around the edge, the flesh of his right hand hammocked between the knots of his knuckles as he twisted the knob back and forth. "You came," he said, blinking like a drunk.

He was red-eyed, but Garrett didn't smell any liquor on him. She strode up crisply, letting her skirts shush about her ankles, and he stepped out of the way. He shut the door; she waited to see if he was likely to shoot the bolt, but there was no thump of the latch. Not that an un-ensorcelled lock could inhibit Garrett when her wand was tucked into her corset.

Apparently, the invitation to dine had been sincere. Several covered salvers and a decanter of wine rested on a round mahogany table before three casement windows. Beyond them, yellow leaves turned in the wind. Garrett waited while Eliot, unspeaking, drew out a chair for her convenience. She permitted him to seat her, the carpet beneath the four legs thick enough that she felt it compress under her weight. The cushions were soft; she might have leaned back on them, but the corset held her up.

Silently, he served her. A green salad, brook trout, and green beans almondine. The wine was an local white, too sweet for Garrett's palate. She wasn't hungry. She buttered tidbits of bread and laid them aside. "Please don't draw it out," she requested, turning her water goblet in her hand.

He laid his fork down. Dining with Sebastien for company could make you forget what a man could eat when he had a will for it, but it seemed to Garrett that the Lord Mayor was no more than picking at his food. He stood and came to his desk, returning shortly with a letter. "You must read this, Crown Investigator."

Silently, she took it. The seal was broken; the address scrawled in a masculine hand. She recognized that writing from an hour on Monday night spent examining Colm Sheridan's desk.

With every appearance of calm, she flipped it open.

It was a plea for help.

"Thank you," she said. "I'll keep this. And authenticate its source, of course."

"Of course," the Lord Mayor said. "May I tell you the rest of the story?"

— ⋘ —

It was the sorcerous work of ten minutes to prove it, once she returned home. The letter was genuine, and genuinely sent from Colm Sheridan— or Emmett Goodwood—to Lord Mayor Peter Eliot. She slipped the flattened paper into a glassine envelope and tucked it into her blue velvet carpetbag. And then she summoned a cab and took herself to Sebastien's house, where Mr. Priest met her at the door.

He helped her off with her coat. He would have taken the bag, but she waved him away, and he was wise enough not to insist. "Is Sebastien in?"

"Waiting for you," Mr. Priest said. Garrett had sent a note ahead, to warn of her arrival, mailed from the Lord Mayor's house. As she came into the den she saw it unfolded on the side table. Sebastien sat in a yellow wing chair beside the cold fireplace. He was knitting.

Or, Garrett reassessed, playing with a ball of yarn and the orange cat. Which did not remove the fact that he *had* been knitting at some point. A sweater, ivory and cabled up the front, sized for a small man. He laid it aside, discomfiting the cat, and stood. Garrett glanced from sweater to wampyr, eyebrow cocked in amusement.

Sebastien shrugged. "I'm not pressed for time."

No, Garrett thought, full of pity again. *You wouldn't be.* "The days are getting shorter," she answered, and he smiled half-gratefully.

"Just so. I got your message. And one from the Colonial Police. There were, unfortunately, unable to recover the envelope in which Mr. Sheridan was sent the paddereen."

"Pity," Mr. Priest said, with a glance at Garrett's burden. "Could you have traced it back to the sender?"

"Confirmed who sent it, if we had a suspect," she said. She shrugged. "There are other ways."

She laid her things down on a coffee table and knelt before it. Unladylike, creasing her dress, but she managed well enough. She opened the carpetbag and pulled out the envelope, mostly unbattered.

Sebastien took it from her and tilted it toward Mr. Priest, and incidentally the light. The cat rubbed against Garrett's thighs and knees while the two men read, ensuring another scolding from her terrier when she got home. When Sebastien looked up, his forehead over his eyebrows was positively corrugated. "Sheridan was looking for a way out?"

"He was laundering money for the Fenians," Garrett confirmed. "And he wanted to escape their machinations. The Lord Mayor was a personal friend, and—upon receipt of this letter—offered to help him escape both his revolutionary creditors and the scaffold, if he would testify."

"And?" Mr. Priest asked. "Is that illegal?"

"No. It's certainly within his rights as the head of the Colonial Police to deal with informants." Her knees hurt from the floor. She pressed the back of her hand to her mouth. When she put it down, Mr. Priest placed a glass of cognac in it; she hadn't even seen him fetch the drink. She closed her eyes and inhaled the fumes, but did not yet partake. The aroma did not soothe her twisting stomach, and she set the glass aside.

"Duke Richard would expect you to destroy this letter," Sebastien said, holding it delicately between thumb and forefinger. She pointed to her luggage, and he slipped the envelope inside. "It could clear the Lord Mayor of any prior knowledge of Sheridan's political leanings."

"Indeed," she said. "I can link the Lord Mayor to Sheridan, and Sheridan to the Fenians. Without that"—she waved at the open carpetbag with the corner of envelope peeking clear—"it's all very tidy, don't you think? It almost solves itself."

"There are," Sebastien said dryly, "more easy ones than not."

"What are you going to do?" Mr. Priest, at Garrett's elbow. He extended a hand to help her to her feet, and she accepted.

She twisted her skirts in her fists, feeling more bitterness than wrath or despair. "Mister Priest," she said, "will you obtain for me a list of names?"

—❦—

Garrett had expected Mr. Priest to temporize, stall, or otherwise attempt in some way to protect whatever familiar friends he had among the Fenians. Instead, he was at his desk within minutes, writing meticulously with a steel-nibbed pen on a torn half-sheet. The scritch-scritch of his writing complemented the clacking of Sebastien's needles; the wampyr had resumed his knitting, this time in the corner by the door.

Neither sound helped Garrett's uneasy concentration as she paced and attempted to distract herself with a book. She flipped pages almost at random, pausing only at the engraved chapter headers. These she tilted so the light caught on the fibers of the paper, studying them to see if she could make out the indentations caused by the pressure of the plates. She had no attention for the actual pictures.

This killing had turned out to be barely a mystery. Garrett was perfectly confident that Colm Sheridan, in the person of Emmett Goodwood, had been murdered because he meant to expose the Fenian organization and in so doing save and free himself. Almost painfully simple.

But there was still the problem of identifying and capturing the man behind the murder, and of course proving the crimes of the Fenians themselves. If they could manage any of those things.

It was rarely a question who was in charge of organized crime or revolutionary conspiracies. The issue was proving it, and while Garrett could arrest anybody she chose, doing it without proof of a crime would only give Finn's Boys another martyr.

And there was no guarantee she'd get the right man. The paddereen might mean nothing at all. It might, she was forced to admit, not even be linked to the crime.

The orange cat miaowed at the kitchen door to be let out into the garden. Garrett heard Consuela, Sebastien's cook, open it for him and cluck. A click, the clamor of outraged birds, and then silence followed.

She shut the book with a snap. Mr. Priest started, blotting his page, but Sebastien did not so much as drop a stitch. "The envelope," she said. "The dustman comes to that neighborhood on Fridays. The Colonial Police don't have it. The son—unless he's concealing it—doesn't have it."

"So a servant took it away," Sebastien said over the clatter of his needles. He reached the end of a row, and bent in concentration as he reversed. The cabling, Garrett must admit, looked tricky, though she could not herself knit. "Or the killer did."

"Or they're one and the same," she said. "It seems I'll need to have the murder squad round up the servants again, for questioning."

"As soon as I'm done with my list I'll take a message," Mr. Priest said. He had lowered his head again and was writing intently. "Forty-one names. I'm better than half done."

It was less than a quarter-hour before he finished, but to Garrett it felt like eight times the duration. Finally, he set the pen down, stood, and came to Garrett to hand her the list, with an odd little bow. She glanced along it and frowned.

It ran onto the back, and a second half-sheet. "Well," she said with a sigh, "it's a start. And it will give the redcoats something to do."

"Redcoats." She suspected, if they hadn't been indoors, Mr. Priest would have turned his head and spat.

When Garrett arrived at the Duke's house, she found herself anticipated. Seamus Gallagher—Richard's butler—was there to greet her and help her off with her coat. She kept her carpetbag. "We received your note, Crown Investigator," he said. "The Duke is out, but I've sent a message."

"Did he say where he was going?" She allowed him to usher her into the study, expecting the headshake before it happened. Seamus was always discreet. That, and his unfailing efficiency, had ensured his employment with the Duke for longer than Garrett had known either of them.

Seamus hesitated as he was leaving, his hand upon the door. "Can I make your wait more comfortable, D.C.I.?"

"Thank you," she answered. "I have everything I need."

He bowed slightly, and seemed about to leave when he hesitated. "Oh. His grace asked if I would return this to you."

He came back across the room and walked around behind the Duke's desk, where he drew an envelope from the cubbyhole secretary against the wall behind it. The niches were filled with paper, paperclips, three colors of ink, fountain pens and quills, lint-padded packets, tape, sealing wax, a rolling blotter, a stub of candle and some lucifers, a tin of candies, and the odds and ends of correspondence, but Seamus unerringly found the right one, and handed it to Garrett with a bow. "His grace said, 'A foolish jewel, to desert so beautiful a lady.'"

Garrett tore the padded envelope open, mindful of scattering lint, and shook a sapphire earring into her palm. She had been missing it.

She didn't need to ask where the Duke had found it, and neither did Seamus. But the butler was in Richard's employ, not the Duchess', and they had relied on his discretion before.

"Thank you," she said, and returned the earring to the packet—her name written on it in Seamus' hand—before tucking it into her carpetbag.

Seamus winked and left her.

The study was cluttered despite its size. The Duke's desk was as big as Garrett's lab table, though not as tall, and the other furniture—bookcases, a reading table, a couch, the chairs—were all to the same heavy standard. Garrett took a position on the edge of a carved maple armchair, beside the Duke's desk and within reach of the afternoon's newspaper, and settled down.

Richard arrived within the half-hour, slightly disheveled and pink-cheeked, still wearing his boots. In the interval, it had begun to rain. Garrett now stood before the window, wondering if the overcast seemed likely enough to hold that Sebastien might venture out by daylight. Maybe he and Mr. Priest would have discovered something useful, on their own or by way of the questioning of the Goodwood's servants, if so. The *Colonial Register* hung by her lilac silk taffeta skirts, the cheap folio sheets folded open to page three. Her sorcerer's tools were sealed in their bag beside the chair she'd been sitting in.

The Duke shut the door behind himself and shot the bolt unsubtly. He came to Garrett, but when he reached to rest a hand on her shoulder and pull her close, she snapped the paper into his palm. He took it, reflexively, and stepped back. "The Lord Mayor has begun a proxy fight, with the intention of assuming control of Goodwood patent shoes," she said. "What does that suggest to you?"

"That he has something to hide," Richard said, scanning columns of print. "I'll have their financial records pulled."

"I've seen a letter that would tend to clear the Lord Mayor of culpability in either the death or any Fenian money-laundering operation," she said. "Do you care?"

He must have finally read the challenge in her voice. He squared his shoulders, dropped the newspaper on the end table, and fisted his hands inside his pockets. "Does it implicate anyone else?"

"Goodwood—Sheridan—was working for the Fenians," she said. "He wanted out. He wrote to the Lord Mayor to ask for assistance and protection, if Sheridan would testify. The letter"—she hesitated—"is confirmed."

"It sounds," he admitted softly, "the twin of one I received. Do you have it with you?"

One you received, Richard my love, and did not trouble yourself to inform me of? It was his privilege as her lord and master, of course.

She was sure there were a thousand things about Richard, Duke of New Amsterdam, that she had not an inkling of.

"No," she lied, without looking down. Her heart beat so hard she felt it in her fingertips. She couldn't imagine how he didn't see it pounding in her throat.

He didn't drop his gaze either. "Did he name the Fenians he was working with?"

"Also no." And that was truth. "We're working on those names. If I can recover a certain piece of evidence, I'll be closer to an answer. Unless it was burned, somewhere exists the envelope in which the rosary bead was posted. If I can find it, I will know who mailed the thing. Then we have a subject for interrogation."

"Or I could arrest the Lord Mayor," Richard said. He took her hand between his own and pressed his lips to it. She suffered the touch, and permitted him to kiss her cheek. "Abby Irene, I have skirmishing on the borders. I have French ships up the St. Lawrence and the Mississippi. I have the Iroquois Confederacy walking out of conferences. It is only a matter of time until we are overrun, and Peter Eliot is the greatest threat to our unity, and our loyalty to the crown. It won't be home rule he gets us. It will be French rule. I need—"

"I won't," she said, her tone like a cracked bell. Without resonance. She lifted her chin. "Do your worst."

He stopped as if run through, and took a breath, and watched her eyes as he said, "Vampirism is a capital crime in the Colonies."

She hadn't actually believed he was capable of what he threatened. But she read his resolve, and knew he would do as he said. He'd burn Sebastien to make her obey.

She'd always admired his ruthlessness before.

"Richard," she said, bending her knees to collect her bag, "it's time you accepted that things are over between us."

"You have a day to decide," he said, and held open the door.

Garrett was still shaking with fury as she settled against the hard cushions of a hansom cab and crossed her arms over her carpet bag. She'd never let Henry make her cry, and she wasn't about to grant any greater power over her to Duke Richard. She drew a shaking breath, experimentally, jolted as the driver shook the reins and the horse jerked into a trot. *Your first breath as a free woman*, she told herself.

It wasn't true, of course. She still owed service to the King. And as long as Richard could extort obedience from her, she had no freedom worth speaking of.

It didn't change the fact that for the first time in years she felt free.

Richard, apparently, had been worse for her than she thought.

It was stupid to go directly to Sebastien's house, but of course she did it anyway, as fast as the rainsoaked driver could get there. Thank God the Lord Mayor had cobbled the streets; just thirty years earlier, they would have been ankle deep in mud already, a death-trap for hurried horses. They were slick, now, and the wheels clicked and squeaked over them, but they were not a mire of earth and refuse.

She made sure to have her money ready when she dismounted the carriage, and paid the miserable cabman while dodging the water that dripped from the brim of his hat. He was eager to be gone; he shook up the reins while she was climbing the three steps to Sebastien's door. Fortunately, there was an awning. She huddled under it, rain spotting her dress, while she fumbled the brass knocker, her carpet bag tucked under her arm.

Silence greeted her. It was Wednesday, the servants' half-day, and she was unhappily reminded of this as she knocked a second time to no reply.

The cab had long since rattled and squeaked out of sight.

"Hell," she muttered, and rattled the door handle. And shockingly, the door swung in.

She stopped it before it opened more than a crack, her pulse—which had subsided a little—thundering again. Surely, the Duke's men could not have come already. Could they have taken Sebastien while she was at Richard's house?

She could still shut the door behind her and leave, walk down the block until she found another cab, go home and let Mary put her into a hot bath. She could lie for Sebastien, do what Richard—do what the *Duke* demanded of her—and Sebastien would have to forgive her, wouldn't he? She held the power in their relationship. And he had said himself, he was disinterested in human politics.

She could walk away right now, and he would never know what the Duke had threatened. She could keep him—at least, for as long as he would stay.

And give the Duke the opportunity to use Sebastien against her any time she showed the slightest disinclination to play the game the way Richard preferred.

She was already pushing the door open completely when she heard the crash. She swung her heel against the door to make sure it shut behind her, then hurried through the dim entry, slipping her wand from its sleeve, the fingers of her left hand white on the handle of her carpetbag. For a moment, she thought of sneaking—but she was a peace officer, and she held her weapon in her hand. "Sebastien?" she called, "Mr. Priest? It's Abby Irene."

There was no answer, but the orange cat catapulted past her ankles and vanished into the entryway. At lest she wouldn't have to worry about tripping over it in the half-lit rooms.

Gaslights did burn in the den where she'd found Sebastien working newspaper puzzles. They shed a rectangle of warm light through the door-frame. As Garrett slipped forward, she heard another loud thump and the sound of something rolling on carpet.

And a moan.

Mr. Priest. Garrett did not drop her carpet bag until she had passed through the door and assured herself that Mr. Priest was the only one in the room.

He was. And he was sprawled on his face, one arm outflung and the other flexed beneath his chest, an overturned end-table and pottery vase upset on the floor beside him. He was breathing—she could see his disarrayed hair fluttering against his cheek—and his fingers flexed as she stood, frozen for a moment, assessing the situation.

She went to him and fell to her knees at his side, her carpetbag falling on its side, this-and-that spilling forth unheeded as the latch was knocked askew. His skin was chill; violent shivers wracked his body. His lips were pale, and when she pulled them back with her thumb his gums were too. Even his mouth felt cold, which—coupled with the lack of convulsions or other symptoms—suggested a thaumaturgic rather than a natural poison. His eyelids fluttered as she felt for his pulse. Thready, quick, and she could not pick one heartbeat out from the next.

She rolled him onto his back. His left hand fell clear, and something dropped from his fingers: the paddereen. Which, by Garrett's own investigations, was clear of both malicious sorcery and latent poison. She flicked it away with the tip of her wand, making sure she noted where it came to rest.

In the few brief moments that she had been holding his wrist, Garrett thought Mr. Priest's heartbeat had become more erratic. She had the medical training all sorcerers received, which included emergency treatment of natural and of thaumaturgic poisoning (intentional and unintentional). The first step would be to establish stasis, while Mr. Priest was still drawing breath. It was a spell she carried prepared, hung in charges on her wand—the most basic of self-defense measures.

She released Mr. Priest's wrist, leveled the wand, and the silver tip wavered. He was almost gone. She'd shared Henry, all the years that she and the Prince had been lovers. And she'd shared Richard, too. But a half-minute's delay, no more than the faintest hesitation, and Sebastien would be hers alone.

Except for whoever else he went to, when he must. She had no idea who the rest of his lovers—*his court, Abby Irene, use the ugly word when it's the right one*—were. But they must exist, five or ten at least, to sustain him without undue risk. And being Sebastien—or whoever he'd been, before he'd forgotten the name—she had no doubt he considered each and every one of them a bosom friend. There was no doubt that Mr. Priest was right. Don Sebastien de Ulloa was, in wampyr terms, a hopeless eccentric.

Mr. Priest's breathing caught. He shivered.

And Garrett leveled her wand and froze him with a gesture, suspended in time. Still alive, on the edge of death.

She was still crouched over him, shuddering—a matter of no more than ninety seconds—when the front door opened again. "Jack?"

"In the den," she called. "He's safe for now—"

She never finished the sentence. Sebastien materialized beside her and dropped on one knee at her left hand, though she'd neither seen nor heard his approach. "What is this?" She couldn't have stopped him when he reached out, but he arrested his own hand before it quite brushed Mr. Priest's cheek.

"Your paddereen, I think," she said, and gestured to where she'd flicked it. "I've put him in a stasis. He isn't dead, Sebastien." Gently, she touched *his* sleeve. "He's quite safe, for the moment, and we have time to attempt a cure."

This time, he leaned his shoulder on her as if to borrow strength. He rested his hands on his raised knee, fabric dimpling under the tightness of a grip whose ferocity did not color his voice in the slightest. "But you tested the bead. No poison and no sorcery."

"No poison," she echoed. "No, nor any sorcery. But—" She let the tip of her wand rest on the carpet as she thought. "What if you took a spell and cut it in half?"

She could sense his impatience, but he held it in check. "Proceed," he said, tightly.

"It wouldn't be detectable as a spell. No active magical principle, not even a stored dweomer. There'd be…no tension on it. So if half the spell were on the paddereen, for example, and the other half—"

Sebastien could not blanch. But his brows drew together and he glanced over his shoulder. "The cat," he said. "When he was out in Sheridan's garden, anyone could have…"

She nodded. "It's the only other thing we brought here from Sheridan's house. And when you became exhausted you had been handling both the cat and the bead."

It was at times such as this that she was reminded of just how unhuman Sebastien was. The façades and japery fell away, his almost-perfect counterfeit of a mild-mannered, breathing, human man. A *man* would have drawn a breath, squared himself, steeled himself. He would have tensed and seemed to enlarge as he filled his lungs.

Sebastien, the predator, simply settled into himself and became profoundly still. "Well," he said, his eyes mad with red glints, "we know a wampyr can survive it. What if he were of the blood?"

Oh, God, Garrett thought. "Would he thank you?"

"He could curse me all his nights," Sebastien said. Garrett glanced down, not wanting to see the curved needle-sharp canines pressing into his pale lower lip. "He'd not be the first."

His voice, the scent of him, the blown pupils in the narrowed eyes—she quailed, as she had never quailed from him before. And somehow, nevertheless, reached out and put a hand on his steely arm.

"Let me try first," she said. "He's safe for a few hours. And I can treat the spell if I can discover the original casting. I need to construct an exact complement, which will absorb and neutralize the malevolent sorcery, and for that I need the spell itself. And better, the sorcerer. Because anyone this clever will have false trails and deceptions worked into the structure."

"Then we're no better situated than we were this morning."

"Did they find the envelope?"

"Since you ask, I'm just back from the Colonial Police. I helped question the servants. Sometimes I notice when people are lying, after all." That wolfish curve of his lips chilled her every time she caught a glimpse of it. "And yes, I have the envelope. It seems my skills were not needed; a downstairs maid had taken it for the paper. Apparently," he said, his voice rich with irony, "she fancies herself something of an artist, and she's covered the back with sketches."

Garrett winced. "That will muddle the correspondence, but I can work through it. Perhaps."

Sebastien glanced at the young man sprawled insensate on the rug. "What about Jack?"

Garrett said, "I'll see to him. Because now I have a spell cast by an unknown sorcerer. And I have a list of names. And that, my dear Sebastien, is all I really need."

He stared. And then he leaned over and kissed her on the forehead, his fangs scratching like thorns. "Lioness," he said. "Use whatever you need. I'm going to carry Jack to bed."

"Wait," she said. "There's something I need to tell you."

He did not stop working Mr. Priest's limp body into his arms. "Is it likely to result in our collective deaths in the next five minutes?"

"No," she said, as she collected the spilled contents of her carpet bag and stood. "Not in the next five minutes, no."

Again, Sebastien's dining-room table was pressed into service as a workbench, and again, Garrett improvised her altar from a linen handkerchief and whatever else she could borrow from the kitchen or dig from her carpet bag. Her hands shook as she lit the candles and poured the wine. Her hands shook as she laid out her tools, the paddereen and Mr. Priest's list of names.

Sebastien let her hear him coming, the careful scuff of his boot on the carpet as he paused where her line of salt would have been, if she had cast one. "Shall I roll up the rugs for you, Abby Irene?"

She straightened the black handle of her silver knife. "That would be very kind, Sebastien. Thank you."

She rummaged through the carpet bag and found the sack of sea-salt, gritty and gray-white, sticky-damp from the rain. She crunched it in her palm while Sebastien stripped up the rugs, and when he withdrew to a corner of the room, she cast a circle around the table, only leaving open a gap wide enough for one to pass. "Would you bring me the cat, please, Sebastien?"

He arched an eyebrow, but sidestepped and vanished through the door. "You were about to tell me something," he called back. She brushed salt from her fingers into the bag, and some of it scattered the floor.

"The Duke tendered me an ultimatum today," she said. Sebastien didn't answer, but she heard the clucking noises as he coaxed the cat. Apparently, the animal's name would remain *el Capitán*, for when Sebastien reappeared, he cradled seventeen pounds of marmalade tomcat.

"How shall you keep him in the circle?" Sebastien asked. "I would rather you did not touch him."

"No, that would be unwise. Just put him within the line; animals understand protective circles."

Sebastien did as she instructed, and Garrett closed the circle before the cat identified the gap. Whiskers trembling, it began a slow circuit of her improvised workspace, inspecting the line on the floorboards. But as she had predicted, it respected the barrier, and having made one and a half circuits, sat down beside a table leg and began to wash a forepaw, pretending vast unconcern.

With tongs held in gloved hands, Garrett lifted the paddereen and touched it to the tip of the cat's tail. The cat twitched its appendage aside, but on the second try, Garrett managed to make good contact. She spoke three harsh, ancient words of Aramaic and a fragile green-blue aura stretched like cobweb from the cat to the rosary bead, coiling around the latter and tearing free. The cat stared over its shoulder at her with greatly affronted dignity. Garrett lifted the tongs, holding the paddereen up to Sebastien with a chuckle of triumph.

"Should I be seeing something?"

"Only if you were a sorcerer," she said, and laid the glowing rosary bead gently in an empty watch glass. "If you were trained, or very powerfully gifted, you would see that the bead has, through contagion, become the receptacle for the entirety of the sundered spell, and is now exhibiting a typical luminescent quality which we may term limerence."

She took up the lint-padded envelope she'd laid on the table and placed it near the watch-glass. It was, as Sebastien had noted, covered in pencil sketches, rather good ones. For a moment, Garrett permitted herself a frown at the waste of talent, though she could not say if it was because artistry was wasted on a maid, or because an artist was wasted as one.

She sketched circles and diagrams around each one with the silver-bladed knife, connecting them with straight and wavy lines. And then she calmed her mind, and with her knife in her left hand and her wand in her right, crossed them over envelope and bead and spoke a word.

With a whisking sound, the rosary bead shot back into the envelope. "Well," Garrett said. "I'd say that was conclusive. The address is block-printed, though. I fear we've no hope of a handwriting match."

She put the bead back in the watch-glass and set the envelope aside.

"So," Sebastien said, "Tell me about the ultimatum."

She smoothed Jack's list beside the watch-glass, weighing the corners with copper pennies and dome-shaped beads of tempered glass. "Sebastien, you will have to flee."

And that was all. She heard him shift—he let her hear him shift—and she knew in that gesture that he understood the Duke's threat, and her decision, as plainly as if she'd laid the whole thing out for him, point by point.

"Not for the first time," he said. "I can't leave Jack."

"In a moment I'll be ready to set him right." She feigned confidence; he'd know she was pretending, but that was fine. "He's not in danger."

Sebastien harrumphed. "And in any case, this is his house. I am but a lodger."

Garrett refrained from pointing out that she had guessed correctly, contenting herself with a quiet gloat. She spoke words over the paddereen and made a little heap of iron filings in the same watch glass, then sketched runes and sigils in the air with the tip of her wand. Real sorcery was not particularly spectacular, despite the flash and gunpowder one might see devoted to making ritual convincing when it came to stage plays.

She tapped the glass once, twice, a third time, and blew across the filings in the general direction of Jack's handwritten list. If the name of the sorcerer appeared there, and if she'd done everything correctly, the iron filings would wing through the air, clump and stick and find themselves attracted to it, as if by magnetism.

They flew, all right. Past the paper, out of the scope of the altar, past the startled cat, and into the open top of Garrett's carpet bag.

She almost dropped her wand.

"Abigail Irene?"

She crouched, her corset biting into her hips, and reached gingerly into the blue velvet satchel. Her gloves protected her fingers, but she still felt iron grit against paper.

She drew forth the envelope with her earring in it. Her name was perfectly outlined in the metal filaments.

But of course, they hadn't found just the name of the mage who cast the spell. They'd found an even tighter correspondence of identity to cling to: the handwriting of Seamus Gallagher.

"Shit," she said, who was a lady and who never swore. "Sebastien, shall we go upstairs to Mr. Priest? I think I know how to take the spell off him, now."

—⁓—

And it was as simple as that in the end. A few snapped meta- thaumaturgical threads, and Jack Priest blinked muzzily, tried to sit up under the heavy blankets and comforters that Garrett had heaped upon him, and fell back against the pillows, shivering so violently that Garrett was eventually obliged to climb up on the bed beside him and hold him in her arms, sharing body warmth until Sebastien could make shift to bring a pot of tea.

By the time Sebastien returned, Garrett had Jack laughing weakly.

She decided to leave it up to Sebastien to explain about the Duke's ultimatum.

―⁘―

Garrett marshaled her evidence and wrote up three copies of a deposition and report. She'd have them notarized along the way to the Duke's house and deposit one copy with the Colonial Police, as it was still, impossible though it seemed, within business hours.

She set out with a kiss to Sebastien's cheek. Before she went, he placed a hand on her shoulder and squeezed.

And that was all. No confessions, no promises, no tokens, no sundered rings. She might never see him again.

―⁘―

It was an odd thing, to find one's self greeting a murderous sorcerer by name, making casual conversation while he helped one off with one's coat and escorted one to the usual place. The study was gray with the rain and with evening darkening the sky. She could not make herself sit on the couch where she and Richard, on occasion, had done somewhat more than kiss, and so she set her carpet bag on the Duke's blotter and stood beside it, having availed herself of the excellent brandy.

Richard, for once, was prompt. She said nothing but the barest greeting, handed him her deposition, and fixed herself another brandy while he seated himself and read.

She hadn't eaten all day. The liquor went straight to her head, and she welcomed it—its warmth, the disassociation that it brought. *Abby Irene, you pathetic old drunk.*

When Richard lifted his eyes from the paper, she felt the stare upon her back. She finished her brandy, discarded the glass, and turned to stare him down.

"I think you may find when the Fenians are questioned that the ultimate source of their funding is French," she said, as an opening gambit. "Any enemy of the Commonwealth is a friend of the Frogs, after all."

"It's the French that concern me," he said. "Phillip can worry about the damned Fenians. If this is true—"

She saw him formulate the question and dismiss it. Of course Seamus wouldn't have acted against the Duke. The Fenians didn't give any more of a damn about the colonies than the colonies gave about the Fenians; Richard might be a useful source of information, but killing or compromising him wouldn't ensure home rule in Eire. They'd take money from the French. They'd take money from anyone, but they were a one-issue revolution. Meanwhile, the French would support anything that might drain British colonial resources.

And Richard being Richard, he wouldn't bother asking a question he already thought he knew the answer to.

Instead, his thumbnail caressed the notary's embossed seal. "Tell me this is the only copy."

She lowered her voice. You never knew who might be listening at keyholes. "So you can deal with Seamus quietly, yourself?"

He stood and came to her, towering over her, his height and breadth no longer the comfort she had been used to find them. His voice was cold and tattered as mist on the Hudson of a morning. "It would be nice to think you'd allow me the privilege."

Garrett would not allow him the triumph of forcing her to step away. She drew herself up and lifted her chin. Good she'd set her snifter down, or the clench of her hand would have broken the stem. Her head spun from the liquor; she could still taste it up her sinuses.

"It's on deposit, Richard. Your servant is in the pay of the Fenians, who I believe are in the pay of the French. I've provided a copy of my findings and of the list of names provided by Don Sebastien's agent"—and how strange, now, to dismiss the old-eyed, magnanimous young Mr. Priest with that cold description, as if he were no more than Sebastien's extended hand—"to the Colonial Police."

And as her comment was interrupted by the sound of the door knocker, she concluded, "I rather expect that's them now."

And the wonder of it was, *Richard* stepped back. "Abby Irene, this will ruin me."

"Nonsense," she answered. "You're unsinkable."

But he was always so clever, so ruthless. And this was no exception. "We can salvage this," he said. "If you'll say that you left out the Lord Mayor's part in the plot under duress, under threat or ensorcelment, and testify that Seamus is Eliot's agent, we can still salvage this."

One may, Garrett mused, flee an island nation for colonial shores and leave a handsome prince behind. One may set one's self well back from the centers of power—or as far back as one's temperament and inclination will allow. One may limit one's options and remove opportunities for conflict, for temptation.

It will find one anyway.

She had been here before, metaphorically speaking. She knew the signs of a tipping point as well as she knew anything: the damp palms, the cold across her neck. She was intoxicated, perhaps not the best state in which to be making life-altering decisions, but she'd never let that stop her.

She said, "Not without an order from my King."

—⊱—

In the small hours of the morning, Garrett answered a tap on her front door. Mary was long abed, and Garrett had been drinking that night, rather than sleeping.

She swayed as she pulled the handle, but managed the operation with only a little awkwardness. Say what you would about the Crown Investigator; she was a lady who could hold her liquor. She chortled at the thought: most unladylike, which made her laugh the more.

At the top of her stair, cloaked against the night's deep chill and with a hood drawn over his bright hair, stood Mr. Priest.

"Oh," she said. "Mr. Priest. Come in."

A moment later, she remembered to stand aside to let him enter, but he remained where he was. "I'm just here to deliver a message," he said. "Against my counsel—not, please, that I do not think you can be trusted— Sebastien sends to tell you that a letter may find him in Boston at the home of Mrs. Phoebe Smith. Under the name of Nast. Will you remember that, Crown Investigator?"

"I'm drunk, young man, not incapacitated." Her show of indignation was admittedly somewhat undermined when she was obliged to clutch the doorframe to stay upright.

He smiled, a cherub with a wicked secret. "Also, he sent this." He held out a gloved hand with the back toward the sky, something concealed in the palm. When she reached, he laid a crisp, green-bloomed red apple in her grasp. A van den Broeck, grown in New Amsterdam since the first Dutch settlers brought over seeds sewn into their petticoats.

She closed her fingers over the cool, waxy globe and lifted it to smell. Tart, sweet. The aroma cleared her head a little.

Comfort me with apples, she'd said, quoting the Song of Solomon—

and had Sebastien answered in kind? *My beloved spoke, and said unto me, "Rise up, my love, my fair one, and come away."* "Was there a message with it, Mr. Priest?"

The young man shook his head. "He said you'd understand. And please call me Jack, Abby Irene."

CHATOYANT
(December, 1902)

DON SEBASTIEN DE ULLOA turned the silver ring between his fingers, refusing—quite—to frown. The metal stayed cool; Sebastien's touch could warm nothing. He watched the light bend across a cloudy cat's-eye sapphire set level with the broad flat band, and licked his lips.

"Chatoyant," he said, and when he looked up felt the frown get away from him. Jack Priest, his friend and courtier, stared at him across the width of a cherrywood table in the chintz-and-lace front parlor of the Boston townhouse of Mrs. Phoebe Smith. His head cocked under a cherubic blond tangle, he frowned right back.

"Said of a mineral's luster," Sebastien continued, "'containing numerous threadlike inclusions, aligned to produce catseye figures with reflected light.'" He held up the ring so the glow from the gaslamps caught in those selfsame inclusions. It was not yet evening, but Sebastien could not venture into sunlight. And so the draperies were drawn.

Jack's frown deepened. "I don't know whose is that stone."

"Good," Sebastien said. "Go upstairs and put on your ring, please. And bring another down for Mrs. Smith."

Under other circumstances, Jack might have argued. Sebastien had no patience for the roles of blood and courtesan, freighted with tradition, and demanded only that his court treat him as a friend. He did Jack the dignity of never using that tone of flat command unless it was absolutely necessary, and Jack returned the respect with occasional considered obedience.

Now, he stared at Sebastien for a moment, obviously contemplating what it meant that another wampyr had braved the long Atlantic journey by dirigible or steamship, and come to the colony of Massachusetts. And sent a courtesan's ring by way of announcing his presence to Sebastien.

Jack vanished up Mrs. Smith's front stairs as with the speed of the adolescent he still resembled.

Sebastien pressed the cold ring between his fingers, and his fingers to the bridge of his nose.

Jack was gone longer than anticipated. When he reappeared, a silver ring flashed on his wedding finger, a trillion-cut garnet like a drop of blood bezel-set flush with the broad band. Except in the choice and shape of stone, it was identical to the ring Sebastien held. Jack wiggled a third between uplifted fingers. "I couldn't remember where I'd packed them. I had to guess at the size for Phoebe."

"I'll want to courier some to New Amsterdam as well," Sebastien said.

Jack nodded. He bounded the last three steps—Sebastien winced—and came bouncing over. "It's too late tonight. I'll take care of it in the morning. In the meantime, you can compose a telegram to Abby Irene and I will run it down to Atlantic Telegraph before sunset. Sebastien?…"

He slipped the spare ring into his waistcoat pocket and reached for the one Sebastien still clutched. Reluctantly, Sebastien laid it on his palm, not sure whether he was loath to let the cool metal leave his grasp, or concerned that its touch might somehow infect Jack.

Jack could have asked why Sebastien worried, why he required Jack to wear the band that advertised to those with eyes to see that he was under Sebastien's protection. Instead, he glanced at Sebastien, once more, and then stood for a moment turning the ring to admire the play of light snarled on the stone. "Whose is it?"

"Epaphras Bull," Sebastien said. His orange cat appeared from wherever he had been entertaining himself and coiled Sebastien's ankles, miaowing. Sebastien did not have the heart to nudge it away. "He was an Englishman."

The widow Mrs. Phoebe Smith—authoress, friend, and owner of the house where Sebastien, Jack, and el Capitán were lodgers—returned while Jack was wiring Sebastien's message to New Amsterdam. She came through the door flustered and windblown, her milk-pale skin flushed, her pale hair escaping the pins. Sebastien's hearing was too good for her to have startled him; he was halfway across the room to her before she shut the door.

But she did not greet Sebastien. Instead she lowered her parasol, shook it closed, and drew two deep breaths he assumed were meant to be calming. She smelled of perfume, like roses and rain, of powder and woman and the street.

"Have you heard about the murder?" she asked.

His heart did not beat. There was no sensation of his pulse accelerating, or the tingle of apprehension in his throat and chest. Strange that he could remember so clearly what it felt like, when he could not remember his mother's name. "My dear, I haven't. Murder?"

"A young man found in his flat," she said. "A stylish address on Essex, near Queens Street."

Sebastien took her hand to cover a moment of thought. The very land under the Back Bay neighborhood was less than a hundred years old, the fill construction an engineering and thaumaturgic marvel that had occupied the first two thirds of the nineteenth century. Finished in 1862, it had converted a useless stretch of tidal bay to valuable—and fashionable—real estate.

It was true Sebastien had been less than three months in Boston. But his habit was night-time restlessness, and in his wanderings, he had already become quite acquainted with the city's slanted streets and narrow ways.

While the address she mentioned was not as prestigious as Mrs. Smith's on Beacon Hill, it was more than respectable. Sebastien felt an intense frustration that he was in the city under an assumed name—in hiding, not to put too fine a point on it—and could not present himself to the murder investigation as an able assistant.

Mrs. Smith was looking down at his lightly restraining fingers with an elevated eyebrow when he came back to himself, a moment later. "Don Sebastien—"

"One moment," Sebastien said. "Hold that thought." Still holding Mrs. Smith's warm right hand in his left—produced the red-violet garnet ring that Jack had brought downstairs. "I must ask you to wear this, for your safety."

"A ring?" She lifted it to the light, her tone teasing. "I wasn't aware that you felt for me so strongly. Although finding a priest who would perform the sacrament of marriage for a wampyr might be challenging—"

He let her make him laugh. It helped a little. "It indicates that you are under my protection." Reluctantly, he let her hand slip from his grasp. "Should another of the blood come calling."

Her eyes widened, but she didn't flinch. "Is that likely?"

"More likely today than yesterday," he said, and made a needle-threading gesture.

"Well then." But she handed the ring back to him and held out her left hand. It was innocent of her wedding ring; she had switched the emerald band to her right hand when he and Jack moved in. He imagined the neighbors were talking.

He kissed the stone, all mocking courtship, and slipped his signet on her finger just as the front door banged open.

Her breath had quickened, her pupils dilating. She spun at the sound, her newly-adorned hand lifted to her throat. Sebastien stepped back reflexively, away from any possible fall of sunlight, but turned, when he turned, more slowly.

"Hello, Jack."

Jack pushed the door closed and lifted the evening paper by the bottom corner. The cheap newsprint was already ink-smudged and friable. "Sebastien—"

"Yes." Sebastien crossed the parlor with quick small steps, the heavy carpet squishing under his weight. "Phoebe was just telling me. A murder in the Back Bay?"

"No flies on you," Jack said, affecting a peculiarly horrible accent he perhaps imagined to be American. "Did she tell you the gory details?"

"I was just about to," Phoebe said. With a glance at the curtains, she joined Sebastien and Jack by the door. She stepped between them, and while Jack held his hands wide so as not to stain her pale green silk noil dress with ink, she cupped his neck between her hands and kissed him on the lips. Sebastien plucked the paper from his grasp and turned to give them a moment's privacy.

Not that they required it. Jack was a young man, and Phoebe had been widowed for some time. And there were pleasures Sebastien could not provide his still-warm lovers, just as there were pleasures no one living could provide for him. Also, Sebastien suspected that Jack enjoyed rubbing his nose in it.

The banner headline had to do with sinking of two English-flag ships in the North Atlantic, attributed to the French. War was no longer an inevitability: although it had yet to be declared, it had become a fact. But below the fold, Sebastien found the gaudy account of a young man slashed to death in his bath.

When Phoebe and Jack broke the kiss, he turned back. "An insinuatory article."

"Yes," Jack said. He disentangled himself from their hostess, who went to fetch a rag. "I believe you would say the victim had no visible means of support."

"He was a whore," Phoebe called, from the kitchen.

Sebastien entered the dining room, Jack in tow, and craned around the kitchen doorway to blink at her. "Such language."

"Words are my business." When she returned, she dropped a soapy rag into Jack's hands. "I'll use them precisely. Don't put that newspaper on my clean tablecloth, please."

Sebastien stepped into the kitchen to lay the paper on the counter and rinsed his hands under the tap. Boston was the most modern city Sebastien had lived in; there was even a system under the pavements by which water was piped for use in fighting fires. In fact, Boston had largely electrified, a process New Amsterdam was still struggling through, but the residents of Beacon Hill had been resistant to the stringing of unsightly cables.

Here, they were to be buried, and so for now, the wealthier citizens still made do with gas. But electric street cars ran throughout the city. It was only a matter of time until the trunks were tapped, or until the broadcast power that was—supposedly—already being tested in Paris crossed the Atlantic.

That, of course, would have to wait for after the war. But still, this was the age of miracles.

"Whores don't usually have the means to live in the Back Bay," he said, drying his hands.

"Unless they're beautiful and well-spoken," Phoebe said.

Sebastien smiled as he came from the kitchen. Too many women of this era were silenced by its unrelenting primness…or simply as naïve as society expected they remain. He enjoyed Mrs. Smith. She would have been at home in the courts of the Renaissance. "So this young man was kept? How fascinating."

Jack placed one hand lightly on his wrist. "Sebastien. You're not—"

The killer was most likely one of the young man's clients. Or patrons, if one preferred. No mystery worth solving, though that did not ease his compulsion to try.

"Right," he said, and pulled Epaphras' ring from his pocket and showed it to her. "Phoebe," he said, "and Jack. I'm going out tonight. He lifted a hand to forestall Jack's inevitable protest. "I swear to you, Mr. Priest, I will not interfere in the investigation of this killing. But I must refresh myself, and I have dined at home too recently. Please stay in the house, both of you. If anyone comes looking for me—a man about Jack's height, with pale eyes— don't invite him in. He might be wearing a stone such as this."

Phoebe said, "I can survive scandal, but a reputation for plain bad manners will have me cut from society entirely."

"Have him wait in the cottage, then," Sebastien answered. There was a summer house, of sorts, in the back garden, boarded up for the winter now. One of the blood would not mind the cold. "He does not cross your threshold, as you value your safety and mine."

—❧—

In his first weeks in Boston, by virtue of being able to claim a mutual acquaintance in Venice, and through the good offices of Mrs. Smith, Sebastien had garnered an invitation to a certain well-known salon at the home of Miss de Courten, which he now frequented. Miss de Courten—Sebastien assumed it was a *nom d'amour*—was French-speaking Swiss, and still quite European in her habits. She had only recently dropped the style of *mademoiselle*, deeming it unwise in the growing atmosphere of dividedness surrounding relations between the British Empire, the French incursions thereon, and colonial calls for Home Rule.

In any case, the lady, whose Christian name was Verenna, was a daylight sleeper, though quite mortal, and her guests were accustomed to such society hours as one kept on the continent. Lamps still burned in all the windows when Sebastien arrived, though it was well after midnight, and the maid responded immediately when he tapped upon the door.

He was instantly admitted, though he had not taken the precaution of sending ahead a card. The staff knew him, and the party was still in full voice.

Sebastien surrendered hat, gloves, coat, and walking stick, and suffered himself to be led to the parlor.

Miss de Courten had been a courtesan in more than one sense, in the old country. Although she was but recently acquainted with Sebastien, she was well aware of his nature and history…and quite grateful for his attentions. She was growing older, and had left her own patron behind in Nice, crumbled by the sun.

One grew tired. Sebastien understood very well the exhaustion that came with age, and it would be a lie to say he had never been tempted to the same route. But then, those left behind—mortal, or of the blood—grieved so.

Miss de Courten's salon was populated by the demimonde. When Sebastien entered, there were three in attendance. He made his obeisance to Miss de Courten and then greeted each guest in turn: a dark-haired stage actor with a famously burred and rasping voice, Mr. Alexander Frazier—named, like so many, for King Philip's mother, the Iron Queen; Mr. Roderick Chisholm, an author even more scandalous than Mrs. Smith for all he was a man; and a rangy, beaky woman in a domino mask, to whom all did the courtesy of honoring her incognito, though her identity could be no true secret. Even if he hadn't recognized her scent, Sebastien would have known her. Her fame—in impolite society—was undeniable.

"Chouchou," Sebastien said, her preferred alias. He bowed over her broad-knuckled hand and pressed his lips to the red-flashing violet glitter of amethyst on her gloved finger. It did not matter that Sebastien's hands were cold; she'd never notice through the kidskin. She made the demure turn of her head and the drape of a black line of false eyelash across her cheek seem bold as a stare.

"Mr. Nast," she replied—his new alias, and he was almost accustomed to it. The years taught one not to hold any tighter to names than to lovers.

She was the mistress of Michael Penfold, the Colonial Governor, and Sebastien had no more illusions about her nature or profession than Miss de Courten had about Sebastien's. She was a gorgeous creature, artifice and art, and even as he found her intriguing—exciting—he wondered what the child-Sebastien of centuries before, an unworldly young man of different name and no experience, would have made of her breathy, dusty contralto, elaborate scarlet wig, and the corseted curve of her waist.

It might be interesting to know her better. Secret-keepers were often amenable to assisting with the secrets of others. As he bowed himself back, he could not quite keep a smile from his mouth. Abigail Irene would have pretended to be shocked at him, he thought, with a trace of satisfaction. Although given her own—checkered—history, it would have to have been dissimulation.

Sebastien took a seat close by the fire where it could lend some warmth to his winter-clammy flesh. He permitted himself to be poured a brandy that he had no intention of drinking, and bowed his head over the glass with a show of enjoying the fumes. Even that was lost to him; they stung his eyes and burned his sinuses. He blinked as water filled his eyes, and realized the room was still silent. "Please," he said, "don't let me interrupt."

The wearer of the domino sipped tea. Sebastien rather thought it might be fortified. "The conversation," she said, delicately, flicking her nails against the gold-painted-china eggshell rim of her cup, "hinges on matters of scandal."

Mr. Chisholm, the author, chuckled. "Mr. Frazier advanced the suggestion that the architect of last night's murder might be the wampyr escaped from New Amsterdam. We were discussing the possibility—"

"There are no vampire in New Amsterdam," the hostess said, with a sniff. "There isn't a single vampire in America. How would one manage the Atlantic?"

"He could have himself shipped."

"He'd starve along the way," said the one in the domino.

Sebastien smiled at her. She blushed and glanced down, and glanced back. He liked her boldness, the way she did not hide her intellect, and the breadth of her hands and shoulders worried him not at all. It wasn't as if it mattered to him what lay behind her petticoats.

Mr. Frazier ran a hand through thick black hair, snagging a few strands on a sapphire pinky ring. Sebastien looked at it askance, but it was a clear Ceylon stone, powder-blue and velvety, set high in gold—no courtesan's flat band of silver. He was a slight man, and his voice was a pleasant shock with its depth and scratchiness, no trace of defensiveness detectable as he said, "But the City Guard *are* seeking one. So someone is taking the possibility seriously."

"They are?" Chouchou's fan snapped open, hiding her mouth. Kohled eyes widened as she fluttered the device.

"The Duke's men," the actor supplied, while Sebastien caught the hostess's eye and let her read inquiry in his expression. She nodded, slightly, and her color rose.

Though he was dead, Sebastien imagined his pulse racing like a mortal man's. The body had its means of telegraphing excitement to the heart and mind, sensations that did not change simply because the heart beat no longer.

Chisholm interrupted, "As a writer, I have sources that others…may not. I heard that the wampyr"—with painfully correct overpronunciation—"subverted a crown officer, and she's resigned in disgrace."

"Is that so?" Sebastien made a show of boredom. Just an example of how tales grew in the telling: Abby Irene might resign her commission on principle, but never to flee scandal. She was a great believer in the merit of a brazen face. "What do you know of vampires?"

Most of the blood considered the English approximation of the word something of an insult. Sebastien thought it rather silly to draw such lines in the sand. Language was ephemeral as a mortal life, and clinging to it made as little sense. It would change and change again, like the world, and it was not Sebastien's role—as he understood it—to oppose that change, though he and his kind were changeless in the end.

Let the breathing concern themselves with politics and borders and the philosophy of human rights. He'd wager any movement created as many injustices as it redressed.

Chisholm, challenged, deflected the volley. "Far less than Mr. Frazier, obviously. I can't aspire to his levels of erudition."

Sebastien shared an irony-soaked smile with Miss de Courten, who chose to keep whatever special knowledge she might possess quite private. Soon, she would feign tiredness, and escort them all to the door. Moments after, Sebastien would be re-admitted by the servants' entrance, and he and the lady would see to each other's needs. He would give her a ring tonight, for her safety, if she would wear it.

An amicable arrangement.

—⋘—

Sebastien's instincts had not deserted him. When he returned, replete, in the small hours of the morning, a light burned in the parlor window and two bay horses slumbered on three legs apiece before the coach stopped in the street. The coachman—no doubt—slept as well, bundled up inside.

The front door was locked. Sebastien understood it to mean that the household had gone to bed, and though he had a key, he thought perhaps his guest had waited enough.

Sebastien took himself through the garden gate and into the walled yard of the red brick rowhouse. In the one-room cottage a light burned as well. Though the windows were boarded, Sebastien could see it because the door stood ajar. He did not mind the winter cold, nor would Epaphras.

Sebastien pushed the panel open with his fingertips.

Epaphras Bull was not a tall man, as Sebastien had been once, before elapsing centuries had grown men taller. He was slight, finer-boned than Jack, with a priest's delicacy of touch. He lay on the never-used couch, his elegant knobby fingers steepled over his breast, a powdery cat's eye sapphire blinking in soft gold from his left hand. His mouse-blond hair was swept back from a brow pale as skimmed milk.

He smiled faintly when Sebastien closed the door.

When Sebastien paused, Epaphras swung his feet around and sat up, then rose with coltish grace. Opened, his eyes were arresting, the irises ice-blue and thinly ringed with indigo. An admission of superficiality: it was those eerie eyes that had first captured Sebastien's interest, two hundred and fifty years since. That, and the provocation of corrupting the innocent and hypocritical, which had amused him more in those days.

Epaphras had been a Puritan. Now he wore rich linen, a dove-colored silk brocade waistcoat crossed by a platinum chain, a silver and burgundy cravat pinned with another sapphire, and a woolen suit of meticulous cut and press. He watched Sebastien latch the door, and picked a speck of lint from his cuff. "Sebastien," he said.

"John Nast. Are you still Epaphras?" It seemed unlikely. Too memorable a name.

"David." He glanced aside behind veiling lashes. When his tongue flicked over his lips, it left a sheen of moisture. Like Sebastien, he'd fed not long before.

"Beloved." It was the translation of the name. And what Sebastien had called him, once upon a time.

"There were giants in the earth in those days," he quipped, and laughed.

Sebastien felt his teeth sharpen with desire, but managed, "You wished an audience with me."

Icy eyes fixed on him, and this time didn't slip away.

Epaphras—*David*—twined the first two fingers of his left hand in the hair at his nape and half-winced, half-smiled. "This is your city now. The forms must be observed."

A debatable point. Boston was large enough that in Europe it would never be considered Sebastien's exclusive domain. But then, in Europe, there would be a half-dozen or more wampyr in a city this size, and courtiers might host a secret club, a gathering place and refuge for the convenience of travelers.

With so very few of the blood in the New World—if there were any others—they might in conscience invent the forms all over again. So, David owed Sebastien filial piety—if Sebastien chose to believe so.

Sebastien had crossed the room. He was the taller, but only by inches. He smelled the blood on David's breath.

"I've missed you." Either of them might have said it, but it was David's mouth that shaped the words. He picked a tawny hair from Sebastien's lapel and flicked it away, while Sebastien put a cold hand on his cold cheek. And then David's palm cupped Sebastien's nape and pulled him down.

The wetness of David's mouth confirmed recent feasting, and the sharpness of his teeth confirmed his desire. "Who invited you in, David?"

"Your courtesan," David answered, the breath he took only for speaking tickling Sebastien's mouth. "The boy. He told me I could not enter the house, but I could wait in the cottage. You spoil them."

"I spoiled you in your time," Sebastien answered. "You did not complain then. I trust you did nothing...untoward?"

David smiled. It crinkled the corners of his eyes and thinned his lips, and Sebastien jerked away, wrath like a brand in his chest. The predatory, possessive wrath of the blood, so much like lust as to seem identical. Jack's dalliance with Phoebe, he could accept.

A wampyr would be different.

David's hands clenched tight on Sebastien's upper arms, creasing the fabric of his coat. Sebastien could have torn free, but instead he drew up, glowering down his nose at David.

Passion filled him, terrible and sweet, a craving as fierce as ever. It was not something one could turn on a courtesan—that wanton cupidity—and expect him to live. But another wampyr was not prey, was not a courtesan. Another wampyr was an equal and a rival, though David might be less than a quarter Sebastien's age, and quite capable of surviving his unalloyed strength.

And of course David meant to evoke that fury. He delighted in Sebastien's jealousy and anger, and always had.

Sebastien wondered if David knew he hadn't touched another of his own kind since they parted company, more than a century before.

"Sebastien," the Englishman purred, hurt or feigning. "What would I have done? He wears your ring, my love."

"I don't trust you."

David's nails scratched Sebastien's neck, tracing the spine from skull to shoulders. Sebastien shivered.

"Don't trust me," David answered. "I need your goodwill. Use me." He turned his head aside, offered Sebastien his throat, his fingers curled and urging.

Whether he had the power to resist, he did not care to. Sebastien moaned and let his fangs slip into David's cool flesh as David clung against him. Then a twinned mouth was on his own neck, need-sharpness hot where the kiss was cold, the urgency sweet and rich as the old blood that filled Sebastien's mouth. David was a featherweight in his arms, a frail thing that smelled of citrus-musk and lilac cologne and filled him with a rasping, heated pulse. David stifled a sob against his throat, jaws working, lacerating Sebastien's skin as Sebastien bore them both down on the couch.

It would heal.

It would heal quite perfectly. And the sensation of the thick salvaged blood beating from his wounds into David's mouth as David knelt over him, his blond locks stuck willy-nilly between the clenching knuckles of Sebastien's hand—that was a passion worth anything.

—⋙—

Sebastien lay with closed eyes and listened to the silent, cool pressure on the couch, more an absence than a presence. It was as if a ghost lay down beside him. He knew without looking that David would be leaned on one elbow, studying Sebastian over the narrow bridge of his nose. "You left me," David said at last.

"You were angry company."

But the fingers that traced his brow and cheek were anything but angry. "I wasn't angry with you."

"No." David had been angry with the Church, the King, himself, the tissue of lies that he'd been raised on. But not with Sebastien, not except briefly and at first, when Sebastien had taught him that the desires David had been raised to consider anathema were not merely a matter of unconfessable groping in filthy alleys, of lewdness and whoring.

If pressed, Sebastien was certain he could summon up a list of fates worse than being Puritan and a fairy. And effeminate.

But it would take doing.

David had his reasons to be angry. But after a century or two, one did grow tired. Mortal lifetimes were a mercy to love, Sebastien thought. It could endure that long.

His lips brushed Sebastien's cheek. "I wasn't sure you'd see me."

"You sent a ring. You came alone. How else could I respond?"

His nose and lips brushed Sebastien's ear now. Lazily, Sebastien lifted one hand to stroke David's disheveled hair back into place. "You are not like the rest of us, Sebastien," he said. "It never pays to be too sure—"

"I was."

David's hand rested on Sebastien's shirtfront and cravat, over where his heart would have beat when he still lived. The pressure felt like a trap, suddenly, and Sebastien pulled away and stood, flicking his suitjacket straight with his thumbs.

"I was like the rest of you," he said. "I just grew old."

"And now you're the Moggy Molly of the bloodsucking set," David said, coolly, rolling onto his back with one arm cast languidly on the pillow sham. "Picking up half-starved tabbies from the gutter and carting them home to a teeming house."

It was a smarting double entendre, but Sebastien had the self-control not to return the serve. Epaphras had been one of those half-starved "tabbies," a runaway whore in a molly-house, who had had a flat choice between rotting of syphilis or accepting Sebastien's kiss. Which was the only reason Sebastien had considered making him immortal at all.

He hadn't done it since, though he'd been tempted. One Epaphras Bull in the world was enough.

With feigned patience, Sebastien said, "You need my goodwill. And what else?"

When he glanced over, David's eyes were closed, his pale tongue darting between pale lips.

"David," Sebastien said. The new name was already becoming habit. "This is not a game that amuses me. And you must leave. The sun—"

David's face contorted, but he rose and began to sort himself. He rolled a cigarette and lit it in the lamp, then spoke without meeting Sebastien's gaze. "I had thought to ask you to share resources. Until I become established."

The forms, the ring. The Old World etiquette of courtesy and hospitality among the blood.

Courtesy. And hospitality. "I have nothing to offer," Sebastien said. "My court is in New Amsterdam; I am only beginning to build a network here."

"And you maintain your eccentricities with regard to your pets. Moggy Molly."

"I do not keep pets. And this is not my house."

David snorted and shot his cuffs, the smoke curling from his cigarette. Sebastien found the scent revolting—but unlike food or drink, tobacco was a human pleasure the dead could yet enjoy. "If you love them so, make them wampyr."

Sebastien opened the door. His hand trembled like any human's, with spent passion and frustration. "It will be light soon."

"Of course," David said. He let his jeweled hand trail across Sebastien's breast as he passed. "The question remains, if you made them wampyr, would you love them still?"

When Sebastien let himself into the house—a quarter-hour before sunrise—Phoebe was drinking tea in the parlor. He had expected her to be abed.

"Jack?" he asked.

She gestured up the stairs with the backs of two fingers. "Done enough with hating you to sleep a little."

Sebastien winced. "He should—"

Her glare was as effective as a blow to the throat. "No, he should not. And if you are tempted to abandon him for his own good, or out of some misguided assumption as to the nature of our affair—his and mine, I mean—you should consider the traditional outcome of attempts to mastermind the lives of others."

He sat down heavily in the first convenient chair. "Duly noted."

She sipped her tea, and forgave as swiftly as she'd condemned. "Who was that person?"

His turn to reply with an arch expression and a raised brow. He dearly wished he could stomach drink. He'd never tasted tea—or coffee, for that matter: they were both far younger in the Western world than he—but it would have been comforting to have a cup to hide behind, as Mrs. Smith was hiding behind hers.

It was her house, and he was a guest. He owed her an answer.

"My child," he said, and waited for her to ask more.

But she was a New Englander. She just patted his hand with her warm one and nodded, as if she understood him perfectly in all his implications. And then she sat back in the lamplight, let her shoulders relax against the chair in a most unladylike fashion, and silently finished her tea.

A rattle of paper through the mail slot heralded the sunrise. "First post," Sebastien said, more to break the silence than because it needed saying, and forestalled Phoebe when she began to rise. Her skirts swished around her ankles as she settled back in her chair.

He collected the letters and would have presented them to her without examination, but the scent and writing on the topmost caught his attention. It was addressed to Mr. Nast, care of Mrs. Phoebe Smith, and he knew the particular black script very well. He might have expected a telegram in return from Abby Irene so quickly, but a letter would not have arrived from New Amsterdam since the previous evening.

He handed the rest of the mail to Phoebe and slit the envelope with his thumbnail.

Detective Crown Investigator Abigail Irene Garrett was, as her title implied, a wizard sworn in service to the English King. Her conscience and her loyalties were often in conflict, but Sebastien had no lingering doubts about her faithfulness. Nor did he overvalue it.

Her oath was to her king.

He snapped the single folded page open and held it up. A few lines required just a moment's attention.

Her oath *had been* to her king.

"Well," he said. "This may simplify matters. Abby Irene has resigned her commission."

And the gossiping mouths of Miss de Courten's salon had had the story right, in essence if not in detail, before Sebastien himself had any inkling.

It did not pay to underestimate the demimonde, and Sebastien should frankly know better.

"Does that mean you're going back to New Amsterdam?"

Sebastien wished he thought the wistful note in her voice was for himself as much as Jack. "We'll see," he said. He set the letter on a sideboard. "She says she's on her way to Boston. The letter is postmarked two days since, actually, so she may already have arrived."

"But why would she resign?"

"At a guess? Your king asked something of her that she could not accept."

"Oh," Phoebe said, and straightened her spectacles fussily before pouring herself another cup of tea. "Is there another possibility?"

"I am certain there are dozens," Sebastien said. Including one that he had no right to feel like a blow. Abby Irene might be leaving her post in America to go home to London and her dearly beloved prince now that he was no longer Phillip's heir.

"I'm going to go find a book," Sebastien said. "I'll see you again at lunchtime."

Sebastien did not dine, but he did enjoy joining his human friends for meals. Nevertheless, he became so engrossed in a tome of natural history that Phoebe had to ring for him. The bell must have awakened Jack, who joined them shortly.

Either the sleep had benefited Jack or he was determined out of sheer perversity to be pleasant. When he stumbled downstairs, dressed but still blinking sleepily, he seemed genuinely contented by the news that Abby Irene would send to them when she arrived. He didn't ask about Epaphras, even when Sebastien praised Jack for his handling of the other wampyr.

Perhaps it was an effective strategy, because Sebastien found himself volunteering more information than he might have if Jack had pressed. Or perhaps, Sebastien thought, Jack's lack of jealousy was a symptom of growing older, and needing—and wanting—Sebastien less.

Eventually, protégés—whether human or of the blood—grew independent if they were worth having in the first place. David was proof of that.

Abby Irene's second letter, mailed that day from Cambridge, came with the afternoon post.

—⟡—

Sebastien had been hoping for a solid day-long rain that would make travel a reasonable risk. Instead, the day held clear and bright until change-of-weather clouds mackerel-streaked the sunset. It was evening before he dared leave the house. Summer was coming, the days lengthening, and his increasing confinement made him restless.

Abby Irene was ensconced in a good but not extravagant hotel in the Back Bay—not far, Sebastien noted with a share of amusement for synchronicity's sake, from the residence of that murdered boy.

His carriage pulled under the portico some half hour after sunset. He disembarked and paid the driver, a few shillings extra ensuring the man would wait. The doorman smiled and stood aside to let him enter.

He presented himself at the desk, expecting to be made to wait, but Abby Irene had placed his assumed name on the list as her solicitor, and he was shown up. The bellman winked knowingly. Sebastien pretended not to have seen.

A tidy rap on the door provoked a prompt response: the barking of a small dog. Abby Irene unlatched the door as if she had been waiting—with a sorceress, you never could tell: she might have been—and stood aside to allow Sebastien in. He tipped the bellman, stepped over Mike the terrier—who danced like an animated dust-mop underfoot—and waited while Abby Irene shot the bolt behind him.

Their parting had been sudden. He was not at all certain how he should approach her, and so he tousled Mike's ears briefly and waited for her to provide a hint.

"Mr. Nast," she said, and he couldn't tell if it was wry or derisive. She was an imposing beautiful woman of perhaps half a century, her straight blond hair cut to fall around her face like a boy's. He paused for a moment to appreciate her, watching the flush climb her cheeks, and folded his arms.

"Forgive me?" he said, because it was rarely the wrong thing. It was a very typical hotel room, complete with drapes thrown wide over six-paned windows. Sebastien noticed the unobtrusive door to another chamber, which might mean that Abby Irene had brought her housekeeper as a traveling companion.

"If you'll forgive me," she answered, and touched his arm.

One always lost them, this way or that. "You're going back to London?"

Her smile was a flicker, gone as it appeared. "I hadn't planned on it. But I can't protect you any more, Sebastien. I—"

"Your King asked you to lie to protect his brother?"

"His brother? Sebastien, you can be too polite. The love of my life. Although I suppose I knew he would have to take Richard's side in the end."

Richard was the Duke of New Amsterdam. And another of her con-
quests, among whom Sebastien was pleased to number himself.

"You swore an oath to your king."

"The oath goes with the office," she said. She brushed past him and
slipped a wand out of her sleeve, which she dropped back into her insepara-
ble carpetbag. A glass beside it was full of ice and the gin and lime she smelled
of. She swirled the drink to make the contents clink. "I need your help,
Sebastien."

"Tell me," he said.

She gulped gin, three long thoughtful swallows, and cupped the glass before her breasts. There was an inch of liquor left. He took it from her hands,
returned it to its place beside the carpet bag, and pushed her hair behind
her ear. She shivered when his finger brushed her throat, and then she
laughed like a fox crying in a trap.

Sebastien cupped her shoulder, but it would have been a breach of her
dignity to pull her close just then.

"I'm thinking of going into private practice," she said.

"Do you need an investor?" After centuries of existence, he had money.
Nothing but, it sometimes seemed.

"No," she said. "But I could use some business advice. How does one
go about becoming a consulting detective, anyway?"

He stayed with her for hours. She offered herself, but when he kissed her
mouth and confessed himself quite satisfied, she did not ask for details of
where he had been or with whom. Abby Irene, like Phoebe, was a grown
and experienced woman. Sebastien was old enough to appreciate a mini-
mum of histrionics, and her living warmth was comforting when she curled
against his chest, nursing another drink. "You could stay with me," he offered, and she shook her head and didn't answer.

He understood. She wasn't anybody's pet. Not that David—or the rest
of the blood—could be expected to understand that.

Reminded, he lifted his hips and dug in his pocket. Sleepily, she complained, but then he caught her hand and slipped the ring onto her middle
finger after testing two others. "Sebastien?"

"Please wear it." He folded her fingers closed.

She thought about that, examined the garnet glowing in the gaslight,
and said, "I'll keep it if you tell me why."

He was silent so long she shifted against him and poked him in the ribs with an elbow. "Sebastien."

"Someone I knew in Europe has come to Boston," he said unwillingly. "I don't know what he's running from, but I suspect he's looking for me. That ring is merely a mark of my regard."

"Someone. Someone like Jack or me? Someone you left?"

"David is the name he uses now. One of the blood."

"Oh." She breathed steadily; he closed his eyes and listened. "And you don't trust him," she said.

"I trust him to follow the rules as they are writ. The letter and not the intention. Wear the ring."

"You think he wants to hurt you."

"It's what we do," Sebastien admitted, after a moment's thought. He allowed himself the affectation of a sigh. "He carries too much hatred for himself to entirely thank me for keeping him from true death. I hoped he might...reconcile his contradictions, given time, and find some peace."

She jerked forward and turned over her shoulder to stare at him, her hair breaking into locks against her neck. "You turned him against his will?"

"He begged me," Sebastien said. This time, he did tug her back into his embrace and after a moment, she permitted. "He was more afraid to die—"

"Perhaps," she said, "you'd better start at the beginning."

One portentous sigh was enough in any conversation. He contented himself with stroking her hair. Mike jumped up on the sofa beside them and flopped against her thigh. Abby Irene, who spoiled the dog shamelessly, scratched behind his ears.

"He was a whore when I met him," Sebastien said. "A boy whore, and I don't know if he ran away from home or if his family cast him out for who he was. He had told me various versions of the story, which I suspect are all lies. He is...an inveterate liar. But I am certain of a few things: his family were Puritan, and he believed very strongly in his stern and uncompromising God. The earth was a vale of tears, and the only reward was in the afterlife. But you see, David—his name was Epaphras then—was what they called then a Ganymede. A lover of men."

"A sodomite, you mean."

Sebastian nodded. Abby Irene leaned her hair against his cheek to feel the movement. "He was dying. Syphilis. And he was more afraid of Hell than of living...unliving...a sinner. Or, as he said to me then, it is not as if God could damn him twice."

"You still care for him."

Sebastien's hand paused on her hair, and he didn't notice it until she rubbed into his palm to encourage him to continue. "I still *covet* him," he said. "I would consider that somewhat different."

"You tried to save him."

He shook his head. It took some care to stay gentle. "I was already old enough to understand the futility of that. I tried to…give him a chance to save himself. But he…."

How could you explain it?

Abby Irene said, slowly, "If God wouldn't make your David pay for his sins, then David would have to see to it himself?"

"He was just as unforgiving of others. He has no more care for his courtesans than for himself. And yet he had the gall to ask me for an introduction to my court."

"You said no?"

"Of course I did," Sebastien answered. "He'll manage. You know he's still whoring? He never stopped."

"But how can a wampyr—"

"Easily enough," Sebastien said. "He doesn't sell sex, Abby Irene. He sells his kiss, the pleasure of it, to mortals who have grown fond of a wampyr's embrace."

Three days later, Sebastien handed the morning paper unread across the breakfast table to Jack before slitting open a letter from Abby Irene which had arrived in the same post.

Whatever Jack read displeased him. He folded the paper with a snap and dropped it beside his chair, mindful of Phoebe's tablecloth. Phoebe herself entered from the kitchen with a plate of biscuits and eggs balanced atop a pot of tea. She distributed her burden as Jack jumped up to seat her.

Sebastien, engrossed in the letter, pretending oblivion to the little drama until Jack—reseated—served himself breakfast. Phoebe poured the tea. "I hope I didn't end a conversation."

"Not at all," Sebastien said, without looking up. There was no plate or cup before him, of course. He rested the letter in the clear space. "Jack was just trying to prevent me finding out about the second murder."

Phoebe widened her eyes at Jack over the rim of her cup. Jack's fork rattled the plate. "Sebastien—"

Sebastien flicked the ivory laid with a fingernail. "Abby Irene sends rather more details than that yellowing rag has been entrusted with," he said.

"How does *she* know?"

Sebastien permitted himself a rather less pleasant smile than was his wont, and immediately regretted it. David did not bring out the better side of his personality, the humane mask he aspired to. "She's consulting on the investigation. Commencing last night."

"Sebastien—"

"I know I can't." He was in comfortless hiding in Boston because Duke Richard had attempted to use him to extort cooperation from her. While recent events made his position less precarious, he had no doubt that Richard would find a way to threaten him if it became convenient again. "You are aware, young man, that I have managed to keep successfully ahead of the axeman for several centuries without your assistance?"

It might have been unnecessarily sharp. Jack set great store by Sebastien's presumed need for him, and Sebastien normally permitted the illusion.

Silently, Jack picked up his fork again and began pushing eggs around the plate. Sebastien poked the letter with a forefinger. "That doesn't stop me from helping Abby Irene, however. And I am troubled by a second death so soon."

Jack sipped tea and relented, a flirty glance upwards: just the sort of thing that got them dubious looks in public. "And you're bored."

"Undeath is long," Sebastien said, with a shrug.

Jack steepled his delicate hands. "I know some who could put you to work."

"I wish you wouldn't play at politics," Sebastien answered. He wouldn't stop Jack if he wanted to run with Free Irish agitators or Home Rule terrorists. But he hated that his friend took risks over something as ephemeral as a border or a King when they would all change eventually.

However, Sebastien was honest enough to admit that when one had a bare seventy years in which to seek results, such things no doubt took on a greater urgency.

"Phoebe, would you object to Abby Irene coming here?"

"One of your paramours?" Jack might have forgiven him, then, but she hadn't quite, not yet.

"If you insist on having it so, then yes."

She broke her biscuit with her fingertips, quick squirrel-like gestures. He watched the light flashing in the trillion garnet and waited until she nodded.

"I shall think of it as an opportunity to observe an investigation in progress," she said. "Surely the sort of thing a novelist should cultivate."

Sebastien returned a letter in the midmorning post, and Abigail Irene presented herself at Mrs. Smith's door slightly before tea time. She was exquisitely starched and pressed, all the lace on her navy corduroy falling perfectly. As presentation was never a strength, Sebastien surmised both a degree of nervousness and the capable hand of Mary behind the outbreak of tidiness.

Jack took her coat, and Sebastien introduced her to Phoebe, and everyone ignored the profusion of garnet and silver bands with a correctness as exquisite as Abby Irene's dress. When they were all seated stiffly in the parlor, Phoebe fetched tea and sandwiches for everyone who dined. Jack refused cream in his tea, eyeing the chicken sandwiches, and meanwhile Abigail Irene wasted no time in sliding a slender isinglass portfolio from the depths of the omnipresent blue velvet carpet bag and laying it before Sebastien.

"More than you ever cared to know about the illicit trade in young men and women in Boston," she said, and dryly continued, "I detect a certain unevenness to my welcome from the Metropolitan Police that leads me to speculate on the existence of a political struggle within the department."

Boston, for all its age—as America's young cities went, one of the oldest—had been English since its inception. Unlike New Amsterdam's juryrigged system, the police authority here operated on the London model, with patrol and investigative units reporting to sergeants, lieutenants, and eventually the chief. An orderly system, with authority and responsibility clearly delineated and its exercisers ranked like tiers of angels.

"There always is," Sebastien said, and only became aware of the patent irritation in his own voice when Jack grinned fondly. Sebastien tipped his head, acknowledging just mockery, and some of the tension left him.

Jack would forgive.

He cleared his throat and continued, "It affects the investigation, I take it?"

"Indubitably." Abby Irene fussed with the silver sugar tongs, a sapphire glittering in her lobe, behind her hair. "The victims are not common tavern prostitutes. They were comfortably maintained."

"So someone is providing that maintenance," Jack said.

"Someone of money. And influence. Yes."

"Somebody who would have friends in the police department," Sebastien finished, not too shy to state the obvious. "You think the higher echelons of police are protecting the clients?"

"Or the killer," Abby Irene said. "There's a detective inspector—a Byron Pyle, of all the unlikely names—who's grateful for my help. But I'm not sure how well he'll resist pressure from above, if that's where it's coming from." She shrugged, but Sebastien saw the lines of bitterness around her mouth. "There are a number of political appointees at the top of the organization, as you might expect. Including the Colonial Governor's son. Imaginatively named Michael Penfold, Jr." She laughed unhappily. "And one of Richard's brothers-in-law, if you can imagine. His sister married into Boston money."

"Not everyone has your devotion to duty," Jack said.

Abby Irene glanced at him, surprised by his kindness. And paused, her cup to her lips. "Boston is an Irish stronghold in the Americas, is it not?"

Phoebe leaned forward to speak. "Famous for it."

Sebastien nodded. "Are both the boys Irish? You're thinking of the paddereen."

"Yes," Jack said. "According to the newspaper. Although I wish you wouldn't call them boys. They were my age, near enough."

"Young men," Phoebe corrected. Sebastien wished he could read the glance that passed between her and Abby Irene. "Are you thinking, gentlemen, that the victims were murdered to silence them?"

"Irishness could be a coincidence," Sebastien said. "There could be a dozen reasons they were killed. To silence them, yes; to punish their...protectors; because they were extorting those protectors; because they were the bait in a blackmail scheme. It could be a consortium of jealous wives. For all I know."

Phoebe set her cup down. Jack touched her arm lightly, and Abby Irene noticed, but her face gave away nothing. "I have a sense you could go on," the authoress said.

Sebastien smiled back. "Indefinitely."

"There's another prospect," Abby Irene said, when the silence had lingered a moment. "It's rare, but it happens. The possibility exists that somebody is hunting highly-paid male courtesans. For the thrill of it."

"I'll need to see the murder scenes," Sebastien said.

"We'll go tonight," Abby Irene answered, and neither of them looked at Jack, who sat twisting his napkin in his hands.

—❦—

After tea, while Sebastien sat paging through onionskin sheets covered with Abigail Irene's shorthand scrawl, she came to him and settled in a chintz-covered chair. "Richard's wife is divorcing him," she said. "On grounds of infidelity."

"He'll lose the duchy." Richard only held the position through Jacqueline. Her sister's son would inherit.

Abby Irene nodded. Under her powder, color rose across her cheeks. "I resigned for nothing."

"You resigned on a point of honor." Sebastien set the folder aside. It wasn't telling him anything he could not have guessed, and he agreed with Abby Irene's instinct that information was being withheld. He wished he could interview this Detective Inspector Pyle. "And he'd already put the matter before your king."

He watched indirectly, but carefully. Her shoulders eased as she breathed in and out, once each with great concentration. "If only Henry had been the older brother," she said, with an air of bitterness he thought unlike her. And then her hand flew to her mouth, and she pressed the knuckles against her teeth, jaw working as if she bit down.

It was treason, what she'd just said.

"What else was in the telegram?" he asked. "Richard wants you back?"

"He offered to marry me," she said. And dismissed it with a flip of her hand, as beneath even consideration. "I'm afraid I know him rather too well for that."

Despite himself, Sebastien laughed, and caught her hand when she dropped it from her mouth. "Then what will you do?"

"It's too soon to tell," she said. He felt the tendons working as she made a fist in the blue corduroy of her skirt. And he felt her start, as well, at the toll of the doorbell.

Sebastien glanced at the window. The sun was below the horizon, he judged, though the sky still shone pewter and indigo. He stood, giving Abby Irene one last pat, and went to the door with a good idea who he might find.

Jack was on the stairs by the time he turned the latch, and Abby Irene had risen from the chair, her wand half-concealed in her hand. She nodded when Sebastien caught her eye; Jack merely stood relaxed and ready for whatever might follow. Phoebe was nowhere to be seen.

"Hello, David," he said to the man on the stoop.

"Hello." David leaned on a rosewood walking stick, his shoulders contracted under the dove-gray jacket. "Since you're not going to invite me in, will you come out?"

"I have a date tonight," Sebastien said.

David slipped an engraved watch from his pocket and consulted it, glanced at Sebastien, bit his lower lip, and consulted it again. "As it happens, so do I. Am I to presume that conferring on the stoop with wampyr might be the sort of thing that is not done among Bostonians?"

"You might," Sebastien said. He glanced over his shoulder; Abby Irene returned a small ironic smile, and he wasn't about to argue in front of David. He was not meant to hear Abigail Irene whisper in Jack's ear, "Are we *all* blond?"

Or Jack's murmured answer. "Evie was dark."

David, of course, heard it too, and he knew perfectly well who Evie had been. And that Evie had chosen to burn. Sebastien read it in his smirk. Irritated, but unwilling to admit it, he stepped outside and jerked the door shut, hearing it latch.

He was hatless, bereft of a walking stick, without an overcoat—not that the cold could bother him, but remaining unremarked was a chief strategy of the blood. David's smirk widened, dripping mockery; Sebastien descended the steps, took David's elbow, and pulled him around on his heels. "All right. Walk with me," he said, propelling David forward.

David did not stagger, but paced him comfortably, giving no appearance of haste. Sebastien listened, but did not hear the door open behind him. So they had *some* sense, contrary to other evidence.

The two wampyr had gone half a block before David said, "If you want me to beg, Sebastien, I'll do it."

A typically cryptic comment, hurtling over layers of dialogue. Fortunately, though Sebastien was no longer habituated to David's conversational leaps, he recalled their management. "You want my protection."

"It's your city," David said. "I'm within my rights to ask."

It's not mine, Sebastien thought, but caution kept him from a too-facile denial. To refuse to acknowledge power could be as deadly as claiming it unwarranted. Instead he asked, "What do you need protecting from?"

David shrugged. "I left my share of enemies in the old world. It's not inconceivable that one followed."

"Surely, you know who you fled."

David stepped away, tugging the smooth wool of his coat sleeve through Sebastien's fingers. Sebastien could have held on, but he would have torn the fabric to do so. "What makes you think I fled someone?" Faced with Sebastien's brow-arched stare, he frowned and dropped his gaze. "Or that if I fled someone, that's who pursued me?"

The politics of the blood were complex and prickly and devoted to predator games of rank and status, bared fangs and bared throats.

Sebastien was old enough and wily enough, overall, that they need not ever touch him. The others would treat him as a mad old moneyed uncle, and if he caused no offense they would offer him no challenge. And here in America, until today, his isolation had been a protection of its own.

But David had no such protection. And being what he was, he could scarcely avoid offering offense. Sebastien shook his head. "Or that whoever pursued may be slaughtering boy whores as a message to you?"

He said it harshly, without warning, his eyes on David's face. David's flinch was hard and certain. His stride checked, and he rounded on Sebastien. "I beg your pardon?"

"Read the papers," Sebastien said. He could have reached out and taken David's arm again. Instead, he thrust his fist into his pocket and leaned back, from the hips. The street was cold, the cobbles growing slick, the granite pavements gray and hard. Few walked the streets, and the only one close was a lamplighter with his chin sunk deep in his collar. "There's no telling what you might learn."

— ❧ —

They were furious with him, of course. Phoebe shut the door in his face, proof of Jack's wrath. But he had a key, and slipping the lock would have been no challenge if he hadn't; Sebastien merely let himself in the back. Once you've permitted the devil across your threshold, it's not so easy to invite him out again.

And she wasn't actually angry enough to come at him with a fireplace poker. It had been more a gesture than an assault, and when he rejoined the group in the parlor, only Abby Irene looked up. "Are we ready, then?"

Sebastien nodded, not trusting his voice. Despite skirts and corsetry, she rose with grace. Her carpetbag rested on the side table. She slid her wand back in as he watched. "Right then, we'll be back before daylight. Thank you for the tea, Mrs. Smith. Goodnight, Jack."

Phoebe stood to show them out. Jack rose beside her. Before they came to the end of the hall, though, Sebastien checked and waited for them to turn to him.

Something must be understood. He cleared his throat like a nervous human and said, "These things, I must manage on my own, Jack. I'm sorry."

Jack nodded. "Of course you must. The return of the prodigal."

His choice of words, and the sideways flicker of his eyes, gave him away. Sebastien brushed his sleeve, and Jack looked up, meeting his eyes—a dangerous thing to do, when confronted with one of the blood, but Jack and Sebastien both knew this particular wampyr was more tame than not. "Your inheritance is secure," Sebastien said gently. "And jealousy doesn't become you. I cannot appear so frail as to require the assistance of my court for a simple conversation with my own creation."

This was the reason wampyr did not grant their courtesans autonomy, or agency. It was simpler to keep cattle, slaves, servants—with no thought for them beyond maintaining them in health—than to build relationships with one's courtiers. And it hurt less, when the inevitable end came, to lose a servant than a friend.

"Do you think it's Epaphras doing the killing?" Jack asked, right there in front of the other two, and Sebastien knew he was outnumbered.

"David," Sebastien said. He glanced at his fingernails, dull half-moons of dead chitin, sanded smooth along the edge. "I don't know."

He felt the humans staring. He looked up, met their eyes, each in turn. None of the three looked down, and Phoebe took a slight step toward him. "I don't." He shook his head. "But I will. I promise you."

Abby Irene broke the silence. "Shall we see where these young men died?"

Sebastien went with her, in silent gratitude.

—⁂—

They had some trouble entering the room—Abby Irene's official standing was lost to her, and the Boston patrolman assigned to guard the scene did not at first believe in the authority—or perhaps even the existence—of a woman claiming to be a consulting detective, but Sebastien's air of command cowed him. The intercession won him no points with Abby Irene, to judge by her sniff and the stiffness with which she set her carpet bag down inside the door. Or perhaps she was merely as displeased as Sebastien by the damage that had already been inflicted upon the scene.

The body had been removed, the bloodstained bedding stripped from a brown and sticky mattress. Abby Irene's nose wrinkled; Sebastien imagined she was grateful for the chill that pervaded the fireless room, minimizing the presence of flies and stench. By now there might have been maggots, in summer.

"Not a wampyr," Abby Irene said, settling her navy kidskin gloves finger by finger. "Even if one killed, it would not waste so much blood."

"'Yet who would have thought the old man to have had so much blood in him?'" Sebastien quoted softly, to see her smile. But she frowned, only, at the stained bed. "Still, it could be one of the blood. Those who kill, when it is not from desperation—they kill for pleasure, yes? There is no need, when the prey is willing."

"And some prefer unwilling prey?"

"Some do," Sebastien admitted. "Do you think a whore could be paid for blood?"

Her glance said, *yes, of course*. Just as a wampyr could be paid for the pleasure he could bring a mortal lover—paid in money as well as blood. "No one would sell *that*," she said. And then she reconsidered. "No, someone might just, mightn't they? If they needed the money badly enough to die for it?"

"So," Sebastien said, "what sort of monster eats rentboys?"

Abby Irene did not answer immediately. She paced the room, as if measuring dimensions. She selected her wand, and a silver dagger, and a glass rod, and cast circles and muttered and did things with mingled salt and ash. She poured water from a crystal flask into a silver chalice and made passes over it, while Sebastien stood, hands folded, calmly keeping one eye on the unwinding of the clock.

After an hour and a half, she approached the window and threw the shutters wide. Sebastien knew better than to interrupt as she leaned out, breathing the chill. It wasn't good to disturb her when her brain was working.

"I'm not sure it was a monster at all," she said at last. "Or even in any wise magical. I may be here under false pretenses."

"You're not a Crown Investigator any longer," Sebastien reminded her gently. "Your jurisdiction extends to anything that takes your fancy."

"And that they'll pay me for." It might have been said bitterly. He wasn't sure.

She turned to him and scanned the room. "Stand against the wall again, please. I'm going to make one final check for magical residue. And then, when I find nothing—"

"You bow to my deductive skills?"

That netted him a sharply arched eyebrow. "Do you suppose anyone has claimed the bodies yet?"

—⁂—

No one had.

Both murdered men had been brought to the same mortuary, where they lay awaiting either their next of kin, or burial at the expense of their estates, which had been placed in escrow. They were far from the only bodies arranged in drawers and on marble slabs; the chill of the room lessened the stink somewhat, but Sebastien could see from Abby Irene's expression that the wretchedness of rot and cloying blood was apparent even to her merely mortal senses.

The morgue attendant was disinterested, and *he* was willing to accept Abby Irene's credentials. She had a signed writ from the chief homicide detective of the Metropolitan police—and, she explained to Sebastien, a verbal caution that it would not carry much water with the Chief Inspector, who seemed to prefer the murders handled quietly and with little publicity. Sebastien's suspicion of departmental politics and a white-wash were thus uncomfortably supported.

The bodies were slashed and disfigured, throats cut and faces, hands, torsos, buttocks, and thighs sliced open like badly butchered beef. Their investigation confirmed Abby Irene's suspicions: no trace of magic remained on either corpse, and there was no sign Sebastien could detect that a wampyr had been at them before death, for which he at least contemplated a silent sigh of relief, even if he did not breathe one.

"Well," Abby Irene said—tugging the stained sheet over the second boy smooth, tucking it about his shoulders with nervous darting gestures, "if we could identify a suspect, we could see if the corpses bleed at his touch. If a judge will still accept my sworn word as a sorcerer as evidence."

"Is there a reason one wouldn't?"

"I haven't been defrocked," she said. She touched the cloth over the dead man's slashed throat and drew her hand quickly to the side, as if considering force and angle.

"His throat was cut from behind," Sebastien said. He'd noticed the slope of the wound from deep to shallow, as well. "Or by a left-handed assailant."

Abby Irene twisted her hands together and glared doubtfully at the shroud. "How squeamish are you, 'Mr. Nast'?"

The question shocked him into inappropriate laughter, but after a moment's stare, the implications of her question sank in, and she laughed as well. "Not particularly, I take it? Good then. Help me roll this young man over." She rummaged in her bag, and while Sebastien stripped down the sheet again she drew forth a pair of rubberized gloves and various arcane implements: balls of cotton, forceps, covered watch-glasses and the like.

Even on second viewing, the deep bloodless gashes in his flanks and thighs resembled an inept butcher's work. He understood her intent quite plainly. "You think he may have been raped?"

"I think the murderer may have been a…a *trick*," she said. "And if he left behind any traces, then we can prove that both murders were committed by the same person."

"These weren't streetwalkers," Sebastien said. "They had a limited— and exclusive—clientele."

"Indeed. I don't suppose we know anyone who we could ask about their patrons?"

Carefully, impersonally, Sebastien rolled the body onto its stomach, avoiding the worst of the wounds. "Yes," he said. "As a matter of fact, we do."

Sebastien delivered Abby Irene to her hotel and returned to Phoebe's house before sunrise, where he found Jack at the table, either risen early or waiting up. The morning newspaper sat unfolded on the table before him, heedless of Phoebe's white linens.

The headline justified the carelessness.

It read, quite simply, *WAR.*

"Oh," Sebastien said, and sat down beside him.

"I tailed Epaphras last night," Jack said. "While you were out with Lady Abigail Irene."

Sebastien hid a frown with his hand. Yes, she wasn't D.C.I. Garrett any longer, was she? "I wish you'd be more careful."

"And huddle like a rabbit from the shadow of a hawk?"

It wasn't the force of Jack's stare that set Sebastien back in his chair, but it certainly felt like it. "If that's the metaphor that pleases you."

Jack turned his cup on the saucer, one fingertip on the peaked handle. "I know better than the others what's at risk," he said. "But you need to know what dangers he's brought down on you, Sebastien, and if he won't tell you and you won't force the issue, someone needs to find out *for* you."

"And what did you learn?" Sebastien put a hand on Jack's to still him. Jack glanced up, blue eyes quite brilliant in his pallid face.

"Nothing," Jack said. "Nothing useful. He is staying in a pleasant enough rooming house; he had joined a gentleman's club. He did nothing untoward, I noticed no-one else observing him, and he met no one who might have been a courtesan." He shrugged. "I'll try again tonight."

"Be careful," Sebastien said, because it was all he could say. He could forbid Jack, of course.

But Jack would not obey. Any more than he would obey Sebastien if Sebastien asked him to stay out of the kind of pubs where armchair revolutionaries congregated.

He stood, scraped the chair back, and leaned over the table to kiss Sebastien on the mouth. Sebastien let him, hands flat on the ink-marked tablecloth, and stretched without rising to kiss him back. Jack's lips were wet, warm, flavored with the unpleasant herbal pungency of tea and the nauseating sweetness of sugar. "I always am," Jack said, and patted Sebastien's shoulder before he went upstairs to bed.

It wasn't difficult to discover where the courtesan in the domino mask lived: not far from the two murdered boys, which was as Sebastien would have wagered. He presented himself at the servant's door slightly after sunset, when he expected she would still be at home. Of course, if he missed her, there was always the salon for a second chance, but he'd prefer to speak first in private.

His knock apparently startled the scullery maid, but a good suit and a silver-headed cane opened many doors, including this one. And if she seemed inclined to shut it in his face again quite promptly, a silver shilling slipped into her hand with his visiting card corrected the matter. "I must speak with Madame," he said, and doffed his hat as if to a lady.

She shut the door after all, and left him on the cold stoop beside the rubbish bin, but she gave him a smile before she did and really, given his irregular approach, he could expect no better. When she returned, no less than five minutes later, a stout valet followed.

Sebastien did not doubt that the strapping young man had concealed a sap in the sagging pocket of his suitjacket. It would only be sensible.

They conducted him inside with a silent efficiency, and showed him into a sort of study. Velvet draperies of an off-white color that Sebastien associated with the interior of coffins, burgundy burned-velvet wall coverings, and too much dark wood gave it a claustrophobic aspect.

Sebastien recognized the rangy, beaky man within. He was perhaps thirty-three, thirty-five. His eyes were lined with kohl, his cheeks rouged, his forehead pale with powder. But he wore a dark worsted suit, a good waistcoat crossed with a platinum chain, and his hair was cropped quite short and oiled back from a razor-line part. He moved painfully, as if he had been sitting too long and he stretched against the stiffness of his muscles.

The valet seemed inclined to linger, but Sebastien's host—or hostess—gestured him to shut the door with one commandingly whirled finger. "Roger Abernathy," Sebastien said pleasantly, and extended his hand in its glove.

"Mr. John Nast," he said. "You have tracked me to my lair. Dare I ask your business?"

His breath smelled faintly of blood, as from a bitten cheek. His handshake was quite firm, masculine, but not so the delicate squeeze before he disengaged. Meant to be shocking—or alluring—but Sebastien was too old to be shocked, and he had already been allured. After a fashion. "I need a list of clients," he said.

"Is that a test?" With graceful assurance, Mr. Abernathy gestured Sebastien into a chair. He limped only slightly as he crossed and recrossed the room to pour brandies and set one at Sebastien's elbow, where Sebastien calmly ignored it. "I would never reveal the name of an intimate friend."

"Your intimate friends," Sebastien said, "have special needs, do they not?"

Abernathy swirled the amber liquid in his glass, making every appearance of savoring the aroma. When he tasted it, he left a stain of lipstick on the rim. "Do you wish to become one of them?"

"Oh no." Sebastien lifted his own brandy glass in turn. "I have special needs of my own, you see." At Abernathy's arched eyebrow, he felt the need to reassure. Sebastien did, after all, find him quite attractive.

In both his guises.

He continued, "And we might discuss them another day, but I would prefer to first become much better acquainted. No, I am not interested in your clients. But rather those of two young men who have recently come to the attention of the police."

Abernathy's moue was perfect. "Come to their attention in what manner, Mr. Nast?"

"Messily," Sebastien said, and set his brandy down. "And I am very much afraid they will not be the last. Will you help me...Chouchou?"

For a moment, Sebastien thought he'd succeeded. Mr. Abernathy reached out and stroked a fountain pen that rested diagonally across his desk blotter. And then he quaffed his brandy and shut his eyes to shake his head, wincing as if the alcohol stung more than it burned. "No."

Sebastien suddenly understood the why and wherefore of the paint and powder worn in addition to—in spite of—the male dress. "He struck you," he said.

Abernathy licked his lips and put the glass down on the blotter. "I don't take your meaning, Mr. Nast."

"Michael Penfold," Sebastien said. "The Governor of the Colony of Massachusetts. Your protector." As polite a term as he could summon up on such short notice. "He struck you. Your face is bruised beneath the maquillage. Your cheek is cut from your teeth."

Roger Abernathy smiled. "Michael would never strike me," he said, but Sebastien noticed that he pressed the backs of left fingers to his cheek, the amethyst glinting heavily. "Is there anything else I can assist you with?"

He said it suggestively, leaning forward. Sebastien stood, leaving behind his untouched glass. "Yes," he said. "Be cautious, please. I should hate to lose the pleasure of your conversation."

—⁓—

He did not remember mortal life clearly when he remembered it at all, but Sebastien was fairly certain that even then, he'd thought better on his feet. By the time he left Chouchou, a cold misty rain was falling over Boston, and he decided a stroll was the order of the evening.

At first he was surprised by the number of people on the street, walking in groups, entering taverns and coffeehouses. Jack's morning paper had held the explanation, though: in time of war and fear, people clung to one another, shared news and gossip…

…and plotted, he suspected. Jack would be in his taverns before the day was out, the dens of Irish and Home Rule agitators. A Crusade and a conquest or two had cured Sebastien of causes—but Jack had an affinity for them, the more doomed the better. At least, if the streets were full of whispering conspirators and revolutionaries, it would serve as a distraction for a police force whose leaders might be disinclined to trust the direction of Sebastien and Abby Irene's investigation.

As was becoming habit, Sebastien returned to Mrs. Smith's house before sunrise to find Jack waiting up. Not alone this time, however: the entire household was awake, and Sebastien thought the others seemed peaked. Abby Irene looked more her age than usual; Phoebe's hair had escaped its habitual knot and framed her face in frost-pale whorls; and Jack seemed thin. Relationships with the blood put a strain on mortal partners, and though Sebastien tried to spread the burden, he worried.

Especially about Jack.

"The man I am most interested in is Michael Penfold," Sebastien said, dropping into the lone empty chair. "This may present…insurmountable difficulties."

A silence, as those difficulties were considered, was his answer. "You're certain the Governor is the murderer?" Abby Irene would rather he said, "no." Her face gave that much away.

In that, he could oblige her. "No."

"But you have evidence?"

"No," he said again.

"I've been informed that I am to discontinue my investigation," Abby Irene said. "Detective Inspector Pyle seemed most unchuffed to deliver the news." She sat back in her chair, and Jack, beside her, crossed his arms.

With a sigh, Phoebe rose to refill the teapot. "Carry on," she said. "I can hear you from the kitchen."

Abby Irene couldn't quite keep the amusement from her voice. "In the absence of evidence or certainty, I would suggest that your instincts, Sebastien, are nevertheless rather good. Whatever pressure is being brought to bear on D.I. Pyle must be significant."

"I have reason to believe he was a patron of both of the victims. And that he's offered violence to a third young man."

"What about David?" Jack asked, leaning forward. "Have we abandoned that theory?"

Sebastien scratched at the enamel of his teeth with a thumbnail. "We can't. But whoever killed those boys did not drink. Or not much, anyway."

"Just because they were not drained, does not mean that a wampyr did not kill them," said Jack. "Only that he did not dine."

"He is not full of love for himself or those driven to—or choosing—similar extremes." Sebastien shook his head. With a twitch of his thumb, he loosened his cravat. "He might kill out of self-hate. Might."

"I'm sorry," Abby Irene said. Her hand covered his.

Sebastien cocked his head. "I said might. But the fact remains, Abernathy was protecting somebody. Somebody, at the very least, who patronized all three men. I suggest from Abernathy's behavior that the person he's protecting is Michael Penfold."

"You're not suggesting this as confirmed, then?"

"Merely an avenue of investigation."

"Someone sent a coach and pair for David tonight," Jack said, with a glance at Abby Irene. "The two of us—"

"Abby Irene accompanied you?"

"You were worried," Jack said, with a dismissive shrug that warmed

Sebastien as well as any mouthful of blood. Anything that Jack and Abby Irene could not manage together might just as likely be too much for Sebastien. "A black coach, unmarked, drawn by bays. We followed—"

The hesitation wasn't feigned. But they couldn't have found *proof,* or his comment about Penfold would have met a different response. "And found?"

"Well, we entertained the hack," Abby Irene said, when Jack glanced at her hopefully for assistance. "As David was driven in circles for half an hour and then let off at his door again."

"No marks on the carriage, I take it?"

"None," Abby Irene said, as Phoebe emerged from the kitchen with a fresh pot of tea and warmed her cup. Abby Irene touched her wrist approvingly.

Well, Sebastien thought, they might all be furious with him, but at least his court were convivial.

Abby Irene continued, "But after it returned your…offspring to his lodgings, Jack disembarked to continue surveillance, and I followed on."

"Where did it go?"

"It stopped for some time at a townhouse, dropped off a visitor I do not know, and later returned with her to the Back Bay. I have those addresses. I don't know the houses any more than the man, I'm afraid."

But Sebastien did. They were the homes, respectively, of Verenna de Courten and Roger Abernathy.

Phoebe snorted in disbelief when he explained. "Then without a doubt, David is hunting you. That's too nice a coincidence for happenstance."

"It's probably how he found me," Sebastien said. "Jack will confirm; we know where in a strange city to go for succor. If I knew to contact Miss de Courten, he would, as well."

—⤐—

The morning newspaper arrived while they were considering their options. It was Jack who rose to fetch it back, and when he returned to the table, he handed the still-folded sheets directly to Sebastien. "You're a personage," he said, resuming his place and his teacup.

"It doesn't look anything like me," Sebastien said, flicking the edge of an engraving with a fingertip. For which he was profoundly grateful, though he wouldn't let either the worry or the relief show on his face.

A mortal man would have had the excuse of setting the paper aside to lift his cup. Sebastien, bereft of excuses, folded the paper open and read.

The article, though it occupied the position immediately above the advertising circular on the front page, was brief and typically melodramatic, and did little more than spuriously linking a wampyr sought in New Amsterdam with the killings in Boston.

"I'll find other lodging tonight," Sebastien said, and Phoebe laid a hand on his arm. "You'll do no such thing."

The argument that followed was predictable: there was nothing to link him to her, he would be safer here than in a hotel where others might notice drawn curtains and the irregularity of his hours, in the face of the new war hysteria was to be expected. But finally it was Jack who convinced him, as he had secretly expected.

"It's simple," Jack said. "Abigail Irene solves the crime, and everyone in Boston forgets you exist."

"Abby Irene is off the case," she reminded.

"And that's as likely to stop you as…?" Jack flicked the paper from Sebastien's grasp. "You're right. It doesn't look a thing like you, and no one in Boston knows you as anything except John Nast."

"Well," Sebastien said. "Present company excepted."

Abby Irene cleared her throat, with obvious reluctance. "And, of course, Epaphras Bull. I mean David."

"Yes," Sebastien said. "Jack, will you take a message for me?"

"I'm meeting friends for lunch," Jack said, in a manner that did not invite inquiry as to the nature of these *friends*. "I can drop it off along the way. Oh, Sebastien—"

"Yes?"

"I already told Phoebe"—he squeezed her hand—"I'll be out on business most of the night."

Sebastien didn't ask. If Jack wanted him to know, he would tell him. "Phoebe," he said, "Would you consider extending your reputation for eccentricity by claiming a cadaver?"

—◆—

Jack, of course, knew perfectly how to maneuver through the channels of wampyr etiquette. Sebastien could keep himself as separate from society as he liked; whatever deference his age entitled him to, there had always been times when society would seek him out. And it seemed even America was no haven from the politics of the blood, any more.

So when Jack left at lunchtime to deliver Sebastien's invitation to David, Sebastien attempted his best not to fret, or hover, or deliver unneeded remonstrations.

Shortly after sunset, when David's carriage—or, more precisely, when Abernathy's carriage, bearing David—arrived before the house, Jack had not yet returned, and Abby Irene was about her business. Sebastien met him at the door. Phoebe had come home from her errands, and though Sebastien would have ushered her back she reminded him it was her house, and so she stood at his shoulder, just behind him.

The wampyr stared at one another across the threshold, and Sebastien finally squared his shoulders and said, "Whose carriage is that, David?"

"A friend's," David said. "Surely, as I have answered your summons in good faith, you can allow me to enter? I can't imagine you've reconsidered my request, so there must be some manner in which I can assist you."

"It's not my home to issue invitations," Sebastien said. "We can speak in the cottage, if you like."

"Relegated to the garden shed again," David said, glancing down as he fiddled his cufflinks and studied the dove-colored fabric of his coat sleeves.

"Come in," Phoebe said impulsively, her hand on Sebastien's elbow as she stepped into the doorframe. "Come inside and talk."

Sebastien clutched her fingers before he remembered himself, but managed not to protest. It was too late, in any case. The invitation had been issued.

He allowed Phoebe to draw him aside, and David, swinging his amber-handled walking-stick, stepped inside. "More flies with honey, madam?" he inquired of Phoebe, his pale eyes narrowed in a most convincing smile.

She curtseyed; David surprised Sebastien with a brief but impeccable bow. "Your need *must* be great," he said. "Forgive me if I enjoy the reversal of power a little overmuch."

Sebastien shut the door behind him. "Must you be a prat?"

To his surprise, David looked up from his careful adjustments of the walking-stick in Phoebe's umbrella stand. "No," he said. "I don't suppose I must. Very well, Sebastien—or, John, is it now?—how may I be of assistance to you? And if I do owe you fealty, as the summons would seem to suggest, does that mean you owe me in return the protection I asked of you before?"

They stood just inside the door, the aura of tobacco surrounding David as present as his charisma, and his chilly smile. Sebastien stepped back, allowing Phoebe to usher them into the sitting room. So many of the small rituals of human grace and hospitality fell through when confronted with wampyr, and he watched her consider and discard the usual options—the offer of brandy, of tea, or what-have-you—and simply bring him a crystal scallop-shell ash tray and retire to a seat beside the fire where she could observe without intruding.

"I'd like to know what you're seeking my protection from," Sebastien said. He knew better than to suggest Phoebe leave the room, though David gave her a doubtful glance. Yes, by the standards of the blood, his associates were shockingly ill-behaved. As ill-behaved as the orange cat now contemplating David from the doorway.

Still, the silence stretched, so Sebastien added, "David, you must tell me why you fled Europe."

A soft laugh. "Is it not enough to say I missed you?"

"It would be. If it were true."

The rustle of paper bought time as David, without so much as a glance at Phoebe for permission, concentrated on rolling a cigarette. He produced a blue-headed match from the same chamois bag as paper and tobacco, and flicked his nail against the tip to spark it. "It was a foolish enough situation," David said, letting the match burn, the cigarette dangling from his lower lip. "Young Master White struck up a friendship with a certain Epaphras Bull, you see, and members of his family objected. The parents, coming to understand the intimacy of the acquaintanceship"—he held flame to paper, and breathed deeply, an action that seemed dramatic in one who so seldom could be seen to breathe—"and that Mr. White could not be dissuaded from its continuance, retained the services of a certain professional by which to remove me from the equation. This fellow prides himself on thoroughness. Europe simply became too unhealthy for my continued residence."

The last words issued with a coil of cooling smoke. Sebastien wrinkled his nose at the reek, and David smiled and dragged at the cigarette again.

"And you have reason to think this fellow followed you here?"

David shrugged and tapped ash into the tray. Despite himself, Sebastien was fascinated by the delicacy of the motion.

"He has a reputation to maintain," David said dismissively. "But the Atlantic is wide. And it isn't as if I advertised my destination—"

Of course, Sebastien thought, the penny dropping amid all David's evasions. He settled back in his chair. "Or did you think I was more likely to take you back if it seemed you needed me?"

David's faint superior smile slid off his face. "Don't flatter yourself," he said, but he was shaken enough that Sebastien could hear the lie as clearly as the rustling of Phoebe's skirts as she shifted uncomfortably and found—in tending the fire—an excuse to turn away.

"So it wasn't me?" Sebastien let his voice drift lower. "Then you were, what, seeking access to my court?"

"So now you admit you have a court?" But it came out weakly, and despite all their history, Sebastien pitied him.

"No, I don't believe that," he said, and saw David's face relax across the mouth and cheeks. "Do you have the courage to be honest with me?"

"I said I missed you," David answered, with painful dignity. "You called it a lie."

Sebastien licked his lips and sat forward in the chair. Pity, the ugliest emotion, and it snapped his unbeating heart as sharply as the crack of a broken bone.

Of course David's anger was his fault as much as David's. Everything that had gone wrong between them, all the jealousy and sorrow. He might have preserved David's existence—one could not say, *saved his life*—but he hadn't, he thought, made existing any easier for him. And wasn't that what parents were meant to do, teach their children?

He took one deep breath, for speaking, and spoke over the crackle of the log Phoebe had slid onto the fire. "I'm sorry."

The cigarette rose to David's mouth again. Smoke trickled from his nostrils. He stared at Sebastien for a long, smooth moment before he nodded and said softly, "Yes. I see that you are. And I was untruthful."

"It's your nature. Is there any such person as Master White, David?"

"Trevor White," David said. "There is. Not too much chance of pursuit, though, in all honesty. You needn't worry that I'm linked to your murdered whores. Either through omission or commission. Nor is Chouchou—"

"I was more afraid," Sebastien said, "that she would prove a victim. If someone were killing young men as a means to find you."

"I do not think so," David said. "Everyone in Europe thinks I went east."

The truth, Sebastien judged, as much by the unfamiliarity of the tone and expression David wore as by knowing what his lies looked like. "So you're not seeking my help?"

"I am," David said. "But not for that. I just..." He shrugged. "You know."

Sebastien, watching the frown lines at the corners of David's mouth, knew very well. "Can we begin anew, then?"

David laughed. "You wouldn't say that unless you wanted something. Very well, then. Tell me what you want. I'll think about it."

"I want you to convince Roger Abernathy to help me catch the murderer who is slaughtering Ganymedes in their homes, since it definitely isn't any enemy of yours. Or you either, I trust? No? Good."

"Oh."

David crushed out his cigarette.

—⤜⟨⟩⤛—

Abby Irene returned a little before six, with another carriage that they turned out not to need, as—courtesy of David—they had Abernathy's. Once Abby Irene renewed the preservative spells upon the corpse, loading it was simply a matter of carrying the coffin out the front door—Sebastien and David managed quite well, with the women supervising—and manhandling it onto the luggage rack.

Sebastien rode with the cabdriver to steward their unwitting passenger through the brief journey.

This time, he arrived in Chouchou's study by the front door.

—⤜⟨⟩⤛—

Chouchou, resplendent in peach silk and armed with an ostrich plume fan, might have regretted inviting David in, but she was as stuck with him now as Sebastien was. It mattered not that Chouchou stood with her back to the coffin on the piano—and its slightly rain-damp entourage—while David and Sebastien pried up the hastily tacked lid with fingernails.

She turned when David called her name, moving less stiffly this time.

Sebastien, silent, picking pine splinters from dead fingertips, only stood and watched. Chouchou—complexion pale as her powder—pressed the obscuring fan to her mouth as she came to the coffin with mincing steps. Her ring glittered as she reached out and lightly stroked his cheek, the one not laid open deep enough to show his teeth through the gap like a string of red-dyed pearls.

The bathed and bloodless wounds of the young man did what Sebastien's persuasion could not, or perhaps it was David's influence. "Grant Nelson," she said. "Did you even bother to learn his name, Mr. Nast?"

Sebastien didn't answer.

Chouchou looked up, eyes dry and gleaming behind the black false lashes, and said, "It wasn't Michael. How do I prove it?"

Sebastien could not but admire her loyalty and courage.

Of course, Chouchou had a room with a false panel. Sebastien wondered if such things were de rigeur in her profession, and decided, most likely, yes. The space behind it, however, was only large enough for two, and one of them had to be Abby Irene, whose sorceries required she see the subject. Jack wanted to draw straws for the second position, but Sebastien claimed it by fiat.

They had to trust Chouchou to summon Michael Penfold without trickery, but Sebastien read her note and David accompanied the coachman when he delivered it, which were the best assurances they could obtain. The coachman did not return with the Governor, of course. That would have been grossly unsubtle, and there were protocols for such things.

There was time after David returned for Sebastien and Abby Irene to secret themselves, breast to breast in the confined space which quickly grew warm and rank with Abby Irene's body heat and sweat. She seemed impervious, as was her affectation, but he could hear the shallowness of her breathing. In her corset, it must be a test of endurance.

"You think the Governor struck Abernathy?" she whispered, when they were sealed within.

Sebastien nodded in the dark, but of course *she* could not see that. "I do, yes."

"I don't," she said. She pressed a hand against his neck, as if drinking in his coolness. Her perspiration slicked his skin. "He's frightened of someone. But it's not Michael Penfold."

That worthy arrived a comfortless half-hour later, and was shown up the stairs with haste, to the room they watched. They had fallen silent as soon as the carriage drew up in the street, and Sebastien could hear Abby Irene's stays creaking now with the flutter of her breath.

The dead boy—Grant Nelson, Sebastien reminded himself: even the dead might have some dignity—sat with his back to the door, resplendent in a scarlet gown with one of Chouchou's platinum wigs curling delicately across his forehead. His head lolled, as if he dozed; otherwise, the corset under his brocade bodice held him stiffly upright. The Colonial Governor was a stout man, well-favored, with muttonchop sideburns and a rose-gold watch-chain. He did not seem to notice the crunch of gray sea-salt under his boots as he crossed the carpet, quietly calling Chouchou's name, and placed a hand on Nelson's bare shoulder just as Abby Irene murmured a few words of sufficient power to raise the hairs even on magic-deaf Sebastien's neck.

Penfold snatched his hand up and skipped back, covering his mouth with the other hand to stifle his shout. Sebastien breathed deeply, carefully—but while he could smell the man's sudden chill sweat, and Abby Irene's hotter and more stifled one, there was no tang of blood.

He could also hear Penfold's whimpered prayer as he nerved himself and came back, circling the divan upon which the body of Grant Nelson was propped, fist still stuffed against his mouth. "Please no," Sebastien heard him say, and then his combined grunt or relief and horror. "Oh, *Grant.*"

"He's not bleeding," Abby Irene said. "He's not bleeding at all."

"Someone could have done it for him," Sebastien said, but he was snatching at straws and they both knew it. That kind of brutality was not what one expected of a hired killer; it was the product of hate.

"Well," she said, groping for the handle that would release the cubbyhole door, "I suppose I should go explain to his Honor why we've ruined his evening."

— ❧ —

The explaining, which Sebastien effaced himself from as much as possible—he was "Mr. John Nast, my associate," for Abby Irene's purposes as far as this interview went, and that suited him well—was cut short. "I rather strong-armed Mr...that is to say, Miss Abernathy," she offered apologetically, while Chouchou fluttered over the half-prostrated Governor and David remained absent. "You must understand, your Honor, the melodrama was only to clear your name."

"May I inquire, Lady Abigail," he said, hunched over a restorative brandy, "who advanced it as a suspect?" His glare rested on Chouchou, but Abby Irene shook her head and womanfully forbore from correcting him.

"I am afraid, your Honor, that I am not at liberty."

"Weren't you removed from the case?"

"I am no longer in the employ of the city," she admitted. "But I've done nothing illegal."

Chouchou brought another brandy; Sebastien did not miss the gentle manner in which Penfold lifted it from her fingers, or the tenderness with which he stroked her hand. He glanced at Abby Irene.

She had seen. And was nodding softly, bitten-lip. No, perhaps he had not struck her.

Penfold snorted. This brandy, he nursed rather than quaffed. "I'll see you at my offices tomorrow, Lady Abigail. Along with my son, the Chief Inspector, I think. For a more in-depth discussion of your involvement in this case. For now, if that will be quite all—"

"Yes, your Honor."

"Good," Chouchou said, fanning herself. "My carriage will run you home."

"What about Mr. Nelson?"

"I'll see to proper burial," Chouchou and the Governor said, both at once, and then shared a startled glance. Penfold shook his head and said, "It is the very least I can do."

Chouchou patted his shoulder. "But please get that coffin out of my dressing room, if you don't mind?"

Sebastien nodded. "We shall, if we can borrow your carriage again. Lady Abigail Irene?"

He could manage her name. She offered a small grateful smile. "I shall return to my hotel," she said. "If it's all quite the same to everyone."

He nodded. David could help him with the coffin, anyway.

Jack had still not returned by sunrise. Phoebe had done her mortal best to stay awake, but sometime after midnight she'd drifted asleep in a parlor chair, and not awakened when Sebastien propped her head with a bundled shawl. He tucked a strand of hair behind her ear and stroked the warm skin of her neck, but even the chill of his fingertips did no more than make her stir.

The motion did rouse David, though, who materialized at his shoulder with all the softness of an interested cat. "So frail," he said, which should have sounded ridiculous coming from a creature who might have been made of ribbon-jointed twigs. "How can you bear to give your heart to them?"

Sebastien stepped back from her, bringing his shoulder against David's. David leaned; Sebastien slipped an arm around his waist under his coat, without thinking.

"I can't," Sebastien said, trying not to think of Jack's private business, and all the dangerous places it might have taken him in the night. But Abby Irene was sleeping in her hotel room, or awake and preparing for her interview with the Governor. The rain had broken with sunrise, and burning murder fell from the skies.

And in any case, he hadn't the slightest idea where Jack had gone, other than a suspicion that he was indulging his young man's preoccupation with revolutionaries. For lack of anything better, Sebastien shook his head and said to David, "How can you bear not to?"

For answer, David pressed his lips to Sebastien's throat. "He'll come back to you," David said. "Haven't you noticed we all do?"

⁓

The morning post was delayed, which worried Sebastien further, and a strange hush had fallen over the city by midmorning. Even on the Hill, there should have been a bustle of scullery maids on their way to market, the cries of costermongers in the distance, the clatter of delivery carts. But there was none such, and no children in the street. Gunfire, distant, but unmistakable, wakened Phoebe before noon.

"The French?" David asked.

"We would have heard the canon, if they came by sea." It was not Sebastien's first war.

Phoebe rose up, smoothed her crumpled skirts and hair, and went into the kitchen to make tea. The tension around Sebastien crystallized into a shell of silence that even David hesitated to break.

Eventually, Sebastien set down the novel—one of his hostess's, in fact— that he was flipping at ineffectually, and left David in the parlor. Even the cat wanted nothing to do with him in this mood. Perhaps he'd go upstairs and find his knitting; his concentration might be sufficient unto that.

But his route to the back stair—the front had windows—took him through into the dining room, where he found Phoebe at table, picking crumbs from the crust of an otherwise untouched watercress sandwich. The knitting could wait. He sat down across the table; she looked up and proffered a feeble smile.

He was searching for the right words when the lock on the front door clicked. Both of them started, Phoebe knocking her chair backwards as she rose. She did not pause to right it, just gathered her skirts close and stepped over the legs with all the catlike fastidiousness of a saloon girl stepping over sprawled drunkards.

Whatever dignity she mustered, she clutched Sebastien's elbow as they stepped into the front parlor.

Jack and Abby Irene stood shoulder to shoulder within the door, he with his cap askew and she clutching the handles of her carpet bag in both fists, a cape thrown hastily over her shoulders and her short hair spilling from its pins.

"Riots," she said, with all the ice-knife precision of her exquisite enunciation, and slumped against the door, the carpet bag falling unheeded at her feet, though Sebastien noticed she kept her ebony wand clutched in her left hand, concealed in the fall of lace cuff. He turned to fetch brandies for her and Jack; David was still seated not far from the fire.

While Sebastien poured, Phoebe guided the travelers into chairs. "Riots?" Jack waved at the door. "I had a little warning," he said. "The outcry was over rumors of Navy press gangs working near the docks, and I think some Home Rule advocates opining we should be siding with the French against the Crown. It started in the taverns."

Sebastien, setting a drink by Jack's elbow, suspected how Jack knew that, and what his business of the previous night might have been. From Abby Irene's steady gaze, she had an idea as well, and Sebastien wondered what she might choose to do. Her loyalty had always been to the Crown.

But that had been changing recently.

"Were there agitators?" Phoebe asked. She perched on the edge of the divan beside David, who edged over to make room.

"Yes," Jack said. "Although I could not say for a fact that they were French. It would be best to sit tight at home, I think."

"I have to get back to Mary and Mike," Abby Irene said. Mary was her Negro housekeeper. "I can't leave them alone in a strange city."

"Was there fighting on the Hill?" Phoebe, ever practical.

"No, nor in the Back Bay."

"Then sit tight," Sebastien counseled. "Mary will have the sense to stay in the hotel, and she can take care of the terrier. They're as safe there as here. Safer: the building has security and brick walls."

Abby Irene winced, but acquiesced. Sebastien continued, "Could it come to civil war?"

Jack nodded. Abby Irene picked up her brandy—Sebastien had provided her a somewhat larger measure than Jack—and did away with it most professionally. "I should say it's inevitable, in fact. There were some fires, but they've been controlled so far."

Boston boasted an excellent fire-fighting system: water ran through lead-lined hollow logs buried under the streets, which could be chopped into by firefighters in need.

"I spoke with the Governor, briefly, before being escorted out by his son and a pair of burly friends." Abby Irene said, breaking the silence that followed. She held out her glass for a refill, and Sebastien accommodated her before Phoebe could rise. David smiled archly at him, though, and he would have blushed if he could have managed it, because he realized was usurping Phoebe's role as host. *Not my house?* David mouthed, and Sebastien set the carafe down with a click on the white marble bartop and turned back to Abby Irene.

"Tell me more," he said.

"He not-so-gently suggested that I return to New Amsterdam and cease troubling his fair city, if I were concerned for my continued well-being."

"He threatened you?" Jack, who should have been too old for such naivete.

"He offered to pay my train fare," Abby Irene said, placing her wand across her knees. She reached into her sleeve and drew forth a handkerchief, which she draped over the wand and carefully unfolded. "But you should look at this."

In the center of the handkerchief was a stain of palest rose.

"What's that?"

"A thaumaturgical reaction," she said. "This handkerchief is impregnated with samples that Sebastien and I collected evidence from the bodies of the murdered men. I used the magical principle of similarity to lay a spell on it that would cause a color change if it came within a short distance of the…source of the samples."

"But you've already proven Michael Penfold didn't commit the murders. At least with his own hands," David said, abandoning his the calculated expression of boredom to lean forward, craning around Phoebe.

"It didn't change color last night," she said. "It changed color this morning."

David's pale eyes were quite startling when they widened so. "You're insinuating that it's perhaps not the Governor who is ashamed of his…proclivities."

Abby Irene looked up, lips pursed, and nodded to David before she glanced around the room. "Would the Governor's actions make sense, Sebastien, if he were protecting his son? Would a man protect the son who murdered his lovers?"

"Oh, yes," David said. "I should say he might. Especially if he were ashamed himself."

"We'll never get an arrest," Sebastien said. "Never mind a conviction. Not in Massachusetts."

"A Colonial Governor's not too much of a personage in London," Abby Irene said. "There are higher courts."

"Courts you've severed your connections with," Sebastien reminded.

Abby Irene shrugged, and tucked the stained handkerchief into her reticule. Sun streamed down behind the drawn curtains and closed window-shades, bright enough even through the muffling fabric that Sebastien could not look at it directly. He said, "Jack, do you think both David and I can fit in that coffin?"

"*Coffin?*"

"Grant Nelson's coffin. If there's revolution in the streets, I shan't suffer us to be parted. And the mails may not be reliable." The morning post had not arrived, and neither had the forenoon one.

Jack rolled his eyes. "Good God. How…cliché."

"Indeed. But if the Governor's darling son is murdering his lovers, then Chouchou must be warned."

"Oh darling," David answered, laughing hopelessly, "do you think for an instant she doesn't *know?*"

"Nevertheless," Sebastien said. "Nevertheless."

Sebastien was moderately tall, but slender, and David was a small man by anyone's standard. They fit, face-to-face, lying in one another's arms, although Jack gave them a doubtful glance before he settled the lid. "Breathe shallowly," he joked, hefting the hammer.

"I shan't breathe at all," Sebastien reminded.

"Right. This is insane, you realize." Sebastien disdained to answer, instead watching Jack's face as wood ground on wood. The last words he said, before his eyes vanished, were, "And no talking."

No, they did not speak.

But that didn't stop David from silently, stealthily, nuzzling his face into Sebastien's throat and working his fangs into the soft flesh there. Sebastien gasped, first at pain like flame and then pleasure, and somehow scraped his hand through the narrow pace between David's back and the lid so he could knot his fingers in David's hair. He bit his lip, and did not cry out, while they rode in the bumping coffin.

Sebastien quickly came to understand that something was wrong, and to judge by the tension in David's gripping hands, he knew it too. The carriage ride—balanced atop a hired hack whose driver, Sebastien judged, must have been in tight financial straits indeed to venture out on such a day—was longer than it should have been, punctuated by a great deal of pausing and hurrying and the clatter of iron-shod wheels on cobblestones.

He heard shouting, once, and the neigh of a frantic horse—not the hack's gelding, he didn't think—and by his estimation it was almost two hours before the coffin was unloaded, and the lid cracked open. Sebastien flinched from the light for a moment, his eyes adapted to the dark, and fought the ridiculous urge to sit bolt upright and take a deep, cold, unnecessary breath. But David jerked himself back and rocketed to his feet with unsubtle, inhuman grace. And Sebastien, knowing where he was by the scent, arose with better dignity.

He found himself, surprisingly but now not unexpectedly, looking into the eyes of Miss de Courten. "I see," he said. "And how came we here?"

"We were too late for Chouchou," Abby Irene said, from beside her. "I'm sorry. I thought it best we not be discovered there."

"Indeed," Sebastien said, straightening his collar. The marks of David's teeth would have already vanished. "And how did you think to come here?"

Phoebe touched his arm. David, catlike, was still attempting to straighten his crumpled demeanor. "There were patrolmen at my house when we came within sight," she said. "Discretion being presumed the better part of valor, Jack directed us here."

"…Jack?"

Jack, who had been pacing fretfully to the window and back again, peeking around drawn curtains each time, looked over his shoulder and licked his lips. "I know where you go."

"Oh," Sebastien said. He turned to Miss de Courten.

She tipped her head, a lovely feminine shrug. "Perhaps you could manage the introductions, John?"

His manners were slipping. He was not, he admitted, at his best. "I beg your pardon," he said, and obliged. That responsibility dispensed with, he redirected his attention to Phoebe. "Patrolmen. At your house."

Miss de Courten cleared her throat, quite daintily. "There are broadsides," she said. "Wanted posters. All over the city."

"I think we should consider ourselves fugitives until further notice," Phoebe said.

"Wanted posters for all of us?"

"Just for Don Sebastien de Ulloa, wampyr. For the murder of three young vagrants. It seems that the governor has found a scapegoat for his son." Phoebe fiddled with her eyeglasses. "The drawing doesn't look a thing like you, though."

"Oh dear," he said. "I'm so sorry. Miss de Courten, I shall be on my way with sunset, if you'll agree to risk yourself for so long. As for the rest of you—"

Jack nodded. "You know how to find me. I'll look out for the rest." He took Phoebe's hand and squeezed it, as she was about to protest. Abby Irene examined him for some time, expressionless, before she nodded—once. She knew as well as Sebastien that he would travel faster and more safely alone.

"If I may," she said, and unbuttoned her collar. "You can't know when you'll have the chance again, and I imagine I'm freshest."

The rest of his court avoided his eyes as he sought—what, their approval? their permission?—and of course Abby Irene was right. Normally, he would not drink from the throat; he did not care to leave visible scars. But then there were the bounds of public behavior to consider, here in a room with five others, some of whom were strangers to Abby Irene if they were not, quite, to Sebastien.

He moved toward her.

And something shattered at the front of the house.

Miss de Court screamed, her garnet glinting on her finger as she covered her mouth. Sebastien reached for her as she fainted, but David was closer and caught her before she fell. She lolled in his arms, eyelashes fluttering. Sebastien was not distracted.

Abby Irene calmly slipped her ebony wand into her hand.

The doorway to the parlor filled with men. Uniformed patrolmen, and a detective inspector, at least two ranks behind the first and all of them armed. He took in the scene with a scathing glance and shook his head, his lips pursed in disgust above stubborn jowls.

"D.I. Pyle," Abby Irene said, leaving even Sebastien uncertain if her tone of disdain was feigned.

"I should have known I'd find you here," he said. "Bad enough you protected this creature in New Amsterdam, Lady Abigail. If we should find that you knew he was involved in these deaths, it will go ill for you."

One of the patrolmen leaned down to speak in the Detective Inspector's ear. He shook his head. "No," he said. "She's a peer; I won't arrest her without a warrant."

He stared straight at Abby Irene when he said it. Her nod was tiny, but definite.

He could not more plainly have told her to get out of town if he'd sent a telegram. A decent man, Sebastien judged. But weak, as men were.

D.I. Pyle rubbed his hands together, gave Abby Irene a moment of polite silence, as if waiting for her to protest, and turned away from her.

"Don Sebastien de Ulloa," he said, "alias David Bull. You are under arrest for the crime of vampirism, and for the murders of Grant Nelson, Roger Abernathy, and Alexander Dabree. Please come quietly to the test; it's broad daylight and you've nowhere to run."

Sebastien heard Abby Irene's squeak of protest, Jack's indrawn breath. David, of course, made no sound. He simply stared at Sebastien, hard, half-smiling, and then set Miss de Courten down on the divan.

"Of course," David said, and Sebastien realized with a sickening sense of reversal that the inspector was looking at David, not at him. "A fight would endanger my court, wouldn't it? You'd just burn the house, in the end." He stepped around Miss de Courten's outflung skirts and came to the police inspector, wrists extended. More patrolmen filled the doorway, and behind Jack, Sebastien heard steps in the back hall.

"Wait—" Sebastien said. He stepped forward, two quick steps, and then froze where he stood.

Not willingly. He'd seen the flick of Abby Irene's wand. David, chin high, gave him a pitying glance as the manacles closed on his thin wrists. "John," David said, "it's over now. Let me go. If you fight them, they will hurt you."

Sebastien could neither speak nor move. The wand carried a spell that paralyzed the target in a kind of stasis, a forensic sorcerer's tool of arrest and self-defense. Sebastien had always presumed, with—he now understood—inadequate evidence—that it left the target insensible.

He wished it had been so.

"Was it Chouchou?" David asked, standing meekly while they draped his ankles, also, in chains.

"Roger Abernathy, you mean? I shan't reveal who gave us your name, sir."

But of course he already had. Chouchou, protecting his patron. The patron, protecting his son. The Colonial police, corrupt to the core with their secret mission—to protect the aristocracy at all costs.

That was what this was. Refusal to surrender to it, to the great machine of politics that protected the great at any cost to the small. The machine that had driven Abby Irene from her service. The machine Sebastien had thought he could ignore with impunity.

D.I. Pyle took hold of the chains between David's wrists. Sebastien thought that only he saw the quick, sideways glance at the window, the daylight glowing behind the curtain. They would put him to the test; the crime was vampirism, and the test was the sentence as well.

Wampyr only died by burning.

If they could be said to die at all.

"Are you ready, sir?"

David nodded, and now Pyle seemed to treat him with respect. The solemnity due a condemned man, perhaps.

A patrolman in his midnight blue took David's elbow. David looked like a child, his hair still stuck all askew from the coffin. Sebastien thought Phoebe might turn her face into Jack's shoulder as the long train of officers left the room, David walking stolidly in their midst, his chains rattling. In the front room, they paused and attached a long chain to his manacles, to drag him if he balked.

He did not. He turned over his shoulder and caught Sebastien's gaze.

And winked.

Nobody could lie like David.

Sebastien was not in a position to see what happened when they led David out into the sun, but he didn't need to. You only needed to see some things once to remember them forever.

David didn't scream.

But a patrolman did.

He was calm by the time Abby Irene released him, though he shook her hand off when she came to apologize. "They would have just taken us both," he said. And then he bit his lip, his teeth opening bloodless slashes in the dead flesh, and said, "Just don't comfort me with any pretty lies."

"Never," she said, and kissed him on the wounded mouth before she stepped away.

In the next room, sunlight speckled with motes of dust or ash shone through the shattered door. Neither Abby Irene nor Jack had the strength to stop him if he chose to follow David.

Tempting as it was to throw David's unwanted gift in his face…the light stung Sebastien's eyes. He turned his back.

He stared down at his hands; a dead man's hands could not tremble with wrath. Nor could they steady at the moment of decision.

France was no better than Britain. One government was much like another. Sebastien knew these things, objectively.

But it was not the government of France whose corruption, whose protection of a monster worthy of the appellation had brought down death upon Sebastien's house. Upon David, beloved. A monster as well, perhaps, but a monster in name only.

"Jack," he said. "You have friends who do not love the English Crown."

"Oh boy," Jack said, in his terrible American. "Do I ever."

Sebastien looked at Abby Irene. "Cherie, you won't want to hear this."

"I'll stay," she said.

"It's treason."

Her smile made her seem old. "Good," she said. "I don't think I mind."

He looked at Jack. Jack nodded. Phoebe's knuckles were white where she squeezed his hand. Miss de Courten was sitting upright, finally, blinking, her bosom swelling over her corset with each deep breath.

"Of course you may," Sebastien said, smooth-voiced and dry of eye.

He had not recently enough fed, for weeping.

LUMIÈRE
(December 1902 - January, 1903)

"WELL THEN," SAID JACK Priest. "We'll go to Paris."

He gazed steadily at Sebastien when he said it; Sebastien was staring at the backs of his own hands, his fingers interlaced like a dead man's.

Which, Jack supposed, he was.

There were three others arranged around the hotel room they'd taken refuge in: the sorceress Lady Abigail Irene Garrett with her small dog on her knee; Mrs. Phoebe Smith, the noted novelist; and Doctor Garrett's mulatto servant Mary, whom Abby Irene—as Sebastien called her, with fine familiarity and a disregard for rank that seemed to trouble her not at all—had insisted be included in their councils.

Sebastien didn't respond. Jack knew what he held folded between his hands—a silver ring set with a cloudy blue stone. And he supposed Sebastien deserved time to grieve, but the hard fact was they didn't have it, and that wasn't only Jack's jealousy speaking.

"Paris," Abby Irene said. "What would we do in Paris?"

"As a former servant of the Crown, and a member of the peerage, and a bonded sorcerer, and an émigré to the colonies—" Jack shrugged. "You are in a unique position, Doctor Garrett, to negotiate for diplomatic recognition of the Colonial home government from the French."

"There is no Colonial home government," she said.

Jack answered her with a smile, and he knew she would read the answer in it.

"Peter Eliot," she said, articulating each syllable. "You mean to tell me he's set up an entire shadow government."

"He's not alone," Jack said.

Another risk, because if Abby Irene had suspected, before, that the revolutionaries rioting in the streets of Boston and New Amsterdam, stoning redcoats and inscribing graffiti, answered to a central authority, now she knew it. She had known since they met that he had revolutionary friends, but he doubted she had any idea how deep and how high ran disaffection with the Crown.

"You"—she paused, in order to get her thoughts aligned—"wish me to offer an alliance to the French. Against our own government."

"The English."

"Our own government. Our own King. Tell me you're joking, Mr. Priest."

He'd asked her to call him *Jack*, and sometimes she remembered. Not right now, however, and he didn't blame her.

Jack expected her to be his greatest challenge. Loyal as her terrier, but Abby Irene treated the dog far better than her masters had ever treated her. He could see her formulating objections—*but that's treason, Mr. Priest*—and hearing his replies without having to ask—*for you, Doctor Garrett, and Mrs. Smith. It is. But aren't you a traitor already?*

He could mention, if he would, that he'd chosen not to condone murder among the revolutionaries, and had helped her resolve that case—but she knew that already, as well. She sucked her lower lip into her mouth and chewed it, staining her teeth with the waxy red from her rouged lips. She already knew every argument he would make, and while he thought she stood on the edge of open revolt, only she could decide if she would step over. She had been a loyal subject of the Crown all her life, and it had cost her everything.

Jack didn't think a personal betrayal alone would turn her against her old masters. But here she sat, having twice in close succession seen how the powerful would sacrifice anyone to their political aims—or for as petty a reason as protecting a criminal son—and he thought, just possibly, that Abby Irene held justice in better regard than patriotism.

"We could have fought," Phoebe said. She turned a glass of Abby Irene's brandy in her hands, warming it but not drinking. "Two wampyrs, a sorceress. Jack, you're handy in a scuffle."

Of course he was. But just that afternoon, they had all of them stood and watched, helplessly, as Sebastien's old protégé Epaphras Bull was arrested in Sebastien's place and dragged into the sunlight to die. Not that Sebastien had done anything to deserve arrest—nothing other than being a wampyr, and a convenient lever against Abby Irene, and an even more convenient scapegoat to divert attention from a *real* killer who happened to be the Colonial Governor's son.

It was because Abby Irene had chosen her principles over both her loyalty to the crown and her love both for Sebastien and for Richard, the soon-to-be-former Duke of New Amsterdam, that Jack thought she might listen. "I don't need to argue with you," he said, after a long quiet consideration, which she permitted him to take in silence. "You've seen what your king and his lieutenants get about, Doctor Garrett. They kept Prince Henry from satisfying honor because it might be an embarrassment, and they've done the same to you."

"And is revolution a better choice? Or joining the French in a war against England? War is a pain in the *ass*, Jack. People starve. People die."

He smiled to hide his own passionate nausea. This was his single best chance to secure her aid, as he had secured Sebastien's. "What would your prince say?"

Doctor Garrett stared at Jack, her fingernails picking at the arm of the chair. "Damn you."

"Besides that," he said.

A risk, but she stared a moment longer, and then dissolved into tears and laughter. Her terrier gave her a dirty look when her knee started to shake, but then jumped up, planted both small feet on the lip of her corset, and licked her face and eyes while she fended him off unsuccessfully. "Henry would say," she said, when she finally got hold of the dog's collar and wiped her face off on her sleeve, "that it is the duty of the great to police themselves, for there is no other to do so."

"And if the great will not?"

Her lips compressed, and she pulled the little dog close against her chest and let her chin fall on his head. She closed her eyes. "That is what I was sworn to," she said. "When I was sworn to anything."

"We should have fought," Phoebe said, again, into the silence that followed—as if she responded not to Jack and Abby Irene's conversation, but one internal to herself. She raised that glass, at long last, and drank, wincing from the fumes.

Sebastien unfolded his hands and let the silver ring chime on the tabletop. While it was still rolling, he said, "Don't be ridiculous, Phoebe. They only would have fired the house."

Phoebe pinched her eyes closed hard behind her glasses, refusing tears with a violent shake of her head. But Jack knew Sebastien was right, and he had no doubt Phoebe did as well. The Metropolitan Police would no doubt have taken the greatest care to evacuate the street, saturate any neighboring buildings with water, call in sorcerers to attempt to limit the action of the flames—and then they would have burned the infection out at the core.

Wampyrs and those who sheltered them rated no more, in Jack's experience; arrest was only a courtesy. Epaphras Bull had chosen to burn not just for Sebastien, but on behalf of the mortals as well—a peculiar choice for a wampyr. A peculiar choice for *this* wampyr, whom Jack had not held in high regard.

It seemed that even when Sebastien chose poorly, he chose better than most. Jack might have phrased the reminder more gently, all the same.

— ⤫ —

There was no chance of a direct route.

Lady Abigail Irene Garrett, Th.D., knew they were lucky—in that winter of 1902, in time of war—to find an airship making the Atlantic passage at all. That they were not fugitives was only by the grace through which Sebastien was presumed dead—though Garrett doubted the former Don Sebastien de Ulloa, now traveling as Mr. John Nast, would perceive the instrumentality of his salvation as *grace*—and even asking after a direct route to Paris would have been begging for arrest and questioning.

A little research into airship, steamer, and overland routes convinced her that it would be easiest to go by way of Köln out of the great port of New Amsterdam. And she did find an Italian dirigible bound back to Europe and away from the site of colonial squabbling with all haste—which was a massive stroke of luck, and she didn't in the slightest mind spending Christmas and the New Year aloft. She initially purchased passage for herself and her housekeeper Mary only as far as London, where the *Andrea Doria* would pause in its eastward journey for fuel and supplies.

She no longer had any obligations in New Amsterdam. She *could* be seen to be returning to England without arousing suspicion, and once the airship was enroute she could extend her ticket.

A day later, Jack Priest arranged travel for himself and two others—ostensibly his parents, in actuality Sebastien and Mrs. Smith, who had refused to be dissuaded from this adventure, no matter how hair-brained—on the same ship, but continuing on to San Marino. Thus, they would not seem to be travelling with Garrett and Mary until they took train in Germany, and it would not be obvious in advance that all five intended to jump ship in Köln.

Despite the elaborations of her ruse, when Garrett stood on the boarding platform on a winter night at the end of 1902, her hands shook in their fur-lined gloves. And it was not with cold, though she folded her arms across her breast and hugged herself tight, her carpetbag hanging awkwardly to one side. Mary, warm in plain gray felted wool and carrying the flannel-lined basket in which Garrett's little dog traveled, shifted closer, though propriety did not permit her to take her mistress' elbow.

"Come along then, ma'am," she said, when Garrett had stood shivering and staring at the great, fluted, floodlit, dull-silver body of the grounded dirigible curving overhead for at least five minutes. "We'll be warm once we're in, and we can get you a nice cup of tea."

Their trunks and suitcases were already loaded. Garrett had only her blue velvet carpetbag of sorcerer's tools to manage, and Mary only the dog. Garrett nodded, gathered herself, and joined the other passengers queuing at the base of a short flight of stairs. As she climbed them, her ticket and passport in her hand, she forced herself to stop chewing on her lip.

She wondered when she had moved from mere conspiracy to treason.

The journey passed uneventfully, although with a certain clandestine air that leant it spice. "Mr. Nast" took ill on the first night of the journey. His "wife" and "son" were busy tending him, and so barely in evidence. D.C.I. Garrett—or Doctor Garrett, now that she was no longer a Crown Investigator—was all by herself enough of a scandal to serve as a distraction, and with her blue carpetbag never out of arm's reach and her busy terrier and silent servant as a travelling companion, suspected she was very nearly the only topic of conversation among the other passengers and the crew.

They certainly weren't talking to her.

The strangest stage of the journey, for Garrett, was the passage over England. It occurred in daylight, when Sebastien was of necessity confined to his cabin or otherwise the interior of the ship—not that he could have acknowledged her under any circumstances, until they were safely on the ground in Germany. Garrett feigned enjoyment of a solitary luncheon in the salon and watched green English countryside glide by, dotted with copses and the white specks of sheep. The shadow of the *Andrea Doria* scudded across the earth below as clouds scudded across the sky above, and Garrett's bone china teacup rattled in the saucer when she set it down.

England. When she entered her self-imposed exile in the colonies, she'd never expected to see it again. Now, she wondered if she was seeing it for the last time. An unexpected gift, perhaps. Or an unlooked-for cruelty.

When the dirigible made landfall outside London on the last day of the year, although the layover was scheduled at thirteen hours, she did not disembark. She could not bear to feel England's earth and cobblestones under her shoes again, she thought. And if she could bear that, then she might never bear to leave.

She celebrated the arrival of 1903 alone, having given Mary leave to explore the city, as she had never set foot outside of New Holland and New England before.

—⟡—

Debarking in Köln was by means of a railed gangplank rather than a stair, and as soon as Jack Priest set one bull's-blood-colored boot upon it, he breathed a soft and heartfelt sigh. Germany. The continent. Civilization.

Safety, at least for the moment. It was not a crime merely to *be* a wampyr here.

He strode down, all swinging arms and stomping boots, and paused at the bottom when he realized Phoebe and "John"—whom he must stop thinking of as Sebastien, especially in moments of affection and exasperation— were not on his heels. All of them were travelling under the name Nast, which Jack found reprehensibly amusing. He supposed he passed very well for Phoebe's son—she was slight and blond as well, though paler than he—but the recently-minted John Nast was medium-tall and dark, almost swarthy.

And currently standing at the top of the gangplank, when Jack turned, leaning on a cane and his "wife's" arm, pretending to breathe heavily while his wife juggled him and a basket full of more-than-usually irascible orange cat.

A virtuoso performance, but Jack really wished they could just hurry and set aside the charade.

"Mother, oh mother, let me help with your bag," he called, and started up the plank again while "John"—no, *John*, dammit—arched an eyebrow and Phoebe laughed helplessly. A Gallic-nosed fellow, slight with silver-shot dark curls and dark eyes, brushed rudely past them just as Jack regained the top of the plank. He reeked of vetiver and musk; Jack's nose wrinkled as he passed, and he half-smiled at himself to realize how accustomed he'd become to the Puritan cleanliness of American colonials, and their aversion to heavy perfumes.

But then he had Phoebe's bag, and was shepherding her and Sebastien across the broad open lawn of the landing field, under a bright winter moon augmented by newfangled electric floodlights, their breath steaming around them.

Except for Sebastien, of course, who—even though he remembered to feign the rise and fall of his chest—had no warmth or moisture on his breath to frost in the December air.

"I hate winter," he stage-whispered.

Jack reached up and straightened the wing of the wampyr's dux collar. And then none of them spoke again until they were within the airfield terminal and warm beside the tracks that would soon bring an electric tram.

They would stay in Germany only for a little. Long enough for Sebastien to make certain inquiries, ask certain questions, and learn what the blood knew about Armand Renault, the prime minister of France.

In the course of a long unlife, borders might cross one almost as often as one crossed borders. It paid to understand the politics, and for all their prickles the blood had long ago learned the value of shared information.

Sooner or later, in Jack's experience, a wampyr found out everything.

Paris, the city of man. The city of lights. The city of revolutions.

The city of stray dogs, filthy gutters, and chestnut blossoms in spring, Sebastien thought, assisting Abby Irene down the steps of the train and into the airy glass-walled space of the Gare Saint Lazare on the last night of the waxing moon. The name in its implications amused him.

The undead pass through Lazarus.

It echoed with footsteps now, and the curious noisy silence of train stations—so few voices, for so many travelers. When Abby Irene was safely grounded beside him, shaking out her periwinkle corduroy skirts and settling her fur wrap closer about her neck, Sebastien turned his attention to Mary, who seemed a little shocked by his extended hand. She took it, though; the stairs were steel, and high, and bad enough to climb. Sebastien couldn't imagine descending them in a woman's enveloping skirts and little boots.

"Welcome to Paris," he said, in English, because that was all she spoke. He turned back to Abby Irene. "I'm afraid I must hurry on ahead; it won't be long before it's light. Jack will see to your luggage, and pay the power tax for all of us."

Sebastien and the others had all been watching the clock anxiously, having timed their arrival in Paris with great care. Abby Irene nodded, and squeezed his wrist quickly before turning away. No farewell, and no words of caution. She was very much herself, and her assumption that he would understand anything she might care to say was a good deal of her charm, although he imagined other men might not find it so.

He let the crowd sweep him up, and was carried on the tide out of the station.

Paris gleamed in the early morning. Here, there was no longer any darkness, except the darkness that lay puddled in shadows between the electric lights. Here there were no wires, no cables, no unsightly trenches. Rather, Paris was the first major city of the world endowed with broadcast power, the technological marvel of the twentieth century. Yellow light glazed her ancient cobbles, her muck-stained granite curbs, her ice-ringed puddles.

Paris' broadcast electricity was free for anyone to use, which meant that everyone paid for it. Typical of any human society, wasn't it, that the ones who benefited least carried as much of the burden as those who benefited most?

The sweepers with their birch brooms were already in evidence, scraping the previous day's rubbish into piles that would be washed into the cathedral sewers. On their caps they wore electric lanterns, powered by the same miasma of energy that lit the streets. Drunks slumped in doorways, and the iron-shod hooves of a milkman's carthorse rattled on cobbles. But other than that, the streets were strangely barren under the light of the high waxing moon.

It had been a long time since he was in Paris, and the memories crowded close. Not close enough to ease the complex ache that Epaphras' destruction had left him with—this was an additional sorrow, rather than a distraction. Sebastien tucked his nose into his collar, though he felt no chill. It would hide his absent breath, if anyone was watching.

And he did feel someone watching. Not with chill presentiment, as a mortal might, but by the soft prickled lifting of the hairs across his nape, a sense of pressure between his shoulderblades.

He knew better than to turn. Chances were, it was only some bold streetwalker or cutthroat. But there were shop windows, and though he avoided walking too close before them (for even by lamplight, his lack of a reflection might be noticed) they could be twisted to his uses. He watched from the corner of his eye, and at first saw nothing. He heard the shush of the garbagemen's brooms, the clip of his own heels, and something else. A rattling click, the clatter of a dog's nails.

Paris was full of dogs, both leashed and feral. But what Sebastien finally glimpsed in reflection wasn't a dog of any breed he recognized. Its coat was shaggy and gray over lean sides, the eyes pale under prick ears, and it slunk from shadow to shadow like a giant cat.

But surely there could be no wolves on a Paris street.

— ✎ —

He said as much to Jack, when the others—luggage in tow—caught up with him at their reserved hotel, and Jack found him in their room and dropped a stack of papers on the floor beside the bed they were to share. "…but in any case, it was a great hungry-looking dog."

"Werewolves?" Jack said, glancing up from his breakfast with wide eyes and lifted brows, as if he couldn't believe Sebastien hadn't considered it.

"There's no such thing as a werewolf," Sebastien said, pushing his tiny glass of orange juice across the small table in their room so Jack could reach it easily. They ordered two meals, and Jack consumed both. Young men were always hungry, and it didn't hurt Sebastien's charade if he seemed to be dining.

Jack finished his own orange juice before reaching for Sebastien's. "You know," he said, "every time a vampire says he doesn't believe in lycanthropes, a werewolf bursts into flames."

Sebastien eyed him for a moment, trying to decide if his reciprocal sarcasm extended to slow clapping, and instead contented himself drawing on the tablecloth with a finger dipped in water. "I didn't say there were no such thing as lycanthropes. I said there were no such thing as were*wolves*. There are plenty of other were-things in the world."

"Aren't werewolves the iconic lycanthrope?"

"Ironic, isn't it? They were never common, and they were hunted to extinction by the *Inquisitio*—"

"English, John," Jack reminded, gently.

"That was Latin," Sebastien answered, hurt. "In Spanish, *la Inquisición*. Or *el Santo Oficio*."

"Neither of which is English. Which is what we are supposed to be."

"Don Sebastien de Ulloa is probably safer in Paris than Mr. John Nast, under the current circumstances."

Jack, plying his butter knife, did not answer. Sebastien took advantage of the silence to watch him, the dim light through the shades dull in his pale curls. Sebastien had never seen Jack's hair in the sunlight.

He never would.

He put his hand over his mouth, and muttered into his palm. "'Eh bien, cria Satan, soit! Je puis encor voir! Il aura le ciel bleu, moi j'aurai le ciel noir.'"

"Beg pardon? Still not English, sir."

"Will you permit me French in France, mother?" Sebastien repeated it, and translated, though he knew Jack did not need him to. "'Very well,' cried Satan. 'So be it! I can still see! He will have the blue sky, and I will have the black!'"

"'Et déjà le soleil n'était plus qu'une étoile,'" Jack answered, skipping ahead in the poem. *And already the sun was no more than a star.* "Victor Hugo. 'La fin de Satan.' Pray God, tell me you're not succumbing to vampire *Angst.*"

"Satan's forgiven in the end," Sebastien said, because he hadn't words for what he felt—and anyway Jack would come to understand it himself, in some human approximation, should he live long enough. An old man might smile in the back row of a wedding, knowing from the vantage of his years all the joys and travails that will come. Sebastien had more centuries than that old man could have decades, and what he loved was as bright, and as frail. "In any case, werewolves did not long survive the advent of gunpowder. Silver bullets."

Jack broke open his second croissant and reached for the jam pot. "So then what did you see on the street?"

Sebastien lifted one shoulder and let it fall. And then corrected himself to a less continental mannerism, and worked his shrug again. "Perhaps it was a werewolf's ghost. Get some rest when you've eaten. Tonight we work."

"Yes," Jack said. "But first, I have a letter to deliver."

The letter was a formality, but an important one. Sebastien was unsurprised to discover Jack's revolutionary friends used the time-honored method of keeping in touch through the classified advertisements. Or that Jack had managed to contact them through the august pages of *L'Aurore*—and the less august pages of the *New Amsterdam Record*, and alert them to his coup: an English peer willing to deal with French authorities on behalf of the Colonial revolution.

Abby Irene hid it well, but Sebastien knew she must be imagining Peter Eliot's ill-concealed delight over her cooperation.

Jack's letter, hand-delivered, had not been addressed to any accessible member of the government, or even the inevitable nimbus of lobbyists, attaches, secretaries, and major domos that surrounded the elected officials—for France, since the deposition of the Emperor, had existed under a series of democratic governments, a grand experiment that, in Sebastien's estimation, had offered no significant increase in human dignity—but which seemed to content the plebeian classes.

Rather, Jack had written directly to the Prime Minister, although he had been forced by circumstance to place the letter not in the man's own hand, but (accompanied, of course, by an honorarium) that of his mistress.

In Sebastien's experience—which was vast, and at least as precisely honed as his estimation, if he did not flatter himself to think so—above a certain level, there was *always* a mistress.

His own duty tonight was simply to ensure that the letter made the next crucial step, into the hands of the man that Abby Irene would need to contact on the morrow. It was a task well-suited to Sebastien's special abilities.

As the sun set, he dressed by the light of Paris's ubiquitous electric lamps. Their glow was far brighter than gaslight or candles, and he took care to powder his cheeks with color. He would need to importune one of his courtiers for sustenance soon, but with only three to choose between, he would suffer the discomfort of some hunger rather than risk their health.

In any case, he chose black, and occluding clothes that masked the outline of his body. A caped coat, leather gloves, a beaver topper—not for poetic associations, or any theatrical effect, but because he did not care to be noticed as he went about his business.

Jack stepped before him before his hand settled on the knob, though. Under warmer circumstances, Sebastien suspected Jack might have justified the gesture by handing him an umbrella. Instead, the young man stared him in the eye and then grabbed his shoulders and kissed him before allowing him to pass.

Sebastien said nothing, but his lips burned with Jack's transferred warmth as he shut the door behind himself and turned to face the stair.

Neither Phoebe nor Abby Irene came out to bid him farewell. He hoped they were dressing for dinner: the short days of winter gave him more latitude, and meant as well that his warm and breathing friends carried out far more of their own lives after dark. He understood that Jack was taking the women someplace fabulously well-regarded for supper, a trip predicated upon an equally extravagant expenditure and the opportunity to see and be seen. Sebastien might have felt a moment's jealousy, but he schooled himself with a reminder: if he were the sort of person who could still enjoy an elaborate supper, he would have been dust a millennium since, long before he had any chance to see Paris lit up like an electrical jewel…or, in all honesty, to travel far beyond his childhood village.

He might be a dead man. He might sometimes find himself grown very tired. Every year, there was more to mourn. But he could not find it in himself to regret the circumstances of his death, no matter how unusual.

No one paid him untoward attention as he crossed the lobby or stepped into the street. He looked respectable, and though cabbies hailed him from the curb as he passed he dismissed them with a flat, hip-high gesture of his hand. He would walk.

A cab ride meant someone who knew his destination. And it wasn't a very great distance.

The dead, for all their frailties, did not suffer bodily fatigue.

The night, if anything, was colder than the night before. A mortal man might have been quite grateful for the scarf wrapped across his face and tucked into the vee of his heavy wool caped coat. A mortal man might have shivered despite it.

Like London, like Mayrit, Paris was older than Sebastien. He found its permanence comforting, the winding streets unchanged since medieval days. The city plan was almost entirely unmodernized, which made the occasional entrances to its new Metro and the regular metal posts of the electrical lights seem as if they had been transplanted from another time and place.

In truth, *la Ville-lumière* had earned her name by being the first in Europe to install gaslamps, and now less than a hundred years later, she was the first in the world with the new broadcast power, the invention of a scientist and theurgist who had come to her as a refugee from Russia's ambitions of empire.

So it was untrue what some said, that Paris was eternal. She had changed in a few hundred years, changed a great deal—trains under the streets and glowing lights upon them—but her plan, that remained as it had always been, the old buildings leaning shoulder to shoulder, nearly closing over the narrow streets. And so Sebastien knew where he was going, and knew as well that although they were peculiarly deserted, the ancient city's byways would take him there.

He did not feel competent to risk the Metro.

It was not long at all before he felt, again, the same sense of being observed. There were no street-level shop windows along his route tonight, no convenient reflective surfaces in which to survey the pursuit. He lost discipline enough to turn once, suddenly, in the hopes of catching a glimpse of whatever trailed him, but managed not even so much as a flash of movement—although he could cozen himself all night with the possibility that he had seen something.

There were too few people on the streets to conceal a pursuer, though he did notice that everyone who walked walked warily—heads up and arms swinging with purpose.

Disturbed air stroked the fine hairs of his nape, above the scarf. But there was no sound, no scent, no sense of movement. And certainly, there was nothing to see. Still, one of the blood knew when he was followed.

He had allowed extra time, and with it he forged a random path that crossed and recrossed itself. He finally found a neighborhood that was better-populated, the streets filled with streams of tradesmen and secretaries and office workers returning home at day's end. He might not be able to scent his observers, but he could smell the warm bread and the bloody meat these folk carried, paper-wrapped parcels in string shopping bags. He could scent the bundled violets and roses, wrapped in newspaper against the chill and pressed close to coat-covered bosoms. A gift for a lover, a gift for a wife, a little color to brighten a bare, spare chamber. So many of them had nothing.

So many of them, Sebastien thought, would never have more.

But none of his doubling-back or pretending to crisscrossing errands gave him any clue of who might be watching, and in the end he was forced to admit that either he was merely feeling the effect of nerves, and not pursuit…or that he was simply going to have to take his chances with whomever might be observing.

He let the thinning crowd carry him to the street upon which stood the hotel within which Jack had said the prime minister's mistress awaited her lover, and stepped out of the bright-lit thoroughfare.

The radiant globes on their high wrought-iron towers were an advantage to the dark-adapted eye, if one could manage to not be dazzled. For the shadows between were cool and velvet, and a man—or something shaped like a man—in muffling black could vanish into them.

And so, Sebastien turned up his coat collar, stripped off his gloves and secured them in a buttoning pocket, and did exactly that.

When you watched a mortal move, you could see the weight of his or her body in the gestures, the resistance of the muscles against gravity, the way the strength and elasticity of tendon and sinew fought the hungry pull of earth. There was a grave at the end of that struggle, and mortals, however straight and young, eventually bowed under the weight of it.

Sebastien faced no such fate. His body was light and hard and cool, animated not by the transformation of sunlight and soil nutrients and water into energy, nor by the digestion of sustenance in the gut, but by the harvesting of that energy refined and re-refined in its passage up the chain of being. The sunlight that gave green grass strength to grow and flourish was the ultimate source of life in the cow that cropped the grass, and the man that butchered the cow.

And so it was Sebastien's nourishment, he thought, as surely as it was his destruction. Nourishment which he drew with blood from the veins of his court. Pure and refined, concentrated—as the suet was the richest bite of beef, as the fruit was sweetest of the harvest. The blood was only a metaphor.

It was that strength—and the lightness of body of the dead, freed of the weight of the grave by having passed through it—that gave Sebastien the ability to thrust his fingertips into the mortared cracks between the bricks, flex and press until fingertip ridges caught, and rise effortlessly along the hotel's soot-stained facade.

He felt, for the moment, a right bastard of a cliché. Still, despite his chagrin, it was effective.

It was early in the evening, though the winter made sure of the dark, and as he edged around the corner of the building toward a lighted window, he contemplated how long his wait might last. Minutes? Or hours?

Time enough to feel the roughness of mortar and the grit of rain-etched brick under his fingertips, and brood.

Abby Irene, he thought, was here out of complex and primarily noble motivations, rooted deep in her patriotism and personal honor, and her sense of justice: she would see Michael Penfold brought to book if it meant overthrowing a corrupt government to do so. Jack was here because he was young, and young men needed to feel that they were carving their mark on the world in the name of idealism. Phoebe was here because she was not the sort to pass up on adventure, especially if it were the sort of adventure that was generally considered radically inappropriate for women.

Sebastien was here for revenge, though he could pretty it up with Justice's blindfold if he cared to play the hypocrite. The self-absorbed machinations of Duke Richard and Governor Penfold had led to the destruction of a friend. Sebastien…was not always of a forgiving disposition.

He might be an eccentric. But he was still of the blood. And he could afford his eccentricities because other wampyr knew the cost of rousing him.

It seemed odd that his height gave him no greater vantage, but the street was narrow and here he was above the lights, which made observing what occurred on the pavement a nigh-impossibility. He could see a good way in two directions, but only above the lamp posts. Still, what concerned him was what occurred in the lady's rented room.

Passers-by were only a concern if they happened to notice him…and he was as shielded from their vision by the wall of electric light as they were from his.

Her window was closed against the cold, of course, and the curtains drawn against the night—or perhaps to ensure the privacy of those within.

But Sebastien had anticipated this, and the ledge offered an easy purchase for one hand while he slipped the other inside his coat. A drinking glass liberated from his own hotel rested there, wrapped in ivory silk.

He raised himself on a flexed arm, worked the toes of his shoes into the crevices between the bricks, shifted the grip of his hand, and pressed the glass to the window and his ear to the glass.

There was no conversation within. Not yet, anyway, though Sebastien heard the click of heels and the rattle of ice. Like the lady, if he was not content to wait, he could feign it from practice.

And wait he did. For some time, while from below he heard not just the conversation and passage of pedestrians, but the occasional few words spared the doorman, and then the thud of a door opened and let close again.

Finally, the sound of someone entering the hotel was followed, two or three minutes later, the click of an interior latch and the sound of a chain slid from the catch. Greetings, and kissings, and a few words Sebastien didn't understand. More ice and more drinks, while he held himself suspended, a black tatter dangled from the windowledge, until—as other sounds came from within—it began to snow.

If Sebastien believed in a God, it would have been a giving God, just then. The cold could not sting him, nor the snow do more than heap and hush upon his coat; his flesh could no more melt the crystals than he could frost the air with a breath he had no need of. But the snow blurred the lamplight, and blinded vision, and hid him more thoroughly than even the sympathetic shadows.

No human could even in extremis have done what he did in ease. Muscles would have cramped, hands frozen, fingers slipped from the ledge. Sebastien only waited, his body an appendage to his will. And eventually the sound of lovemaking stopped, and he heard other, relaxed conversation.

She gave him the envelope, and he opened it. They argued; he accused her of gullibility and she protested that she had promised nothing, but to place the letter in his hand.

"Armand," she said—Sebastien could picture the clasped hands and the lowered lashes from her tone—"It was only an English boy. What harm could have been in it?"

"Dearest, you do not think."

The wampyr at the window was pleased to note that his French was not so rusty as to be insufficient to the task of eavesdropping. He could picture the prime minister holding the offending letter by a corner, the other hand pinching the collar of his dressing gown closed. "In any case, this is quite a quandary." He sighed, and the way he said her name was part of the sigh. "Frederique, you must destroy this letter. I smell a trap: this is far too good to be true."

Sebastien assumed she was about to ask, with patent innocence and well-wrung fingers, something along the lines of *Oh, Armand, what on earth are you talking of?*

Several cross-streets east, a swirl of snow or an eddy in the broadcast power caused several lamps to seem to ripple and dim. They flared bright again in instants.

Sebastien was bored.

Blessing the Continent, illicit affairs, and hotel rooms—which he required no invitation to enter—Sebastien came in through the window. It was a casement, opening in and latching across the window frames without benefit of a center post.

He left the glass upon the ledge and hoisted himself until he could grasp the upper edge of the frame with both hands. Snow made the cement slick, but the unknown architect had left him a detail of vines to find purchase on, so when he swung his feet up and kicked, he did not hurl himself four mortifying stories into the street below.

The latch—only wood—shattered dramatically under his boots, and Sebastien entered the room amid a whirl of snowflakes and draperies and a rain of broken glass.

Of course, he lost his hat.

"Armand Renault, I presume? There's no need to shout, and please pardon the drama of my entrance. I will of course make recompense to the hotel for the damage."

The prime minister was, indeed, clutching his dressing down at his throat, and Sebastien awarded himself points for accuracy. He shook the caped coat out with a snap, showering snow and shards of glass to the carpet, and dusted cold hands.

The prime minister squeaked. The mistress—Frédérique Glibert, according to Jack—remained calmer, as Sebastien would expect of any ally of Jack's numerous friends.

Sebastien finished rubbing his palms together, amused by the cynicism of his own performance, and smiled at Renault, who still had not answered. But Sebastien could deliver his line without a cue. "Believe me," he said, "it's anything but too good to be true. You see, we need your help rather badly, monsieur."

Monsieur Renault stood. He let go of his collar and raked his fingers through his hair. "Sir, who are you?"

In a flash of his sense of the dramatic, Sebastien bowed, spread his arms to make his caped coat flare, and delivered a line he'd heard repeated on more than one penny stage. "Amédée Gosselin, at your service, monsieur."

It was gratifying, the way the man's eyes went wide.

—⁓—

As for Jack, he spent the night pub-crawling. He was of no use to Sebastien when it came to feats of physical prowess—the wampyr, although he generally preferred to downplay his puissance, had that aspect of the operation under complete control—but frankly, Jack was Sebastien's superior when it came to striking up casual friendships and earning confidences.

And it was Jack who numbered among those friendships the assortment of revolutionaries and agitators upon whom they had been reliant to get them this far.

Even in Paris, however, those were not men with the ear of the government. And getting the ear of the government, through suitably impressive display, was thankfully not Jack's problem. Rather, that fell to Sebastien and Abby Irene. For which Jack was grateful.

No, this first night, Jack was only formalizing relationships that had previously been two or three links removed. In America or occupied Eire, or England herself, he would have named this the underground and it would have been much harder to locate—but in Paris, there was nothing treasonous in calling for the overthrow of the English king. Since the deposition of the Emperor, it was far more likely in Paris for one to be hauled into jail for espousing monarchist sympathies than republican ones.

Jack adored it. A cramped, gorgeous, antique city full of drunks and poets, artists and gardens, whorehouses and opium dens, crooked streets and tilted buildings. He wished Sebastien had brought him here ten or fifteen years before.

Of course, he could have come on his own. Sebastien would never have prevented it.

But Jack didn't like to let Sebastien get too used to doing without him. He considered it a poor trend, and one that should not become established.

Much as he never allowed himself to become established in any one bar, this first night. This was for exploring, for listening, for locating men who might eventually become friends. Not that he would need them, if Sebastien and Abby Irene's plan came to fruition.

But Jack believed in redundancy and in fallback positions. He assumed that the others were also making contingency plans.

None of them were dumb.

Sebastien had convinced him that counterfeiting an Englishman or American was entirely too unsafe, and so Jack allowed himself to slip into his native accent and gave his name as Hlavach, although he was careful never to hint that he was not merely a Czech by birth, but also a Jew. Better to be thought a refugee from Russian expansionism: there were enough of those in Paris these days.

The blond hair and blue eyes helped. And he had, after hours of exploring, finally found the right bar.

For a moment, sighing over his wine, his workman's cap folded and shoved into his hip pocket, Jack allowed himself to wish they were back in New Amsterdam, the greatest concern of any night a suitable entertainment to carry them through to morning. He checked his pocket watch idly and was surprised to notice the time.

When he stood, excusing himself from his new acquaintances, they encouraged his return. Another small victory. Pile enough of them together, and they became like bricks in the wall.

One of the drinkers—a tradesman named Rene whose last name Jack had not managed to catch (Sebastien would be disappointed in him)—stood when Jack did. "You're too new for wandering Paris at night," he said. "Especially on the full moon. I'll see you safe back where you belong."

For a moment, Jack wondered what Rene expected in return for the escort, but then he shrugged and got his coat without a protest. Jack was a slight man, but Rene was classically Gallic: dark, not tall, with a distinctive nose. Jack thought he could defend himself if it became necessary. "All right," he said, and Rene wrapped his scarf, buttoned his overcoat, pulled on his gloves, and was ready while Jack was still fussing with his cap.

They walked in silence through empty streets, breath steaming under cold lamplight, between swirling flat broad snowflakes, and chins scrunched into collars, while Jack considered what he'd do if Rene made a pass.

It was the downside of being slight and pretty. If you considered it a downside, exactly.

But Rene seemed mostly nervous of ambush, or something. And so Jack was still contemplating his options when he noticed the streetlights down the block flickering and then brightening once more, one at a time, like a ripple rolling over still water. The effect was moving away from them, slightly faster than the pace of a walking man, and he nudged Rene with an elbow to get his attention. "What's that?"

"Just an eddy in the power. You see them sometimes." Rene sounded bored. "You know, it doesn't snow like this every year, in Paris."

Jack speeded his steps. His boots left a wet black trail pressed through to pavement. "There's something there."

"Where?"

"Under the first lamp." The lamp where he'd seen the beginning of the ripple effect burned bright as ever. Under it, something black and lumpy stretched on the cobbles, the snow about it a soaked outline of red. With a nasty creeping feeling, Jack recognized the shape. "There's someone in the street."

"Oh God," said Rene, folding his gloved hands into the bends of his elbows. "Not another."

—⁂—

The conversation proceeded along absolutely predictable lines. Celeste, a sister in the blood to whom Sebastien had spoken in Köln, had been very forthcoming about Monsieur Renault's predilections. Celeste was young, as such things went, and still maintained a few lingering human friendships; some of them touched on the demimonde of Paris.

She had seemed flattered by the attentions of an elder, and had put herself out to be an entertaining and informative conversationalist while Sebastien had allowed her to think he might be seduced to more. He was no fool; he knew that just the evidence of his regard would lend her cachet in the social games the blood played to alleviate their long boredom.

Celeste had assured him that Monsieur Renault considered himself something of an adventurer and a master of intrigue, and would find it hard to avoid being beguiled by a suitably glamorous proposal. And thus, all the nonsense with scaling buildings and hand-delivered letters and misled courtesans.

By the end of the conversation, however, Sebastien was confident that he not only had the prime minister's attention—but also his interest.

He exited the hotel not by the window, but more simply: down the corridor and the stair—he had not yet learned to trust lifts, especially new ones installed in old buildings—with only a pause at the bell desk to alert them to the need for a porter in Mademoiselle Glibert's room.

The street beyond was still well-lit, the electric lights unflickering despite the risen wind and deepening chill, but entirely deserted now. Dry snow scoured the cobbles and drifted into doorways, and flakes blew horizontally, swirling around Sebastien's limbs. He turned his collar up for the sake of appearances and hasted his steps.

There was no repeat illusion of dimming street lamps, but Sebastien again found himself with the creeping sensation of being watched. The snow and the chill emptied the streets. He walked, now, nearly alone. And so, when he felt the pressure of someone's regard most fiercely on his spine, he stopped, and turned, and stared directly back along the path he had just walked.

There was no benefit in pretending that one believed one's self unobserved when there were no bystanders to perturb. It only made the stalker bold.

Not that this stalker was in any need of additional boldness, apparently.

Sebastien turned to face yellow eyes through eddying snow, a gray four-legged shape almost the color of the grey city behind. The wolf stared levelly, and Sebastien stared back. It was of a height such that he could have rested a hand on its shoulder without stooping, an animal the weight of a man. Behind it, dimmer in the shadows and veiled by snow, Sebastien made out two more.

The lead wolf stepped forward, ears up and hackles down, and Sebastien awaited it with hands at his sides and chin up, a silent answer. He had the empty street at his back, and he strained his ears for the answering click of claws, but all he heard were echoes from the wolf's advance, hushed and made furry by the snow.

The lead wolf crouched, and Sebastien saw the cobbles through its outline, the gleam of the lamplight on white bones under its shaggy hide. When it rested its elbows on the stones, the trailing guard hairs of its coat traced no lacework in the powder it lay upon.

"Amédée Gosselin." The voice resonated, a sound like the wind scraping the corners of old buildings and racing down narrow streets.

"I was he." Not, *I am he.* That could never be the answer: what was dead was dead, and the seventeenth century lay buried deep and cold.

"The wolves of Paris are not your enemy."

The other two had faded from sight while Sebastien spoke to the leader, and he was left with the uneasy conviction that they had indeed faded, rather than withdrawn. "Have I an enemy?"

"Paris has an enemy," the gray wolf said. "The enemy has a dog."

Before Sebastien could answer, it rose up—not a bound to its feet, but simply a bound, like a cat springing from a crouch. It flew at Sebastien, ears down now, and all he saw were the yellow eyes and the teeth like shattered bones in the skull behind its transparent face.

He kept his hands at his sides, and he did not cringe.

The wolf passed through him, a chill that even he could feel lifting the fine hairs of his hackles. He had just time to notice that there was no snow heaped on its coat as the snow heaped on Sebastien's shoulders and his hair.

For the snow had fallen through it.

—⁂—

Mrs. Smith was already sleeping, worn out with travel, but Garrett was still engrossed in a book beside the fire, her hated reading glasses perched on her nose and Mike drowsing on the hearth edge beside the orange cat in a détente composed of scorn, when Sebastien came in to her room with a snowflake cupped in the hollows of his ungloved palms. He lifted the upper hand to show her how it lay on his flesh like white embroidery on a white nightgown, as pristine and as crisp.

"A gift," he said, and reached out to her as she stood. She cupped her warm hands around his—cold enough to burn—and bent down to see. It was symmetrical, more fragile than spun glass, and she imagined the delicacy it must have taken to catch it unharmed, and carry it to her unharmed.

Her breath melted the crystal into a bead of water on his skin. "Oh," she said, and straightened.

He put the cold hand into her hair and kissed her with lips like ice, and said, "Forgive me. I've been too long from the fire."

"Sit," she said, and moved to bring another chair. Mrs. Smith, awakened by voices, sat up in her bed. "Sebastien?"

"Back safe," he answered. "Any word from Jack?"

"Not yet." Garrett shoed him into her old chair and settled in the new one while Mrs. Smith slid from under the covers and shrugged into her dressing gown. *Her* glasses were perched on her nose within instants; Garrett slipped hers into her pocket and patted them to make sure they would stay. "So," she said, "What happened?"

Before he could answer, Jack came in and had to be plied with brandy and hot water before he stopped shaking. When he, too, was huddled by the fire, wrapped in the coverlet from Mrs. Smith's bed, he insisted that Sebastien speak first. "My story might be longer."

From the snow thawing on his lashes and the dark circles under his eyes, Garrett believed him.

Sebastien stared at Jack contemplatively for a moment, but then he shrugged, and told them. When he got to the wolves, though, she stopped him with a hand on his wrist. He'd taken his coat off by then and sat by the fire in shirt sleeves, cravat untied and collar unbuttoned, cuffs rolled up so the warmth could soak in, but the skin still didn't feel human. It was resilient, but too...dry.

"Wait," Garrett said. "Amédée Gosselin? The ghost *spoke* to you? And called you by the name of a character in a book?"

Sebastien smiled. His forelock fell into his eyes, but he didn't pull his hand from her grip to smooth it back. "Not just a character in a book."

Jack roused himself enough to grin. "Oh, yes, Dumas père is well-known for historical accuracy. The D'Artagnans still operate a chain of pubs and hotels, I understand."

"Actually," Sebastien said, "the story predates Dumas by more than a little. In the seventeenth century, it was easy enough to pass among men in a city such as Paris, where the salons were full of glittering clothing and the faces hidden under layers of powder and rouge. Amédée Gosselin was real, I assure you. It caused a scandal, when it came out that most of the court had known what he was, and none had been willing to unmask him. It's said there was a portrait painted, even, though I do not know if it has survived."

Mrs. Smith had helped herself to the brandy when she prepared Jack's toddy. She dipped her nose over the glass and said, "And now you're going to spin us some tale of the real existence of Dracula, I suppose?"

"The Draculas existed," Sebastien said, chafing his hands together delicately. "Exist, I should say. They are not of the blood. And I can vouch for the absolute nonexistence of Lord Varney and his nonsensical tricks with moonlight."

"Camilla?" Mrs. Smith asked, bright as a robin after a worm.

"Millarca von Karnstein, quite real. Although not by any means an actual German Countess. Very few of the blood have any trace of mortal nobility, though many of us—"

"Adopt the titles, Don Sebastien?"

"Surely one ancient bloodline's as good as the next?"

Garrett fiddled her ring, the silver ring he'd given her, and interjected, "You're actually Amédée Gosselin."

"No less so than I am actually Don Sebastien de Ulloa," he said, gently. "Or Mr. John Nast. One uses up a good many names in but a single century, and the centuries…add up."

"Ah," Jack said. "You never told me—"

"Never gave you a list of my abandoned guises? No, I never did. Why should I?"

"You never told me you were famous."

"Infamous."

"Still."

"I made a series of rather bad mistakes," Sebastien said. He looked very directly at Jack, until Jack glanced down, and then he gave the same courtesy or perhaps begged the same indulgence of Garrett. "And now Don Sebastien de Ulloa is infamous as well, and so lost to me. And in a hundred years—or less, my dears, mi cariño, mis corazones—there will be some scandalous novel about him as well. We learn to let go of our former selves, if we are to live in the world forever. Or we burn."

Garrett, dimly aware that Sebastien had stopped speaking, that Jack was staring at the floor between his feet, nodded. She let go the wampyr's wrist and rubbed her hands together, to chafe some warmth into her chilled fingers. "And when ghosts come looking for your former self?"

"All debts are paid when the ship sails," Sebastien said, but he did not sound as if he believed.

Jack sank down in his chair and snorted, tossing back his head. He spoke as if to the shadowed ceiling. "I thought there were no werewolves."

"There are no werewolves," Sebastien answered. "Anymore."

— ❧ —

During the following silence, Garrett was drawn to the window again. She had long since given up any hope of sleeping. The snow was still falling, though, and the nigh-unheard-of spectacle of the streets of Paris clogged with six inches of accumulation drew citizens onto the pavement to marvel. The earlier emptiness had given way to a flood of people. Among them walked children, boys and girls, awakened by their parents to wander through a city filled with rosy reflected light, a sweet amorphous glow.

It was beautiful, and eerie. It was like another city all together—Prague, or Vienna. Not Paris at all.

Except for the radiance that filled every crevice.

"We won't see the sunrise," Mrs. Smith remarked.

"Good," Sebastien said. He sounded weary, but he had insisted he did not require sustenance. He turned to Jack, and nudged him. "I know you're not eager to tell us about your night. But I'll ring for coffee, and you can start."

Jack jerked alert, and cleared his throat. "Of course," he said, as Sebastien rose to find the bell-pull by the door. "I've been to the police. There was a dead man under a streetlight, you see."

Sebastien had raised Jack Priest, and for all his fey flighty affectation, Garrett's estimation of the young man was that he was a keenly trained observer, and one who knew that the most relevant clues were sometimes those that seemed incomprehensible at the time. And that that ostensible delicacy masked a galvanized will.

She kept a terrier.

She knew the type.

In any case, she leaned forward—not slouching: even with her corset hung for airing, Garrett still was far too much a product of finishing school to slouch—and listened carefully while Jack explained what he had witnessed.

She saw Sebastien's eyebrows rise when Jack described the dimming streetlights, one of the considered gestures by which he practiced courtesy to his human associates. It meant that he was listening, and that he'd have something to add in his turn. But then Jack detailed the condition of the corpse, the gnawed hands and torn throat, the clawed footprints in the snow, and the information that this death was not the first—and Sebastien sat back and crossed his arms.

Jack stopped, and spread his hands. "You'll probably take the blame for that, the way our luck is running lately."

"I also saw the lights dim," Sebastien said. "When I was on the building."

The coffee arrived, and Mrs. Smith arose to answer the tap on the door. Although the winter dawn would not break for hours, it was by now late enough that the bakers had warmed their ovens, and the tray arrived with fresh crescent rolls, steaming and crusted lightly on the top with egg wash, and a little glass pot of strawberry jam.

Jack and Mrs. Smith fell upon the breakfast, with rapt attention and willing assistance from Mike. While Garrett was still stirring cream into her coffee the adjoining door to the valet's chamber opened and Mary came in, wearing her dressing gown. "I would have gone down," she said.

"You're in Paris, Mary," Jack said. "Sleep in."

Her laugh was strained, Abby Irene thought, but she sat down by the fire and folded her hands on her knees.

"We could leave," Jack said. "Leave Paris."

Sebastien didn't shake his head as a human might, but he inclined it perceptibly. "After we've come all this way? That will never do. We've business."

"And you're coming to the interview with Monsieur Renault today, are you not?" Garrett asked.

"I wouldn't sacrifice any of you on the altar of my politics, is all." Jack sipped his coffee, set the china cup aside. It rattled on the saucer, and his fingers left buttery prints on the delicate gold-painted handle.

"We've all our personal reasons," Sebastien answered, and Garrett restrained herself from pointing out to Jack that he, himself, was Mrs. Smith's own personal reason.

And then regretted her self-discipline, when he looked Sebastien in the eye and said archly, "Which is sweeter, Mr. Nast, love or remorse?"

"Love," Sebastien answered. "For it is fleeting."

Even the Parisian sunrise papers carried news of the American revolt, although it was below the dispatches on the French war with England. Garrett finished her coffee while Mary chose the clothes in which she would beard Monsieur Renault.

When she had laid out the garments and combed Garrett's hair, Mary stood behind her, hands on her shoulders, and caught her eye in the mirror. "Ma'am," she said, "I don't mean to be impertinent—"

"There's a first time for everything," Garrett said, softening it with a smile. Mary's tone honestly concerned her: it wasn't like her to be so hesitant. "Please, Mary. Speak plainly."

"Ma'am, I'm just wondering. Are we staying in Paris?"

Garrett looked at Mary's tensed fingers, the lines etched between her nose and the corners of her mouth. "I don't know yet," Garrett said, taking pity. "But you'll have employment with me where ever I may end."

"Thank you." Garrett gestured her to go on, or excuse herself. But she paused and hesitated. "Ma'am?"

"Mary?"

"Then will you teach me to speak French?"

Garrett smiled into her coffee cup. "Of course," she said.

"You travel with interesting company," the prime minister said by way of introduction, as his secretary permitted Doctor Garrett—and her companion—into the office. His English was flawless.

Jack stepped in at Abby Irene's back and made sure the door latch caught as the secretary departed again, a discreet push with the gloved heel of his hand. Then he flanked the sorceress as she stepped forward.

She carried her own bag, to his chagrin, though he couldn't fault her the caution. And she set it down on the corner of the prime minister's desk and commandeered a chair opposite before she answered.

Jack preferred to stand.

"We apologize for the dramatics," Abby Irene said, also in English. "Monsieur Renault, this is Mr. Jack Priest. It is he, actually, who wishes to negotiate with you."

"Then what are you here for, Lady Abigail?"

If Jack hadn't been waiting for it, he wouldn't have noticed her cringe at the hated shortened version of her name. She also seemed impervious to the lack of any courtesy, an offer of refreshment or even a chair. "To reassure you of his bonafides, monsieur. Communications with the Americans are not what we would wish, and"—she shrugged delicately—"the new government wants you to understand their commitment to a lasting French-American friendship."

"And the word of an agent of the English crown is meant to reassure me?"

"Former agent," she said. Jack almost set his hand on her shoulder. He could *see* the tension therein, but she spoke delicately. "I have a reputation for forthrightness that I had hoped might precede me even here."

Renault smiled at his desk blotter. "You have another reputation as well, Lady Abigail. One as a sort of distaff Nimrod. A mighty slayer of monsters."

She shrugged, lacing her fingers together, Jack thought so that she could fiddle with the haft of her ebony wand unobserved. "A career I've left behind in New Amsterdam."

The prime minister still hadn't looked at Jack, except in brief dismissive flickers. He did not alter the behavior now. "Pity," he said. "We appear to have a monster here in Paris that is in want of slaying. Three victims each month, for a year and a half, always on the three nights of the full moon. The city is all but paralyzed those nights: no one walks the street unless he must. I imagine the government might be far more amenable to offering aid if they were not distracted by these crimes."

Jack started. "Certainly, you're not going to blame that on...on Amédée."

"When he has only just arrived in the city, in your company, Mr. Priest? No, of course not." Renault snapped his fingers. "In any case, he is a national hero, your wampyr friend. I've seen his portrait, you know. It's a very good likeness. Let us hear no more of that. No, I'm simply suggesting that, if you wish the ear of the assembly, especially in a time of war, it might not be remiss to present them with a token of your esteem."

"The head of a monster," Jack answered slowly.

Renault's bright soft smile vanished, leaving graven jowls to hand sternly beside his abruptly narrowed mouth. "It does seem suited to your partnership's particular skills, young man. And it would lend a little weight to your request."

Doctor Garrett turned to catch Jack's eye. He nodded, trusting her to take the lead. "Why would you wish to help us, then?"

Renault turned a half-sheet of paper on his desk with a forefinger, but he met Doctor Garrett's eyes, and then Jack's, with apparent candor. "I'm not inclined to trust Phillip any further than I can toss him. We're sharing a continent with you—and the native nations—no matter what happens, we have enemies in common. And there's a monster in my city, Doctor, or there's someone pretending to be one. I don't believe for an instant you're stupid enough to require an explanation, when you came here yourself in the expectation of assistance."

"I'll want to see the bodies," Doctor Garrett said.

The earlier dead were buried, although not in the ancient and notorious cemetery of Les Innocents, where in medieval days the bodies had sometimes floated up from the flooded, death-soaked earth. It was all tidied these days, charnel houses and sorted bones, centuries of plagues and murders and childbed deaths stacked and organized by femur, tibia, jawbone, skull.

The dead were buried outside the city now.

The most recent victim, however, still lay cold on a marble slab, a white sheet tucked about him to keep the chill not out, but in. The coroner had been with him, but had not dissected, and Garrett was anything but squeamish. She drew glass rods and oiled gloves from her bag, probed wounds, measured lacerations, examined the depth of bruising on throat and thigh and arm. Jack proved an able assistant, which should not have surprised her as much as it did, and strong enough to help her roll the body up.

The marks of jaws were mastiff-sized, she thought, and the femur had snapped under the pressure of that bite, though living bone was not so easy to break. Fibers from the victim's workman's dungarees had been driven into the wounds. His flank had been torn open, postmortem she thought, and the innards feasted on, as was the way of predators. The rich organ meat would always be devoured first.

What was strange, however, was that the man's skull had been stripped of flesh. His dead eyes stared from lidless sockets, and his clenched teeth gleamed like pearls in the lipless jaw. His tongue had been torn out and—Garrett presumed—devoured. In her experience, *that* did not seem very like a wolf.

"Are you learning anything?" Jack asked, as she probed delicately in yet another wound with the forceps and a rod.

"Yes," she said. The end of the glass rod caught and scratched on something at the bottom of the wound. "May I have a scalpel, please?"

He gave it to her, and with a few slices and scrapes she laid the red bone bare. The marrow showed in the break. She thought of a sawn soup bone.

A little work with the forceps, and she tugged the imbedded object free and held it up, ivory-yellow on the conical surface and whiter on the shell-shaped, concave break. "Do ghosts chip teeth?" she asked.

Later, when Jack and Abby Irene had returned and joined Sebastien and Phoebe in the café, Sebastien heard their story related in hushed tones. "Jack," he said. "The giant-killer."

He glanced up, trying to catch Jack's eye, but Jack's attention was firmly fixed on his hands. Even Phoebe's hand on his shoulder didn't rouse him, although he winced when she squeezed.

"So it would appear." Phoebe said. "Jack? Are you with us?"

"Not a bit of it." He shook his head, though, and grinned brightly. "I was just contemplating our options. Renault said you were a national hero, Monsieur Gosselin—"

Sebastien stuck his tongue out, feeling it slide cool and bloodless between dry lips. "Don't do that in public," Abby Irene said, from her bench beside the fire. Her dog lay along her knee, chin on his paws, ears up, eyes shining. "Unless you eat first."

"Explain?"

A mirror would benefit him not. The dead cast no shadows; nor did they reflect. It was Jack who said, "Your tongue is the color of chalk, Mr. Nast. Are you certain you're not hungry?"

"I'm fine," Sebastien said, knowing he lied. He could last another day. Perhaps two. "So we're hunting monsters, then?"

"If you'd seen the dead man you wouldn't be so facile," Jack said. But of course he would, and of course Jack knew it. They'd seen any number of dead men between them. Sebastien steepled his fingers and waited. "Yes, damn you. We're hunting monsters. And I haven't the barest idea how."

"I do," said Abby Irene, and at the tone of her voice Mike picked up his head. "But it will have to wait for nightfall. First we have to catch a werewolf."

"There aren't werewolves," Sebastian said. "They're dead. Long dead."

"And yet, they eat people," Jack said, but when Sebastien stared at him he sat back and folded his arms over his chest.

"The ghost wolves could be a coincidence. I swear they meant to warn me, not to threaten."

Abby Irene smiled. And when she did, Sebastien loved her, that brittle mortality and all its mad, fragile bravery. "Which is fortunate," she said. "Because catching ghosts is easy, and that, I have practice of."

The snow broke after lunch, and the party returned to their rooms. Only Phoebe had slept, and she insufficiently, so Sebastien was left to his knitting.

He was to rouse the others at moonrise, but when he went to awaken Jack he found him sitting up in bed, his arms wrapped around knees drawn up under the bedclothes and a pinched expression above his eyes.

"You're not worried about a little monster."

"I'm worried about you."

Sebastien put his hand over Jack's interlaced ones, knowing his hands were warm from sitting beside the fire. "Because of David?"

"Because you're starving yourself, and you can't hide it."

"A little hunger won't hurt me," Sebastien said. "I need you all strong, and I'm not about to go running off to clubs unless I must."

"Hah. By now, you know, I'm capable of estimating if I'm strong enough. I don't need you to daddy me, Monsieur Gosselin."

"Of course you don't. I just—"

Jack stiffened, shuddered. Sebastien was already leaning in, drawn by the enticing heat of blood, when he recollected himself and jerked back.

"Jack! What have you—"

Jack silently held up a glistening pin. A smear of red dulled the tip. Sebastien's teeth sharped, his mouth flooding with anticoagulant saliva.

"Just a prick," he said, and while Sebastien sat frozen he smeared his left hand across the wampyr's mouth.

Hot. Sharp. Rich and round and full-bodied, full of life. Sebastien moaned and caught Jack's wrist. "*Jack.*"

"What do you think you prove by waiting?" Jack pushed him back, knelt up, let the covers slide down. "That you're its master? That you are more powerful than the hunger?"

"That I'm free," Sebastien said, though the scent of blood roared through him, brain and fingertips and quivering need.

"As free as I am of the need to breathe," Jack said, and freed himself entirely of the sheets. He kept pushing, his unbloodied hand on Sebastien's chest, until Sebastien lay on his back and Jack knelt over him. "Darling, you're ridiculous. Drink."

There was no resisting. Sebastien released Jack's wrist, wrapped his arms around the young man's thighs, and obeyed. And with the hem of Jack's nightshirt falling across his face, the thumping of Jack's heartbeat in his ears, the taste of blood and the weight of Jack's body on his chest, he wondered. He wondered if a werewolf's bloodlust, its passion, its compulsion, could possibly be more unendurable than his thirst.

Which of them was weaker?

And how on earth were ghosts grown solid enough to rend and tear?

Garrett knew as soon as she saw them what they'd been up to, and made a point of her pretense of equanimity. It wasn't exactly that she was jealous, though she *was* jealous, irrational as she knew the reaction to be. It was more that her pride had been worn down to the unyielding nubbin by years of playing the other woman, and what was left of it was adamant. Admit nothing. An iron dignity is the unbroachable defense.

Bloody but unbowed, she thought, packing her velvet carpetbag, and then laughed at her own pretensions. When Jack, wan and pale and gulping beef broth from a mug, arched an eyebrow at her, she laughed. "Me and Lucifer," she said, by way of explanation.

Jack set his mug aside. "Don't be ridiculous. You're much better looking, for one thing."

Out in the side streets, there was still a certain depth of snow, and in places even untrammeled. One tended to walk where another had broken trail, and so there were great muddy washes of slush in the middles of the streets, where gallant cart-horses had dragged the beer waggons through, and then along the walls were narrower trails like the winter paths of deer. Garrett was amused: six inches of snow would not have provoked more than a shrug and a shake of the umbrella, in New Amsterdam.

Of course, these streets had emptied out again with the dimming of the day as those afraid of the full-moon killer stayed close to home, and that made the going easier. And the ruts more apparent.

"So," Garrett said. "Who would want to train the citizens of Paris to stay off the streets on the night of the full moon?"

"The English," Mrs. Smith answered. "If they wanted to send in troops."

Garrett hmmed her answer, and wondered about New Amsterdam.

Perhaps because centuries of living in them had given him a sense of how they were constructed, Sebastien had a gift for cities. Mary and Mike and el Capitán were left behind at the hotel, but he brought the other three without hesitation back to where he'd met the wolves, though by then the sky had burned black and the only light was from the streetlamps and Mrs. Smith's new electric torch, which ran off the same radiant power supply as the street lamps. Jack eyed it covetously; Garrett had to admit that he was not alone in plotting the purchase of such an item as soon as time permitted.

"The wolves were here when I saw them," Sebastien said, gesturing around the narrow street rowed with slouched Gothic buildings. Garrett noticed that, with his new identity, any trace of a Spanish accent had left him. It shook her; she never would have known it for an affectation, and usually she excelled at such things.

She thought of him shedding names and lives and lovers across the centuries, and wondered how he bore it. And then he turned and caught her eye and smiled, and thought that rather, perhaps the shedding *was* how he bore it.

Open your hands and let go.

She went to stand behind him, where he crouched at the edge of the light, close by a patch of less-trammeled snow. He didn't need it. She would, for a while yet. The moon wasn't over the rooftops, but merely silvering the East.

"Second night of the full moon," she said. Or the true full moon, if one preferred. "Are the ghosts of lycanthropes bound to the lunar cycle?"

"You're the expert on ghosts," he said, and she nudged him in the back with a knee.

He absorbed the impact easily, without losing his balance. "No footprints," he said. "No scent. Is that ghosty?"

"It can be. They follow their own rules."

He grunted and stood; she stepped back to give him room when he turned. "Well, this is where they were, anyway."

"Good," she said. She tucked her carpetbag under her arm, contents shifting. "Then there's residue. Let us catch one."

Casting a circle in the trodden snow was a challenge. She used salt and ashes, as she would have on stone, but of course the results were anything but permanent. The snow would melt, the salt dissolve, and the ashes blur. At best, a temporary measure.

Fortunately, she had three willing—or at least compliant—assistants, and apprentices to mark off the cardinal points could only reinforce the spellcasting. In a few moments with a compass she established north and placed Sebastien in it. He was eldest and coldest, after all. By the same logic, Jack went to the south, and that was easy.

But Garrett found that east and west, for a few moments, eluded her. She and Phoebe were simply too similar, in too many ways: sharp old bluestockings, the both. In the end, she took east and placed Phoebe to the west.

Phoebe had been married. Symbolically, that made her the matron, and Garrett, no matter how laughable such a description might be in fact, the maid. Garrett tucked her wand into her bodice (it would not avail her against an immaterial enemy, but anything that had teeth to rend with might not be entirely a ghost) and pulled from her carpet bag four twists of lead foil that she had prepared before they left the hotel. She gave one to each of her companions and kept the fourth for herself. Then she leaned her umbrella against the wall of the building beside her, hung her bag from the handle to keep it out of the snow, and took her place at the circle.

There was, as far as Garrett understood, no actual reason why incantations were in Latin or Greek, Aramaic or Hebrew, other than tradition and mystique. But she found the discipline useful.

She took a breath, and began to speak, enumerating the parameters and limitations of the spell. When she worked in her own laboratory, many of the protections were built in to the architecture—the design of the floor, the resonances laced into the slate-topped tables. Here, in the field, she must construct those limitations on the fly, as she built the structure of her spell from scratch and will and the salt and ashes strewn upon the snow.

"This is a spell of summoning—" she began, and tried to ignore Jack smirking at her.

Of course, Sebastien having seen to his education, he would understand what she said. And its absolute lawyerly mundanity. Which was another reason for the dead languages.

Everything sounded more official in Greek.

Once the parameters and limitations were set, however, there was a refrain. She had drilled her companions, and they came in on the chant when she lifted her hands, the twist of lead foil in the left one.

Sebastien stood as if carved, only his jaw moving as he spoke, and of them all only his words escaped without a veil. Mrs. Smith wrung her hands together around the twist, her shoulders contracted with chill and her face scrunched around her spectacles. She never took her eyes from Garrett's face.

And Jack watched all three of them, glancing from face to face, a perfect counterfeit of placid confidence. Garrett would have believed it if she hadn't seen the tremor transmitted through his twist of foil.

The chant went on. She would have expected them to draw a crowd—in New Amsterdam, they would have been surrounded by now with gawkers—but on the rare occasions that someone passed the mouth of the side street or appeared about to turn down it, that person glanced down quickly and turned away. The Parisian attitude toward sorcery—that its public practice was little more interesting and certainly more gauche than sex in doorways or pissing in the gutter—was refreshing.

And the Parisians were, she realized, afraid of the death in the moonlight. Which in honesty Garrett was as well.

By the third iteration of the chant, Garrett noticed the mist clouding her breath was no longer dissipating, but instead drifting to the middle of the circle on long streamers, curved like tendrils of ink dripped into a vortex. Jack's breath did so too, and Mrs. Smith's, and the air seemed to grow thicker. Jack's eyes widened when he noticed, and he moved as if to clap one hand over his mouth, but stilled himself when his forearm had only jerked up parallel with the earth.

Garrett fixed her attention on the shape forming in the center. It grew, resolved, sharpened. Fur, delineated in lines as sharp as a pencil sketch. Eyes full of the cold blue radiance of moonlight on mist. Great paws, arched nails that left no dimple on the snow. One wolf. Two.

A third, with soft jowls over its teeth and plumed tail held high, ears up, flanks rising and falling with the rhythm of its breathing.

The rhythm of Garrett's chant.

The first wolf stepped forward. She felt a tug, a sharp uncomfortable sensation as if she had swallowed a portion of a string and someone was drawing it back up her esophagus. Her breath came faster, with the wolf's, and she saw Jack's free hand go to his throat. Sebastien turned to stare, grimacing as if he reminded himself forcefully not to break the circle, not to reach out.

Jack's voice was strained, Mrs. Smith's thin, like that of an untrained singer at the end of a breath. The wolves firmed, darkened. Garrett saw the gray shadows of their masks, the dusting of dark color over their rumps and hackles. The biggest breathed in and tilted back its head.

She grasped the free end of her foil twist, held it straight before her, and snapped both hands as if pulling a Christmas popper. And the packet detonated like one, the thump of gunpowder like the bang of a revolver, so that her hands were shrouded in a fine mist of silver dust and powdered aconite.

Her gesture was echoed around the circle in near-simultaneity, and then they each stepped back in haste and held their breaths, as she had instructed. She wanted no-one breathing the wolvesbane: it was deadly.

In the silence that followed, the wolf that had been about to howl dropped its head again and snuffed audibly. It was still translucent. Within, she saw the hard outline of bones like straws in watered milk. "Sorceress," it said. "Why have you bound us?"

Its teeth meshed like the serrated edge of shears, behind the cloudy lip. Its jaw did not move when it spoke.

There was an art to talking to ghosts, when you could trap one long enough to give it a talking to. "Is it you that kills in the city?"

All three wolves laughed, white tongues lolling. Their teeth were white and straight. *I wonder if anyone's ever thought of looking for strong teeth as a sign of lycanthropy.* Garrett ran her tongue across her own crooked ones.

"Ghosts don't bite."

She thought it was the same one speaking. The voice in her head sounded identical.

If they had individual identities. If the haunt of three wolves was more than one consciousness, more than one...creature. If a ghost was more than a pattern of memories and responses graved by violence into the city's stones.

"Then what *does* bite?"

"Besides your lover?" The wolf on the right turned to regard Sebastien— who did not so much as shrug. "Beasts. Beasts bite, sorceress."

She tugged off her glove—remembering at the last moment not to use her teeth, lest there be any lingering aconite or lead upon the leather—and reached into her pocket, where the tooth rested in a glassine envelope. "This beast?"

Now six eyes watched her. "*The* Beast." *La bête*, it said, and she heard two other voices echo.

"Why would you care that another beast hunts here? Why would you want to help us?"

"This was our city to hunt. Ours. Our pack-earth. Not the beast's that comes by moonlight."

"Like you."

"We are the wolves of Paris," the lead wolf said, and was there perhaps something unwolflike about the shape of its skull? It was bigger than any wolf had a right to be, as tall at the shoulder as a wolfhound. But its jaws, she thought, were not so broad as the jaws of the beast that had done the gnawing, after all. "We come in the bright of the moon or its dark. For us, it matters not at all."

"You lie. Werewolves hunt at the full moon," she said. *Les loups-garou.*

"There is no man in us," it answered. "No. No man. Though we endure in the memories of man. Break the circle. Let us free, Sorceress."

Her breath still misted when she breathed, but now it flowed to the invisible wall that circled the wolves and parted upon it, and faded into the air. "You would steal my breath if I did."

"You used your breath to lure us here." Delicately, it sniffed. Three plumed tails waved gently, and she saw that the tail of the leader was bobbed halfway, cut or bitten off. "Your breath would give us strength, strength in our jaws and strength in our tendons."

"And you would hunt again."

"We are the wolves of Paris," it answered. "We have hunted here since your kind cringed behind walls and would not walk in winter, lest we gnaw their bones. We are the wolves of Paris, and even the stones remember us, Sorceress. Your pitiable werewolves feared *us*, in our time."

"Abby Irene," Sebastien said, with all the gentle quiet of a man who does not wish to startle someone in the presence of a snake, "please look up."

She raised her eyes from the wolf who was too big to be a wolf, and turned her head, and bit her tongue so as to stifle a breathy and uncharacteristic shriek.

All around her, shadows with moon-silver eyes stood blinking. One, two, twenty, three dozen. So many ghosty wolves that they filled the narrow street, ringed the spellcasters, vanished half-concealed into walls of brick and stone. Garrett could not count them; they were a troop of wolves, a garrison, a regiment. "Oh," she said, and even across the width of the circle, she heard Mrs. Smith breathing through gritted teeth.

"If our teeth still tore meat," the lead wolf said, "doubt not they would rend thine."

"Well," Sebastien said. "Shall we visit your corpse's place of dying, Jack?"

The body had been found at the base of a streetlamp, and the snow around it was gone, trod into mire by the feet of coroners and officers and inspectors. Sebastien could still smell the blood, however, and a deeper, ranker scent. That smell made him cringe. Even he. No predator cares to encounter another as wicked.

He snuffed deeply, lips curled to concentrate the odors. "Well, something was here."

Jack and Phoebe clustered in silence by Abby Irene as he ranged out. The sorceress was doing something arcane with chalk and tiny candles, a task the other two seemed content to be pressed into. Sebastien was following the scent.

The fear that emptied the streets favored him. The snow around the body might be trodden, but that further back in a connecting alley was pristine, crusted, frozen firm so it had not blown in the wind. There was a third scent here, under the musty one, under the blood.

Sebastien crouched, his coat brushing the ground beside his boots, and touched cold fingers to the marks of pads and claws in the snow, and the marks of a man's boots beside them.

The collective resources of an authoress, a sorceress, and a wampyr and his valet are not to be underestimated. They visited, in quick succession, a certain dusty-windowed bookstore bearing no sign except the name of the proprietor in scraped gold letters on the glass; a library wherein Abby Irene had been obliged to unpin her pleated shirtwaist and display the sorcerer's tattoo over her breastbone; and last, the home of a certain Monsieur Armitage, noted author of Gothic romances and dear correspondent of Mrs. Phoebe Smith. He was not only overjoyed, if startled, to meet her in the flesh, he was equally thrilled by the opportunity to speak with Sebastien and

Abby Irene. There was, they conceded, no point in pretending any longer to be other than they were, as it seemed their presence was not secret and never had been.

In any case, Monsieur Armitage had an extensive—and esoteric—library, and was certainly well-equipped to help them educate themselves on the weirder aspects of French history. Sebastien supposed there were worse deals he might have had to make for information than an hour's conversation with an earnest and pleasant author.

When the four of them returned to the hotel—long after dark, but barely after suppertime—Sebastien and Jack were both mightily weighed down with books, and even Abby Irene and Phoebe were not unencumbered. Within short order, they were arranged around the room, and the silence was broken mostly the sound of flipping pages.

"Courtaut," Phoebe said, holding up a slender blue-bound book with gilt page-ends. "I have found him. You lived here, honestly, Sebastien, and never heard of these wolves?"

Lived was the wrong word, of course, but he wouldn't correct her when she prided herself on care of speech. "Not a word," he answered. "But I did not associate greatly with those who repeated tales of bogeymen."

"Bogey-wolves," said Jack. "Let's hear it."

Mrs. Smith lowered her book into the light, and read aloud in French: "In the winter of the year of our Lord fourteen hundred and thirty nine, when famine lay upon the land and civil war smoldered between the followers of the Count of Armagnac and those of the Duke of Burgundy, the countryside was locked in snow such as none had seen. The city of Paris was laid under siege by a pack of wolves such that none could enter or leave the city for fear of being cast down and devoured. Many starved, and many travelers were slain, and livestock was raided away by beasts with no fear of man. The wolves came into Paris along the Seine, which was frozen with the great cold of that year, and their leader was the bandit wolf called Couped, for he had lost his tail in a trap. In those days, some kennelmasters crossed wolves and hunting-dogs to create the fiercest hounds, but as happens when one meddles in God's affairs, they bred a monster. The dog was untamable, and so he was sent to the baiting.

"Couped feared not men, for men had made him. But he had a hatred of them. In the fullness of time, he escaped from the fighting pits and fled into the wild.

"When he returned, it was with an army at his back."

Phoebe lowered the book, her finger still marking her page. She cleared her throat and spoke in English. "Sparing you any further moralization or melodrama, it goes on to say they held the city under siege for three months, and in no less than a fortnight killed and devoured fourteen men, women, and children. Courtaut was captured on St. Martin's Eve and paraded through the city in a cart before being dispatched. The total death count is given as nearly a hundred, but I wonder how many of those froze or starved and were, you know, gnawed. It also says the wolves dug up corpses in cemeteries—I suspect that's embroidery, because if the Seine were frozen, the ground certainly would be too—and stole from larders—and it says they ran through the very streets of Paris herself."

"They still do," Abby Irene pointed out.

Sebastien folded his arms. "*Les loups du Paris*," he said. "*Les bêtes de la Ville-lumière.*"

"But not the beasts we have to catch."

"No," Sebastien said. "Abby Irene, do you suppose the legend could have inspired a…man? A slasher? Such things do happen—"

"Maybe," she said, her mouth twisted with thought or skepticism. "But that doesn't do anything to explain the nature of the dead man's wounds. Or why you found a man's footprints beside those of a beast, in the alley."

They were still sitting, staring at one another, when Mary opened the door after a quick tap. She stepped within and pushed the door to the frame behind her, one hand still resting on the handle to prevent the latch from clicking. She looked directly at Abby Irene, and waited until she nodded. "Ma'am?"

"Yes, Mary?"

"Someone is here to see you." Her voice was tight. She came forward, and extended a hand that shook visibly. Abby Irene lifted the visiting card from Mary's fingers; her eyes widened when she read it. She made as if to slip it into her décolletage, and then hesitated and handed it to Sebastien. Her kid gloves brushed his palm. He felt her warmth through them, and folded his fingers around the card.

It read, *Henri LeBlanc.* Sebastien read it twice, disbelieving. "Your prince has balls," he said.

And Abby Irene, shaking her head, burst out laughing. "Have the desk send him up, Mary? I'll see him alone. In the other bedroom."

Henry looked the part he'd assumed, with his black curls unpomaded and crushed out of shape by a tweed cap that was still in evidence, tucked under his arm. He'd let himself go unshaven, too, and the creases down his cheeks left by an outdoorsman's squint made him look older, now, rather than dashing. He paused just inside the door, shoulders squared in a tweed jacket, hands shoved into his pockets, and stared at her.

She had thought herself prepared. But, looking at him, she understood her numb detachment as shock.

The last time she'd seen him, she'd walked away with a sensation like fish-hooks ripping her throat and chest. But it didn't hurt any longer. What she felt now was a lack of sensation, as if whatever she was feeling under the numbness was so vast that she could not compass it. She thought of a bad burn, bad enough that sensation failed, only the red ring around the injury still alive enough even to sting. "Henri LeBlanc, I presume?"

"It's a good name," Prince Henry of England answered. "And as much mine as any."

Garrett pressed her fingers to her wrist, to assure herself that her heart was still beating, and went to him. She didn't realize that she had been braced for his cologne, the scent of citrus and ambergris, until she smelled damp wool and tobacco instead. "France has been without kings for a long time, Henry. Don't you think taking the name of a conquering ancestor when slipping over borders unnoticed is a little gauche?"

He leaned his shoulders against the closed door and didn't answer.

Garrett drew herself up, though he still topped her height. "What are you doing in Paris, Henry?"

He drew his hands from his pockets and folded his arms, frowning behind the scruffy beard. She could see him deciding what lie to relate. And she saw the moment when he decided not to bother pretending she wouldn't catch him at it. "I don't suppose you'd believe I followed you here?"

She shook her head, because it was expected, and fiddled with an earring for something to do with her hands. "That's Paris mud on your boot," she said. "And it's been frozen since I got here. Would you care to try again?"

"I could ask what *you're* doing here. Other than patronizing overpriced restaurants."

"Oh, it was well worth the price." But he wouldn't be diverted. He stared at her until she stepped back and folded her own arms over her corset. The defensive posture mashed boning into her skin with a pressure in direct proportion to the thinning of his mouth. Finally, she sighed and let her arms fall. "I'm here to commit treason, Henry. What did you think?"

"I assumed it was something like that," he said, and stepped away from the door. "Are you going to invite me to sit, Abby Irene? Or must I hover at your threshold?"

Wordlessly, she turned sideways and gestured to the chairs beside the fire, the exact mirror of those in hers-and-Mrs. Smith's room. The hotel no doubt purchased them in bulk. He waited for her to seat herself, with a courtesy beyond his rank, and then perched opposite, his elbows on his knees. "I'm here to stop a war, if I can. But I can't exactly get caught doing it."

"It's a war I need, you—" she stopped herself. She couldn't remember exactly when they had slipped into English, but under no circumstances could she call him *your highness* here.

"So you've gone over entirely to the rebels? There's no hope for us?" He sounded tired when he said it, however. He leaned back in his chair, closed his eyes, and folded his arms behind his head, the sleeves of his jacket rasping against the shirtcuffs. His cap rested on his thigh. She heard the banked fire pop.

"Phillip would not be so calm—"

"Fuck Phillip," Henry said. "I'm not the heir anymore. I have the luxury of being an embarrassment now. You want to get the colonies out from under Duke Richard and his cronies—"

"I wouldn't quite put it that way."

He didn't even crack an eye, and she realized with some trepidation that she'd just bluntly interrupted—and contradicted—a prince. Of course, Henry wouldn't *be* Henry if he cared about such things, except when it was useful to care. That pang in Garrett's throat—ah, there it was, finally. The pain. "Of course you wouldn't, Abby Irene," he said. "For some reason, you never did notice what a twat Richard was."

"I have now," she shot back.

This time, Henry laughed. And then he sat up. "Come back to England with me. You're not going to change the world, you know. And your little revolution is doomed, and silly also."

Garrett wished she had a brush in her hands. It was the sort of conversation that called for the dismissive symbolism of hair-combing, if ever she'd had one. She shrugged. "Henry, I've made up my mind."

"You're still with your wampyr."

"I am."

He hesitated, but after that moment forged ahead. "I was wrong about him. You will extend, I hope, my apologies. What I said to and about him, in New Amsterdam, was unpardonable. And also, I was wrong."

"You're trying to win back my sympathy," Garrett said, both because it was true and because it kept her from saying *you're right, it was unpardonable, and so why should I pardon you?* "If you wish to apologize, I will arrange for you to do it yourself, of course."

"Of course," he said. "Now tell me why you're in Paris."

"You know why I'm in Paris. You tell me first."

A long rattling sigh, and then he leaned forward. "I'm here to stop a war, if I can, but I can't exactly get caught doing it. Because my brother is a puffed up incompetent who has lost his grip on the colonies, who is going to draw us into a war on three fronts, and who I only hope will pass on Mother's blood to his son, because he certainly isn't manifesting any of it."

"That's treason too," Garrett said mildly.

Henry snorted. "So it is. You may send Phillip a note. In any case, Englishmen are going to die, and we're going to lose more territory than we strictly must. Renault's a reasonable man, or at least he used to be, and with the Russians pressing west again, I think he'll be willing to deal rather than to fight."

"Leaving England to put down the revolt in the colonies unfettered. Unless you have to cede us to France to seal the deal."

Henry shrugged. "Protecting England's imperial interests is part of my duty."

And yours. He didn't need to say it: Abby Irene could muster the guilt perfectly well on her own. "You should go," she said, while she could still manage to make herself say it.

He stood and bowed over her hand. "Then, so I shall."

— ❦ —

The remainder of the night, the four of them spent in the study of the books they had collected, divided up by language as appropriate. They spoke only rarely, to ask questions or seek Sebastien's help with a difficult or archaic word.

Except once, while Mrs. Smith was powdering her nose and Jack had dozed off, head tilted back against his chair, some fifteen minutes before (in mercy, Garrett and the others hadn't wakened him), Garrett looked up from her book and said to Sebastien, not quite knowing what she would say until the words were out of her mouth, "Are you afraid to die?"

It wasn't quite the right word, of course. He was dead, and had been dead a thousand years. But he didn't correct her. "No," he said. "I don't believe in an afterlife. So there is nothing to fear. But I would regret it, should I miss the rest of your life."

"You don't believe in an afterlife."

"I don't."

"What about the wolves?"

"Ah, the wolves." He smiled. "I believe in an unlife, Abby Irene." And looked down at the book spread open before him, again.

One more night of the full moon. One day to learn enough about the beast to anticipate where it might appear, and have the tools to stop it.

One chance.

The crack that they heard before sunrise, even through the windows and the shutters, was the sound of the Seine freezing from bank to bank. Garrett knew it for what it was, because she had heard, once or twice, the mighty Hudson do the same. Across the table, Jack lifted his head in the lamplight.

He rubbed his eyes, poured cold coffee from the pot set in the center of the table, and bent over his tome again.

In the morning, the papers reported a woman dead.

They stopped for breakfast before sunrise, to compare notes. Jack came to the table bearing the last book he had been working from and a sheet of paper, both sides of which were covered in his precise small hand.

"I have a name," he said, while Sebastien set a cup of coffee beside his elbow.

"Then speak it." Abby Irene, of course. Phoebe was too tired to respond with more than a flicker of her eyes, and Sebastien was inclined to let Jack bask in his triumph a moment longer.

Jack didn't seem to prickle at Abby Irene's teasing the way he once would have, though, and that gave Sebastien hope. *Yes,* mocked a voice in his head—Epaphras's voice—*perhaps your pets are learning to get along together.*

Something you and I were never good at, Sebastien answered, aware even as he did so of the uselessness of arguing with the sort of ghosts that only lived in one's own skull. He'd have better luck with Courtaut. Hell, he'd never been able to win an argument with Epaphras when he was real. And he had no delusions that the voice would stop if he managed his indirect vengeance.

But however long it took, Sebastien would pursue it. One thing about being old, and ageless, and immortal.

One learned to wait.

It was perfectly possible to love someone abjectly when you could barely stand to be in a room with them. Of all the mysteries of life, Sebastien thought, that one might be greatest.

"*La bête anthropophage du Gévaudan,*" Jack said. "The cannibal beast of Languedoc, I should say."

"I know where Gévaudan was," Sebastien said. "And it was a long way from Paris."

Jack stopped speaking and hooked the cup of tea Sebastien had served him closer with one finger. He sipped with closed eyes, and Abby Irene kicked Sebastien under the table with the side of her foot.

"Well, I didn't," she lied, and Jack opened his eyes and smiled at her over the rim of the cup. "Tell me of *la bête.*"

"There are certain inconsistencies," Jack admitted, setting his coffee aside. "Both between the different stories of *la bête* herself, and between those stories and our current murderer. But I think the similarities outweigh, in this case."

Phoebe was already pouring herself a second cup of coffee. The circles under her eyes were heavy, but she looked brighter. She took bread and placed butter on it, then dripped jam from a spoon. "Herself," she said. "What sort of beast was the beast, Jack? A wolf?"

"Ah," he said. "That's the romance of it. No one knows. And it was less than a hundred and forty years ago." He picked up his sheet of notes and consulted it. "The first attack was in late spring of 1764; a young girl tending her family's cattle was pursued by a great beast and only saved when the bulls drove it away. The attacks continued for several years, although a number of wolves were killed, and each of them was claimed for a time to be the beast. However, every time, the attacks were swiftly resumed."

"But she was killed eventually?" Sebastien asked. He picked at the linen tablecloth with a thumbnail, hearing the tick as he scraped it over the fibers.

"She was not. Or rather, perhaps she was. In June of 1767, a hunter named Jean Chastel killed an animal described as a large malformed wolf with two silver bullets. After that, there were no more killings."

"But?" Abby Irene asked, and Jack gave her a strained grin.

"But *la bête* did not act much like a wolf. She attacked during the day; she preferred children and women to sheep and cattle; she liked to leap from high places and ledges and carry off her prey. She consumed the corpses so completely that in some cases not enough remains were left for a church burial." Jack caught Abby Irene's eye before he delivered the next sentence, and Sebastien saw her hands tighten on her spoon when she heard it. His own blood could not chill, but it might as well have, from the prickling sensation that crept along his arms. "She is said to have sucked or licked the blood of the victim, devoured the entrails, stripped the flesh from the face, and in some cases severed heads with a bite or a blow."

"That sounds more like a cougar than a wolf," Phoebe said, just as Abby Irene said, "But our creature hunts by moonlight."

"Ah, but that's not the best of it." He smiled, half-gloating. "She was sometimes associated with a man. A sorcerer, said to control her actions."

Sebastien's fingers moved on the table, as if he stroked something.

Jack continued, "She wasn't the only one of her kind, either. Histories of such black beasts are not uncommon, all over Europe."

"And none of this helps us find him." Sebastien said. "Her. Pardon." He gave Jack an eyebrow, and Jack smiled and shook his head.

"Well, I have a bullet-mold, and I shall be making silver bullets. For anyone who wants them. That's the only thing I've found that might be of use. Those who hunted *la bête* tried bait, poison, dogs. She never returned to a kill. She never took a slaughtered sheep or a poisoned carcass."

"A ghost," Phoebe said. She wasn't eating, only playing with her food. "A very smart ghost."

"Oh," Abby Irene said. "What if it *is* a ghost?"

"You don't mean the wolf ghosts?"

"No, the ghost wolves are hungry, but they can't do anything about it. But there are ghosts that can."

"Shades," Sebastien said, understanding. "But why the moonlight?"

Abby Irene ran both hands through her hair, strands pulling between fingers, the insides of her wrists pale as skimmed milk and veined with blue. "Damned if I—oh."

They waited while she lifted her butter knife and turned it over in her hand, examining her reflection in the silver blade. She tucked a stand of hair behind her ear and frowned, then flicked the metal with a fingernail to hear it ring. You'd get no such tone from flatware.

"Doctor Garrett?"

Jack's voice seemed to break her contemplation. She held the knife vertical beside her face and smiled. "Basic thaumaturgy," she said. "What's the alchemical symbol for silver, Mr. Priest? What's the symbolic association between a beast killed by a silver bullet and the moon?"

"Oh." Jack's tone of voice was almost exactly what hers had been. Sebastien prevented a chuckle only through strength of will. "You're brilliant, Abby Irene."

She inclined her head. "Thank you, Jack. And yet, it also doesn't help us catch the monster."

She bit her lip and lay the silver knife across the gold rim of her plate. Her fingers stroked the lilies in its handle. Dawn was breaking outside, finally, the indigo sky—washed of stars by Paris's hungry steetlights—paling to pewter.

Sebastien stood to draw the windowshade, the light already too much for his eyes although the sun was safely below the horizon.

"We're asking ourselves the wrong questions," Sebastien said. "So we know why it attacks on the full moon. The right question is, what happened to trigger the killings? What happened in Paris eighteen months ago? What changed."

"The Metro," Jack said, promptly, but Phoebe touched his wrist and said, "Three years."

"Sebastien knows," Abby Irene said. "He's smirking."

He gestured to the window. "La Ville-lumière, Abby Irene. The broadcast power. Do you suppose it's intentional?"

Abby Irene closed her eyes and pinched the bridge of her nose. "A sacrifice to power the system? Possible, but—you must speak with the theurgist, then. After my conversation last night with Pr—with Henry, *I* must speak to the prime minister, I'm afraid. This morning."

"Well, any visit by me to the…theurgist will have to wait until sunset," Sebastien said. "So you may certainly expect to come. But I shall advance him a letter, so he'll know to expect us."

"Oh," said Phoebe, her face crumpled in feigned disappointment. "You mean we'll not just show up on his doorstep and crash our way in?"

"I have heard he has a death ray," Sebastien answered. "I shall prefer caution, just this once."

—⁂—

On the second occasion when Garrett presented herself to Monsieur Renault, she did so alone. Jack and Phoebe were still at the books; Sebastien was probably knitting and reading the papers.

The cold, if anything, was worse, and Garrett had stomped into boots and layered on petticoats before she ventured outside. This time, she dared the Metro. She had ridden the subways of New Amsterdam, and also the Tube in London—if Paris was the city of light, London was the city of the Underground, it having been the first in the world—but somehow the character of the Metro was different.

For one thing, there was even more smoking. And there was a beautiful black woman—Algerian, she supposed—tall and fine, gold flashing in her ears when she moved. Her hands burrowed into a fur muff; her kohled eyes watched moodily above her shawl. She huddled even in the comparative warmth of the tunnels. Garrett, accustomed by now to New England's bitter winters, could not imagine the suffering of those born to tropical climes. Paris should, this time of year, be far warmer than New Amsterdam.

The blacks of Paris were nothing like the blacks of America. Garrett tried to imagine Mary among them, and bit her lip in consideration.

She wondered if either of them would ever be returning home. She didn't think she'd stay in Paris though. Not because of the uncharacteristic cold, the snow, the Seine freezing in the night—those, of course, were only temporary, and she had proven to herself that she could bear New Amsterdam. No, Paris was not usually so cold.

Although it had been in the winter of 1439, hadn't it? She remembered Phoebe's story of the wolves entering medieval Paris, loping along the icelocked Seine, and heard again the crack of the ice as it sealed over the mighty river.

She almost missed her station stop.

Ghosts might not, in general and with a few notable exceptions (such as the shades Sebastien had mentioned) have much wherewithal for harming the living.

But if they had one power in all the afterworld, it was the power to make cold. And if it stayed cold enough, long enough—did the cold give power to the ghosts as the ghosts gave power to the cold?

"*Sang froid,*" Garrett said under her breath, and she was only a little joking. The others on the Metro bench did not bother to slide away, although the quarters were not cramped. She was clean and well-dressed, as subway mutterers went. And then she remembered herself, lurched to her feet, and escaped through the closing doors. If she had been an instant slower, she suspected the departing train might have whisked her skirt right off, or dragged her under as it went.

The prime minister appeared to be expecting her. She was swept inside only moments after presenting her card—her new card, still foreign to her without the D.C.I. before her name. Now it read *Lady Abigail Irene Garrett, Th.D.*, after the fashion of a lady doctor's, and if she let herself regard it overlong, she could muster some distinctly mixed emotions.

He met her standing, took her hat and laid it on a chair, and ushered her to his desk. "How may I be of service, Lady Abigail?"

"Please, prime minister," she said. "I don't mean to correct you, but if you must call me Lady anything, could it be Abigail Irene? Or Doctor Garrett, if that's too much of a mouthful. I prefer my full name."

"Of course, Lady Abigail Irene. Again, how may I be of service?"

She smiled and set her carpetbag beside her chair. She was thoroughly a sorcerer and only a Lady by courtesy, but most men hated to acknowledge her doctorate. However, she already liked Renault rather better than she had ever liked Peter Eliot, the Lord Mayor of New Amsterdam. And it was not inapt to compare the two: New Holland was less than a fourth the size of France and had a fifth the population, but that still had the advantage over some European nations. "I was approached last night by an emissary of the English crown," she said. "Monsieur Renault, I worry that perhaps you have already come to another treaty arrangement, and you are misleading me to obtain my assistance in the matter of the beast."

He snorted, and fetched her a cup of coffee from the urn on the sideboard. It was scorched from the heating ring, and the black French roast she did not care for, but she tugged her gloves off—most unladylike—and cupped chilled hands around the warmth. "Henry has been in touch," he admitted. He proffered a tin of biscuits, selecting one himself only when she waved the container away. "The disposition of his suit is by no means decided. Did you know the English and the Russians have been sending emissaries back and forth?"

Her cup rattled on her saucer, enough of an admission that she had not. "An alliance?"

"I imagine that is the likeliest outcome. I am not, my Lady, overly inclined to trust King Phillip's goodwill, or his lack of imperial desires. But I am at an impasse, you see. I am not a king. I gave you what advice I have to give, Lady Abigail. Bring me the head of the beast, if it is a beast and not a ripper. Prove yourselves to the Assembly, and perhaps the Assembly can be moved to be of service in return."

"You're incurring a debt," she said. "In the name of France. You're intentionally placing yourself in our debt."

Monsieur Renault smiled. "Oh, I wouldn't say that," he said. "But I don't trust Phillip as far as I can throw him, my lady. And even Henry's assurances go so far. His brother is not a king to hold to honor or treaties or his word, if benefit is to be gained from abrogating them. I wouldn't put it past him to maintain a truce with France for exactly as long as it took for him to muster strength of arms enough to take from us anything he thought he'd like to have, while sealing some deal with the Russians."

Jack spent the day hunched over books, and by the time Doctor Garrett returned the old paper had dehydrated his fingertips and his cuticles cracked and bled. Phoebe's hands were better off: she'd had the sense to smear on lotion and don cotton gloves, which Jack had refused—although his hands were small enough to have worn her extra pair.

"Did you find anything?" the sorceress asked, crouched on the edge of a stool by the door so she could unbutton her mucky boots.

Sebastien went to her and stopped her, a hand on her elbow. "We're only going back out again."

She sighed, but let him crouch beside her and wipe the slush from the leather with a towel. "Jack?"

He reached out, with no little relief, and flipped the latest book closed. A silken puff of dust rose from the pages. "It might have gone better if I were a magician," he said. "Or an engineer. Or if my association with clerical orders were more intimate than that afforded by a borrowed last name. No, we found nothing immediately useful. But"—he waved vaguely at the room service tray on the writing table—"I can offer you some supper before you tell us what Renault had to say."

"Please," she said, and let Phoebe bring her a plate and a glass, which Doctor Garrett balanced upon her knees as she ate. Despite her corset and the awkward position, she made a fair accounting of herself on roast chicken and potatoes, while Sebastien knelt and watched her—Jack thought—wistfully, the towel forgotten in his hand. When she had finished, she drank water, dabbed her mouth, and said, "Renault, peculiar as it sounds, is most likely an ally."

Precisely, she related her brief conversation with the prime minister, while Jack relieved her of her plate. Although her coat hung open and the room was chill, a light sheen covered her face. She was still wrapped in enough petticoats and sweaters to furnish a bed, given a little clever needlework. "You're going to freeze when we get outside."

"When are we leaving, Jack?"

Phoebe carefully pulled back a corner of the blinds, checking first to see where Sebastien sat, and peered through to the window. "Now," she said. "While we have the twilight."

They shod and girded themselves with the air of warriors going to battle, Jack thought, and contrived to brush his coatsleeve against Sebastien's on the way out the door. Sebastien winked, and let Jack precede.

Paris's electricity came from coal plants beyond the city boundaries, from whence it was somehow transmitted to a redistribution facility within the medieval walls. The theurgist lived beside the warehouse along the Seine where his equipment was housed. He was—not precisely a recluse, but reserved, and Jack hoped he would consent to see them.

He had not responded to Sebastien's note.

Even Sebastien consented to the Metro tonight. Time was of the essence, if they were to reach the theurgist before the lamps were lit.

They made the journey—which included hiring a cab for a three-mile dash from the Metro station—in under eighteen minutes, by Jack's pocketwatch, and drew up before a tall narrow house while the twilight still lingered. The house stood cheek to cheek with an imposing granite building whose bulk could not hide the tall mushroom-shaped mast or transmitter that rose from the riverbank behind. Jack stared, and was not ashamed: the thing was an engineering marvel.

The streets were still bright enough that Sebastien squinted under the brim of his hat. And then they were at the anonymous gray door, and Doctor Garrett had collected visiting cards and was tapping, and it seemed as if what happened, happened fast.

The door opened; the face of the servant beyond was impassive as any English butler's. He was a wiry fellow, his gray-shot curls pomaded carefully, and like many servants, he carried an unsettling air of familiarity, the sense that surely one had but recently seen his face somewhere. Doctor Garrett extended the cards, fanned so that he could see that there were four. "We have arranged to see the Doctor," she said. "I am Doctor Garrett, a colleague."

The servant took the cards in a white-gloved hand and frowned, and Sebastien bumped Jack's arm. Jack turned, saw the way Sebastien's head turned, the sidelong glance at the servant, the flared nostrils and pursed lips and the lift of his brows. *Him*, the gesture implied, and Jack—who had been with Sebastien the better part of fifteen years—could read it perfectly.

This was the man whose scent Sebastien had detected commingled with that of blood and *la bête*, at the site of the murder two nights previous.

"I'm sorry," the servant said, in a clipped Slavic accent. "Doctor Tesla is not at home today."

—⟨≈⟩—

"We must come in before the lamps are lit," Sebastien said, the reek of the servant's coat filling his sinuses. This was the man, and if Sebastien had harbored any doubts, they would be allayed by the smell of *la bête* hanging heavy upon him. His hands were still and calm, pressed against his thighs. The peace of the predator descended upon him.

He smiled, and the man blanched a little. But held fast, and began to swing shut the door. And just as Sebastien was making up his mind to grab it, Abby Irene stepped forward, fumbling with gloved hands in her reticule, and placed one dainty dove-gray boot between the panel and the jamb.

She never felt the impact, although the servant swung with intent. Sebastien, reaching over her head, caught the edge of the closing panel before it touched the leather.

The door thudded into his palm with a sound as if it had struck wood, and he didn't bother flexing his elbow to absorb the force. It rebounded, out of the servant's hand, and Abby Irene stepped forward into the hall, flashing the warrant card she was no longer entitled to carry and sweeping the servant before her. "I am here as a representative of the government of Prime Minister Armand Renault," she said, as Sebastien and Jack stepped into the doorway behind her, Phoebe hard upon their heels. "Doctor Tesla is at home to me. What is your name?"

The servant stammered, and frankly broke and ran, leaving them standing about the hall.

"So hard to get good help," Jack muttered, and shut the door behind himself, careful that the latch caught.

"You lied," Sebastien said to Abby Irene, one hand on her warm elbow.

"I'll pay the note in Hell," she answered, and went forward like a man o'war, her skirts trailing.

Sebastien let her sweep him up, and followed through the entry and into the hall. It was all bright, the walls glowing with sconces—and extraordinarily clean, each object dusted and polished and arranged precisely, even on the disused hallway furniture.

They were met at the bottom of the stair by a gaunt man of quite shocking tallness. Sebastien actually thought his head might strike the ceiling at the bottom of the stair, but he stooped slightly as passed the newel post and came through unharmed. He was elegantly dressed, his hands clad in gray kid, his thick hair severely parted and swept back. A silk handkerchief peeked from his coat pocket.

He drew himself up, his dark mustache quivering with outrage, and spluttered something in a language that might have been Serbian, because it certainly wasn't Russian, Polish, or Czech. Sebastien answered in French: "I am sorry, sir, I did not understand."

Abby Irene looked at Sebastien. Sebastien shrugged. "There are languages I don't speak, you know."

The theurgist rubbed his gloved hands together, once, twice, and a third time, and visibly composed himself. "I said, sir, what is the meaning of this…invasion?"

"You did not receive my note?" Sebastien asked, and then interrupted himself before Doctor Tesla could answer. "No, I see you did not. Your servant, sir, did he pass you on the stair?"

"What? No. Sir, I demand you explain your—"

"Phoebe," Sebastien said, "please handle the exposition. Don't let him turn on any lights! Jack, with me!"

The hall extended to the rear of the narrow house, and Sebastien all but flew along it, his overcoat flaring. His footsteps made almost no sound on the runner, though Jack's thudded sternly at his heels.

The servant was nowhere in evidence, but Sebastien had his scent, and a cold draft gave him all the information he needed. He sidestepped into the kitchen, broke stride at the unlatched back door only long enough to pull it open, and plunged through, making sure he stayed ahead of Jack.

The night air slapped him, followed a split second later by a sharp blow to the chest. Sebastien turned to face his assailant, felt resistance and bone grating on steel.

There was no pain, not from an injury as slight as a knife in the chest. He struck out, slammed his palm into the servant's shoulder, and knocked the man away. The knife stayed lodged; there was a faint tug when Sebastien drew in breath to scent the breeze, and the hiss of air escaping. "Bother," he said, and jumped down the single stone step to clear the doorway for Jack.

The servant scrambled backwards, never quite getting his feet under him. Behind, Sebastien heard not just one set of footsteps but four, and knew the others—and the theurgist—had arrived. A moment later, he saw what the servant was scrambling towards, through the increasing dusk.

A lamp post, at the corner of the cobbled yard, beside the hip-height wall that overlooked the gray and frozen Seine. "Doctor Tesla," Sebastien said, keeping his back turned to hide the knife, "the lamps must not go on."

Advancing slowly upon the servant, hands outstretched as one might advance upon a large dog of questionable character, Sebastien counted three before Doctor Tesla answered. Which was not, to be sure, such a great time for a mortal man—but for one of the blood, on the hunt, it was a painful eternity.

"Monsieur," Doctor Tesla said, in his good eastern-accented French, "the lamps are on timers. Who exactly the hell are you?"

Sebastien heard the words as if they echoed.

Unlike the theurgist, he did not hesitate. He took one running step and lunged.

And as his rear foot left the ground, as he committed to the leap, the lights across all Paris flickered and came on. Sebastien heard Jack shout, he saw from the corner of his eye the flutter of blue and black that was Abby Irene drawing her wand.

The servant, hands raised, froze in her stasis field a moment before Sebastien struck him and took him from his feet. He heard the snap of the servant's ankle bone as they went over, and felt nothing of pity. Impact drove the blade deeper into Seabstien's breast, his shoulders and hips striking hard on cobbles when they rolled.

And then he stood, and dragged their quarry to his feet. Doctor Tesla sidestepped Phoebe, careful not to let his coat brush her dress, and hopped down to the yard. "What, precisely, are you doing with my assistant? Identify yourself, sir—my *God*."

Sebastien glanced down, following Doctor Tesla's gaze, and with the hand that was not occupied with bearing up the servant—or assistant, if that was what he was—touched the hilt of the dagger protruding from his coat. "Fear not," he said, and tugged it loose. The blade came into his hand clean and dry, and Doctor Tesla took a step back, his towering height suddenly making him seem willowy and unstable rather than imposing.

"I'm a wampyr," Sebastien said, and handed the dagger hilt-first to Jack, who had appeared at his elbow. He maintained his grip on the assistant, however. "I'll be all right. Doctor Tesla, do you have the facilities here to shut down the streetlights?"

"Why would I care to do such a thing?"

Doctor Tesla's tone surprised Sebastien. It gave every evidence that the question he asked was an honest one.

"Show us where," Sebastien said, giving the assistant a little shake by the coat-collar, "and I'll explain."

"I must protest. You have burst into my house, incapacitated Monsieur Kostov, and now you demand that I direct you in shutting Paris' power off?"

"Right," Sebastien said. He lowered the assistant—Monsieur Kostov, and wasn't that a Russian name?—to the cold pavement and knelt beside him. Doctor Tesla closed the distance, but Abby Irene stepped forward, one hand upraised and her wand concealed in the other. The theurgist drew back rather than confront her.

Sebastien went through Kostov's clothes. In the inside breast pocket, his fingers brushed crackling paper, and her drew out an envelope with the flap roughly broken. He extended it to Doctor Tesla, who took it gingerly, at arm's length, from his hand. "The letter I sent this morning," Sebastien explained, as Doctor Tesla extracted it and began to skim. "We believed then that your broadcast power was being used by parties unknown as a sort of…carrier wave for the sorcery that summons a cannibalistic beast on full moon nights."

"And now you believe the unknown party to be my assistant."

"He was at the scene of last attack, Doctor Tesla," Jack said. And Sebastien, having nothing to add, pointed at the damning, opened letter.

"Come with me," Doctor Tesla said, crumpling envelope and paper as he shoved the letter back into Sebastien's hand. "All of you. Bring Kostov." As he turned away, he seemed to remember himself, and turned back. "Please."

His eye fell on Phoebe, and he hesitated. "And Madam, if you would please remove your earrings, I would be most grateful. I find them…distracting."

Wordlessly, Phoebe reached up, unclipped the pearl drops pendant from her lobes, and dropped them into her reticule. "Right," she said. "Anything else I must remove for your pleasure, Doctor Tesla? Or are you quite satisfied?"

He flushed furiously and turned away, his suitcoat flapping as only a tall, discomfitted man's can. And so, Sebastien dragging Kostov and Jack escorting Phoebe and Abby Irene, they went. Doctor Tesla did not lead them back into the house, although he did turn and, after checking his pocket for the keys, transferring them to another pocket, and then absentmindedly checking them again, latch the door and tug the handle three times to ascertain himself that it was locked.

Instead he brought them across the yard, under the light of the single lamp, and—producing the same ring of keys and searching through it at length—unlocked a steel door set in the wall of the big building that ran alongside the house. He ducked to enter, and held the door for the ladies—averting his eyes as they passed—and incidentally the burdened Sebastien, and Jack. The room they entered was vast and brightly lit, the ceiling laddered with shining new aluminum support lattices and equipment, the floors snaked with heavy black cables thick as a big man's arm. "Please put him there," Doctor Tesla said, switching accented English for his accented French, and gesturing to a wooden chair beside the wall. "Unless he must be restrained?"

"He is restrained," Abby Irene said. "My spell will hold him."

"Just so." Doctor Tesla locked the door behind himself and checked it thrice while Sebastien set the unresisting Kostov in the chair. From his own hard experience, he knew that Kostov was perfectly conscious, and cognizant of everything that went on around him—simply unable to breathe, or move, or react in any manner.

All four, trailing the much taller Doctor Tesla like hatchlings behind the duck, let themselves be lead to a brass-studded, black-leather swivel chair set before a board of dials and pull switches and electrical cables patched together with clips and locks. "Here," he said, and touched one unassuming white ceramic knob. This place, too, was immaculately clean, which surprised Sebastien more than the state of the front hall. "You are quite certain?"

Sebastien would have answered, but he realized that the theurgist was looking at Abby Irene—or, in the very least, at her chin—appearing both deferential and ready to trust her judgement. "Please," Abby Irene said. "Throw the switch."

He had long, fabulously gaunt hands in the gray gloves, with triangular palms that were much broader at the knuckles than the wrist. A spasm of his hand, a flex of the fingers, a gesture repeated thrice—and it was done.

At first there was no sign that anything had changed. But then Sebastien became aware of an easing, as if the pressure of deep water on his ears had been lessened. A hum or vibration he had barely been aware of faded, and in the silence, he heard water dripping.

The lights within the vast room burned still. "Those are wired," Doctor Tesla explained. "In case of emergency. Monsieur—"

"Gosselin," Sebastien said, pressing the back of his left hand to the hole in the breast of his overcoat. "My Christian name is Amédée."

Tesla's eyebrows rose, but his composure never suffered. "Monsieur Gosselin, we cannot leave the city in darkness."

Sebastien nodded, and while he nibbled his lip in thought, Phoebe craned her head back and stared up at the ceiling. "You run this whole thing by yourself?" she said, quite awed.

"Kostov and I—" He paused. "It requires only two. And I do not care for strangers wandering through my research space unsupervised. It might be unsafe."

"Or they might steal your work."

The theurgist shrugged. "It has certainly happened before. Now, how are we going to catch your monster, Monsieur Gosselin?"

It was Sebastien's turn to look at Abby Irene and lift an eyebrow. She was, after all, the sorcerer.

"Doctor Tesla," she said, "can you limit the size of your broadcast field? Create power only in a tiny location, the smaller the better?"

He stopped, a frown creasing his hollow-cheeked face. "You aren't Jewish, by any chance?"

"No," Sebastien said, with great dignity, and did not look at Jack.

And Tesla seemed to have on that moment forgotten that he had said a word about it. "I can concentrate the field," he said. "It will not be safe, that is to say, it will not be survivable, for anyone within."

Jack cleared his throat. "Excellent," he said. "While you magicians work on that, with your permission, Doctor Tesla, I would very much like to search Monsieur Kostov's room."

To Sebastien's surprise, once the round of introductions was completed, Doctor Tesla left them alone in the lab with Kostov and conducted Jack back to the house himself. He wondered if Tesla was going to lock Jack into each room in turn, and he did hear the rattle of keys in the door after the two men left.

"He's locked us in," he said.

Phoebe straightened up, but Abby Irene looked unconcerned. "He's a compulsive," Abby Irene said. "Everything in threes. All doors locked and checked and checked again. Everything in its place. It's not uncommon." She paused. "Especially in geniuses. Who are all a little mad, I find."

Sebastien reached out and touched the white ceramic knob that Doctor Tesla had used to shut down the power. Slowly, he felt his hair lift on his neck, the finer hairs of his arms standing on end under his shirt sleeves. When he pulled his finger back a heavy blue spark arched across the distance.

He put it in his mouth out of habit rather than discomfort, and Phoebe reached out and touched the bloodless hole in his coat with her palm. "He stabbed you in the heart."

"Lung," Sebastien said. "Not that it would have mattered." Her fingers dimpled fabric. He covered them with his own.

Abby Irene reached out and nudged a pencil on the countertop. "Do we trust him?"

Doctor Tesla, she meant. Not Jack. Sebastien kissed Phoebe's ring and let her hand fall. "The evidence," he said, "would indicate that Kostov was withholding information from him. And we need him."

"Yes, but do we *trust* him?"

"No." Sebastien sighed. "Not yet."

The rattle of the lock alerted Garrett and the others in advance, but though she was forewarned of their return, the grimness on Jack's and Doctor Tesla's faces was distressing. Tesla locked the door behind himself again while Jack came across the rubber-matt covered wooden floor. "It appears that Kostov is a Russian agent," he said. "I found one-time code pads and the like. We can only presume that he's been sending details of Doctor Tesla's work to Moscow, and using *la bête* here to instill panic in the citizens of Paris and destroy their morale. Unfortunately—"

"We found no means of summoning the beast," Doctor Tesla said. He walked around the console, rather than reaching past Sebastien, and straightened the pencil on the desk. When he looked up, he saw Garrett watching, and shrugged a little. "I fear it *is* my work that is being used to call up monsters."

He turned and surveyed the warehouse, the wires and knobs, transformers and capacitors and coils. Ceramic and copper and glass and steel. "We cannot leave the city in the dark."

Wordlessly, Jack reached into his pocket and handed the Doctor a revolver. "Silver bullets," he said. "Whatever manifests is material enough to eat people, and they worked on the beast of Gevaudan."

Doctor Tesla weighed it in his hand. "I am not sanguine about the discharge of firearms here." He gestured about the lab with his free hand, and offered the gun awkwardly back to Jack. "But perhaps I have another solution. When the electrical field is concentrated—as it must be, if we are to lure the beast where we wish it—presuming in advance of experiment that your circumstantial evidence is correct, and it is the interaction of the electrical standing wave with moonlight that permits the monster to materialize in the first place—in any case, when the electrical field is concentrated, it is quite inimical to life."

"The death ray," Sebastien said.

"Some melodramatically so call it," he said. "It unsettles me to consider that the Russian empire may have that technology as well."

And so do the French, thought Garrett. No wonder they were so unconcerned regarding the possible cost of war with England. She rubbed her hands against a chill that had more to do with her divided loyalties than the cavernous and ill-heated space in which she stood. Images of ships adrift at sea, the crews scattered like dropped sticks upon the deck, filled her mind's eye. "What is its range?"

Doctor Tesla winked and turned away. "I intend eventually to build a transmitter that will cover the entire Earth with broadcast electricity," he said. "But that of course will not be concentrated enough to cause death. Very well then"—he straightened dramatically, thrusting his coat aside so he could plunge his hands into his trouser pockets—"if we are agreed? Let us relocate the pigeons, so we may have at your beast while there is still moonlight to work with."

"…pigeons?"

Doctor Tesla was already in motion, surging toward a spiral stair that led to the catwalks among the ceiling lattice. "Yes," he said. "My cote is over the laboratory. If we are to concentrate the electrical field, I can't permit any risk to the birds."

"Why don't we set the field in the yard?" Jack asked, as they clambered up the metal treads.

"I've not yet uncovered how to distance it from the transmitter," Tesla said. "We'll set the device on a timer, as we cannot re-enter the structure while it is active."

They rattled along the catwalk, Garrett quite uncomfortable with the way it shook under the strides of five hurrying people, and followed Doctor Tesla as he burst through a door onto a flat area of the moonlit roof. Indeed, as promised, there was a small cote, within it some fifteen birds. The theurgist handled the sleepy animals with great care, tucking them into wicker baskets, and rescuing the eggs which two roosted on.

"Winter eggs," he said, wrapping them carefully in a linen handkerchief, each clutch knotted into a separate corner. "I don't believe they'll hatch, but who am I to make such decisions?"

He stowed them tenderly in his pocket while Garrett, a basket of pigeons in her hands, stood on the rooftop and shivered, and thought of the casual manner in which he had discussed blanketing the whole earth with his murderous electrical machine. Mrs. Smith, at her elbow with another basket, caught Garrett's gaze and widened her eyes.

Yes, precisely.

Pigeons rescued, roof door locked and checked and checked again, down they went. Sebastien, carrying his pigeon basket one-handed, rescued Kostov with the other, and the four of them exited hastily to the yard while Doctor Tesla made his arrangements with timers and levers within. "Is this safe?" Jack asked, as the door shut behind them.

Garrett handed Mrs. Smith her pigeon basket. "Eminently not," she said, and made sure both her wand and the revolver loaded with silver bullets that Jack had given her were within reach. When she reached into her pocket for the gun, her glove snagged on something sharp-edged, and she drew that out too.

It was the glassine envelope containing the chipped tooth of the beast. "Oh," she said. "It's a pity I can't cast a circle to keep material monsters out."

Just then the door to the laboratory opened, and Doctor Tesla emerged, burdened with the last of the pigeon baskets. "Stand back, please," he said. He locked and fussed, and then unlocked and fussed the kitchen door of the house itself. Garrett made sure she had her carpetbag within reach, and she saw the others making their small preparations for war.

When each basket of birds—and the still-immobilized Kostov—was placed inside, in the relative warmth of the hall, he returned and drew a hasty chalk line on the cobbles. "You will stay south of that, if you are wise."

"What if it doesn't die?" Sebastien asked. "How will we know if it's summoned at all?"

"Watch the lamp." The post in the yard was north of the curved chalk line.

Garrett felt a moment of spontaneous pity for Doctor Tesla's neighbors, and concentrated her attention where he directed. Tesla himself was focused on a silver pocket watch. "Now," he said, and before the word had died on the cold night air, the lamp flared savagely, brighter than Garrett had imagined an electrical filament could burn.

It could not burn so for long, apparently. The filament burst with a pop like a gunshot, and she supposed it was only by blind luck that the glass did not shatter. Behind the laboratory windows other lights flickered into brilliance, and a curious insectile hum, like the sawing of cicadas, made Garrett wince—but apparently those filaments were sterner stuff. Beside her, Mrs. Smith covered one ear with her palm. The derringer she held in her right hand prevented her from covering both.

Cold moonlight lay over the stones.

There was no sign of the beast.

—⁓—

Shoulder to shoulder, they stood and watched. Garrett let her shoulder brush Sebastien's; he wasn't warm, but he was solid, and that comforted her. She would have expected Doctor Tesla to pace, but he stood as solidly as Jack, occasionally rising on tiptoe to peer through windows too high for her to see through.

"Nothing," he said at last. "Perhaps it is too wise to come where it must perish."

The chip of tooth was back in Garrett's pocket. She handed Mrs. Smith her wand and fished the envelope out again, then shook the contents out. Juggling revolver and tooth, she tugged her gloves off with her teeth, and let Mrs. Smith take them.

Cold wind stung her hands. She felt the skin drying, but the cool rippled texture of the tooth was more important. "How do you suppose he controlled it?"

"Kostov?" Sebastien asked, without turning his head. His wariness kept them all alert, she thought, although Jack—bony and slight as he was—was stamping now to keep warm. "He must have had a means, mustn't he? He was there when it killed."

"I'll check his pockets," Jack said, when Doctor Tesla gave a doubtful glance at the house, rubbing his gloved hands together. No, Garrett thought, he would not care to rummage through another man's clothes.

"No," Garrett said. "Let me try this, first." She dropped to one knee and laid her revolver on the cobbles by her hand. From the carpetbag, she drew a silk envelope. "Doctor Tesla, do you have a bit of copper? Silver? Anything that might conduct?"

As the Doctor rummaged in his pockets, Sebastien cleared his throat. She glanced up, and saw him glance at the silver and garnet ring upon her finger. "Oh, of course," she said, and pried it loose. Fortunately, her hand as well as the ring has shrunk slightly in the cold; it slid off easily.

She dropped ring and tooth into the envelope and tied the strings. Then she re-arrayed herself in gloves and wand and pistol, closed the carpetbag, stood up, recited a few sharp words in Latin, and tossed the package under-hand over the curved chalk line.

Doctor Tesla nodded in understanding, and the others were used to her by now. There was no bang, no flash of light, nothing but the peal of silver on stone.

It rang for a long time, though, and did not die away. Rather, it seemed to be picked up by the steady electrical hum, rising like a church bell some-how struck and unfading.

And as it rose, something bounded to the top of the stones along the Seine.

In the moonlight, the beast was black as a cat, and big as a bear. It moved with powerful lightness, though, paws flexing on the stones, and Gar-rett could see, quite plainly, its lean body and the dense moon-frosted coat as fluffy as any mink stole. The tail was longer, thicker than a cat's, lashing sinuously. A vertical slash of white dripped down its chest; its eyes trapped and amplified the light from the laboratory, reflecting back a greenish shine. It had a longer face than a panther, and a shorter face than a wolf, and all its teeth were bared.

"It's not dying," Jack said mildly. Doctor Tesla stepped back, although Garrett was not certain if that was in response to Jack's words, or the ani-mal's stare.

And Mrs. Smith raised her derringer and gave it both barrels.

The little gun no more than stung it. The thing turned quickly on paws like a big man's mittened fists, its curved nails scratching the stone. Garrett leveled her pistol too, drawing a meticulous bead on the eye. Six shots, and a gun like this had a laughable range. They should have had rifles.

Getting rifles would not have been easy, though, and there had been no time.

She squeezed the trigger, and saw the bullet strike. High. There was no sense of motion, of the bullet acting upon flesh: a red furrow only appeared in the thing's head above the eye, and there was a spray of fur and blood hanging in the air about it. By that long red line, Garrett knew that the bul-let had glanced off the skull.

She fired again, and Jack was firing too. Fanning the hammer, she thought, getting two bullets for every one of hers. Emptying his gun, hop-ing to slow and distract it while she chose her target with more care.

Brave child. Good boy.

The beast uncoiled into a spring.

It was thirty feet away, across the entire width of the yard. Garrett fired once more while it was in the air, the eye a lost cause, aiming now for the white patch so beautifully visible on its chest and belly and hoping somehow that her bullet would penetrate the muscle and the rib cage, bounce into the gut and tear something vital wide.

She tracked it as it came, one single leap carrying it the entire distance, and realized only as it landed that she had not been the target of its wrath. Jack was on the far side of Mrs. Smith; his sixth shot struck the animal's body as its paws slammed down on his shoulders and he vanished beneath its black-furred shape. He did not scream. The sound he made was the whuff of a man who's had the wind shoved from his lungs.

Mrs. Smith fell too, scrambling or knocked aside. And then someone else was screaming—shouting—Sebastien, so fast now that Garrett did not see him go past until he hurled himself onto the monster's back. His arms locked around its long throat, dragging the head back, the gnashing teeth away from Jack's upraised arms as Jack fought to block its bite at his head and throat.

Garrett, for fear of striking him, held her fire.

And then the monster turned, writhed, its white teeth slicked with red as it turned its head over its shoulder on a longer neck than a wolf's or a lion's, rolling in Sebastien's grip and rolling with Sebastien, taking him over, taking him down, off Jack, trying to scrape the wampyr off on the cold cold ground.

And—as Doctor Tesla bounded past her, something in his hands and his arms uplifted—showing Abby Irene its belly.

She had four bullets. She put each one, methodically, in a line from the animal's groin to the center of its chest, while Doctor Tesla stood over it, silently and savagely chopping at the beast's head with the edge of a flat coal shovel.

The monster's blood was not savory in his mouth. Sebastien shoved the body—half-headless, from Doctor Tesla's efforts—off his chest and rolled to his knees, spitting. He didn't bother to stand—no time—but crawled across the corpse and across the slick stones toward Jack, and Phoebe, who bent over him, her dress shredded all down the side, her hands covered with something that looked black in the moonlight. Ten feet, only, and before Sebastien had covered three of them Abby Irene was grabbing at his coatsleeve, trying to hold him back.

He brushed her aside like a ghost. Phoebe, seeing him coming, ducked aside.

No need to tear his wrist with his teeth for the blood; the beast had bitten and clawed him to the bone. His coat hung in tatters, his shirt shredded. He willed blood into his wounds, felt it swell his dry flesh, saw it drip from the gashes. "Jack. *Jack.*"

Heartbeat, there must be a heartbeat. Something other than glazed eyes and the smell of piss. He had still been fighting when Sebastien hauled the animal away. "Jack, damn you, drink—" and he smeared blood on Jack's lips, on his tongue, trying not to see the crushed chest, the torn throat dripping blood rather than spurting.

Whatever was on the stones soaked through his trousers. There was a hand on his shoulder. From across Jack's body, Phoebe reached out and grabbed his wrist, and when Sebastien would have shaken her off the pulped ribs gave under his hand and he made a sound that hurt his own ears more than that damned ringing, or the evil buzz of the useless death ray.

A wind even colder than the midnight air stroked his neck, and when he turned his head, he saw the wolves. A ring three deep, surrounding him and Abby Irene, Doctor Tesla, Phoebe…and Jack. Their bones showed through the ghosty skin, and their eyes reflected the moon, but not the electric light. They lay atop the wall and they sat upon the stones and they paced and circled, walking through each other as often as they walked past.

At their center and front was Courtaut, his cropped tail held low, his ears pricked.

If there had been a stone in Sebastien's hand, he would have hurled it. If he breathed, he would have held his breath. But all he could do was stare.

The wolf stared back. And then, when he expected it to leap, or fade, or something—it turned and vanished over the wall, towards the frozen river, and all its brothers and sisters followed after like a wall of fog rolling down a bank.

In half a minute they were gone, blended and torn and blown away, nothing but mist and memory.

In their wake the air felt warm.

Sebastien raised his eyes to Phoebe, her torn dress, the blood smearing her cheek and matting her hair. Long gashes bled freely along her thigh, her skirt and petticoats torn aside, but it looked as if the glancing blow had been otherwise defeated by her corset, and the blood wasn't spurting.

"You're hurt, Mrs. Smith," Sebastien said, Abby Irene's hand tightening on his shoulder, her calf and knee and thigh pressed to his side.

"So are you," she said.

Sebastien slipped his wrist from her grasp and knelt back on his toes, his hands open on his knees. "I'll heal," he said.

And wished it wasn't true.

In the hours while they waited for Renault's summons, Garrett barely slept. Sebastien was brittle and silent—though never less than courteous with her or with Phoebe. Phoebe seemed to deal with her own loss by caretaking Sebastien during the day, when he was trapped inside by the winter sun— pressing him to eat, so he would heal, hobbling on her bandaged leg more than Garrett thought was good for her, reading to him from her novel in progress, refusing to cry where anyone could see her. Once night fell, he wandered, and Garrett and Phoebe were left to their own devices.

Sebastien must have found some courtiers' club, because he returned the first night of the waning moon with his wounds healed—although he would not touch Phoebe while she was recovering, and he had not inquired of Garrett. She was already up, fragrant from her bath and sipping chocolate, when he let himself into the room. "Hello," she said.

"You didn't wait up?"

Garrett shook her head and he knelt to scritch the orange cat. "We didn't sleep much either, though, I fear. Phoebe just dropped off an hour ago. I hung the card on her door."

In the dark, in their shared bed that first night, Garrett had felt Phoebe shaking and heard her labored breaths.

And reached out and took her arm, and turned her, and wrapped both arms around her shoulders and head, to shelter Phoebe while she cried. Phoebe clutched Garrett's wrists, their forearms parallel and Phoebe's head pressed to Garrett's chin, and when Garrett sobbed out loud Mike woke and burrowed between them, licking and poking.

"It hurts," Phoebe had said.

And Garrett had said, "I know."

But that wasn't in her voice when she set her chocolate aside and went to him. There was no blame, no blame for either of them. He had his own grief, as Phoebe had hers. Garrett's was just a shadow, a grief in anticipation.

Renault's letter was on the table, open, pages scattered like kicked leaves. It had come in with the cocoa, in Mary's hand. Garrett picked it up as she passed, and offered it to Sebastien.

He could read very fast when he cared to. His eyes skimmed down the page; the paper crinkled when he turned it. "Rostov was a Russian agent," he said. "This is not a surprise."

"Read on," she said, "to the results of the interrogation."

"The English deal with Russia for an invasion of France," he read. "Night of the full moon, February…next month? They were planning an invasion next month? Hello. Did your Henry know this?"

His voice promised soft murder. But Garrett shook her head. "I don't believe so. I don't believe Phillip would tell him. I don't believe he would be here trying to broker peace if he knew."

"You still defend him."

"A good man can pick a bad cause," she said. "It doesn't matter. Renault will give us the treaty. Financial and military support. Richard and the rest are going to pay, Sebastien. There's going to be a war."

"There already is," Sebastien said, and dropped the letter aside. "Jack's war. The war he wanted. And in fifty years, another corrupt government will rise up out of the ideals of revolution." If he was human, she imagined he would have had to spit, to clear the taste of bitterness. "Abby Irene—"

"Don't," she said. "I'm staying with you. So is Phoebe."

"You speak for her?"

"She speaks for herself. We talked while you were gone." She put a hand on his arm and pressed until she felt the unyielding flesh with her palm. He was warm, full of blood, cheeks flushed and eyes sparkling. "We're staying, Sebastien."

"I'm not interested in taking responsibility for a court," he said. "I can't. I can't—care for people anymore."

"You can't help caring for people," she answered. "And we're both grown women. Grown people. We make our own choices, Monsieur Gosselin."

He stared.

"Now if you'll excuse me, I have to find Prince Henry, and tell him he'd better get out of Paris before he's arrested as a spy. You know, I think his brother might be trying to get him killed?"

The staring continued as Garrett gathered her things, slid on her gloves, found her earmuffs and coat and shawl. He was still staring when she paused, hand on the door, and winked at him. "Don't wait up," she said.

But when the door clicked shut behind her, Garrett was not alone in the hall. Mary stood staring at her, a tray balanced on one palm, her apron pressed and tied.

"I overheard," she said.

"Mary, I—" Garrett swallowed, already sweating in her layers. "I'll pay your fare home. A letter of reference. Severance. I know you wouldn't be happy dragged all over Europe. I know it's not fair to ask—"

"I want to stay in Paris," Mary said.

"Stay in Paris," Garrett repeated dumbly. "All on your own? Are you sure?"

Mary nodded, the tray rocking slightly on her hand. And Garrett thought of the Algerian woman on the Metro, tall and decked in gold, unbeholden to anyone.

"Stay in Paris," Garrett said. And caught Mary's face between her gloved hands, while Mary stood too shocked to intervene, and kissed her on the cheek like a sister, like a friend.

"On your head be it," she said.